PRAISE FOR
That Bligh Girl

'Williams brings meticulous research to this fascinating historical novel about a woman from colonial Sydney whose story should be widely known.' *Who Magazine*

'Engrossing and well-researched ... in *That Bligh Girl*, Williams spins a fascinating yarn of a strong-willed, untold female character from our colonial past. Sue Williams charts the life and times of this remarkable father and daughter double-act, making history come alive by fleshing out the characters admirably. A compelling tale of a flawed father and daughter.' *Newcastle Herald*

'Of course Williams covers the legendary story of how Mary confronted soldiers from the NSW Corps with only a parasol for protection during the rebellion of 1808. But she also delves a lot deeper into Mary's story and consequently that of her father and the early years of Sydney post-European occupation. And she does it in a fabulously engrossing, dramatised way, revealing the often-secretive world hidden behind the better-known scenes of our history.' *Daily Telegraph*

'Well written and interesting, *That Bligh Girl* is an engaging historical novel about adversity, courage, friendship, and love.' *Book'd Out*

'Sue Williams has done us a great service with *That Bligh Girl*, a rollicking read about a dramatic part in the life of one woman and the entire Colony of NSW.' *Australia Explained*

'Superb narration and engrossing drama.' Tom Keneally

PRAISE FOR

Elizabeth & Elizabeth

'In Sue Williams' hands [Macarthur and Macquarie] become vividly real . . . I feel as if I have lived through these times with these two incredibly courageous women.' *Good Reading*

'Williams' journalistic training and love of the colonial era shine through in what is an interesting tale that takes the reader right through highly significant years in the nation's history.' *RM Williams Outback Magazine*

'Williams skillfully shows how both Elizabeths are moulded, pulled apart and pushed together by the times they live through . . . [*Elizabeth & Elizabeth*] provides a record of the too-often overlooked impact both women had on the early development of the colony.' Meg Keneally, *Weekend Australian*

'Williams draws a touching portrait of a friendship that manages to thrive despite difficulties small and large.' *Sydney Morning Herald/The Age*

'*Elizabeth & Elizabeth* is a fascinating look at how these two remarkable women navigated themselves through difficulties and heartbreaks to leave a legacy felt nearly two hundred years later.' *The Historical Novel Society*

'Gripping . . . pulls Elizabeth Macquarie and Elizabeth Macarthur out of their husbands' shadows to give them the attention they deserve.' *Weekly Times*

'In this engrossing novel, Sue Williams draws vivid portraits of two visionary, resilient and charming women who triumphed over innumerable trials and tribulations.' *The Chronicle*

Sue Williams' first two historical novels, *Elizabeth & Elizabeth*, about Elizabeth Macquarie and Elizabeth Macarthur, and *That Bligh Girl*, with Mary Bligh and her father, the notorious mutiny survivor and governor William Bligh, both proved bestsellers. Now this is her third, the prequel to her series about the early days of colonial Australia.

She believes we have one of the most colourful pasts in the world and is always eager to explore it and give a voice to some of the most fascinating characters, usually women, who have been the most unheard until now.

Sue is also an award-winning journalist, travel writer and bestselling author of non-fiction. Her previous books include *Run For Your Life: The remarkable true story of a family forced into hiding after leaking Russian secrets*; *Under Her Skin: The life and work of Professor Fiona Wood*; *Mean Streets, Kind Heart: The Father Chris Riley Story*; *Father Bob: The larrikin priest*; *The Last Showman: Fred Brophy*; *No Time For Fear: Paul de Gelder*; *Peter Ryan: The inside story*; *And Then The Darkness* and *Daughter of the River Country*. Other books are about travel, true crime and genetics, while she has also had a children's book published.

Sue lives in Sydney with her partner Jimmy Thomson, who writes crime thriller novels as James Dunbar, and their cat who remains steadfastly unimpressed by anything they do.

The GOVERNOR, HIS WIFE and His Mistress

SUE WILLIAMS

ALLEN&UNWIN
SYDNEY · MELBOURNE · AUCKLAND · LONDON

This is a work of fiction. Names, characters, places and incidents are based on historical events, but are used fictitiously.

First published in 2025

Copyright © Sue Williams 2025

All rights reserved. No part of this book may be reproduced or transmitted in any form or by any means, electronic or mechanical, including photocopying, recording or by any information storage and retrieval system, without prior permission in writing from the publisher. The Australian *Copyright Act 1968* (the Act) allows a maximum of one chapter or 10 per cent of this book, whichever is the greater, to be photocopied by any educational institution for its educational purposes provided that the educational institution (or body that administers it) has given a remuneration notice to the Copyright Agency (Australia) under the Act.

Allen & Unwin
Cammeraygal Country
83 Alexander Street
Crows Nest NSW 2065
Australia
Phone: (61 2) 8425 0100
Email: info@allenandunwin.com
Web: www.allenandunwin.com

Allen & Unwin acknowledges the Traditional Owners of the Country on which we live and work. We pay our respects to all Aboriginal and Torres Strait Islander Elders, past and present.

 A catalogue record for this book is available from the National Library of Australia

ISBN 978 1 76147 104 9

Set in 12.5/18.5 pt Garamond Premier Pro by Bookhouse, Sydney
Printed and bound in Australia by the Opus Group

10 9 8 7 6 5 4 3

 The paper in this book is FSC® certified. FSC® promotes environmentally responsible, socially beneficial and economically viable management of the world's forests.

To anyone who's ever had to pick up the pieces when love goes wrong

'One fine day, we'll see a thin thread of smoke rising on the horizon where the sky meets the ocean. And then a ship appears. The white ship enters the harbor, booming its salute. You see? He's come!'

Madama Butterfly, Giacomo Puccini, 1904

WARNING: This book is about colonial Australia and contains words and descriptions of Aboriginal people by non-Indigenous characters, as well as the recounting of events from a colonial standpoint that today may be considered insulting or inappropriate.

Part one

BANISHMENT

1

THE HOMECOMING

Ann Inett
24 DECEMBER 1783, GRIMLEY, WORCESTERSHIRE, ENGLAND

She hasn't slept a wink all night but Ann Inett doesn't care. She spent every hour of the hushed darkness impatiently waiting for dawn to finally break and for first light to creep under the door and the faded sackcloth curtains. For this day, she believes, she feels, she *knows*, will be the happiest of her life—of all their lives. It's the day Joseph is due home.

She bustles around the single room of their home, sweeping the already clean stone floor, polishing again the spotless surfaces and shaking out, one more time, the children's best outfits. Everything must be perfect for this day; it's one they will cherish forever, and she wants to imprint every detail on her memory. She stokes the fire at the hearth back to life, pulls on her boots and cloak and carefully lifts the latch on the front door and slips outside, pulling the door closed behind her.

The shock of the cold takes her breath away but she crunches through the snow, making straight for the village green. There, she carefully cuts two pieces of holly embedded in one of the icy hedgerows and then tries to fold her apron around the sprigs for the journey home. As she does so, a thorn snags in the skin of the third finger of her left hand. She flinches and eases it free but not before a dribble of blood stains the snow below. She stares at it for a moment, transfixed, then puts her finger to her mouth to stop the bleeding, pulls up the apron and hurries home. Nothing will be allowed to spoil this day.

Back in the room, she places both cuttings of holly on the table, fills a basin with water from the jug and walks softly to the corner where her children lie on home-made mattresses filled with corn husks. Thomas, who's just turned five, became excited yesterday when she explained that his father was returning to them, even though he can barely remember him. He was only two years old, after all, when Joseph left. Little Constance, now two and a half, has never even met her father and she's still too young to understand.

'Thomas! Constance!' Ann calls, rustling the mattress. 'Time to wake up. It's nearly Christmas, and your daddy's coming home. Come on, hurry!'

Constance stirs first and her face lights up when she opens her eyes and sees her mother.

Ann leans down to kiss her on the forehead. 'Good morning, darling,' she whispers. 'Now let's wake up your brother.'

The little girl giggles and rolls over onto Thomas who grunts in irritation and tries to push her away. She pushes him back until

The Governor, His Wife and His Mistress

Ann snatches her up, puts her on her feet and points her towards the basin. 'Wash your face and hands, and then we'll get you dressed.'

Thomas is rubbing his eyes with his fists and then swings his legs over the edge of the mattress. He catches sight of the holly and smiles. 'It's nearly Christmas.'

'But what's more important than Christmas?' Ann asks him, in a mock teasing voice.

He pauses and looks blank. Then his face clears. 'Daddy's coming home!'

'That's right, you clever boy.' Ann beams. 'Now let's get ready. We don't want to keep him waiting.'

It takes a good hour, but finally the three are dressed in their Sunday best and ready to head out. Ann tries to explain to them again what's happening. The local army regiment have returned after their defeat in the American Revolutionary War and, despite their loss, they'll be parading through the village with bands playing and everyone turning out to cheer them. And Joseph, dear Joseph, will be there among them.

The three hold hands tightly and Ann steers them out of the house and towards the centre of the small village of Grimley, about three miles north of the city of Worcester in west-central England. She heads back towards the green, where she'd cut the holly, and then past the old gravel pools towards Main Street, close by the muddy banks of the River Severn. Constance is having trouble keeping up, and Ann's so keen to reach the village before the soldiers, she hoists her up on her back so she and Thomas can walk faster. The trio finally reach the street to find it already lined with smiling villagers.

'Ann!' one shouts, recognising her. 'Come through this way. You don't want to keep your Joseph waiting!'

'Thanks so much,' Ann calls back, shepherding Thomas through the crowd. 'That's very kind.'

'Come right up to the front, dear,' another one calls, seeing her struggling. 'Your children will have a better view here.'

Ann pushes her way further in, past a woman to her left in a familiar sage-green linen gown, until the little threesome are now at the very front of the crowd, with a clear view of the road where the troops will advance. Ann stamps her feet to bring the feeling back and laughs to see Thomas carefully imitating her. Then she shows him how to blow on his hands to try to keep them warm. They hear the approach of the troops before they see them: the regimental band playing 'Rule, Britannia!'.

The irony that Britannia no longer rules over the waves of the American colonies—confirmed by the Treaty of Paris—is lost on no one, but today few care. Their men are back from foreign soil after a long and harrowing ordeal so far away, and everyone's keen to welcome them as if they're returning heroes. Ann was horrified when Joseph first suggested he volunteer for the war. But when Parliament passed that damned Enclosure of Common Lands Act, enabling the local gentry to snatch land for their sheep, he'd lost the small plot of common land he'd been farming.

'Can't you fight it?' she'd asked him the day he came home with the news.

'I'd love to, Ann, but it's hopeless.' He looked so beaten, her heart went out to him. 'The government wants more people to grow wool and using common land is one way to achieve that.'

The Governor, His Wife and His Mistress

'But what about the rest of us?' Ann cried. 'What are we to do?'

'We can only do the best we can,' Joseph said evenly. 'They've given us some other land as compensation, but it's so poor, nothing will grow there. We'll have to look for another way.'

Ann was dismayed. 'I can make some money with my dressmaking and mending, but that's not enough to pay the rent and feed us. There is no other way.'

Joseph, however, insisted there was: going off to war. It would mean a three-pound bounty on recruitment, which felt like a small fortune, plus the army wage. Ann didn't like it but, after arguing it through for hours, she had to admit it made sense. With one small child and another on the way, and now no decent land to farm, there was little option.

So it was with an exceedingly heavy heart, and a swollen belly, that she'd farewelled him, and told him to hurry back. She'd been just twenty-six, and he, a fresh-faced twenty-five. They'd both wept when the time came, but he'd cupped her face in his hands, kissed her tenderly on the lips and told her he would think of her every day. She would always be by his side, wherever he was. And then he was gone. She'd heard nothing since, except for grim reports that the war was turning against their Redcoats, that their officers frequently made stupid tactical blunders, and that the enemy was determined and single-minded in defending its home ground.

She feels Thomas twist his hand free from hers, and looks down to see him waving furiously at the advancing parade. She lifts Constance higher, onto her shoulders, and then peers hard at the faces of the soldiers coming towards her. Some are already breaking free from the ranks to hurriedly hug and kiss family members, before

7

slipping back into position. Others are looking eagerly around to see who might be there, while still others are staring blankly out. Ann gazes into every row, searching for a blond, tousle-headed man with an adorable lopsided grin, but she can't see any sign of him. Instead, she feels panic steadily rising in her throat.

She glances down at Thomas who is plainly puzzled. He meets her gaze. 'Where's Daddy?' he asks her.

Ann forces herself to be calm. 'He'll be here soon,' she says, with a conviction she's struggling to feel. 'We have to be patient.' She clasps her hands together and notices her finger is still bleeding from the holly scratch.

The regiment of soldiers is thinning out now and, towards the rear, a good number have bandages wound around their heads and criss-crossed over their chests, arms or legs. Some are limping, plainly in difficulty. *Please God, don't let him have been injured.* One soldier staggers, and two men from the crowd rush over to hold him up between them so he can continue marching in line.

Ann darts over to him, with one hand keeping Constance steady on her shoulders, the other dragging Thomas beside her.

'Excuse me, sir,' she says. 'I'm looking for Joseph Corbett. He went over three years ago . . . Do you know where he might be?'

The soldier turns to look at her, his eyes weary and, she can now see, spotted with blood. 'Joseph Corbett?' he echoes. He looks around. 'Aye, lass, Joe served with us.'

Ann feels her heart constrict with fear. What does he mean, 'served'? But just as she summons the courage to ask, the man continues, 'Look, there's the sergeant.' He nods towards a man in a tattered red jacket a few rows back. 'Go and ask him where he is.'

The Governor, His Wife and His Mistress

'Thank you,' she says, a wave of relief passing through her. And, as an afterthought, 'God bless!'

She then darts in front of the sergeant. 'Sir, I'm looking for Joseph Corbett. That soldier there said you'd be able to tell me where he is.'

The sergeant's eyes run over her, Constance and Thomas, and he sighs. 'He's in Yorktown, Virginia.'

'But he was supposed to be coming back today with you all,' Ann says, confused. 'What's he doing still over there?'

'I'm sorry,' the sergeant says. 'He fought valiantly but we were hopelessly outnumbered and . . .'

He trails off and looks at her with an expression of such deep sorrow that Ann finally understands.

2

MAKING THINGS RIGHT

Ann Inett
29 DECEMBER 1783, GRIMLEY, WORCESTERSHIRE, ENGLAND

It's Monday morning and Ann wakes to a sharp pounding on the door. For a moment, she's confused; not sure whether the steady thudding is part of a fitful dream. She squirms under her thin blanket and screws her eyes up tight, willing the noise to stop. But when she opens her eyes and sees her front door trembling under the weight of fists, she knows it's no dream. She hopes whoever it is will give up and go away. Little Constance is stirring in the corner, however, and Ann knows it won't be long before Thomas wakens, too.

She climbs off her mattress and wraps the blanket over her nightdress.

'Who is it?' she calls, hearing the tremor in her voice.

'You know full well who it is,' the gruff voice comes back. 'It's Mansfield. I've come to collect your rent. You're late *again*.'

The Governor, His Wife and His Mistress

Ann pulls the latch free and opens the door. The man immediately barges in.

'Mr Mansfield,' she says, politely. 'I'm so sorry but we were expecting Joseph home and—'

He doesn't give her a chance to finish. 'I know, I know,' he says impatiently. 'And I'm sorry for your loss. But what do you expect me to do about it? I have a family to look after, too. If you can't afford the rent then you have no business staying here. I need to free it up for another family who can afford to pay.'

'Yes, of course,' Ann replies, trying to swallow back her misery as she sees Thomas rubbing his eyes at the sound of voices. 'But could we speak of this outside?'

Her visitor looks confused but then notices her small son starting to sit up. He marches back towards the door and walks outside, waiting for her to follow. She pulls the blanket around her more tightly, and shadows him out.

'You know, there's a very simple solution to this,' Mr Mansfield leers as he stands too close to her shivering body. 'It doesn't only have to be about money.'

She steps away from him smartly and notices his eyes harden. 'Oh, not good enough for m'lady, am I?' he taunts. 'But tell me, who else do you have offering to pay you for it?'

Ann says nothing and Mr Mansfield draws himself up to his full height and moves closer.

'No one that's who,' he continues, and she notices his fat hand moving down to his groin. 'There's precious few men who'd be willing to look twice at a slut like you, with two bastards in tow. Not even your precious Joseph was prepared to marry you, was he? You put it about for him, so you should be grateful that I'm even considering making you an offer. A respectable man like me, a strumpet like you . . . I'm doing this from the kindness of my heart.'

Ann observes him now rubbing himself, and it takes all her strength to disguise her disgust. 'Thank you, Mr Mansfield,' she says through gritted teeth. 'I do appreciate your offer. But I'm still in mourning, I couldn't possibly . . .'

'Well, then, I need my money,' he says roughly, still keeping his hand over his trousers. 'And if you can't raise it, then remember what I've said.'

He looks at her body greedily and when she glances down she sees that the cold has made her nipples harden under her nightdress. She adjusts the blanket to hide them. 'A customer is about to pay a bill,' she says, 'so I should have the money by next week.'

He smirks. 'We'll see,' he says. 'I'll be round next week, and you'd better have the money if you know what's good for you. Otherwise, it'll be the workhouse for you and those brats of yours. Unless you decide to take me up on my offer . . .'

'Thank you, Mr Mansfield,' she says, turning on her heel. 'Good day to you.' And then she walks inside and closes the door firmly between them.

The wave of relief she feels at safely seeing him off doesn't last long. She's exhausted with the effort of keeping the depths of her grief hidden from the children. Everywhere she looks in the little room, she can see Joseph's ghost. Sitting on the chair at the kitchen table telling a funny story, his eyes crinkling with laughter. Crouched on the floor with Thomas, both of their heads bowed in concentration as father shows son how to make the home-made spinning top spin. And lying on the mattress, with Thomas asleep in the corner, holding Ann tenderly in his arms and telling her of his plans when he's back from the war: to give her the wedding he's always wanted for her, to find a bigger home, to meet the baby tucked away in her belly.

A tear slides down Ann's face and she brushes it impatiently away. She can't give in to sorrow; she has two young children to look after.

Thomas was disappointed his father hadn't come home from the war with the other soldiers but seems content to think he might simply return at a later date. Ann can't work out how to put into words the fact that his father will never come through that door again and light up their world with his smile, holding his arms out wide for whoever rushed into them first. The time will come to be truthful, but not yet. Thank God that Constance is too small to understand.

Ann had tried to make Christmas Day a happy one for them, with little treats of an orange each and a home-made Redcoat soldier doll she'd secretly sewn for her son, and a rag doll for her daughter. But whenever she saw Thomas playing with the soldier, she felt her eyes prickle, and she had to stifle a moan.

Now, with the start of the new week, she'll have to draw on all her strength to work out how the three of them are going to survive without the prospect of Joseph, dear Joseph, ever returning with his army wages to look after them. She already owes two weeks' rent and has no idea how she might pay.

When Mr Mansfield mentioned the workhouse, she'd shuddered but she knows only too well that it could be a distinct possibility. Worcester had set one up eighty years before, and she'd passed it once on a visit to the city: a grim prison-like place, with only one entrance guarded by a porter. Of course, it kept people off the streets but she heard plenty of tales about how the dormitories were infested with rats and other vermin and, with ten or more people to each room, it meant when anyone got sick, with smallpox, fever or, worse, the white plague, everyone succumbed. You had to work hard for your food and lodgings, too, with gruelling physical labour like rock-breaking or crushing bones to make fertiliser. Mortality rates were high and children were usually apprenticed for a minimum of seven years, and then stood little chance of ever bettering themselves.

If it was a choice between that and prostituting herself for that vile Mr Mansfield, Ann can't be sure which might be the greatest evil. She has to try everything else she possibly can first.

She washes and dresses, then gets the children up and dressed and takes them to her kindly neighbour, Mrs Thompson.

'Would you mind looking after the children for me today?' she asks, as Thomas and Constance both stand shyly behind her skirts. 'I could take yours later this week.'

'Of course.' Mrs Thompson smiles. 'Come along in, you two. I have pencils and paper out and we're drawing inside.'

Ann bends to kiss them each then pushes them gently over the hearth. 'Thank you so much,' she says, her relief plain.

Mrs Thompson nods in understanding. 'I heard about your Joseph and saw that ghastly Mr Mansfield at your door this morning, my dear. I do hope everything is all right.'

Ann sets her shoulders. 'It has to be,' she replies. 'I'm going now to make it right.'

The village of Grimley is a small place, with only around four hundred people, and most of those Ann knows by sight. Ann's grateful to her neighbours for making her and Joseph feel so welcome when they'd first moved here five years ago from their village of Abberley, just over a three-hour walk to the north-west, halfway between Worcester and Tenbury. A young unmarried couple with a small baby in tow wasn't everyone's idea of respectability but the villagers here had treated them well. Ann has never forgotten it.

When people learned that Ann was a talented seamstress and dressmaker, they were also keen to sample her wares. For a while, she'd been inundated with orders that she worked hard to fill while she tended to the needs of her husband and their small son. But more recently, many people in Grimley seem to have fallen on harder times. There have been a couple of bad harvests and those enclosures of common lands had affected many people who used them for growing crops or keeping animals. And then there's the dwindling demand for the goods made by the area's small cottage industries and craftsmen as the new factories swing into production.

But Ann has worked hard to make herself valuable to some of Grimley's wealthier female inhabitants. She's careful to keep up with the latest fashions from London and adapt them to flatter any shape of client. Sometimes, that's quite a challenge, but she hasn't failed yet.

So now that she is in a hurry to raise some extra rent money, her first stop is a regular haunt: the draper's shop in the village's main street. Mr Roberts beams as he sees her come through his door.

'Miss Inett!' he exclaims. 'I didn't expect to see you here this week. Why aren't you at home with that dashing young soldier of yours celebrating?'

Ann's face falls and immediately the draper claps his hand to his mouth. 'Oh no! Oh my dear, I'm so sorry!'

Ann shakes her head. She doesn't trust herself to speak. Mr Roberts sees her struggling and changes the subject. 'Are you after some material? We've had some beautiful silk come in over the holiday. Look at this!' He heaves a bolt of cobalt blue silk up onto the counter, and Ann reaches out to touch it, feeling how perfectly smooth it is, and watching it glisten in the light.

'That's gorgeous,' she breathes. 'Absolutely gorgeous. Can you give me a snippet so I can show a customer, as well as a sample of that gold over there, and the pale pink?'

'Certainly,' says Mr Roberts. 'We've also had a fresh delivery of muslin. Do you need any? And don't forget, you still owe me for that green linen you took last month. I'm sorry to remind you of it, but times are difficult at the moment. Those new textile factories are driving down prices and hitting us all hard.'

'I won't forget,' she replies. 'I'm so sorry for the delay in bringing you what I owe. I'm still waiting for payment from Mrs Brookes for that one. I saw a glimpse of her in the new dress at the parade—' she hesitates for a split second as she says it '—and it looked marvellous.'

'I don't doubt it,' Mr Roberts replies. 'You have a rare gift.'

Ann smiles, packs up the samples and heads off towards the homes of some of her regular clients to see if anyone would like a new gown. After three hours of traipsing around the village, as well as Sinton Green and Monkwood Green, in the same parish nearby, Ann has one order and two women interested but not yet ready to decide. It's time to make her last call of the day, the one she's been dreading.

She trudges up the long walkway to the front door of Mrs Susannah Brookes' manse house, tucked away behind the village green. It's an imposing two-storey residence, said to be among the finest houses in Worcestershire. Ann has been there many times and although Mrs Brookes is certainly wealthy, and therefore a much-valued client for anyone whose services she uses, she never makes it easy. Most of her riches have come courtesy of her late husband but it's rumoured that she's now better off than when he died. Ann doesn't doubt it. Everyone knows how difficult it is to persuade her to pay her bills.

She hammers the brass knocker against the door, and then calls out, 'Mrs Brookes! Mrs Brookes! It's Ann Inett here!'

She waits until she's almost ready to give up but finally hears footsteps on the rug leading up to the door. It swings opens and Mrs Brookes stands there, a small, squat presence, her face creased with anger.

'Mrs Brookes!' Ann exclaims in as cheery a voice as she can summon. 'So good to see you. And how are you today?'

The woman grunts. She is obviously not in the best of moods. 'I was taking a nap,' she replies. 'You have woken me with your knocking.'

Ann tries to look remorseful. 'I'm so sorry, Mrs Brookes,' she says, thinking what a wonderful luxury a sleep in the afternoon might be. 'Please forgive me.'

'What do you want?' Mrs Brookes barks.

'Well, again, I'm very sorry to trouble you, but I'm calling to see if you might be able to pay your bill.'

'What bill?' comes the response, with an even deeper scowl.

Ann takes a deep breath. 'For the last gown I made you,' she says, patiently. 'You remember, the sage green linen with the white trim that I delivered two weeks ago? I'm very sorry to call round, but the draper needs the money for the material and my rent is due.'

'That's no business of mine,' the woman snaps.

'No, of course not, bu—' Ann starts.

'It doesn't fit me,' Mrs Brookes interrupts. 'It's badly made.'

Ann stares at her in disbelief. They'd had two fittings and the gown had fitted perfectly well in those. 'What do you mean?' she asks.

'Are you deaf? The gown doesn't fit me.'

'But I saw you wearing it at the parade,' Ann says meekly. 'It looked magnificent.'

And at that, Mrs Brookes slams the door shut.

3

A MAN WITHOUT A SON, A SON WITHOUT A FATHER

Philip Gidley King
29 DECEMBER 1783, MADRAS, INDIA

Lieutenant Philip Gidley King stands on the deck of his ship, the HMS *Europe*, and looks out over the Bay of Bengal. He sniffs the air. He could swear he can smell cloves on the warm sea breeze, but maybe he's just being romantic.

It's a good morning. The Indian port of Madras has been captured from the combined French and Dutch forces, helped largely by the British reinforcements his ship had helped bring. Peace is a wonderful thing, and long may it last. But he knows that aspiration is also not in his long-term interests. If Britain stopped fighting its many enemies to preserve its colonies, what kind of life would he lead? Naval men receive the richest rewards and the greatest approbation in times of war, and he's eager to stay at the very centre of things with the Royal Navy, however much it may end up costing him.

He couldn't be a draper like his father, and his father before him, since the great factories had crushed the small craft industries. As a child, growing up in the Cornish town of Launceston, close to the Devon border in the south of England, he'd sometimes imagined working in the local courts or in the gaol, but he'd heard so many terrible stories about both, he knew that wasn't for him. Could he perhaps turn his hand to farming? He doubts the quiet life would suit him after so many adventures at sea around far-flung lands, but he wouldn't be averse to giving it a try.

For while still only twenty-five, Gidley King feels he's truly had more than his fill of war, although he knows better than to admit that to any other living man. He's already cheated death once, and hopefully he'll be able to skirt it the next time it threatens. And the next. He shudders at the thought. During the American Revolutionary War, he'd been transferred from training ships in the East Indies to the twenty-eight-gun frigate, the *Liverpool*, to patrol the American seaboard and protect it against the actions of rebel colonists and the French who were supporting them. Nearly three years into his posting, the ship was attacked in Delaware Bay, near New York, and, with no other British warships to support her, she caught fire and sank, with a catastrophic loss of life.

Gidley King was one of only a handful of the two hundred men on board who managed to avoid injury and swim away from the scene. He still has nightmares about clawing his way through those waters, with fire raining down on his head, helping untangle those who'd been caught up in the ship's rigging, and trying to keep afloat those who couldn't swim. He'd been forced to free himself from the arms of those who were doomed, fighting a losing battle, until the British ship the *Princess Royal* chanced by and hauled the bedraggled survivors on board. The admiral, John Byron, had commended him for his valour and promoted him to lieutenant as a result of his actions, but even today, five years on, he wakes up regularly in a cold sweat with his sheets damp and snarled around him where he's been kicking and grappling in his sleep.

'King!' the sharp shout penetrates his thoughts and he turns to see his captain approach.

'Yes, sir!' he barks in reply, as Captain Arthur Phillip draws level with him. 'What can I do for you?'

The short, olive-skinned captain smiles and looks up at his young officer, almost a foot taller than him. 'Nothing at all,' he replies. 'Are you just taking in the morning air?'

'Would you care to join me?'

'For a moment. But then I have to be off. You did a good job over the last week, King. Well done!'

'Thank you, sir.' Gidley King bows his head. 'I learned from the best.'

Phillip laughs. 'You may have learned many things from me, but your charm wasn't one of them,' he says. 'That's all yours.'

Gidley King smiles and the captain puts a hand on the younger man's shoulder. 'A better result than at Delaware, eh?'

'It makes a difference when you have the whole navy behind you, and an excellent captain.'

Phillip shakes his head. 'That charm again,' he says. 'You'll go far, my boy. You're smart, you're personable and you're not lacking in courage. It's been a privilege to serve with you.'

'You're very kind, sir,' Gidley King replies as the captain nods and heads back towards the aft deck.

He means it, too. He'd first met Phillip the year before, aboard the HMS *Ariadne*, a twenty-gun post ship that he'd been commanding. Gidley King's father had just died, and he'd left his previous ship to help his mother settle her affairs back at home. As soon as that was done, he started looking for another posting and Phillip had welcomed him on board.

Gidley King—the Gidley was his mother's maiden name and well known as a high-standing legal family—had first joined His Majesty's Royal Navy at the age of twelve as a captain's servant, so he learned at close quarters what a captain's work entailed, and how he could be of assistance. He became expert at anticipating what his master would need, using his initiative to get jobs done before being asked and generally working hard to make himself indispensable. He put all those new skills to good use with his new captain, and soon won his favour. While Phillip was twenty years older, the two men also bonded further over a shared love of reading, good conversation, their devout Christian faith and a keenness to faithfully record anything of note in their journals. Phillip had separated from his wife Margaret Denison and had no children; Gidley King now had no father. It seemed each man found in the other something they'd been lacking in the past.

The Governor, His Wife and His Mistress

When, at the beginning of 1783, Phillip was appointed to the sixty-four-gun, two-gun-deck warship, the HMS *Europe*, he insisted the younger man come with him. Gidley King was thrilled.

He leans on the ship rail now and gazes towards Madras. He wonders where they'll be given orders to sail next. With Phillip held in such regard by the Admiralty, he imagines they'll be in the thick of the action wherever the navy is needed. For his mentor is tipped as a captain going places, and maybe, just maybe, it won't do Gidley King's career any harm to be allied with him.

4

ASKING FOR HELP

Ann Inett
23 JUNE 1784, GRIMLEY, WORCESTERSHIRE, ENGLAND

As the distance steadily closes between the stagecoach and her parents' house in Abberley, ten miles to the north of Grimley, Ann Inett's grip on her children, Thomas and Constance, grows tighter.

'Ma!' Thomas cries, trying to wriggle out of her grasp. 'You're hurting!'

'Oh, I'm so sorry!' Ann says. 'I wasn't thinking.'

In truth, she is doing nothing but thinking; going over and over what she might say when the little party arrives, how her parents might respond, and then what she can say in reply. However she frames it, she knows it sounds feeble. But she has no choice. She has to win them over.

This stagecoach has taken the last of her pennies but while she would have been happy to walk the ten miles, she couldn't expect her children to do the same. Besides, she wants them to arrive in

The Governor, His Wife and His Mistress

good temper as she needs them at their very best to impress their grandparents. She had to smile, too, when the horses arrived, to see how excited the children had been to be lifted up inside the coach. It has no springs so all the passengers are continually being jolted as the three horses strain to pull it forward, but the children giggle as they're tossed and tumbled every time the coach bucks over the bumps in the road and bangs down the gullies. They'll all have to walk home, but it has been worth every penny to see them so elated.

Inside the coach, the children both sit on Ann's lap in order to lower the fare, but the five others taking up the space on the two bench seats give them little room. The blinds are down to keep out the unseasonably chill draught, so it's dark, but the portly man to Ann's left is sweating so heavily that the air soon turns rank. In addition, there are three passengers on the roof and more scrambling on at every stop, so the coach travels slower and slower by the minute.

It takes a long two and a half hours to travel the short distance but at last they arrive in the village of her birth. She scrambles out and another of the passengers jammed into the carriage lifts the children down into her arms. She dusts them off, straightens Constance's dress and then, with one child either side of her, walks determinedly towards the house she once knew so well.

'Now be on your best behaviour,' she implores her son and daughter. 'You're going to meet your grandmother and grandfather.'

They both look confused, but Ann marches on regardless, then veers left to walk up a path towards a squat white house. She knocks firmly on the door. It feels like an age before it opens but when it finally does, it reveals a woman Ann has to look at closely before she recognises her.

'Mother!' she exclaims with a forced gaiety. 'Look who I've brought to see you. This is Thomas—' and she beckons him forward '—and this wee mite is Constance.'

'Hello,' Thomas says politely, just as he's been schooled to do. 'It's very nice to meet you.'

The woman stands still, saying nothing.

'Mother,' Ann says again. 'These are your grandchildren. Thomas is six now and good with his letters. Constance is three and she's learning fast and—'

'What do you want from us?' the woman barks, completely ignoring the children. 'What are you doing here after all these years, Ann? Joseph left you, has he?'

Ann flinches at the words, but tries to retain her calm. 'No, Mother. Joseph . . .' she stumbles. 'Joseph—' she glances at the children to check they're not looking at her, and mouths the words '—is dead. In the war.'

'Dead?' her mother repeats as Ann quails to see Thomas looking at her, mystified.

'Can we come in?' Ann asks hurriedly.

'I suppose so,' her mother replies begrudgingly.

'Is Father in?'

'*SAMUEL!*'

He appears at the door so quickly, Ann suspects he was loitering close by, listening to every word.

'Father!' she whispers, but he looks straight past her at the children.

'Hello, young man!' he says to Thomas. 'What a handsome boy you are. And you, young lady, my, what a pretty little girl!' He gathers them in his arms and they squeal with pleasure. Ann realises that Thomas is probably missing his dad's cuddles, and Constance has never known the rough embrace of a man.

'These are beauties, Mary, eh?' Ann's father says as he carries both children in through the door. Ann follows, takes a chair and watches her father playing with his grandchildren, hoping this might be a good sign.

'What do you want from us?' her mother repeats and her father looks expectantly at her, too.

She takes a deep breath. 'Joseph signed up to the war after our land was taken away, but he hasn't returned,' Ann says. 'I've been trying to make do, but one of my dressmaking customers refuses to pay up and our debts are mounting.'

'And now you're back begging for our help, are you?' her mother asks. 'We told you that boy would be no good for you, and we were right. But you refused to listen to us. Now look at you. Two children and he didn't even marry you by the look of your hand. You brought so much shame on us. Why should we help you now?'

Ann bows her head, trying to keep her composure and scratches the mark on her ring finger left by the holly. It still hasn't healed. 'I'm sorry,' she mutters. 'But I was in love with Joseph, and he with me. We planned to marry later.'

'And if you'd listened to us, you wouldn't be in the mess you are in now,' her mother snaps. 'You could have married Mr Woodward, the accountant who was sweet on you back when you still had your looks. He's doing very well, you know. He ended up marrying your old friend Emily and they now have two lovely children and the most beautiful house up the road.'

'But I didn't love him,' Ann protests bluntly.

'Love!' her mother sneers. 'Love doesn't pay the bills, as you now know. Love doesn't give you respectability. Love—'

'Mary!' Ann's father says suddenly. 'Let's leave it alone now. What's done is done. Ann, what do you want us to do?'

Ann looks over at the children. 'I wondered if you could lend us a little money for the rent, just until we've got straight,' she says. 'That would be wonderful. I can't see how we're going to get through otherwise.'

There's a tense silence. It looks as though Ann's father is about to say something, but just as he starts to speak, her mother silences him with a glare. Then she finally speaks. 'I tell you what we'll do,' she says.

Ann's spirits lift. Maybe her parents aren't as unreasonable as she's always thought.

'What we'll do,' her mother continues thoughtfully, 'is take your children and look after them.'

'What?' Ann asks, shocked.

'We'll have the children,' her mother repeats slowly as if she's explaining something to a halfwit. 'We have enough room here, and can afford to feed and clothe them properly. In return, you'll agree to have no more contact with them.'

'No!' Ann cries. 'I won't ever give up my children. You can't expect me to do that.'

'We've long given up expecting anything of you,' her mother replies, narrowing her eyes. 'That's the offer. Take it or leave it.'

The Governor, His Wife and His Mistress

Ann looks at her father. 'You won't agree to this, will you, Father?' she implores, tears beginning to course down her face. 'You can't ask me to leave my children. They're all I have left.'

Her father looks away and, with a sinking heart, Ann understands that he won't speak up against her mother. This is exactly how it was seven years ago, when she and Joseph first got together, and her mother insisted she drop him for the beau of their choice, a man so dull she would have preferred to have remained a spinster. Instead, she chose her darling Joseph, the man who swept her off her feet with his keen appetite for life, his kindness and his loyalty and, when she fell pregnant and was kicked out of home by her mother, the man who took her in with his own parents until the baby was born and with whom she then set up home elsewhere to spare hers the shame.

Back then, they were unmoved by her entreaties. And it seems nothing has changed. She was wrong to have come, to have dared hope.

'Thomas, Constance,' she says, rising to her feet. 'Say goodbye to your grandmother and grandfather. Unfortunately, they won't be seeing you again for some time.'

Then, hand in hand with her children, she walks back out into the cold grey afternoon, ready for the long walk home.

5

TAKING LIFE INTO HER HANDS

Ann Inett
10 JULY 1785, GRIMLEY, WORCESTERSHIRE, ENGLAND

It's been a year and a half since Joseph failed to come home from war, and every day has been a battle for Ann. She's been forced to take on more and more mending tasks and has had to lower her rates to compete with other women in similar circumstances also trying to make ends meet.

She's working from dawn to well past midnight most nights, trying to get her work finished before the children wake again in the morning. They have to accompany her on her rounds, too, as she knocks on all the doors of the village, and then those of the neighbouring villages, hamlets and towns, further and further away, to find work.

Before Joseph's death, her little business had been thriving as her dressmaking skills became wider known, and admired, but Mrs Brookes' failure to pay her outstanding bill is leaving a huge

The Governor, His Wife and His Mistress

dent in Ann's income. And the draper Mr Roberts is reluctant to forward her much more credit in terms of fresh material for new orders, and most of her customers are reluctant to pay good money up front first.

Consequently, Ann is increasingly having to rely on income from merely mending dresses and petticoats and shirts and stockings, which tends to be far more labour-intensive and far less lucrative. She's called round to Mrs Brookes' home several more times, but with no man now in Ann's life to stand up for her, the woman simply refuses to speak to her.

One time Ann even takes her children, hoping the sight of them might melt the woman's heart.

'Mrs Brookes,' Ann says brightly when she opens the door to see the three of them standing there. 'I wanted you to meet my children, Thomas and Constance. Children, this is Mrs Brookes, a friend and customer.'

Mrs Brookes stares at the trio, off balance for a moment.

'Hello, madam,' Thomas says politely. 'It's nice to meet you.'

Then Constance steps forward, shyly. 'Hello!' she says, with a big smile.

Ann feels her heart burn with love for her son and her daughter. What person could resist two such charming children?

'Yes,' Mrs Brookes says finally. 'It is nice to meet you, too.' Then she turns to Ann. 'To what do I owe this pleasure?'

Ann takes a deep breath. 'We were just wondering, Mrs Brookes, your bill for your dress? You said it doesn't fit, so I'd be happy to alter it if that is so. Or if you no longer want it, I would be happy to take it off your hands so I can resell it.'

Mrs Brookes frowns, realising she's been cornered. Then another expression passes over her face. Ann, describing the scene later to her neighbour Mrs Thompson, says it looked like 'rat cunning'.

'Thank you, Ann,' she says, 'but I'm afraid it's too late. The dress was so poorly made, and the fabric so cheap, I have thrown the whole thing away.'

'But I saw you in the dress just earlier this week,' Ann protests. 'And it looked—*you* looked—stunning.'

'No, that's not true.' Mrs Brookes curls her lip. 'I tried wearing it once but the seams started coming loose.'

Ann blanches, but keeps on going, trying to sound reasonable and not too wheedling. The children are starting to look upset. 'But I must have seen you in that sage-green dress at least five times now, Madam,' she says. 'Every time it looked as if it fitted you, and suited you, perfectly.'

'What nonsense you talk, Ann,' responds the older woman coldly. 'I think you should take your children and be gone, before I call the parish constable.'

'But Mrs Brookes!' Ann exclaims. 'For the love of God, please be reasonable. We both know that the dress is perfectly fine, and that you can well afford to pay for it. I, on the other hand, am behind with my rent and am unable to buy more material on credit because I haven't yet paid for yours. I have two children to feed. You can see them here. Please have a heart.'

'Maybe you should have thought of your finances before you had two children,' Mrs Brookes says sharply. 'That is no business of mine. Good day to you all.' And then she slams the door shut.

Constance bursts into tears and young Thomas puts his arm around her to comfort his sister. Ann is close to tears, too, but is determined not to frighten her children.

'Let's go home,' she says cheerfully instead. 'We'll leave this wicked witch to her own devices.' She is heartened to see Thomas grin and, at that moment, decides she'll have to take life into her own hands. She has to be bold; she has to be daring. There doesn't seem to be any alternative if her little family aren't to be flung out onto the streets.

The pounding of her heart is almost deafening to her ears as she gently eases the door open, freezing at the squeak of the hinge. 'Courage,' she whispers to herself. 'Courage.'

This is something Ann never imagined she'd ever have the hide to do, but needs must when the devil drives. She pushes open the door a little further and listens intently for any movement. Nothing stirs and she takes a deep breath and slips silently inside.

It's dark, but Ann makes her way sure-footedly towards the drawing room. She's confident of where she's going and how to get there; goodness only knows how many times she's been in this house in happier times. In those days, there was no need for subterfuge or stockinged feet. She'd march in and call a cheery 'Hello' to the mistress of the mansion and then go about her business. But that was then and this is now. And things are different. Very different.

She continues through the winding corridor and concentrates on controlling her breath, but she imagines she can hear the material of her skirt sweeping along and her feet padding on the thick rugs, while her heart feels as if it's beating out of her chest. At every creak of the floorboards, at every sigh of the wind outside, she can feel the hair on the back of her neck stiffen to attention and she stops to listen for movement. At any moment, she's ready for a ghostly figure to appear or a scream to signal she's been heard. But, thankfully, not yet. Finally, she swings open the door to the drawing room and can see everything is almost as she imagined. Almost. With one critical exception.

The sage-green linen gown with a tight bodice topped by a white frill, a full skirt with a matching panel of white at the front and three-quarter-length sleeves trimmed with white is lying over the back of a chair. It's one of her finest creations and, even tonight, she can't help feeling a flush of pride at the sight of it. As if Mrs Brookes would ever have dreamt of throwing it away! But then she reminds herself why she's here. She creeps over and picks up the gown, feeling the soft lustre of the material under her calloused hands. She admires it for just a moment before folding it carefully and slipping it into the sack she's been carrying under her arm.

With her eyes now adjusting to the gloom of the room, she can see the petticoat she sewed to go under it tossed onto the floor, and the two matching aprons hanging where she left them, alongside the white gauze cap and the dark green silk hood. She seizes them, too, but notices a couple of threads hanging down from one of the aprons she hadn't quite finished. Without even thinking about it, she takes the scissors out of her pocket where they habitually live, and snips them off, and then slides all the garments into the same sack, flinching at the soft rustle of the fabric. Finally, she spies the shoes that go with the dress and the cotton stockings to be worn under it and, on an impulse, stuffs them in as well.

Ann heaves the sack over her shoulder, turns away from the scene of her crime and sneaks as quietly as she can out of the room, back down the corridor and out of the front door. Once there, she pauses for a moment to replace the heavy latch, pulling up the leather thong looped around it and gently dropping it back into place, then runs as fast as she can through the dark, deserted streets, past the village green and up the rough path to home.

As soon as she opens the door, she realises she's panting, and her breath sounds forced and raspy. She wills herself to stop. She drops the sack, sits down on a stool and forces herself to calm down. Then, when her breathing is less laboured, she moves over to check on Thomas and Constance.

She still can't quite believe what she's done, but she can't have disturbed Mrs Brookes, otherwise she would have come running after her, and she saw no one on the route back. She's clear. And it was for a good cause. The very best: her children.

The days following the break-in are tense for Ann. She hides the dress and everything that goes with it underneath the children's mattress and keeps a low profile. She ventures out occasionally to the village shop to make sure she'll be seen out and about and won't raise any suspicion, but it seems all anyone can talk about is the burglary at Mrs Brookes' house.

Ann had imagined Mrs Brookes wouldn't report it to the constable, as she'd be embarrassed at not having paid for the dress and would most likely want to forget all about it, but Ann is wrong. Four days after the event, on 14 July 1785, a report appears in the local newspaper, *Berrow's Worcester Journal*:

The dwelling-house of Susannah Brookes in Grimley has been broken open and several articles of her wearing apparel taken thereout.

Even more worryingly, further back in the same newspaper is a public notice offering a reward to anyone giving information leading to the conviction of the house-breaker involved.

Ann has a plan to take the dress far away from Grimley to sell it, and now decides to take it further still, maybe as far as Worcester or Tenbury, to offer it at the local markets. No one there would ever know. She just has to wait until the coast is clear to spirit it away. In the meantime, she can't help feeling sick every time she sees the lump in the children's mattress, or hears a knock at the door.

Two days later, and the day before she's organised her ticket to Worcester, that fateful knock finally comes. It's 4 pm and she's been sitting at the table when there is the sound of footsteps at the door, and then a strident rapping. Her heart sinks.

She tells the children to sit on their bed, and opens the door. Two constables are standing there, and she can see Mrs Thompson in her doorway watching.

'Ann Inett?' the first asks. 'We have reason to believe that you broke into the house of Susannah Brookes and stole items that belonged to her.'

The Governor, His Wife and His Mistress

Ann stands stock still, gaping. She doesn't know what to say or do. The children look fascinated by the drama. One of the constables walks straight into her home and starts opening cupboards and looking on shelves. When he sees the children sitting on the bed, he asks them to get up and lifts the mattress to reveal her plunder.

The two constables exchange satisfied glances. 'Ann Inett, you are under arrest,' the first one says as he slips handcuffs around her wrists and pushes her out of the door. 'You'll be coming with us.'

Ann tries her best to smile reassuringly at Thomas and Constance. 'It's going to be all right,' she says. 'Mrs Thompson will look after you,' she adds, looking beseechingly at her neighbour, standing open-mouthed in shock. 'It's all right, children, everything is going to be all right.'

But even as she says it, she knows in her heart that it isn't true.

6

AS YE SOW, SO SHALL YE REAP

Philip Gidley King

10 OCTOBER 1786, LAUNCESTON, CORNWALL, ENGLAND

It's the day of the hiring fair in Launceston, the de facto county capital of Cornwall, and Philip Gidley King sighs as he ties his boots ready to attend. His dairyman was recently caught stealing pails of milk and selling them down at the local alehouse, and now he needs a replacement.

He's been farming now for two years since the ending of both wars in America and India. England is at peace and, just as he'd suspected, that period of calm has cut short his vocation. Much to his disappointment, he's been retired on half-pay from His Majesty's Royal Navy.

With his savings from his naval pay and the money his father left him, he's bought a small beef and dairy farm close to where his mother lives. He thought farming might suit him, especially since he seems to have little experience that would qualify him for much else. Being sent away at the age of seven for school on the Isle of Wight, well known for its naval training, had equipped him well for a career at sea, but nothing else.

His mother, Utricia, watches his progress. 'How are you finding farming life, son? Have you got used to it now?'

'I suppose so,' he says dutifully. 'I like being in the country where I can walk over the fields, around the hedgerows and along the little laneways to my heart's content. I love the peace and the quiet and the turn of the seasons.'

She nods. She can understand that. As a boy, he'd walk for miles and miles around their village and every time he came back from time at sea, he did the same. He'd return from those walks with drawings of what he'd seen—farm animals, trees, people he'd passed by, scenery. She often wonders how he survived in a ship with nowhere to walk to, and precious little to sketch except those blasted endless oceans.

'We're lucky, too,' he continues now, 'that the market for meat and milk is very strong. There's so much demand from the cities, as they're growing so quickly. But . . .' He stops and looks down at his hands.

'But *what*?' she asks him softly, as if she doesn't already know.

He smiles apologetically. 'It's a good life, but I'm not sure it's for me. I miss the camaraderie of life in the navy on a big ship, and the excitement of sailing ocean passages.'

'And battle?' she asks.

'No, not that at all,' Gidley King says, thinking of so many broken nights' sleep pushing his way through a tangle of bodies at sea. 'That's the one thing I don't miss. But I suppose you can't have one without the other.'

'You could join a merchant ship, with the English East India Company?'

'I suppose so. But . . . we'll see.'

Today, his thoughts are concentrated on the hiring fair and the man he'd had to dismiss. He'd confronted the dairyman after the farm manager, Jethro, caught him red-handed at the bar. Gidley King had asked him why he'd done it, thinking that maybe his wife was sick or his children were going without, and he desperately needed the extra money. Times were tough for rural workers in England, and Gidley King was known to be a kindly and generous employer.

The man, however, had bowed his head. 'No, sir, I'm not married,' he told Gidley King. 'Nor do I have children. I suppose I just did it because I could.'

'Because you could?' Gidley King repeated slowly, trying to understand. 'Do we not pay you fairly here?'

'You do,' the man replied, hanging his head even lower. 'I am sorry, sir. I don't know what came over me.'

Gidley King pondered his position, and looked over at Jethro. He was scowling. But Gidley King remained composed. 'How old are you?' he asked.

'Nineteen, sir.'

'And how long have you been working here?'

'Since I was twelve, sir.'

'Have you been selling the milk all that time?'

The man jolted his head up with a horrified expression. 'No, sir,' he exclaimed. 'I've only done it three times. There's a lassie I'm keen on, and I wanted to take her out and . . .' He ran out of courage.

The Governor, His Wife and His Mistress

'You know I'm going to have to dismiss you, don't you?' Gidley King asked him.

'Yes, of course, sir,' the man said.

'And you know the gaol here is one of the worst in the whole country, don't you?' Gidley King continued. 'The gaols everywhere are overcrowded and full of vermin and disease, so this Launceston one is absolutely shocking. I heard so many stories about it from the customers at my father's drapery store. Tiny cells, mud floors, filth, sickness, and poor rations dropped down through the bars to the prisoners below.'

He noted, with some satisfaction, how the man's face had turned white.

Pausing for effect, he let his words sink in. 'But,' he said finally, 'I'm not going to report you to the constabulary.'

The man looked up again, as if he couldn't believe his ears.

'Losing your job after such a long time here will be punishment enough,' Gidley King said. 'Do you promise me you will never do such a dishonest thing again?'

'Sir! Sir!' the man cried. 'I promise. I promise as God is my witness.'

'Then get out of my sight before I change my mind,' Gidley King said.

'Thank you, sir, thank you,' the man muttered as he raced away.

The farm manager turned to Gidley King. 'That was very kind of you, sir,' he said. 'Maybe too kind, if you want my opinion.'

'I think he's learned his lesson, Jethro,' Gidley King replied. 'Those gaols are terrible places. You go in a simple milk-thief and you come out a highway robber. He's young enough to change. He's had a fright. Everyone deserves a second chance.'

Now, Gidley King walks down the laneway towards the marketplace, keeping his eyes open for anyone holding a few wisps of straw to indicate that they are a dairyman for hire. Along the way, he passes a few shepherds with tufts of wool in their lapels and some housemaids holding mops, keen to be hired for the next year.

But just before he arrives at the main marketplace, he's stopped by the Royal Mailman. 'Lieutenant, I have a letter for you,' the man says, reaching into his bag. 'Saves me the trouble of delivering it.'

'Thank you.' Gidley King notices the envelope bears the Royal Navy seal. He tears it open impatiently, and sees it's from his old friend, Captain Arthur Phillip. He walks away to get free of the throng of people so he can read it in peace.

It seems Phillip has also been spending his time since the end of the wars farming, but he's in the New Forest, nine miles south-west of Southampton; land he describes as perfect for grazing cattle and pigs. Yet he has also been finding the change of pace unwelcome.

Happily, he's since received an offer of a challenging new position back in the navy, and he'd like to know if his old friend might be interested in joining him. Gidley King can barely believe his eyes.

LAWS FOR THE RICH

Ann Inett
1 NOVEMBER 1786, WORCESTER, ENGLAND

It's as if Ann Inett is trapped inside a ghastly nightmare that has absolutely no end—*ever*—in sight. At first, she's terrified not so much about what will happen to her, but what will befall her children. Then she's angry that life can be so cruelly unfair. And finally, she feels absolutely devoid of hope and utterly drained of even the will to live.

'I was only doing the best I could for my children,' Ann whispers, doubled over in loud sobs when her neighbour Mrs Thompson visits her in the gaol in Worcester where she was taken two days after her arrest. 'What else could I have done? That Mrs Brookes, she's the one who should be in here! If only she'd have paid her debt, none of this would have happened.'

Mrs Thompson remains silent. Her heart goes out to her neighbour. She's ten years older than Ann, but can see that, at thirty-two, and with no man in her life, two small children to provide for, and parents who'd refused to help her, Ann didn't have many options. But she should never have broken into Mrs Brookes' house. That was a step too far.

Ann, however, can't bring herself to believe that the court won't see her side of the story. '*Surely*, they'll believe me?' she says to her friend. 'They'll see I'm an honest woman. They can see I've never broken the law before. They'll understand.'

'Ann, don't get your hopes up,' Mrs Thompson gently warns her. 'Judges aren't drawn from the likes of us. They're from the class way above. Above Mrs Brookes, even. But they'll have much more in common with her than they do with us. They could see her as a poor, helpless middle-class woman who lives on her own being preyed on by the nasty lower classes.'

'No!' Ann cries. 'They won't. Not when I tell them my story. They'll realise—'

'Ann, you've got to be realistic. They'll think they have to protect people like her from people like you. The rich make the laws to protect their own interests.'

Ann stares at her in disbelief, then breaks down again in loud, racking sobs. Mrs Thompson sits quietly, rubbing her back until a warden walks by and pushes her hand away.

'No touching!' he barks.

Ann breaks off, startled, and Mrs Thompson seizes the moment. 'Now, Ann, I've had Thomas and Constance with me for three weeks now and while they're delightful children, I can barely afford to feed my brood, let alone yours as well.'

She pauses to let the words sink in. 'I'm so sorry, my dear, but you're going to have to think about who else could take them. There's the workhouse, but surely there's someone else?'

Ann falls silent. 'Yes, there is,' she says finally. 'My parents. They'd like to have my children but that might mean I won't ever get them back. But I don't want my parents to know what I've done.'

Mrs Thompson shakes her head. 'I think it's too late for that,' she says. 'The week after you were arrested, *Berrow's Worcester Journal* reported that you'd been apprehended for the crime and taken into custody.'

'They used my name?' Ann asks, wide-eyed.

Her friend nods. 'Everyone in the county knows about it by now so it won't have escaped your parents' notice. I could take the children up at the weekend. I'm sorry I can't keep them any longer, but it's just not possible.'

'I understand,' Ann says. 'And I am so grateful to you for taking them as long as you have. Tell me, how are they faring?'

'They ask every day for you,' Mrs Thompson says. 'Constance has been having nightmares, but Thomas is trying to be brave for his little sister. They're a real credit to you.'

'Please God I'll be free soon so I can pick them up again from my parents,' Ann says, looking into the distance. 'And could you ask my parents to write to me regularly to tell me how the children are? They can't be so hard-hearted that they'd refuse me that.'

'Of course I will,' her friend replies. 'I'm sure they'll be glad to take them and be happy to write to you often.'

By the time the day of the trial dawns, eight long months after her arrest, Ann is so nervous, she can barely speak. She knows her parents have the children, but she's heard nothing from them since. Dear Mrs Thompson has made it her business to visit them twice, though, and has reported back that they're settling down well. Ann begs her to bring them to visit her, but her parents have expressly forbidden it. Instead, she writes them long letters 'from their dear mama' saying how much she misses them, and how much she loves them and how much she hopes, one day, they'll all be reunited. Mrs Thompson tells her she hands them over to Ann's parents in the hope they'll read them to the children, but doubts that they do. She says that maybe, in time, their attitude will soften and they'll agree to read the letters and write themselves, and maybe even let her see Thomas, now eight, and five-year-old Constance again. Ann feels such an ache in her heart that she wonders if she'll even survive this separation.

Meantime, life in the cells is far worse than she could ever have imagined. The gaol is so crowded, Ann is sharing her cell with ten other women and men, and it's so small, they have to take turns to lie down on the cold, earthen floor. The wardens throw in the meagre rations—usually just stale bread—and watch the prisoners scrabble to win a share. There's one overflowing bucket in the corner for everyone to relieve themselves in, which they empty just once a day, and another bucket in another corner with water to wash in. That's usually fetid, and finished, by early morning. As a result, the cells stink, there are rats and the constant scurrying of beetles, and fights frequently break out between the exhausted inmates.

The Governor, His Wife and His Mistress

Ann tries to keep out of everyone's way, but now the prospect of the trial is terrifying. She's heard the others say that the courts are weighted against them, and often the judges suffer from gout and are extremely bad-tempered and harsh as a result, but she can't really believe it. Instead, she's rehearsed what she has to say, over and over. The dress. Mrs Brookes. Joseph fighting, and dying, for his country. Their children. The landlord. Mr Mansfield. Her despair over the unpaid debt. Mrs Brookes' refusal to pay.

When she's finally handcuffed and led up into the dock at the Worcester Assizes in the Guild Hall from the basement cells on 11 March 1786, she's never been more ready in her life. She looks around and is shocked to see her parents frowning from the back of the court, but Mrs Thompson smiling encouragingly next to them. She strains her neck, but she can see no sign of Thomas nor Constance. Maybe that's just as well.

A booming voice breaks the hush as the court officer reads the charge: that Ann Inett did, with force and arms, break and enter the house of Susannah Brookes, and steal a petticoat, two aprons, a pair of shoes, three muslin handkerchiefs, a silk hood, a gauze cap, a linen gown, cotton stockings and a muslin cap, all to the value of twenty-one shillings.

Ann is aghast to be charged with breaking in with arms, and can't help interrupting, declaring that the charge is wrong. 'No,' the judge says, looking bored. 'You had scissors with you. They can be a dangerous weapon in the wrong hands.'

'But . . . but I always carry scissors,' she protests. 'They're my stock-in-trade. I'm a dressmaker.'

'Silence!' shouts the court officer. 'Only speak when you're ordered to.'

Ann is then forced to stay silent as Mrs Brookes takes the stand and gives an obviously well-practised speech, interspersed with equally well-practised tears, about how she felt sorry for Ann as the mother of two illegitimate children and so gave her some work as a seamstress. She quickly realised, however, that she had no talent for dressmaking and ruined the piece of material Mrs Brookes had bought for a new frock. After that, she says, Ann had frequently called round to threaten her and ask for money. Then, finally, when she was sleeping upstairs, Ann had broken into her home and stolen many precious items. Luckily for Mrs Brookes, she hadn't heard her intruder; if she had, and had gone down to confront her, she could have well been stabbed to death by those scissors.

At first, Mrs Brookes says she had no idea who had burgled her home. But then she noticed a stray thread on the ground—the one that Ann had snipped off one of the aprons. Who else would ever have done such a thing but her recalcitrant dressmaker? That was evidence, too, that she'd been carrying scissors.

Ann listens in horror to Mrs Brookes' lies about her dressmaking. It makes it worse that she's wearing a dark plum-coloured gown that Ann had made for her maybe two years before. She remembers even then the woman had argued about the price and paid her less than she'd asked. And being so conscientious in her craft by snipping that thread has cost her dearly.

The judge is making notes, and Ann waits patiently for her turn to speak. But it never comes. The judge addresses the court, saying a woman's home is her refuge and it is unforgiveable for anyone to invade her territory, especially when carrying a weapon.

'But, sir,' Ann interjects, 'can I explain? Mrs Brookes wouldn't pay her bills and look at the dress she is wearing today—'

'Silence!' thunders the court officer. 'You haven't given us a written statement, so you can't speak now.'

'But . . . but . . . I never knew . . . I was never asked for a written statement,' Ann stumbles.

'Enough!' says the judge, who she can see is already turning over the page to look at his next case. Her words trail out and in their place the booming voice delivers the verdict: 'Guilty!'

Ann looks around her in bewilderment. But the judge hasn't finished. 'You will pay dearly for your crime,' he says. 'You will be hanged by the neck until dead.'

Hanged! Ann stands open-mouthed and feels numb with shock. Empty. Completely spent. She can see Mrs Thompson in tears, and her parents looking stonily at the floor. Then she's led back down into the cells, moving as if in a dream, or that never-ending nightmare.

Her cellmates offer her no sympathy. They've generally fared no better. Many—found guilty variously of burglary, theft, sheep-stealing, horse-stealing and robbery—have received the same crushing death sentence.

Two mornings later, seven of the prisoners who'd been tried the same day as Ann are roughly dragged to their feet by the prison guards and bundled away.

'Where are they taking them?' Ann asks, although dreading the answer.

'They're off to Red Hill,' another cellmate tells her. 'Two miles away. The gallows there have never been busier.'

Now there is a little more room, Ann can sleep every night on the rough earth floor of the cell, but wakes every few minutes in terror, waiting for the warden to drag her out to be hanged. After three weeks, she can't bear the tension and fear anymore and longs for her death. Then, after the passing of yet another week, two guards clang the cell door open.

'Inett!' one of them shouts, and she stands stiffly to attention. 'Get here,' he says.

She moves to him obediently and is handcuffed again. She feels sick to the stomach. The time has obviously come for her to be taken to Red Hill and hanged. She says a silent prayer: *Forgive me, Lord, for I have sinned, but please look after my children.*

But after the gaoler pushes her out of the cell, he doesn't lead her outside into the dull light. Instead, he shoves her towards the stairs that go up to the courtroom.

Ann is bewildered. 'What's happening, where are we going?' she asks.

'Shut up if you know what's good for you,' is the reply.

When Ann emerges back into the dock, she can see the court is virtually empty but for the judge—a different one this time—and the court officials.

'Ann Inett?' the judge asks.

'Yes, sir.'

'It's your lucky day,' he says. 'Your life is to be spared. Your death sentence is instead commuted to seven years' transportation beyond the seas.'

Ann gapes at him. Transportation? She doesn't understand. She knows that prisoners used to be sent over to America, but the colonists banned taking convicts when they won the war. In some ways, she wouldn't have minded being taken to America; at least she'd be much closer to Joseph.

The judge sees she doesn't understand and, in a softer voice this time, says, 'You are to be banished to Botany Bay to serve out your sentence.'

'Botany Bay?' she echoes. Everyone knew that was the place on that Great South Land Captain Cook discovered in 1770, sixteen years before, and she'd heard all the recent talk of sending convicts there, in place of America. But she had no idea it was real, nor imminent. And it was so far away, on the other side of the world.

'But my children,' she says. 'My children are here. I can't leave them.'

There's a sound like a snort from the judge's bench. 'You'll be taken to your transport in November,' he growls, losing patience. 'And better you leave them behind when you go to Botany Bay than you leave them behind from the end of a noose. Now take her away, out of my sight.'

Ann spends seven more months in prison before word comes that the ships are ready to transport the convicts to Botany Bay. She's desperate to see her children again, one last time, and begs the warden to smuggle a letter out to Mrs Thompson, pleading with her to bring Thomas and Constance. Every day, she prays to hear from her, but every day, there's silence.

Seven days later, Mrs Thompson arrives. 'I'm so sorry, my dear,' she says. 'But your parents won't hear of it. They won't allow me to bring the children.'

Ann hangs her head, tears blinding her eyes. 'I understand,' she says. 'But please tell the children, one day I will come back for them. One day I will. I promise. Don't let them forget me.'

Two days on, a wagon and brace of horses, accompanied by a team of armed guards, arrive at Worcester and a guard snaps an iron ring around one of Ann's legs and shackles her to those holding other female prisoners. The women are then shuffled onto the wagon, which joins others stopping off at various gaols along the way to pick up more female prisoners. The armed guards aren't only to keep the women in check; it seems from their whispered conversations that they're also there to defend the convoy against highwaymen, notorious on this stretch of road around Blackheath, London. It's two full days before they arrive at their final destination, Gravesend, Kent, the last port on the River Thames.

It's November 1786, a full sixteen months since Ann broke into her customer's house to take back her dress, and her mood is grim. It isn't helped either when one of her fellow passengers tells her about the town. 'It's called Gravesend because it was a burial ground during the plague,' she says. 'There were so many bodies, they ran out of space in London, so they dug mass graves here. It's said at night you can still meet the restless spirits roaming the land.'

The Governor, His Wife and His Mistress

But once there, they're herded aboard a 338-ton, two-deck transport, the *Lady Penrhyn*, the ship earmarked to carry female convicts as part of what would become known as the First Fleet, and pushed into the darkness below. There are no portholes for light and the ceiling is so low most have to crouch to stay upright.

Ann learns the ship was originally designed to carry slaves as part of the Atlantic slave trade. As such, it seems the perfect vessel to take them to Portsmouth, their departure point from England, and then to continue on to oblivion.

8

A FINE ADVENTURE

Philip Gidley King
15 MARCH 1787, LAUNCESTON, CORNWALL, ENGLAND

The horses shuffle and stamp as if they can't wait to be off, the steam blasting from their nostrils like a dragon's breath in the cold morning air. The grass by the roadside is crisp with morning frost and the tower of the nearby Launceston Castle perched on the hilltop is swathed in mist.

Philip Gidley King regards it for a moment. 'Castle Terrible' it's been dubbed, as it's now the county gaol for Cornwall and notorious for its cruel treatment of inmates. It's good, he thinks, that it's now partly hidden from view from the townspeople. But it should neither be ignored, nor forgotten. He hopes he can contribute, in time, to a far better solution than cramming so many people into Britain's sordid gaols.

He turns back towards the coach and hefts his kitbag onto the roof. A strapping man of about thirty-five, unshaven but neatly

The Governor, His Wife and His Mistress

turned out nonetheless, hands him his valise as he prepares to take the step to the interior of the coach.

'Don't you worry, sir, about anything,' the man says in a broad Cornish accent. 'The farm will be in even better shape when you come back than it is now. Me and the missus will take care of that.'

Gidley King looks him in the eye as they share a firm handshake. He'd been warned not to hire this fellow, but there were worse crimes in the world than punching the nose of a tyrant and bully as Jethro's previous employer was known to have been. In the three years Gidley King had retained him, he'd been impressed by his strong sense of right and wrong. Take that dairyman, for example. Jethro hadn't hesitated to step in when he discovered he was doing the wrong thing, and even felt he should have been punished more harshly than he was. He'd approved wholeheartedly of the new young dairyman Gidley King had brought back from the hiring fair, too, and the pair had already talked about ways in which they could increase yields.

'Thanks so much, Jethro,' he says. 'I know I'm leaving the farm in capable hands. I shall write often and will be glad to hear news of the farm's affairs. I could be away two years, maybe more. But I will stay in touch.'

'Yessir,' Jethro says, touching his forelock. 'God bless you on your new venture.'

Gidley King nods and then steps up into the carriage, feeling the familiar prickle of excitement running up his spine at the prospect of returning to his beloved ocean, and the adventures that lay ahead. He feels his whole life is now before him. His dear friend and mentor Captain Arthur Phillip had surprised him with his generous offer to join him on the historic First Fleet of convicts to be sent to Botany Bay—some, perhaps, from Launceston's gaols—and he will be forever grateful. However it turns out.

Because, in truth, he has little idea of how this ambitious endeavour will shape up. He knows only the basics, and has been following the debate in the newspapers keenly about the rising crime rate and the crackdown by the judiciary with tougher sentences. As a result, the gaols have been overflowing and conditions are becoming ever more appalling both there and in the floating hulks—decommissioned ships used as prisons—to accommodate the excess. There are constant reports of multiple deaths among inmates from fever and poor hygiene amid the crush of bodies. In March, there'd actually been a riot on one of the hulks in Plymouth with forty-four convicts shot, eight of them dead. Previously, the government had the chance to relieve the situation by transporting convicts to America, but that finished with the war. They'd tried transporting them later to the slave forts of West Africa but had to abandon that plan after the disastrous first voyage on which half of them died, and most of the rest deserted. The influential botanist Sir Joseph Banks, who has the ear of the king, then pushed for a new convict colony in Botany Bay, and now preparations are well advanced for the First Fleet of eleven ships to take them.

What actually awaits them there will be anyone's guess.

It takes Gidley King two long days to reach London for his rendezvous with Phillip at The Admiralty in Whitehall. The two

The Governor, His Wife and His Mistress

men shake hands, then warmly embrace. They have dinner together, and Gidley King can see how animated Phillip becomes when he starts talking of their upcoming voyage.

'By God, King, it's going to be a fine adventure!' Phillip tells him. 'Just think of it: eleven ships carrying what's going to be around fourteen thousand people on an eight-month voyage of about fifteen thousand nautical miles. Nothing like this has ever been attempted before in the history of the world. It's going to be monumental. This is why I need good people around me and you, King, I already know are one of the best. I'll be on the flagship HMS *Sirius*, and you'll be serving as my aide-de-camp and the second lieutenant on the ship, below Captain John Hunter and First Lieutenant William Bradley. Are you up for that?'

'Of course, sir,' Gidley King says. He's trying to retain his cool but, in truth, he's thrilled. This is a major promotion and, always ambitious, it could be the making of him and his naval career. With only a few weeks till his twenty-ninth birthday, he's well aware that it could also enormously help his marital prospects. Like any young man, he'd dearly love to marry and have a family, and a position like this would give him access to a much better class of woman. He smiles at Phillip. 'It feels like a great honour,' he says.

'Nonsense!' Phillip barks. 'You deserve it. You're an extremely hard worker, conscientious and very able, with great perseverance. I know you to be extremely enterprising, too, although I know the navy hasn't always appreciated that.'

His protégé blanches. Eight years earlier, he'd stained his spotless record of service while aboard the HMS *Renown* when he'd captured an enemy ship and approved an agent to sell the cargo—without consulting his captain. Within such a strict hierarchy, he'd paid dearly for that error of overstepping his authority, being court-martialled and dismissed from the ship. He realised he'd acted wrongly, but is pleased to hear Phillip recast it as something of a virtue.

But his captain is still speaking, and Gidley King focuses back on his words. 'I can't say it'll be an easy task,' he's saying. 'We'll doubtless have many challenges in front of us, and who knows what it will be like trying to establish a colony of convicts and settlers at such a vast distance from Britain.'

Gidley King nods. 'It certainly is a big task,' he agrees.

'I've prepared for it as much as I can,' continues Phillip. 'Captain Cook kept an excellent daily journal from his time on the *Endeavour*, and wrote plenty of descriptions of the places and people of New Holland. I feel he has done us proud. Sir Joseph has also been generous with his time, and we've met on several occasions now for briefings. I think I know as much as it is possible to know, without, of course, having been there.'

Not for the first time, Gidley King is impressed by Phillip. He knows the man isn't the most charismatic of leaders, and hadn't been the pick of the First Lord of the Admiralty, Lord Richard Howe, who'd even gone so far as to say he didn't feel Captain Arthur Phillip would be suitable as the leader of such an important expedition. But, on the other hand, he was known to be immensely steady and reliable, and, now at forty-eight years old, a wise old hand and, most usefully, an experienced farmer. While others doubted his capability, it's possible that a friend, and near neighbour of his farm in the New

The Governor, His Wife and His Mistress

Forest, the future Navy Treasurer Sir George Rose, had weighed in on the decision to appoint him.

Yet he's won the admiration of Gidley King, time and time again. Both are from similarly humble backgrounds—the shopkeeper's son and Phillip, the son of a teacher—and Gidley King knows how hard it is to haul yourself up the ranks of such an established institution as the navy.

Phillip was far from the usual kind of captain, too. For a start, he spoke no fewer than five languages with his father a language teacher from Germany, which enabled him to work for a spell as a spy for the British in the naval facilities in the south of France, reporting to a spymaster who ended up Secretary of the Admiralty. He'd also served a stint in the Portuguese Navy, assisting them in their battles against Spain and transporting convicts from Lisbon to Brazil, becoming, in that country, something of a national hero.

Gidley King has done his own fair share of reading about New Holland, too: the first British voyage there, Cook's and Banks's notes and speculation on the quality of its land, observations of the 'native inhabitants', and what's known of its topography. He believes that Phillip's farming experience will more than likely stand him in good stead when assessing the land beyond Botany Bay for such ventures. In addition, he has a kindly Christian humanity that Gidley King believes will serve them well. In the New Forest, Phillip had taken on the post of overseer of the poor and appeared genuinely concerned for their plight. While he believes in firm discipline when it comes to convicts, he's also keen on the opportunities for reform.

'I want this to be more, far more, than just a penal settlement,' Phillip is saying, as Gidley King remembers he's not only going to be in charge of this voyage, but he's also going to take charge as the first Governor of New South Wales when they finally arrive. 'There is so much potential. I want to encourage free settlers to migrate, and eventually have the British Government treat them as British residents and protect them from the convicts.'

'And have you thought anything of the natives?' Gidley King asks him. 'I know Cook found them fascinating and felt they were generally far happier than us Europeans, not coveting the kind of modern conveniences, clothes and possessions we prize.'

Phillip nods in reply. 'I admire how he wrote in his journal that they live in tranquillity, with the earth and the sea furnishing them all things necessary for life. I hope we can treat them kindly and establish a peaceful co-existence with them.'

Gidley King travels the seventy-five miles south onto Portsmouth, his heart beating with excitement for what lies ahead. But when he arrives and sees the eleven ships of the expedition at anchor out on the Motherbank between Portsmouth and the Isle of Wight, he's appalled. Some look so decrepit, he fears they won't even survive the voyage. Of the total, there are only two navy escort ships. The first is the sixth-rate 540-ton HMS *Sirius*, the flagship for the fleet, which is actually an overhauled former food and beverage supply ship, fitted with twenty guns. Gidley King is horrified by the state of it and writes in his journal that it has been 'rebuilt with the refuse of the yard'. The second is a tender with eight guns, the 170-ton HMS *Supply*, that he immediately complains that, at just seventy feet long,

The Governor, His Wife and His Mistress

is too small for such a long time at sea. That night, he prays more fervently than he can ever before remember.

As he inspects the other nine ships, Gidley King realises they're all merchant vessels that the government has hired, with most of their owners planning to use the convicts as ballast to reach the other side of the world, and then sail back to Britain with goods from the Far East. He's told that six will carry convicts, including the largest, the *Alexander*, the next down in size, the *Scarborough*, the *Prince of Wales*, the *Charlotte*, the *Lady Penrhyn* for one hundred and one female convicts, and the *Friendship*. There'll be around five hundred and forty-eight male convicts, one hundred and eighty-eight female convicts and seventeen of their children, officials like the Governor-designate Phillip, and his deputy and the next governor-to-be, Captain John Hunter, as well as other officers, the chaplain, the judge advocate, the surgeon and assistant surgeon, and a number of soldiers along with the ships' crews, marines and their wives and children.

Gidley King is eager to get this adventure underway, but the departure date keeps being put back while Captain Phillip lobbies for more money, guns, seed, tools and medical supplies, with the government dragging its feet on supplying enough of everything. Although it's now been eight months since the order was given to establish the penal colony, Gidley King starts to suspect that the government doesn't consider it much of a priority. Just as they want to get the convicts out of sight as cheaply as possible, and then out of mind, he thinks sourly, so too does it seem with those tasked with getting them there.

While they await departure, he volunteers to accompany Phillip on regular inspections of the ships, the crews and their miserable cargo as they await departure. Their visit to the *Lady Penrhyn* to check on the female convicts presents a sight he will never forget.

As his eyes adjust to the gloom on the lower deck, he sees the women are chained together to prevent them escaping but, beyond that, he can make out that they have few clothes between them, with many almost naked. In addition, they're absolutely filthy, their hair looks dull and matted, and it would be a safe bet that most would be infested with lice and God knows what else. He assumes they have little access to water to wash, but it's a shock to see them in such a state, living in this kind of filth. The stench hits him, too, probably from so many bodies in close proximity, as well as the rudimentary open buckets for toilets. Gidley King is horrified and dismayed and feels his eyes begin to water. He wipes them impatiently.

'It's the smell,' he says to Phillip hurriedly, to mask his distress. It would never do to appear so weak even before the voyage has begun.

'Yes, it is appalling,' Phillip agrees, putting a handkerchief over his own nose.

'This is so much worse than I expected,' Gidley King says. 'And we haven't set sail yet! These conditions are intolerable. This isn't right.'

Phillip agrees. 'They will be defenceless against any kind of fever if that starts to spread,' he says. 'I've been asking the government for extra supplies of clothes for them but have heard nothing back. I think there's nothing for it but to commandeer some of the material from the *Sirius*'s stores.'

The Governor, His Wife and His Mistress

Gidley King is relieved that the captain feels the same, although Phillip's manner is admirably detached and businesslike. 'That's an excellent idea,' Gidley King says. 'I'll give the order and have them handed out.'

The captain then departs for London to continue his entreaties for the clothes, as well as the other supplies—most of which fall on deaf ears. He arrives back in Portsmouth on 9 May and tells Gidley King, Hunter and Bradley that they'll be sailing on 12 May. Already, seventeen convicts have died in the cramped conditions on the ships as they float on the Motherbank, and fever is spreading so rapidly, they can hold on for no longer. But then, on the very day of departure, the seamen who've been employed by the ship owners refuse to work and, without them, it's impossible to leave. Gidley King again is the first to volunteer to sort out the situation and goes off to talk to the men.

Many are surprised he's so sympathetic to their cause. 'They've been working here for seven months on the ships and have received little pay in all that time,' he reports back. 'They need money to prepare for the voyage, but their masters have been withholding their pay so they'll be forced to buy provisions from the ships en route at vastly inflated prices.'

Perhaps remarkably, he manages to negotiate a solution, with Phillip ordering those not wanting to sail to be put ashore and be replaced by seamen from the escort naval ship. Then, at last, on 13 May at 3 am, the First Fleet weighs anchor and sets sail for Botany Bay with, below deck, its cargo of absolute human misery.

A PIT OF DESPAIR

Ann Inett

15 MAY 1787, PORTSMOUTH, ENGLAND

Ann Inett is one of the lucky ones. She's given a length of material to wrap around herself after the dress she'd been wearing since her arrest nearly two years before has frayed, torn, tattered and finally fallen apart. But by now, she's lost any modesty she might once have had. She simply can't afford it in the conditions she now finds herself in aboard the *Lady Penrhyn*.

The space the women are crowded into below deck is cold and damp and stinks of body odour, acrid bilge water, urine and faeces from the overflowing pots. The bulkheads—which run vertically through the ship to divide it into sections to reduce floodwaters pouring from one into another, and keep the convicts, seamen and marines separate—are filled with nails and dotted with holes to allow the crew to poke their guns through in case of any mutiny. Often the women see eyes at the holes, peering at them and their

The Governor, His Wife and His Mistress

bodies. When she was first brought on board, Ann had glimpsed a three-foot-high barricade on the upper deck, topped with iron prongs, to separate the ship's crew from the prisoners.

'Surely they can't be *that* scared of us?' Ann mutters in surprise to one of the other women. 'It's not as if we're murderers!'

'By the time this voyage is over,' the woman replies, 'we might well be.'

Another woman lets out an earthy cackle. 'I don't think it's to protect them from us,' she interjects. 'It's more likely to protect us from them.'

Ann turns to her, eyes wide. 'What do you mean?' she asks. 'What would they have against us?'

'As much as they possibly could,' the woman replies to a general outbreak of laughter.

Before they set sail, Commodore of the Fleet Arthur Phillip orders the hatches, with access to the sunlight and fresh air of the upper deck, be flung open to help give the women some relief. Everyone is mystified until news filters through the deck about one of their number collapsing and dying a day later. The diagnosis turns out to be 'gaol fever', the typhus spread by rats and fleas to humans.

Phillip is apparently so alarmed at the thought of it spreading rapidly throughout the human cargo that the women are moved up to the top deck while the crew whitewash the lower one with quick lime and igniting gunpowder to try to disinfect it. Ann relishes the two hours in the fresh air, but stands transfixed as a corpse sewn up in a hammock, weighted with shot, is jettisoned overboard before slowly sinking below the surface.

Now they have finally set sail, past the Isle of Wight and out into the open sea, conditions are deteriorating rapidly. While the chains have been taken off the women, the hatches are secured back down with cross bars, bolts and locks, and there's absolutely no fresh air. There's no light either as candles and lanterns are banned for fear of fire and everyone has to stoop down as the ceiling is so low when they stand. In addition, Ann, like nearly all her fellow convicts, has never been on a ship before, and finds both the confined space and the constant motion terrifying. She seems constantly to be sick and, once one woman starts, the smell makes everyone else join in. They're constantly slushing around in a pool of vomit and soon give up trying to mop it away. The only relief comes when they lie like sardines at four to a mattress set on the sleeping racks soldered into the hull. At least then they can stay partly dry. But it's not long before fresh vermin crawls back out from the ship's wood.

Ann can't stop thinking about Thomas and Constance, and is terrified that one day she'll no longer be able to remember their faces, nor hear their voices in her head. She continues to write them letters, which she hopes a ship at Botany Bay might carry back to England, and daydreams of one day returning to her children, and the excitement she'd see on their faces. But the happy vision is always edged out by the crushing fear that it might never happen.

She tries to focus on other things, knowing the anguish and sense of hopelessness could so easily overwhelm her. She silently thanks the young naval officer who'd come with Captain Phillip to inspect the women and obviously been horrified by what he'd found. Some of the crew had been down before, but only to ogle the women. Before their gaze, she and the others had tried to cover themselves and shrink away into the shadows as best they could. But that officer seemed different. He'd come down with the captain, who'd looked all business and matter of fact, but Ann thought she saw a glint of a tear in the eye of his lieutenant. She felt oddly grateful for that rare sign of humanity, and perhaps sympathy. As a result, she and a number of other women had been given fabric, which she quickly wrapped around herself, then tore and sewed into a type of tunic.

'How did you manage that?' one of the women asks her, in what sounds a little like her own Worcestershire accent. 'I couldn't have done that even with scissors and endless thread and needles.'

'I am—' Ann quickly corrects herself, 'I was a dressmaker. It's easy if you know how. Let me show you.'

Ann has befriended a number of the other women on her part of the lower deck. The one who made the joke about them needing protection from the crew is Ann Green, a fellow dressmaker who, at twenty-eight, is closest to her years, but seems so much more worldly-wise. She'd been found guilty at the Old Bailey of stealing crockery from a china-mending business in central London.

'I was desperate,' she tells Ann, when they first meet. 'My husband died three months before our son, William, was born. I'd been trying hard to feed and clothe us, but then our money ran out. I had no one else in the world I could turn to. And so when I saw an opportunity, I took it. But if I'd have known then what I know now, I would never have done it. I've lost everything.'

Ann puts her hand on the other's arm. 'Were you forced to leave your son behind?' she asks.

'No, I was able to bring him with me.'

Ann looks around. 'Is he not with you now?'

She sees a terrible flicker of pain pass over the woman's eyes. 'No, he isn't,' she says in a dull, flat voice. 'He died on the eighth of February in prison before we were brought to this ship. He wasn't strong enough and slipped away.'

Ann puts her arms around the woman as she breaks down into agonising sobs. It's as much as Ann can do not to join her. They sit like that for a full five minutes before the woman recovers.

'I'm so sorry,' she says. 'It's still so fresh.'

When Ann tells the others her own story, there's a hushed silence, with murmurings of sympathy at various points. She weeps as she describes the last time she saw her two children, as she was being dragged away by the constables, and how much she misses them both.

'I just want to die, really,' she finishes up. 'I can't imagine life without them. I want all the pain and hurt to end. I don't want to feel like this anymore.'

'You can't think that way,' says Olivia Gascoigne, the woman who'd asked her how she'd managed to turn her material so quickly into a robe, who is indeed from Worcester close to her. 'One day, when your sentence is over, maybe you'll be able to return home and be reunited with them. Think how awful it would be for them if they discover they are orphans, and that their mother has died.'

A tear slips down Ann's face as she listens.

'I'm sure your parents will be doing their very best by them,' Olivia continues. 'They may not be kind to you, but they won't be able to resist their grandchildren. You have to stop worrying about them. I know it's easy to say but, in here, you have to look after yourself. You've got to put all your energy into surviving this God-awful voyage. It won't do them any good if you don't.'

Olivia's twenty-six, and had been in service, but was found guilty of stealing thirteen gold coins to the value of thirteen pounds and thirteen pence, and one foreign silver coin, from a neighbour's house.

'You would have done better to have stolen that woman's money rather than her dress,' Olivia advises Ann. 'But then again, we've both ended up here, so I suppose neither of us covered ourselves in glory.' Ann can't help smiling. She liked Olivia from the moment she met her.

There are two much younger women on a nearby bunk. One is Nancy Yeates, who's just nineteen and broke into a house to steal cotton, and the other is seventeen-year-old Esther Abrahams with her baby daughter, Rosanna. She's a milliner, convicted of stealing fifty shillings worth of black lace.

'Let's hope we're all around at the end of this voyage,' Ann says one day after the group sit and talk. 'I can't imagine what's in store for us.'

'I can,' says Nancy. 'And none of it's good. But if we all try to look after each other, we might stand a better chance.'

The days start gradually to blur into each other, with boredom the greatest enemy. After the first week, however, things start to improve. The hatches are re-opened to give the women slight relief from the rising stink of the bilge waters. They have to be closed again, however, when heavy rain soon sweeps in and threatens to drown them all.

They're also allowed on deck occasionally, weather permitting, for exercise, although the space they're given is so tiny, some of the women complain they feel faint after trying to walk in such tight circles. On Phillip's orders, the food they're given is unexpectedly good, too, with rations of fresh meat, vegetables, bread and oatmeal.

It isn't long, however, before Ann discovers what her first friend, Ann Green, had meant when she talked about the barrier between them and the sailors. They overhear the mariners one day talking about the *Friendship* where the crew had been threatening to strike. It turned out that they'd been demanding more meat in their rations after a few of the men cut their way through the bulkhead to proposition some of the convict women there for sex, offering part of their rum provision to secure a deal. When they were refused, they pushed for more meat instead as a more compelling bargaining tool. Commodore Phillip had uncovered the plot and punished them instead. A chalk message on a blackboard at the stern of their ship now warned the sailors on the *Lady Penrhyn* about the consequences of similar bad behaviour.

Ann is shocked, but Green tells her not to be. 'These are desperate times,' she says. 'You can't blame these women for looking for some way out.'

'But they're treating us all like prostitutes,' Ann protests. 'We might have been convicted of thieving and robbery and perjury, but none of us have been selling our bodies.'

'No one's ever been transported for prostitution,' Green agrees, 'probably because too many rich men in England wouldn't be able to survive without it. But don't blame the women for doing what they feel they have to.'

The Governor, His Wife and His Mistress

'I'm not,' Ann replies slowly. 'But they've taken away every-thing from us: our homes, our children, our families, our country, our freedom. All we have left is our pride. And it feels like it's going to be a huge battle now to hold on to that, too.'

10

MUTINY, SCURVY AND SEX

Philip Gidley King

6 AUGUST 1787, JUST OFF THE COAST OF RIO DE JANEIRO

The ships of the First Fleet are now nearly three months into their voyage, getting ready to drop anchor in Rio de Janeiro, their second-last port of call, and Gidley King is both amazed that they've managed to reach this point, and horror-struck at the enormity of the task they still have before them.

He knew it would be an eventful expedition, but he didn't truly appreciate its scale before, or anticipate the difficulties that arise at almost every turn. In just the first ten days alone, they had seamen flogged for breaking through the barricades to demand sex from the convict women; they had some of the women put back into irons or had their hair shaved off as punishment for obliging them; and then they had a mutiny. He bites his lip at the memory. And they still have the toughest four months ahead of them.

The Governor, His Wife and His Mistress

'Try to take it in your stride, King,' Phillip advises him over dinner one night on the *Sirius*. 'It's never going to be a perfect outcome; you just have to work towards the best that's available. Our main goal is to get as many men, women and children as we can safely to Botany Bay, and in the best health possible. We have to remember that taking the convicts to America was a six-week passage. This will be over five times longer. And, of course, we all know what can go wrong. You just have to look at the experience of Commodore George Anson.'

Gidley King nods. Every sailor knew about that. In 1740, during England's war with Spain, the commodore had sailed around the world with six ships and had lost over seventy per cent of the crew to disease or starvation in the ensuing four years. More than one thousand of the seamen died as a result of scurvy alone, while a mere four deaths were from enemy action. Before Cook had introduced mandatory lemons and limes on board, scurvy was always the navy's greatest threat on long voyages and some of the convicts were already showing signs of the disease.

'Happily, we'll be in Rio shortly and we should be able to load as many fresh provisions as we can hold,' Gidley King replies. 'I know the value you place on oranges and lemons, so we'll purchase those as a priority.'

'Good man!' Phillip responds. 'I've seen with my own eyes the curative effect of citrus and I can't for the life of me understand why the navy's Sick and Hurt Board dismiss such evidence. Instead, they keep on pushing malt, wort and sauerkraut as the remedy, which do absolutely nothing. The pompous fools!'

'I couldn't possibly comment on that, sir.' Gidley King smiles.

The captain grunts his amusement. 'You'll go far, young man.'

While the health of most on the ships is fair, the attempted mutiny had been a challenge of a different kind, although fortunately foiled in time. It had been plotted by two male convicts on board the *Scarborough* who planned to seize control of the ship, free all their fellow convicts and then sail away from the convoy in the middle of the night, when no one would notice. The two men were eminently qualified for such a task, too. One, Phillip Farrell, was a former boatswain's mate before being convicted of stealing a one-shilling handkerchief and sentenced to transportation, while the other, Thomas Griffiths, had been in charge of a French privateer during the American War, before stealing two pounds' worth of cloth. Had they not been betrayed by one of their fellow convicts to a ship's officer, they might well have been successful.

That afternoon, Gidley King watched gloomily as the two conspirators, under armed guard, were rowed over to the *Sirius*. Phillip's instructions were that they be flogged, transferred to the *Prince of Wales* and placed in irons. His second lieutenant didn't argue. The flogging would be a deterrent to any other convicts trying to plan an escape, and it was wise to move them off the *Scarborough*, to avoid them being treated like martyrs and attracting any more support. It would also, hopefully, keep the attempted mutiny quiet.

Yet, generally, things seem to be proceeding as well as they could under the circumstances, although he still can't get out of his mind that image of human misery when he and Captain Phillip had inspected the female convicts on the *Lady Penrhyn*. He'd checked on the women again when they made their first stop in Tenerife in the Madeiras on 2 June and, despite the stifling heat and tropical rainstorms that prevented them exercising on deck and meant the hatches had to be battened down again, he was pleased to find they all looked a great deal better than when he'd first seen them.

They were, in fact, a stark contrast with the male convicts on board the largest of the ships, the *Alexander*. No fewer than sixteen died there from the bitter winter's cold, lack of fresh air and disease-spreading vermin even before departure from Portsmouth, and another five perished en route to Tenerife. One man, John Powell, slid down the side of the ship and escaped—but was discovered hiding on an island nearby and re-arrested. Many fell ill afterwards too but the cause was later discovered to be the foul-smelling bilge water, a putrid soup of dead rats, rotting food, seawater, urine, faeces and vomit. Since it had been drained and washed out, the men had been in much better health.

That stop in Tenerife two months before had been enjoyable for Gidley King. Much to his surprise, he was put in charge of acquiring more supplies and dispatched to visit the Spanish Governor while, as protocol demanded, everyone else stayed behind on the ships. He'd imagined Post Captain Hunter, as the second most important man on the voyage, would have been delegated to go or, after him, First Lieutenant Bradley as the third in command. Instead, Phillip chose Gidley King as his personal emissary. It turned out to be a good move. When the governor expressed his displeasure that the *Sirius* hadn't saluted the fort at the entrance of the port with the customary cannon fire, Gidley King was quick-witted and humble enough to apologise profusely and explain that it hadn't been possible with so many stores littering the deck and creating a potential fire hazard. The governor was charmed, reassured him he could have all the further supplies he needed, and invited the whole official party to a lavish dinner at his palace. Phillip was delighted with his protégé's success.

In Gidley King's spare time, he walked the whole of the island's port city of Santa Cruz and the old city of La Laguna to the north, and made copious notes about, and sketches of, everything he saw. He looked at the buildings, the churches, the crops and the prices of goods for sale, as well as investigating how the island cared for its poor, orphans and unmarried women. There might well be valuable lessons there for Botany Bay, he had already decided. If his experience with the female convicts had taught him anything, it was that they might need all the help they could get. He often wondered what kind of life might await them in New Holland. If the male convicts obeyed orders and worked hard, he was convinced that they might thrive. But the women ... What kind of work could they be expected to do, and how could they make their way, especially if they had children, fell pregnant or were already sickly? Life was undoubtedly going to be much harder in the new colony for them.

Afterwards, crossing the North Atlantic for the eight-week journey from Tenerife to Rio had not been pleasant. There'd been stormy seas and winds that had prevented them landing in the Cape Verde Islands off Africa, and then warm weather that had rotted some of the food in the stores, heightened the stench of unwashed people and set off successive plagues of diarrhoea. Phillip's meticulous planning and preparations had helped enormously, however,

The Governor, His Wife and His Mistress

and Gidley King admires him even more for both that and his fair-mindedness, especially with his actions to improve conditions for the female convicts on the *Lady Penrhyn*.

Mind you, there seemed to be a few convict women who were incredibly resourceful. One in particular, Sarah MacCormack, had been causing no end of problems on her ship, the *Friendship*. Convicted of stealing two pieces of gold, she was twenty-one years old when the fleet set sail from Portsmouth. But shortly afterwards, she was discovered to be making regular trips through the bulk-head to visit various seamen. On 3 July, she was placed in irons, but shortly afterwards she'd become very sick with what the doctor assumed was 'the pox', or syphilis. He spent two days bleeding her in an attempted cure, and she rallied. The men she'd slept with, however, were panic-stricken.

Another female convict, he heard, back on the *Lady Penrhyn*, was also consorting with the crew, but this time with none other than the captain of the ship, Captain Sever. This was trickier. As well as being in charge of the ship, he was also a part-owner. With so few qualified master mariners in the fleet, it would be nigh impossible to replace him, especially with his ownership, and it would not do to raise his ire by punishing his new mistress, either. Gidley King had scratched his head over the quandary many times. Was it fair that someone in a powerful position use the advantages of his rank to start a liaison with a woman with absolutely no standing at all? What happened if one or the other wanted to finish the affair? And, finally, did he himself have any right to interfere?

The actual ship, too, is proving a huge headache for everyone. The *Lady Penrhyn* handles so badly, and is so slow, she constantly trails the rest of the fleet, forcing them to wait for her to catch up. She also lists badly in inclement weather, slopping seawater through the portholes of the upper deck. God only knows how the women below manage to cope.

Gidley King resolves that when they reach Rio, in a few days' time, he'll conduct a further check to see how the women there are faring. He might even take the opportunity to have a quiet word with Captain Sever. Most importantly, he wants to make sure the women are being kept in as humane a state as possible on a voyage like this. After all, it was Phillip's stated aim that he'd like to see their prisoners reformed, as well as punished, and sailing on that ship would be punishment enough for anyone.

11

THREE FIRM FRIENDS

Ann Inett

13 OCTOBER 1787, CAPE OF GOOD HOPE

The fleet is just anchoring at the Cape of Good Hope, and Ann Inett sighs with relief that there'll now be a few weeks' respite from the ship bucking and twisting below them in the wild high seas. The weeks since they left Rio to cross the South Atlantic in mid-winter have been a torturous nightmare of storms and rain and heat—often all at the same time—and everyone's looking forward to the next stop, the last before they strike out on the final leg of this godforsaken voyage to Botany Bay.

'This journey feels like it's never going to end,' Ann remarks to her friend Olivia. 'How long do you think it is since we left Rio?'

'I heard the sailors talking about it above us on the deck this morning,' Olivia replies. 'It's been five weeks.'

'Is that all?' Ann asks. 'It feels like it's been much longer.'

'Well, it's been five months since we left Portsmouth.'

'And how much longer have we got to go?'

'No idea. But surely it can't be much further. We'll drop off the edge of the world soon!'

Ann laughs. 'Talking about dropping off the edge, have you seen Ann Green? I saw one of the sailors coming down yesterday and taking her off somewhere—and she didn't come back. I hope she's not in trouble.'

Olivia shakes her head. 'She's up to something, that one, but I don't know what. She's not been on our bunk at night a few times before. Maybe she's been seeing one of the sailors, but she won't tell.'

Ann shrugs. 'She told me that you shouldn't blame women for looking for a way out. Maybe she's found one of her own.'

'And good luck to her,' Olivia says.

The ship creaks and shudders beneath them, and there's a sudden grinding and shouting and clatter of activity above. 'This must be it,' Olivia says. 'The Cape. Now hopefully we'll get the chance to spend more time on deck and get another round of good food and fresh water.'

The women still remember Rio fondly for the abundance that port had brought them. They'd heard that Commodore Phillip had once served Portugal in its colony of Brazil and, as a result, when they dropped anchor, he'd been greeted with huge respect and been given open slather with supplies of fresh food, wine, plants and seeds. In addition, the young officer who'd first accompanied Phillip on the inspection of their quarters at Portsmouth had appeared several times since with a look of concern on his face that Ann had seen on no one else on this ship, either before or since. One time, she smiled shyly at him and was surprised to see him blush. As a result

The Governor, His Wife and His Mistress

of one of his visits, or maybe Phillip's standing, or perhaps both, the women were thrilled to be given fresh beef, fresh vegetables and more oranges than they could possibly eat. That continued for the whole month at port. Spirits were high and they could often hear the seamen in a good mood, too, heartened by the purchase of over fourteen thousand gallons of rum for the new colony. The men spent the evenings when they weren't on shore leave, drinking and singing and carousing up on deck.

A couple of them who'd been frequent visitors to the convict women's quarters had been tried by the officers, found guilty of breaking the rules about consorting, and flogged. From some of the conversations the women overheard, a number had spent their time on shore with prostitutes; news greeted with a mixture of relief from those women keen to keep their distance, and irritation from those who'd got used to the extra rations of rum they'd received as payment. Two of the regulars were now with child as a result, so were assured of extra allocations of milk and meat. They heard that Mary Broad, a convict on the *Charlotte*, gave birth a few days after Rio to the baby of her prison hulk gaol warden, named her Charlotte and was now planning to marry a fellow convict, William Bryant, as soon as they arrived in Botany Bay.

It had only been about a month after leaving Rio, however, that the fresh food had run out, and it was back to salted meat and weevil-infested rice. With the winter seas so rough, and so many of the women seasick, they hadn't had much of an appetite, or been able to keep anything down. The *Lady Penrhyn* often listed so far in the wind and the storms that the women were forced to cling to each other and their bed shelves in order to stay upright, while water poured in from the deck above down the gaps around the hatch, soaking them all.

Just the week before, news had swept the ship about a fresh attempted mutiny among the male convicts on the *Alexander*. A number of the men there, led by John Powers, the man who'd tried to escape in Tenerife but had been recaptured, had armed themselves with iron bars, with the help of a few seamen, and were plotting to take over the ship before arriving at the Cape. One of the loyal marines, however, informed the captain who managed to foil the plan. The leader of the insurgency was chained to the deck and the rebel seamen were flogged.

All the female convicts were hoping their stay at the Dutch settlement at the Cape would be a great deal more peaceful and see the allocation of more good food. But their first sight of the Table Bay shore when they are finally allowed up on deck is a shock. It's lined with horrifying makeshift gallows and breaking wheels—large wooden wheels that are either run over victims' bodies with the aim of breaking bones and causing as much pain as possible before their execution, or to which bodies are tied as the wheel is cranked round. There are still mutilated bodies draped over several.

Ann shudders to see them. 'Don't look,' Nancy Yeates hisses at her.

'But . . .' Ann says, struggling to find the words to express her horror.

'Yes, I know,' Nancy says. 'Let's go down again now. We can come back later when it's dark.'

Ann allows herself to be led back down below deck. As she steps off the last rung, they encounter Olivia about to make her way up.

'Stay down here,' Nancy tells her. 'We'll all go up later when night falls.'

Olivia nods obediently. Over the weeks and months of this voyage, the three have become firm friends and have learned to trust each other implicitly. They know that, in this strange new world they're going to, they'll need all the support they can find. Ann has never had many female friends and she finds these women's honesty and eagerness to help each other refreshing.

Nancy seems so much more worldly than any other woman she's ever met, that she actually finds her quite intimidating. But she admires her, too. Nancy has made no secret of an affair she's been having with a seaman she started a conversation with once up on deck, and has now confided she's with his child. The baby will be due in March, hopefully after they arrive in Botany Bay. She says she hopes her lover, Joseph Theakston, will stay with her and look after them both, but reports, with a shrug, that his ardour seems to have cooled somewhat since she told him about his child. She has no idea what might happen, but Ann has no doubt that she'll survive—and admirably so—on her wits.

In contrast, Olivia is so shy and sweet-natured, Ann warms to her immediately. Neither woman would dream of going with a sailor, although, equally, they'd never criticise any of the other female convicts for their choices. In the meantime, one of the other women they first met, Esther Abrahams, is often too absorbed with her baby to spend much time talking with them, and Ann Green seems to have vanished into thin air.

A few days into their stay at the Cape, the sailor who delivers their rations seems eager for female companionship and a chat so

Nancy seizes the moment. 'Sir, we have lost one of our number and we're worried about her,' Nancy tells him. 'We wondered if you might have any news of her?'

He looks taken aback. 'What's her name?' he asks.

'Ann,' Nancy replies. 'Ann Green. She's small and dark and pretty.'

'Long black hair?' he asks.

'Yes, that's the one.'

'Ah, yes,' he says. 'She's Captain Sever's whore.'

Nancy, Ann and Olivia are stunned.

He smiles, enjoying being the centre of their attention. 'She's staying in his quarters,' he continues. 'He's taken quite a fancy to her. She knows what side her bread's buttered, that one.'

'And who can best butter it,' Nancy adds.

That afternoon, when he's gone, the three discuss the news. 'But what will happen to her when we arrive in New Holland?' Ann asks.

'Who knows?' Nancy replies. 'I suppose it's about whether he's planning to stay, or whether he's been contracted to sail on. I'd imagine he would be, being part-owner of this ship. I guess it'll depend on just how much of a fancy he's taken to her. It's always a bargain with the devil . . .' She looks suddenly wistful, as if considering her own position.

Olivia is thoughtful. 'But her sentence is for transportation for seven years, so she won't be allowed to leave if he sails on.'

'And I'd bet anything he's married, too,' Ann adds. 'I suppose her best hope is that he'll stay.'

'But in the meantime, she'll have a better voyage than any of us.' Nancy shrugs. 'I bet she's up there in his quarters now, eating

The Governor, His Wife and His Mistress

some of his roast beef and drinking his wine. Good luck to her! That's probably the best any of us can hope for—to attract the eye of someone with a bit of authority and power.'

Ann looks horrified, and Nancy laughs to see her expression. 'Come on, Ann,' she says. 'We've got to be practical here. Survival, remember? We know all about your love story with Joseph, but when we finally arrive on this god-damned ship, we're going to be the lowest of the low. True love will be a luxury beyond any of us.'

'But . . .' Ann starts, colouring.

Olivia weighs in. 'She's right, Ann,' she says. 'And your Joseph would want you to survive, wouldn't he? If not for yourself, then certainly for those two beautiful children you talk about so often. And who knows? Maybe it'll help you get back one day.'

Ann nods, not trusting herself to speak. They're right, she knows it. And although at this moment it feels like an impossible dream, she has to keep going just in case one day she could see her children again.

POSSESSION

Philip Gidley King

20 NOVEMBER 1787, INDIAN OCEAN, BETWEEN THE CAPE OF GOOD
HOPE AND NEW HOLLAND

The stop at the Cape had been an immensely difficult time for the
naval officers of the First Fleet. They'd been looking forward to
loading many more supplies on board their ships, but the surly Dutch
Governor told them there was little grain available as a result of
poor harvests. On the other hand, there was plenty of livestock to
buy at hugely inflated prices. Since they couldn't afford the risk of
running out of food or animals to stock the new colony, they'd dug
deep into their reserves and loaded cattle, sheep, pigs, goats, horses,
ducks and chickens onto the ships, filling every available space for
what was set to be the longest leg of the voyage over the Indian
Ocean. Bringing the livestock on board wasn't easy, either. Table
Bay was exposed to winds gusting down from Table Mountain,
which were strong enough to tear anchors up from the seabed and

The Governor, His Wife and His Mistress

often led to ships being swept off and wrecked at the heads. It took all the seamen's skill to keep the ships steady enough to bring on the animals.

It was tough, too, on the convicts. On the *Lady Penrhyn*, the urine from the livestock frequently seeped down through the cracks in the decking onto the women below. Their quarters were, in addition, used as storage for all the extra seeds, plants, hay and animal feed brought on, as well as the additional water for the stock. Very soon the smell of animal urine and dung became overpowering.

The journey from the Cape had been horrific. Although the strong westerly winds blew in their favour on their departure on 13 November, the storms had been the worst anyone had encountered or could ever imagine. Fears were strongest for the *Lady Penrhyn*, as one of the least seaworthy vessels. Whenever it was within sight of the *Sirius* during a storm, Philip Gidley King would look anxiously to see how far over it was listing, and wonder about the scenes below deck with the women and beasts it was carrying.

He made sure he was rowed over to check on them when there was a lull in the westerlies, becalming the Fleet mid-passage.

'Ahoy there!' he shouted, standing up as his longboat drew alongside the *Lady Penrhyn* the morning after a particularly ferocious storm. 'Permission to come aboard?'

'Good morning, sir,' a seaman called back, alerting deckhands to throw over the rope, and drop the ladder for Gidley King to climb aboard. 'I'll ask the captain permission.'

A few minutes later, Captain William Cropton Sever hove into sight. 'Good morning, Lieutenant,' he said somewhat stiffly.

'Permission granted. Thank you for coming to check on us. Glad to report all is well.'

'Excellent news,' Gidley King replied. 'That was a hell of a storm last night, and it looked like hard work keeping all in order.'

Sever looked pleased. 'Yes, it was,' he said. 'But I run a tight ship here and we're a well-disciplined lot. The women below are doing well, no casualties at all to report. We've been doing everything possible to safeguard their wellbeing.'

Gidley King nodded, even though he believed the situation to be, in fact, quite the opposite. Once before, in Sever's quarters, he'd glimpsed a woman flitting through the background and assumed that was the convict the captain had been consorting with. So how could Gidley King be sure that the captain was protecting the women from other seamen when he was setting such a bad example himself?

'Thank you, Captain,' he said, curtly. 'Now may I be permitted to go below to check on them so I can report back to Commodore Phillip?'

Sever looked irritated but kept an even tone. 'Of course,' he said. 'I'll have someone escort you down.'

'And would your surgeon be available this morning to come along with me, too?'

'I'm sure he would,' Sever replied, in a voice rigid with annoyance.

It was only five minutes before Arthur Bowes Smyth was standing at Gidley King's side down in the women's quarters. 'The women's health is generally pretty good,' Smyth told him. 'It has been difficult for them during the storms, but most are managing well. As soon as the westerlies and waves abate, they usually recover quite quickly.'

The Governor, His Wife and His Mistress

'Do you check on them regularly?'

'Yes, Lieutenant, I do,' replied the surgeon. 'If one of the women falls ill with fever, it's important to keep a close eye on the others to make sure they don't succumb. I tell them to send a message via a seaman if any of the women look poorly. And most of them are very cooperative.'

Much to Gidley King's relief, it did indeed look as if the women were faring if not well, then not too badly. He noticed the woman who'd smiled at him during a previous visit had a great deal more colour in her cheeks on this occasion, and he nodded at her before turning back to the surgeon. 'Thank you very much,' he told him. 'Please don't hesitate to let me know, as the commodore's aide-de-camp, if anything changes at any time.'

Bowes Smyth looked momentarily confused; it would normally be Captain Sever who would let the officers in charge of the expedition know if anything was awry. But he was no fool. He had seen the way the young officer looked at Sever as if he didn't quite approve. And he had a sneaking suspicion why. 'Yes, Lieutenant, of course,' he replied.

Gidley King had raised his doubts about the captain with Phillip, but the commodore had so much on his plate already, he didn't have room for more. The two men remained close, however, and just lately Phillip had raised the possibility that Gidley King be sent over to Norfolk Island, off the coast of New Holland, to establish a sub-colony and be its commandant. He wasn't sure about such a move. He didn't know much about the island, but others assured him it was another promotion.

When the news went around, the other officers seemed pleased for him.

'Congratulations!' beamed David Collins, the affable and outgoing former naval captain who'd been commissioned deputy judge advocate of the new colony, despite knowing little of the law. 'That's a great move for you.'

Gidley King smiled and thanked him. He was always a little wary around Collins. The man had once confessed he hated the 'salt sea ocean', which Gidley King found odd, considering his seafaring profession. But when he confided how much he missed his wife, Maria, Gidley King felt much more kindly disposed towards him.

'Did you not consider bringing her with you?' he asked one day.

'No,' Collins replied, flatly. 'I didn't think she'd enjoy it.'

'But you're not enjoying it either, and you might have been good company for each other.'

A strange expression passed over Collins' face, which Gidley King couldn't quite fathom. 'No, I didn't want that,' Collins eventually said. Gidley King waited for the explanation, but none came. It seemed that was the end of the conversation.

A couple of weeks into the voyage from the Cape, Gidley King is approached by Phillip to accompany him off the *Sirius* to transfer by longboat to the faster ship, the *Supply*, in the hope of arriving in Botany Bay before the rest of the Fleet. Gidley King is thrilled to be chosen. Phillip tells him that he wants to get the lay of the land and start the clearing work and building shelter for the livestock and storage for the plants and grain.

The Governor, His Wife and His Mistress

They're now very short on food, scurvy is again threatening the convicts, and it's important that the journey ends for the faster ships as soon as possible, to set up camp ready to feed and water the convicts and whatever animals remain alive. As they sail south into the Roaring Forties, the westerlies whip up the sea, and it's some of the most difficult sailing of the entire voyage.

Nearly two months after leaving the Cape, land is finally sighted again, and excitement is at fever pitch. Gidley King gazes out from the deck of the *Supply* at Van Diemen's Land and marvels at how green and lush it looks over the bleakness of this seemingly never-ending ocean. He wonders if Norfolk Island will be such an idyll. He itches to drop anchor and go ashore but knows that they'll have to wait till Botany Bay. They have no time to waste.

Christmas comes and goes in another blast of stormy weather and high seas. They're now so close to their final destination, but life still feels tenuous. Many of the livestock have perished, with the survivors weak from hunger, thirst and being battered so severely by the movement of the ships. Many of the precious seedlings intended to provide food for the new colony are washed off the main decks in the surging waters, and all of the ships, bar the *Sirius*, sustain terrible damage. Even sailing north after rounding the treacherous southern tip of Van Diemen's Land and up the six hundred miles along the New South Wales coast, the seas show no sign of abating, and the Fleet is forced to move further out to sea to stay upright.

The weather is dark and gloomy, the skies are black, the sea is white with angry foam and the winds are ferocious. Gidley King ponders how the women on the *Lady Penrhyn* are faring. He's heard most have spent the last few days on their knees in constant prayer, and terror. He feels they're in good hands with Bowes Smyth, if not Sever, but still he worries about the welfare of the oldest, the sickest and the most fragile. It's going to be a miracle, he thinks to himself, if the Fleet makes it intact and all those still living make it to shore.

13

BOUND FOR BOTANY BAY

Philip Gidley King
18 JANUARY 1788, BOTANY BAY, NEW HOLLAND

The *Supply* finally arrives in Botany Bay on the afternoon of 18 January 1788, just over eight months, and fifteen thousand miles, since they departed England, and Gidley King says his own prayer of thanks for them all being spared. Then he, Phillip and a number of the other officers are rowed in on two longboats, being carried the last few yards on the backs of seamen wading ashore, as is the naval custom. In the confusion, marines' Captain George Johnston claims he is the first Englishman to step on the shore of New Holland, but Gidley King doubts it. In reality, it was the seamen on whose backs they rode, and his steed might well have beaten Johnston's.

Gidley King and Phillip notice a group of ebony black natives, naked and with spears, who have been watching them come to shore, and they try to gesture to them in a friendly way that they mean no harm. The natives brandish their spears at first, but then seem to understand and when they ask them if they could show them fresh water, the natives point them to a stream close by. Phillip offers them beads but they signal they want them laid on the ground so they can pick them up from a safe distance. They obviously don't trust their visitors. Gidley King is intrigued, and later, back on the ship, makes careful notes in his journal about their behaviour and sketches their portraits. It's the first exquisite sketch of many he completes of the new colony and its peoples, and also the first sent back on returning ships to England, where the artist-poet William Blake redraws some of them to sell as exotic postcards.

Despite the presence of fresh water, Gidley King notices how disappointed Phillip seems by Botany Bay, and shares his dismay. Cook and Banks had reported that the bay was sheltered from the winds, and that the pasture was rich and fertile. But the two men aren't finding that to be true.

'This bay is very open to the winds,' Gidley King remarks to Phillip, looking over at the sails of the *Supply* being buffeted by the gusts. 'It doesn't feel very protected at all.'

Phillip nods, his face grave. Gidley King continues. 'And the water is so shallow by the shore, it's not possible for the ships to come in far enough. Also, that stream is not enough to sustain so many arrivals.'

He sees Phillip smile tightly.

'Let's look around more tomorrow,' he tells his aide-de-camp. 'Maybe a new day will yield new surprises.'

The next day does bring a surprise, but not the one the two men had hoped for. While, happily, the other faster ships of the

The Governor, His Wife and His Mistress

Fleet—the *Alexander,* the *Scarborough* and the *Friendship*—sail in, further surveys of the shoreline provide little reason for optimism. The strong winds continue to blast the ships and they don't come across any more substantial sources of water. They continue to make contact with other natives, who are more hostile this time and indicate that they want them to get back on their ships and sail away. One throws a spear close to Gidley King to make the point, forcing him to walk backwards in retreat and, when more natives join in, he ends up ordering a marine to fire into the air to scare them off.

A day later, the final ships, including the *Lady Penrhyn,* arrive. Gidley King is enormously relieved that the entire Fleet has made it, with not a single ship lost, and only forty-eight of the more than fourteen hundred people on board having perished on the journey. But there's no time for celebration. The hunt for good fertile land and water is going badly. Instead, they're simply finding more marshland with poor soil, in which nothing of much use is likely to grow—both Phillip's and Gidley King's farming experience are now proving invaluable in surveying the land—and the group sent off to fish, sadly, catch very little.

Relations with the natives seem to be improving, however. Gidley King passes two of them a glass of wine which they sip then immediately spit out but, in the sign language conversation that follows, it turns out they believe their visitors to be women because they're clean-shaven without beards. When Gidley King realises this, he orders one of his sailors to unbutton his fly to make their gender clear. The locals are amazed, and point to some women on the shore, offering the new arrivals the opportunity for sex. Politely declining, Gidley King tries to give one of the women a gift of a handkerchief which he delicately places 'where Eve did the fig leaf'. Peace, and some kind of cross-cultural understanding, may have been restored.

Finally, on 21 January, Phillip announces that he's going to sail north to visit the next bay along, Port Jackson, to see if that would be more suitable for settlement. He tells Gidley King to continue surveying Botany Bay in case there is no alternative, and takes a small party, including Hunter and Collins, with him. He returns two days later and seeks out Gidley King.

He looks triumphant, and Gidley King's heart leaps. 'How was it, sir?' he asks him impatiently. 'What did you find?'

'We found—' Phillip pauses for effect '—without exception, the finest harbour in the world! Here, a thousand sail of the line may ride in the most perfect security.'

Gidley King gasps with excitement. 'Really?' he asks. 'That's wonderful.'

'It's more than wonderful, it's a bloody miracle, that's what it is.'

'So could we settle there?' Gidley King asks.

'Without doubt,' Phillip replies. 'It has a freshwater spring of water at its head flowing into the cove, and the ships could anchor close to the shore.'

Gidley King grins. 'So when can we go?'

'Immediately!' the commodore says. 'Please give the order that everyone should re-pack, re-embark on their ships and sail north.'

A frenzy of activity ensues but, just before they leave, they sight two other ships at the entrance of the bay—two French exploration vessels. They turn out to be ships under the command of Jean-François de Galaup, Comte de La Pérouse, sponsored by King Louis XVI who'd been inspired by Cook's voyages. They try to meet,

The Governor, His Wife and His Mistress

but the winds aren't in their favour, so finally they give up and the *Supply* starts back out north on 25 January, followed by the other ships. That evening, just before sunset, Phillip sails deep into the harbour to a snug cove with a steady stream of water.

The next morning, on 26 January 1788, a number of officers disembark the *Supply*, erect a flagpole on the shoreline, name the area Sydney Cove after the British Home Secretary Lord Sydney, and hold a foundation ceremony.

Gidley King carefully records the event in his journal: *At daylight, the English colours were displayed on shore and possession was taken for His Majesty*, he writes.

And then the convicts from the *Supply* are set to work clearing the land. The other ships arrive and more convicts are brought on shore to unload provisions, cut down trees to build rudimentary shelters and animal pens with the wood, collect water from the stream, light fires to make food and plant gardens.

Despite this orderly beginning, however, it's not long before absolute hell breaks loose.

14

DRUNKEN DEBAUCHERY

Ann Inett
6 FEBRUARY 1788, PORT JACKSON, NEW HOLLAND

The atmosphere aboard the *Lady Penrhyn* is one of a heady excitement mixed with a gut-wrenching fear. Everyone's eager to feel the thrill of treading on dry land once more after so many long months at sea, but no one knows what landing in such a place will bring.

From the deck of the ship, the women can see a mass of people on the shore in a frenzy of activity, and they can hear the chopping, the clanging and the cries of those urging the convicts to work harder and faster. They're going to be the last to disembark at Port Jackson, or Sydney Cove, and have little idea of what they'll face.

Ann Inett stands silently with her friends Olivia, Nancy and Esther, who is holding hands with her daughter Rosanna. Nancy has already found out what this landing will bring: even more uncertainty. Her seaman lover has told her he wants nothing more to do with her and their child. They had some fun, didn't they, he asked

The Governor, His Wife and His Mistress

her blithely the night before, but soon it'll be time for him to return to sea with his mates to pick up their next lot of cargo en route back to England. She pleads with him—what about their unborn child? Doesn't he want to be a father? He shakes his head and turns his back on her. How can he even be sure it's his? he asks. And only then does she weep hot tears of remorse and anger.

'I think I knew this would be coming,' she tells Ann that morning. 'But maybe not quite like that, and so soon. I don't regret it, though. That could have been my last chance for some tenderness, and I took it, and now I'm going to have a child. I won't ever be alone again.'

Ann nods. She can understand how Nancy feels. She aches so painfully with the loss of her own children, and knows how absolutely life-affirming a child is. 'Your baby will bring you great joy,' she says. 'I'm sure of it. And it will be a new start in this land, however difficult.'

The five wait in silence, until Olivia stirs. 'Still no news of Ann Green?' she asks the others. 'I thought she might have come back to disembark with us.'

Nancy raises her eyebrows. 'Maybe she's having more luck with her man than I had with mine,' she says. 'If she's still with the captain, I'd imagine he'd try to smuggle her off the ship with him, rather than let her go with us. That's if he hasn't tired of her yet.'

'Oh, I hope not,' Ann says. 'I really hope not.'

The first of a flurry of longboats draws up alongside the *Lady Penrhyn* and, as the women watch, the surgeon Arthur Bowes Smyth clambers back on board. He looks up at the women waiting patiently on deck, then climbs up the rope ladder and heads for the little group.

He looks straight at Nancy and then down at the bulge beneath her frock, and shakes his head, while ignoring Esther and Rosanna completely. Instead, he addresses Ann and Olivia. 'You two, come with me,' he says brusquely. 'No, not you, Nancy Yeates, not this time.'

'But where are we going?' Ann asks. 'We'd like to stay together.'

'You'll find out in due course,' Bowes Smyth says pompously. 'But hurry, say your goodbyes, and let's get going.'

Ann and Olivia both hug Nancy, Esther and Rosanna. Nancy clings onto them tightly and Ann realises that, despite her bravado, Nancy is as scared as the rest of them. Ann prises herself free and can barely trust herself to speak. 'Good luck and God speed, my dear friends,' she whispers. 'We'll see you ashore!'

The two women are helped into the longboat, alongside four other women, and are rowed, with Bowes Smyth, to shore. As Ann steps out, she splashes in the shallow water, but can't help a smile spreading over her face. Land once more. Even though her feet are sinking into the soft sand and mud, it's amazing to be back on terra firma, to know she's survived the voyage and now, if she can somehow endure the next seven years of her sentence, and then make it back to England . . . her children might still remember her. She hugs the thought close. Then she and the other women are led to a tent just back from the shore. It's made up of timber-framed panels covered with oil cloth, and seems to have been reserved specifically for them. 'What's happening?' Ann asks the surgeon when they've been safely deposited inside. 'Why have we been singled out?'

'Orders,' he replies cagily. 'You'll be told later. Now I'd advise you to stay inside. Many of these men haven't seen a woman for over a year. I have no idea how they'll react. We'll put an armed guard outside.'

The Governor, His Wife and His Mistress

The women sit quietly on the ground inside the tent, wondering what's going to become of them. Through the slit at the front, they can see more longboats are going out to the *Lady Penrhyn* and to the *Prince of Wales* to bring more of the female convicts to shore. But while the disembarkation starts as an orderly operation, soon the word goes around Port Jackson that the women are coming, and male convicts and seamen alike wade out and jump into the boats the women are in. The seamen have already been drinking their extra rations of rum and soon there are wild scenes of drunken debauchery all along the shoreline.

A number of the women are screaming as what's left of their clothing is torn off them, and they are helpless to defend themselves. To add to the horror of the scene, a violent storm breaks, rain lashes the shore, a number of the tents are blown away and many of the newly landed women become so mired in the mud, it's even harder for them to get away. It becomes one incredibly chaotic, terrifying free-for-all. Ann, Olivia and the other women cling for dear life onto the walls of their tent, and each other, as they watch the scenes outside, in absolute terror.

By the next morning, 7 February, the storm has blown itself out and the broken huts, torn tents and exhausted people are strewn across the land that is going to form the new Sydney settlement. It looks like a terrible start. But, regardless, Phillip orders everyone to gather and issues a stern warning that scenes like those should never be repeated. Moreover, if the convicts henceforth behave well, they will be rewarded; if they break the rules, punishment will be immediate and severe. Then he has Collins read the commission given to now Governor Phillip by King George III that formally inaugurates the colony's first government.

Bowes Smyth follows Ann, Olivia and the other women to their tent after the ceremony. 'You six women have been chosen as being of good character, relatively speaking.' He coughs at that point. 'And having been the best behaved or the least exceptional on the voyage.'

Least exceptional? The women exchange pointed glances with each other. The surgeon doesn't notice, and they wait patiently to hear their prize for being the least exceptional. A reduction in their sentences? A chance to set up their own businesses in Sydney? Special roles in the new town, keeping house for the officers? The surgeon puffs out his chest. He knows they're hanging on to his every word, and is relishing the attention.

He adjusts his cuffs. 'As a result,' he finally continues grandly, 'you are being sent to accompany Lieutenant Gidley King to set up a second colony on Norfolk Island.'

Ann feels a tightness in her chest. *Another* colony? Somewhere else? An *island*? She can see the other women around her looking similarly horror-struck. Surely this won't mean getting back on board one of those damned ships again, after having only been on land for one night?

She takes a deep breath and tries to keep her voice steady. Perhaps this island is closer to England, to her children. 'Norfolk Island?' she asks. 'Where's that?'

'Well you may ask,' he replies with a smirk. 'It's a further one thousand miles out into the Pacific Ocean, pretty much in the middle of absolutely nowhere.'

Part Two

ISOLATION

FIT ONLY FOR ANGELS OR EAGLES

Philip Gidley King

14 FEBRUARY 1788, PORT JACKSON, NEW SOUTH WALES

Norfolk Island . . . a tiny speck of land in the middle of the South Pacific Ocean, which Captain James Cook discovered thirteen years before and believed had never been trod by human feet.

Philip Gidley King has read about it in Cook's journal, but paid it little attention, never imagining he'd have any reason to visit. He'd be far too busy with helping establish the new settlement at Botany Bay, he believed, or Port Jackson where it is now. Such a remote, inaccessible piece of land to Sydney's north-east would be far too insignificant an outpost to merit any consideration.

But he'd been wrong. And now he is being sent to set up a second colony on the island Cook had described as being covered by giant spruce pines, flax plants and little else. A place Cook had paused at only long enough to take a walk, cut down the smallest tree he and his men could find, and name the island after the Duchess of Norfolk.

Gidley King can't help but feel disappointed. The work is continuing apace in Sydney Cove and, although everyone is encountering terrible difficulties clearing the dense tangle of greenery, cutting the ancient hardwoods and building with the soft buttery bark of the gum trees, he would prefer to stay there, at the centre of the action. He wants to make his mark, to contribute to this new colony and continue to impress those above him. Being sent to Norfolk Island feels strangely like banishment. He wonders if this is what transportation feels like to the convicts.

He's a practical man, however, and needs to come to terms with his new mission. Phillip had explained that King George III had himself stressed the importance of establishing a colony on Norfolk Island to prevent it being occupied by France or any other European power. In addition, it could prove a helpful adjunct to Sydney, as a stop on trade routes east, especially with the start of whaling and sealing. The flax could be extremely useful for sails and canvas—currently sourced from the Baltic Sea ports but now under threat from Empress Catherine II of Russia who wants to restrict the supply to England, to reduce its power at sea. Those tall straight pine trees could also be put to use for the masts of sailing ships, now they can no longer rely on the supply of timbers from New England following the American War. At the same time, the rest of the interior could well be developed into a garden to help feed the colony at Port Jackson.

Gidley King is in no doubt that he still has Phillip's favour and tries to be heartened that the Governor trusts him with such a

The Governor, His Wife and His Mistress

demanding task. Just a few days after landing in Port Jackson, he'd even been asked to return to Botany Bay to talk to the French captain, La Pérouse, see what he was doing, and offer him any help he might need. Gidley King had accepted gladly. He spoke French well and he liked these diplomatic tasks; they seemed to suit him.

Back at the bay to the south, he finds La Pérouse a charming host and is impressed with how well the French expedition is funded and organised with scientists, including botanists and an astronomer, and plentiful resources, quite unlike their own First Fleet. As a bonus, the French count had also earlier visited Norfolk Island and says he has advice to offer the Englishman.

But as La Pérouse talks about how difficult the island was to land on, and describes how vital it is to negotiate the treacherous rocks and to avoid being dashed by the wild seas onto the towering cliff faces, Gidley King's smile gradually freezes on his face. The count himself failed to land, and talks about the place, much to Gidley King's mounting dismay as somewhere 'fit only for angels or eagles'.

By the time he returns to Port Jackson, Gidley King has written his report on the French, and Phillip is pleased with it and thanks him warmly. La Pérouse—who said he's had a premonition of impending disaster—has also given him letters and official journals to deliver back to Europe with the first ships that will return. Then, preparations begin for his voyage to Norfolk Island on the *Supply*. He consoles himself with the thought that Phillip is treating it as a great honour. He tries to think of it in the same light, but doesn't quite succeed. Still, he's being given labour and tools for the task of settling the island, and setting it up for sending timber, flax, cotton, corn and other grains, vegetables and fattened cattle back to Port Jackson. This is perhaps another chance to shine. And, Phillip reassures him, it won't be forever.

Gidley King leaves Sydney on 14 February, with six months' worth of supplies, fifteen convicts and seven free men on board to form the first settlement on the island. He's been appointed superintendent and commandant of the island, and his fellow passengers include the surgeon of the *Sirius* Thomas Jamison, the assistant surgeon of the *Lady Penrhyn* John Turnpenny Altree, carpenter William Westbrook, weaver Roger Morley, various marines, nine male convicts and six female convicts. Among the male convicts is carpenter and builder Nathaniel Lucas, and among the women are Ann and Olivia. Gidley King casts an eye over the group set to be his companions for the next . . . He has no idea for how long.

He is pleased to see the small, dark-haired female who'd once smiled at him, and to whom he'd nodded another time, among the group. He likes the look of her, and she appears to have a good figure under a neat dress.

He approaches her on their first day sailing. 'What's your name?' he asks.

'Ann Inett, sir,' she replies. Her voice has a soft English Midlands lilt to it, which he immediately warms to.

'I am looking for a housekeeper, as soon as I have a house—or my tent—up,' he says. 'What would you say?'

He can see her hesitating and wonders why. Surely, she'd be delighted to be the housekeeper to the most important man on Norfolk Island? It would be much easier work than clearing the land. He can see she's weighing it up, though, and can't help but admire her poise. As a convict, she has no rights at all, and could never refuse his offer even if she wanted to, but he likes the idea that she's spirited enough to actually look as though this is a choice. He waits patiently.

'Thank you, sir,' she says finally. 'I would be happy to be your housekeeper.'

'Excellent, Ann,' he replies. 'Then that's settled.'

After a week's sailing, the little party pass by another, smaller island that they name after the Admiralty's Lord Howe, and then, on 29 February, two weeks and one day after leaving Sydney, they finally spot Norfolk Island. It's an unedifying sight. The land surges steeply up into thick bush from rock-littered shores and the sea around it is rough and choppy, slapping up against the jagged peaks guarding seemingly every bay. Gidley King immediately realises that La Pérouse wasn't exaggerating the difficulties of finding a landing place. Captain Cook had landed at Duncombe Bay on the north of the island, but it had obviously been uncharacteristically calm the day he'd chanced upon the place. Today, it looks virtually impenetrable.

The mood on the ship had been one of elation when they'd first caught sight of the island but now, as everyone stares at the foaming surf battering the 300-foot-high cliffs, there's an air of despair.

'No matter,' Gidley King says, breaking the silence on board. 'We'll find a way in.'

He looks meaningfully at the *Supply*'s master, Lieutenant Henry Ball. The man is grim-faced. 'Yes, sir,' he says quietly.

The group spends five days sailing around the island, charting all possible landing places. It seems to be five miles long and three miles wide, but has few places to land safely around its circumference. Gidley King decides to take their small four-oared longboat and five men to take a closer look. They manage to row into Duncombe Bay and pull their boat up on the shoreline. Then they head up into the interior.

It's hard going, with the men's shirts soon soaked with sweat from the effort of hacking their way through the thick greenery, tangles of irises and groves of tall pine trees. At one point, the bush is so dense, the men barely notice that the ground falls away ninety feet down the side of a cliff until it's almost too late. Almost.

They also find Cascade Bay, further south on the east coast, which Cook had named after the nearby waterfall, but that also seems a treacherous landing place. Gidley King is enjoying walking around the island but the surgeon gets so lost in the thick forest, he ends up spending the night alone, surrounded by the sound of animals nibbling. He assumes they are rabbits. The soil looks rich and deep, and there is fresh water and seems to be plenty of wildlife.

They return to the ship full of enthusiasm and continue their hunt for a landing spot. Eventually, on 6 March, on the south side of the island, Gidley King glimpses something promising.

'Ball!' he cries out to the lieutenant. 'Look yonder.'

Ball raises his telescope and peers in the direction that Gidley King is pointing.

'That looks like a channel through the reef,' Gidley King says, excitement in his voice. 'What do you think?'

Ball frowns with concentration, then lowers the telescope. 'I think you're right, sir,' he says. 'Let's try.'

The Governor, His Wife and His Mistress

The ship is carefully navigated through the gap in the reef, and drops anchor off shore.

Gidley King is elated. 'Good man!' he says, thumping Ball on the back. 'I'm going to name this place Sydney Bay. And now let's get to work.'

The men disembark first with their tools, supplies and tents, and then the six women are brought ashore.

Gidley King helps the women off the longboat onto land, and smiles at how relieved Ann looks. 'Welcome to Norfolk Island,' he tells her.

She looks down to avoid his eyes. 'Thank you, sir,' she replies softly.

'Tonight we shall celebrate our safe arrival,' he announces, to no one in particular. 'This is the beginning of a whole new chapter in our lives, and of Britain's.'

That evening, Gidley King formally takes possession of the island in the name of the king, and drinks toasts to the health of the royal family and to Governor Phillip back in Sydney. He tries to make it a cheerful occasion, but, despite his outward demeanour, he can't help a terrible sense of foreboding creeping in.

The fresh water is plentiful, there are towering trees that shoot straight up, fifty to sixty feet in the air, before branches appear that would make perfect masts, and a riot of birds flying everywhere above. But the ground itself is bare, with not a single blade of grass or flower, and as for the flax that they've come here to farm, there's no sign of any whatsoever.

III

THE HOUSE ON THE RIDGE

Ann Inett

14 FEBRUARY 1788, IN THE SOUTHERN OCEAN
EN ROUTE TO NORFOLK ISLAND

Ann Inett is startled when she climbs aboard the *Supply* to see the young officer who'd carried out the regular inspections of the *Lady Penrhyn* and seemed so concerned about the welfare of the female convicts. But she is even more astonished to be approached by him on their first day at sea and offered a job as his housekeeper.

She makes a concerted effort to lift herself from the gloom she is feeling as she watched the tiny settlement of tents in Sydney Cove disappear in the distance and sailed even further away from her children back in England. She doesn't want to be his housekeeper, *anybody's* housekeeper, in fact, but what choice does she honestly have? From what she's heard, they are going to start a new settlement on Norfolk Island so it's not as though there'll be any demand for her dressmaking skills. And her friends on board the *Lady Penrhyn* have talked a lot about the need to catch the eye of a man, preferably one with some kind of rank, in order to survive. However much she loathes the idea, perhaps this is her lifeline.

Ann looks Gidley King full in the face and can see his puzzlement. She imagines he's maybe just a few years younger than herself and can see he's a handsome man with a finely chiselled nose and such an air of self-assurance she supposes no one has ever said 'No' to him. But, she has to give him due credit, he stands there patiently waiting for her answer.

Finally, she realises she can delay no more.

'Thank you, sir,' she says. 'I would be happy to be your housekeeper.'

Gidley King turns away to talk to a crew member waiting for his attention and Olivia races over.

'Ann! What did he want?' she asks, breathlessly.

Ann smiles to see her friend looking so anxious. 'He wants me to be his housekeeper.'

Olivia gasps. 'Oh, that's great news,' she says. Then she notices the uncertain expression on Ann's face. 'You did say "Yes", didn't you?'

Ann frowns. 'I did,' she says, 'but I'm not sure I had much choice in the matter.'

'Choice?' Olivia rolls the word around in her mouth. 'Why on earth would you even think to say "No"?'

'I don't know,' Ann replies. 'But it may also mean living with him in his house, or tent,' she corrects herself hurriedly, 'and I don't know him at all. It feels strange.'

Olivia laughs. 'And this *doesn't* feel strange, being taken away from your family and sent to the ends of the earth and not being allowed back home to England for another seven years?'

Ann feels herself blush. 'I suppose you're right.'

'Remember what Nancy said?' Olivia asks. 'That the best any of us can hope for is to attract the protection of someone with a bit of authority? Ann Green seems to have that with Captain Sever, although Lord knows how long that will last.'

Ann nods her agreement, and her friend continues. 'And it looks like Esther Abrahams has found that with Captain Johnston when he suggested on that second day in Sydney that she could be his housekeeper, and bring Rosanna with her. I wouldn't mind betting that—despite her condition—Nancy is casting her wise old eye over the available men to find a likely candidate to tie her fortunes to.'

At that, Ann can't help laughing. Olivia is right. Maybe Gidley King isn't such a bad prospect. And, after all, she's only agreed to be his housekeeper.

Ann feels even more relief this time as she disembarks the ship to wade onto the small beach at Sydney Bay. While the voyage has been comparatively short, she hadn't liked the look of that jagged shoreline being pummelled by spray. But now she's safely on Norfolk Island, she takes a moment to look up at what's set to be her new home.

This Sydney Bay is a relatively flat area, sloping gently up to hills in the distance. There are already men hard at work hacking at the tangle of trees bound together by tough, supplejack vines to make room for the tents and the shelters and the planting of vegetables and fruits that is planned to take place later. She can see they're making good headway, and there are already a few tents erected on the cleared expanse of land. She and the other women are shown one and told this will be their home for the meantime. Ann supposes Gidley King will need to get organised before he calls her over to join him.

The next day, the clearing work continues, and other men are sent off to see if they can catch fish. They return with a bountiful supply and Ann, Olivia and the other women light a fire in the middle of the clearing to cook the catch along with some of their supplies of rice. When Ann serves Gidley King his plate, he smiles warmly at her.

'Thank you, Ann,' he says. 'This looks delicious. Are you comfortable in your tent?'

'Yes, sir, thank you, sir,' she replies. 'It is perfectly adequate for our needs.'

He raises a single eyebrow. 'Well, I hope we can make you more comfortable later,' he says. 'We are making good progress with the shelters and soon I hope to have my own house built.'

'Yes, sir,' she mumbles. In truth, she's perfectly happy where she is, with all the other women.

On 8 March, the *Supply* weighs anchor and departs, as the small group of twenty-three assembles on shore and watches the ship leave. A couple wave a forlorn farewell to the captain, but most are lost in their own thoughts. They're now totally alone on this island in the

middle of nowhere, with only one small longboat between them, and five months before another ship is due to call in. The general air of desolation is palpable.

The next day is Sunday and Gidley King holds a church service as Governor Phillip has instructed him to do each week, and then reads out his commission to the assembled group. He says he wants to reward those among the convicts who work hard, but won't hesitate to punish those who don't pull their weight. He hopes that, together, they'll be able to make a success of this settlement.

As the men work, the women are busy exploring the island and looking for food. Along their walks, they discover a kind of wild spinach, as well as a hard, starchy banana-like fruit they discover later is plantain, and swamp cabbage. Each precious find they take back and experiment with, by trying to cook it over the same open fire, with varying degrees of success. They also help plant some of the seeds they've brought over with them, so the men can continue their clearing work, felling trees and sawing them up for houses and storerooms, and tearing away the undergrowth. There are so many birds on the island, too, like pigeons, seagulls, doves and parrots, which are unused to humans and so tame. The men discover they can walk right up close and snatch them to supplement their rations.

A few days on, Ann sees a group of men staking out a patch of land on a ridge behind the tent settlement. It's on a prime site, overlooking the whole settlement to the waterline. She asks one of the convicts what they're doing.

'This is going to be our new Government House,' he says. 'For our commandant Lieutenant Gidley King.'

It takes a few weeks but every day Ann looks over towards the house on the ridge, she can see it's moving closer to completion. She watches the progress with dread. At some point, she suspects Gidley King is going to ask her to vacate her tent and come over to start work as his housekeeper.

Olivia doesn't understand her. 'It looks as if it's going to be a fine house, much more comfortable than where you're living now,' she reasons one day when the pair are working side by side planting corn in one of the newly raked vegetable plots. 'I don't understand why you wouldn't be looking forward to it. Have you inspected it yet?'

Ann shakes her head. She's never even thought of that. 'I'm quite happy where I am with you and the other women,' she says. 'Can't he come down here with everyone else when he wants his meals?'

'But he's the commandant!' Olivia laughs. 'You can't expect him to live like us forever! And, mark my words, we won't be in this tent for much longer. A couple of the other women have been seeing men and it's likely they'll move in with them before too long. I'm not sure I'll be here long, either.'

'What do you mean?' Ann cuts in.

'I've been talking to one of the men working on Government House. He's a carpenter and joiner from Surrey, called Nathaniel Lucas. He's very, very nice.'

'That man with broad shoulders and fair hair who always has a faraway look in his eyes?' Ann asks.

'That's the one.' Olivia smiles. 'He's very charming and funny. And thoughtful.'

'But you only met him a few weeks ago. How can you possibly know him in that time?'

Olivia's face becomes deathly serious. 'I know everything about him that I need to,' she says. 'He was actually one of the few male convicts on the *Lady Penrhyn*, and I spoke to him a few times there too.'

'But do you know why he's here? He could be a robber or a highwayman or . . . or a murderer for all you know.'

Olivia shakes her head. 'He's actually a lot like you,' she says slowly. 'Someone who shouldn't have been sent here in the first place. He was living in a public house in London, in Holborn, and got on the wrong side of the publican's wife. She was annoyed that he wasn't a drinker and also that he wouldn't pay his rent before the agreed date.'

'What of it?' asks Ann.

'So she set him up. He came home from work one evening, went to bed and the next morning the parish constables arrived, searched his room and found clothing hidden under his mattress belonging to a female neighbour. He was charged with the theft of two pounds' worth of items and given seven years.'

'But didn't he protest his innocence to the court?' Ann queries.

'Oh, Ann!' Olivia looks exasperated. 'You of all people know how the courts work. He didn't stand a chance.'

Ann looks shame-faced. 'I'm sorry,' she says. 'It's just that you're my dearest friend—' She pauses. 'Well, my *only* friend, and I want to make sure that you're making a wise choice.' She holds out her hand, and Olivia takes it.

The Governor, His Wife and His Mistress

'Thank you, Ann,' she says. 'But don't worry. He's probably the kindest and most gentle man I've ever met. He's a lot like how you describe your Joseph. I imagine the pair would have got on very well if they'd ever have met.'

Ann feels her eyes fill with tears at the mention of her dear dead Joseph, her lost lover and the father of her children. 'Then I imagine they would have,' she whispers, her voice croaky. 'And if you're even half as happy as we were, then you have made an excellent decision.'

A sudden shout makes both women start. 'Ann Inett?' calls one of the male convicts, walking towards them. 'The commandant wants to see you.'

GETTING TO KNOW YOU

Philip Gidley King

23 APRIL 1788, NORFOLK ISLAND

It's Philip Gidley King's thirtieth birthday but he doesn't feel he has much reason to celebrate.

A rickety building to serve as Government House has now been erected, but it isn't terribly comfortable. Progress is slow in clearing more land on Norfolk Island as the entire surface is covered in a thick mass of solid vegetation that is exhausting to slash through. Some flax plants have been discovered, but not many. And the tall pines that were going to provide so many masts and spars for sailing ships have, so far, proved bitterly disappointing.

'They just don't seem to have the strength to hold much at all,' Gidley King is told by one of the marines after a group of trees have been sawn down. 'A number of them look as though they'll snap as soon as a gust of wind catches the sail. They could be worse than

The Governor, His Wife and His Mistress

useless. And even if they weren't, Lord knows how we'd get them off the island.'

What's more, his new housekeeper is proving something of a disappointment. He'd liked the look, and gentle manner, of Ann Inett but she is nothing like he'd imagined. She seems diligent around the house, he'll give her that, but she's quiet and withdrawn and doesn't seem particularly pleased to have been picked out for this role. He was hoping for some good company on the evenings when he wasn't working, but she seems more like a ghost flitting around the house. If he didn't know any better, he could swear she was actively avoiding him.

One day, he decides to confront her. He's at his makeshift desk, working out the island's food supplies for the coming months with their stores and likely yields from the crops they've managed to plant, when Ann walks past.

'Ann,' he calls, 'could you come in here please?'

She appears dutifully, her eyes cast down. 'Yes, sir. Do you need anything?'

'Well, yes, I do, as a matter of fact,' he replies. 'Could you sit down? I need to talk to you.'

He notices she looks frightened, and sighs. Obviously, something is the matter, but will she actually tell him?

'Look, Ann, you've been here for two weeks now, and I know next to nothing about you. Could you tell me about yourself?'

She hesitates, and he decides to take a different tack.

'There are so few of us here on the island, we need to get along with each other if we stand any chance of making a success of this settlement,' he says. 'Of course, we come from different backgrounds and upbringings and places, and we represent a big cross-section of society, but we have one thing in common: we've all been hand-picked as the ones most likely to make a go of it. It may not have been our choice to come to this island, and we may not be happy to be here, but it's imperative that we at least make an effort to get along with each other. Wouldn't you agree?'

Ann stares at him, her eyes wide. He wonders if she's understood what he's trying to tell her. Then, to his enormous relief, she smiles and her whole face lights up.

'Did you not choose to come here either, sir?' she asks softly.

'No, I didn't.' He chuckles. 'Look at this place!' He gestures towards the exterior. 'Who on earth would want to come to such a godforsaken spot? I came because it was my duty to king and country, and to Governor Phillip,' he adds hastily. 'They needed a settlement here and he thought I was the man to make it happen. But no, Ann. It wouldn't have been my choice, either.'

There's a moment's silence and then Ann raises her head. She looks, to Gidley King, as if she's made a decision. 'I was horrified when I was told I was coming here,' she says. 'It was bad enough being sent to Botany Bay and then Port Jackson, so far away from my children back in England. But this is further still.'

'You have children?' he asks her.

'A boy and a girl.'

'How lovely!' he replies. 'How old?'

'Thomas is ten soon, and Constance is six—no, has just turned seven.'

'And where are they now?'

'They're back at home near Worcester.'

The Governor, His Wife and His Mistress

'With their father?'

'No.' He notices a cloud pass over Ann's face. 'He died in the American War.'

'Oh, I'm sorry,' Gidley King says. 'I also fought in the American War. We had many casualties. Many brave men lost.' He can feel a flicker of pain pass over his face, too, as he thinks back to the *Liverpool*. 'That must have been very hard for you.'

'Yes,' Ann says. 'It was. But now our children are with my parents.'

Gidley King makes an effort to regather his wits. 'You must miss them very much.'

Ann drops her head, there's a silence again and when she raises her face, he can see she's biting her lip and her eyes have filled with tears. 'I do, terribly,' she says. 'Every day.'

'I am very sorry.' Gidley King is genuinely touched. He's seen from the scant paperwork sent over with the convicts that she was a dressmaker and received a sentence of seven years' transportation for stealing clothing. He has no idea why she would have done such a thing, but he knows his parents had a tough time with their draper's shop when the new factories began opening, and she could well have faced similar difficulties. In addition, if her husband had died, leaving her with two small children to bring up alone, he can imagine what a struggle that could have been.

Without even thinking about it, he reaches over and touches her hand. It's surprisingly soft and smooth and he realises, with a start, that he hasn't touched a woman's hand, apart from his mother's, in . . . It must be years. She doesn't move her hand away but he can see tears are coursing down her face and now dripping onto both their hands.

123

'I didn't mean to upset you, Ann,' he says, finally, withdrawing his hand. 'Please forgive me. It's just that while we're both under this one roof, I thought it would be nice to get to know each other a little more.'

'Yes, sir,' she mumbles, and he can tell she's battling to get her emotions back under control.

'No need to call me "sir",' he says. 'If we're going to get to know each other, too many "sirs" will just get in the way.'

She nods. 'How about I call you Gidley, sir?' she asks. 'Gidley King is a bit of a mouthful and King seems disrespectful, and Philip too . . . familiar.'

'That would be fine,' he says. He smiles encouragingly at her, but he's not sure she can see him.

Some of his fellow officers had warned him that the convicts could be terribly manipulative if they felt there might be something to gain by befriending the crew and officers. They talked of the female convicts on the ship trying everything from tears to entreaties, toying with their captors' emotions and desires, in order to win favour. But this woman seems different. Very different.

The following days are busy for Gidley King as he is giving out orders to the assembled convicts each morning, and supervising the planting on the cleared ground. He directs other houses to be put together, and the building of proper storerooms for the food supplies, as well as pens for the pigs and sheep. He then dispatches most of the female convicts to help support the men on their tasks.

The Governor, His Wife and His Mistress

The search for the elusive flax plants continues, much to Gidley King's puzzlement. Captain Cook had described the island's flax as being 'rather more luxuriant than at New Zealand', but so far, hardly any has been discovered.

That changes, however, when *Sirius* surgeon Thomas Jamison goes for an exploratory walk on the island and discovers that what everyone had been calling an iris could, in fact, be the elusive flax. Gidley King examines one of the plants more closely and sees that the leaves are thicker and larger than the conventional iris, and the fibres through the leaf are extremely flaxy and run down the stalk all the way to the root, giving it surprising strength. He orders the convicts to bring him three bundles, and he puts them in a rivulet to soak, as he's heard that's the first step in the process of treating the flax.

Things are looking up all round. His housekeeper, Ann Inett, also seems much more relaxed around him since their talk a few days before. It might be his imagination, but she seems to be more cheerful as she goes about her daily tasks of cleaning and washing and cooking. The last few evenings, she's even sat with him in his study, doing some mending of both his clothes and hers, and he's admired her fine needlework. They either maintain a companionable silence or chat about the day's events and even, occasionally, laugh at something they heard someone say.

Their relationship, indeed, seems to be progressing well. She's opened up more to tell him about Joseph, about the rift with her parents, about her children and about the crime that saw her so harshly punished. He's also found himself talking about his parents,

125

his childhood, his impressions of the terrible prison in Launceston and his life at sea and love for adventure.

In fact, it's going so smoothly, and he's found himself enjoying her company so much, that he realises how lonely he's been for so much of his life. He's also just lately started wondering if perhaps their relationship could develop into something more. She's an attractive woman of thirty-four, only four years older than himself, and they're both alone here.

That evening, while they're sitting in his study, he decides to broach the subject.

'Ann, could I speak to you about something?' he asks, as he sits with his after-dinner glass of port.

'Did you want more port, sir . . . Gidley?' she asks him, looking up.

'No, no, but—' he suddenly has an idea '—did you want a glass perhaps?'

'Me?' she replies surprised. 'Thank you but no. I have never had much of a taste for alcohol.'

'Admirable!' he says. 'I sometimes wish I didn't either.'

'So, what was it you wanted to speak to me about?'

Gidley King coughs awkwardly. 'Well, I was thinking . . . I was just thinking . . .'

'Yes?' Ann asks expectantly.

And it's then that he notices for the first time how pretty her eyes are.

18

THE PROPOSITION

Ann Inett

6 AUGUST 1788, NORFOLK ISLAND

It was an horrendous loss of life and, what made it even worse, was that it happened right in front of their eyes.

There'd been so much jubilation when the *Supply* returned to Norfolk Island on 26 July with extra stores. Everyone was overjoyed to see them appear on the vast, empty horizon. That initial thrill was, however, tempered by the foul weather that delayed the offloading, and left the settlers on the island gazing longingly at the ship, and at the new faces on board, while the crew stared in absolute frustration back at them.

When the wind finally dies down and the sea settles, everyone races to the shoreline to see the ship unload, Ann and Olivia among them. As the crew are finally able to disembark into a longboat, place the stores in there and row to the bay, there's an atmosphere of incredible elation.

'I wonder what fresh food they're bringing?' Ann muses. 'I never thought I'd be so excited to see a ship arriving in my life!'

Olivia smiles back. 'This is such a different life from any I've ever imagined,' she says. 'But how wonderful we're on dry land, and not on that boat.'

Ann nods her agreement. She's in no rush to climb aboard another ship after the voyage to Sydney Cove and then to the island.

The two women watch in companionable silence as the crew rows to shore, then back to the ship, then unloads more goods and rows back again.

After about an hour of watching, however, Ann shifts uneasily. 'Look! Can you see that surf flowing faster now, and it looks as though the tide is turning!' There is alarm in her voice.

Olivia strains her eyes to see and, just at that moment, a massive wave crashes over the rowboat and tips it over. Ann screams as the water rears up and swallows the four men. The last she sees of them are arms thrashing in the foam as the longboat is swept uncontrollably out to sea.

The two women fall into each other's arms, weeping bitterly.

'Oh my God, that was horrific,' Ann mumbles as soon as she's able to draw breath again. 'What a senseless loss of life!'

Olivia nods numbly.

Ann can see her friend's face is a ghostly white and assumes she looks the same. It was a terrible shock and, in such a tiny community of people, living in tremendous isolation, every single person is precious.

It has only been six weeks, too, since they'd lost marine John Batchelor, who'd drowned after his fishing boat capsized in the tempestuous waters. He was well known as the sailor who, two months after arriving on Norfolk Island on the *Supply*, had run amok, abandoning his work, breaking into stores and stealing rum—and earning three dozen lashes for his trouble. But, to everyone's delight, he'd come good, had been forgiven by Gidley King, and had become one of the most valuable members of the community with his large catches of fish.

But now, they had many more men to grieve from this latest catastrophe. There was William Westbrook, a free man whom everyone had liked for his ever-optimistic outlook; convict John Williams, a hard worker keen to build a new future for himself; the old master's mate of the *Sirius*, John Cunningham; and one more, able seaman Laurence Tomlinson of the *Supply*. All now lost, presumed dead.

'I couldn't believe my eyes,' Ann confides later to Gidley King, back at Government House, breaking down again in loud sobs. 'We were all so happy to see the *Supply*. I'd been talking to William Westbrook just yesterday and he'd been saying how much he was enjoying his work here, and what a difference he felt he was making. I told him to come to Government House for dinner sometime. And now . . .'

Gidley King takes her in his arms, holds her tight and strokes her hair until he can feel the shaking of her shoulders start to subside. 'It is terrible,' he says, 'and it reminds us all how dangerous it is out here. Westbrook was a man of great courage, determination and valour. He was always willing to undertake any project I set him. He was a huge asset and will be sorely missed.'

'Our numbers are diminishing fast,' Ann mumbles against Gidley King's chest. 'We've lost five. Now we're just eighteen.'

'And most of the dead were free men,' he agrees. 'We're now only four with fourteen . . .'

He trails off, and Ann knows he was going to say *convicts*, but had thought better of it.

'The next ship will be bringing more people,' he picks up on his thread. 'Governor Phillip sent me a number of questions with the *Supply*, and I have sent my answers back to him on its return voyage. Among those are how many more people we think we can support. So he will assess what's needed in terms of extra supplies and personnel, and hopefully give us what we've requested.'

Ann pulls away and wipes her eyes. 'I'm sorry for getting so upset,' she says. 'I'm having trouble controlling my emotions at the moment.'

She sits back and looks him in the eyes. He looks blankly back. 'Anyone who'd just witnessed such a scene would be in the same state,' he says, guilelessly. 'It's nothing to apologise for.'

Despite herself, she can't help smiling. 'But it's not just that,' she says.

He shakes his head. 'What is the matter?' he asks her. 'What can I do?'

'I think you've done quite enough,' she responds. 'I'm with child.'

It had taken a while for Gidley King to persuade Ann to join him in his bed. When he'd finally summoned the courage to bring up the subject, she'd looked unsurprised, but wary. He wondered if she'd been expecting it.

The Governor, His Wife and His Mistress

In truth, she had, but she had also expected it to have been couched in far different terms. Ann had anticipated him making warming his bed a condition of her employment. But he hadn't. Instead, she'd been charmed by the shy, timid way in which he'd suggested they might start a relationship if she thought it was a good idea. He'd love to, he said. But only if, and when, she might agree.

Ann left him waiting for two days before she returned to him with an answer. She'd spent many sleepless hours turning the proposition over and over in her mind, and examining it from every angle. She felt as if her heart would always remain with Joseph, and part of it had died with him, but she was practical enough to realise that life had to go on. Stuck on this terrible island so far from everything and everyone she knew, she had to admit that Gidley King was definitely the best option she had—if not the only option. He was kind with strong Christian values, he was thoughtful, and he would never force himself on her. They could, she supposed, actually create some kind of life together.

They wouldn't be on Norfolk Island forever, either. Gidley King was an ambitious man who had the ear of the governor, and he'd confided in her that he'd been commended to the authorities back in London for his conduct both on the First Fleet voyage, and his performance since. In short, he was a man likely to go far and, if that was to take him all the way back to England, she wouldn't mind accompanying him there to reclaim her children. It could be the best chance she'd ever have.

She had to think carefully, however, how she would manage a physical relationship. But she could do far worse than him, she eventually decided. He was a good-looking man, he'd always treated her with respect despite her convict status, and he'd no doubt had a great deal of experience with women.

Gidley King was a good-looking man all right, but as for the experience . . . It was only a few minutes into their first bout of lovemaking when Ann realised that was far from the truth. He was clumsy and awkward and rushed, and the experience was perfunctory, at best. He'd been isolated from female company for a long time, but still . . . She had totally misjudged how practised and skilled he might be. When she thought back to her tender nights with Joseph, how they'd taken their time exploring each other's bodies, found out what gave them pleasure and had whispered affection into each other's ears, there really was no comparison.

She was cautious about bringing up the subject with her new lover. After all, he was a proud man. But he proved touchingly willing to learn, and turned out to be an excellent student. And, gradually, their bodies fell into an easy rhythm and their lovemaking became as pleasurable for her as she knew it now was for him.

'I can't believe you're doing this!' Olivia tells her the next time they meet. 'That's so brave of you!'

'What, exactly?' Ann asks, genuinely mystified.

'Instructing him in bed. That's so . . . well, unusual.'

Ann shrugs. 'It's for the good of both of us. And he seems to be pleased.'

'That's just as well for you.' Olivia smiles. 'I'm glad you decided you would sleep with him. You make a good couple.'

'It still feels a little strange,' Ann says. 'I know it seems to be the done thing to pair up with those in charge but it didn't come easily to me.' She looks at her friend. 'And how are you going with Nathaniel? You're virtually living together now.'

'Yes, that's much less complicated,' Olivia says, colouring slightly. 'He's a good man, and it's easier as we have similar backgrounds. We don't have the complications of position and rank that you face.'

Ann grimaces. 'Rank and position doesn't mean as much out here as it would in Sydney Cove, or in England,' she says. 'I can still scold him for bringing mud from his boots into the house. I don't think I would dare to do that in the fine drawing rooms of England!'

'It looks as though we're going to be here for a fair while yet,' Olivia says, 'so you're safe for the meantime. Has he said anything about returning to the settlement at Sydney Cove? I wouldn't assume we'll be here for the next seven years.'

'I really wouldn't know,' Ann replies. 'But he did write to Governor Phillip saying that he thought it would take two years before we would have more than enough grain and meat here, depending on the supply of stock. He has plenty of barley and expects soon to have corn and rice. He wants twenty more men and women to help clear and cultivate more land.'

'And how is the flax going?' Olivia asks.

'Not so well. He rotted away the plants that were dug up, but no one knows how to separate the wood from the flax. So that doesn't seem to be working. He's hopeful that Britain will send out some flax dressers to show us what to do, and then we'll be able to make new clothes, as well as sails and rope.'

'New clothes!' Olivia sighs. 'Now that I'd love.'

Ann smiles. She feels much the same. 'But the big problem, as we know from that last awful tragedy, is the lack of safe places for ships to drop anchor and send longboats ashore here,' she says, her eyes darkening. 'Hopefully summer will see the ocean a lot calmer so that they can anchor here. And then one day, not too far into the future, God willing, we'll even be able to leave.'

A POPULATION BOOM

Philip Gidley King
12 OCTOBER 1788, NORFOLK ISLAND

The settlement back at Port Jackson was doing it tough. From the letter Governor Phillip had sent over with the *Supply*, Philip Gidley King could tell that his mentor was struggling.

There was the stifling Sydney Cove heat to contend with, as well as heavy rain that continually washed away the clay and mud with which so many convicts had built their huts. It wasn't so easy to repair them, or build sturdier houses anew, either. All the tools brought over on the First Fleet turned out to be either broken, old or manifestly inadequate, nowhere near robust enough to cut the hard wood of the Port Jackson trees and do all the work necessary. The convicts who were dispatched to collect reeds for thatch to replace the canvas tents also encountered hostility from the local Aboriginal people, angry at such bold-faced theft of the rushes they depended on to trap ducks. After a canoe was also purloined, two of the convict rush cutters were speared to death in a spot that became known as 'Bloody Point'; the first European deaths at the hands of Aboriginal people in the Sydney region.

Relations with the natives remained tense, and judge advocate David Collins frequently voiced his fears that, once they realised the newcomers intended to stay, things could turn quite ugly.

The ships of the First Fleet had started sailing off on their homeward-bound voyages, too, but left behind the rapid spread of venereal disease throughout the colony, as a result of liaisons with both convicts and the Aboriginal women, which was ultimately to have a devastating effect on the whole of the Aboriginal population.

Food was also a continual problem. There were equal rations for all males, with females receiving two-thirds as much, but those doing hard physical work complained it was never enough. No one was allowed to touch the livestock; it was far more important that they be allowed to breed for future provisions than be slaughtered for food now. The poor soil in many areas meant the cultivation of grain and vegetables wasn't successful, while attempts to catch turtles had all failed and fishing was poor. As a result, many of the convicts were underfed and, as a consequence, had little energy and worked exceedingly slowly. Phillip despaired at never having enough free men to oversee them, and the theft of food and illegal killing of animals were becoming regular occurrences. On top of all this, further exploration of the new colony was tough-going. *I believe no country can be more difficult to penetrate into than this*, Governor Phillip wrote in one disconsolate letter.

But he did have an idea about how to make the meagre supplies of food last a little longer, since no more ships seemed to be arriving in

Sydney Cove in response to his pleas to London for more provisions. In October 1788, he sent the First Fleet's storeship, the *Golden Grove*, to Norfolk Island with forty-six people on board, thirty-two of them convicts, along with eighteen months' worth of provisions, in the hope that Gidley King could feed them instead. It would now be his problem.

Although the land clearing and planting program is well advanced on Norfolk Island, and the soil is proving rich and fertile, the business of providing more food is never without its hurdles. One day, the wheat and barley are sprouting nicely; the next they're decimated by a plague of the only four-legged creatures found on the island: rats— the animals the surgeon had heard that first night and assumed were rabbits. The vegetables are also growing well—until they're chewed up by grub worms that then transition into the hugest beetles anyone has ever seen. Then there's the harsh sea salt winds and further foes, like the pinhead-sized aphids that chew the leaves and stunt plant growth, and, finally, a blight of caterpillars. Gidley King draws up a program of poisoning the rats with a deadly mix of oatmeal laced with crushed glass splinters, and then getting rid of the insects with a potion made up of ash and everyone's donations of urine. His experience back on his farm in England is finally proving useful.

'But everything is so hard,' he complains to Ann one evening as he pours his second after-dinner port. 'Nothing here is without its complications. And while I can cope with rats and bugs and all manner of creatures on the ground, there's nothing I can do about these terrible storms we've been getting.'

'Nobody expects you to be God,' Ann says, in the most soothing voice she can summon. 'You're doing the best you can, and everyone sees that.'

'But is my best good enough?' Gidley King asks, staring into his glass.

'It has to be,' Ann replies. 'We all appreciate everything you're doing. Look at Port Jackson; it doesn't sound as if things are going too well there and they have access to so much more of everything than you have here.'

'That's true,' he says, turning to her. 'Ann, I'm so glad you're here. I don't know what I'd do without you.'

'Oh, get away with you! You'd manage fine,' Ann says, laughing.

He looks serious. 'I honestly don't think I would. You've been a great help to me these past months. You have so much common sense, and your advice is always invaluable, especially about how to deal with the convicts.'

'You did well with them before me,' Ann says, also now pensive. 'All those times you came and inspected our ship to make sure we were all right. That made a big impression on us.'

'That was just humanity,' Gidley King says. 'You looked so wretched that first time I saw you all.'

Ann smiles. 'But I'm looking very different now, aren't I?'

Gidley King glances up and then down at her swollen belly. 'You certainly are, my dear,' he says. 'You certainly are.'

Two days later, everyone on the island dons their finest clothes—which really aren't terribly fine at all—and gathers in the clearing in front of Government House. This is a big day for the new colony: the occasion of its first wedding.

Gidley King is dressed in his freshly laundered and newly mended uniform, thanks to some more of Ann's skilled needlework, and Ann stands beaming in her best frock, a posy of purple irises in her hands.

The happy couple look blissful. As they walk into the clearing, Gidley King and Ann smile at them: Olivia Gascoigne and Nathaniel Lucas.

Gidley King, holding his Bible, officiates as the Commandant of Norfolk Island, and says how pleased he is to join the couple in holy matrimony. He studiously avoids looking below Olivia's waist; she fell pregnant shortly after Ann.

After the short ceremony, everyone is given a cup of rum to toast the pair. Ann hugs her friend Olivia. 'Congratulations, my dear,' she says. 'You look beautiful.'

'Thank you,' Olivia responds. 'And you do, too. Pregnancy suits you.'

'It feels a mixed blessing,' Ann says. 'I am happy but it does make me think so much more of the ones I left behind.'

Olivia nods. 'Of course. You haven't received any response to your letters, have you?'

'Nothing at all.'

Olivia tries to rally her. 'But think of the thrill you'll get one day introducing Thomas and Constance to their new brother or sister.'

'That's true,' Ann says. 'Thank you for saying that. And how do you feel today?'

'Absolutely wonderful!' Olivia beams as Nathaniel joins the pair. 'And hopefully it won't be long before we have our next wedding.'

'Here's hoping,' Ann replies. 'I keep hinting, but he's not very good at picking up the cues. I had my other two children out of wedlock, and I thought this time it might be different.'

'There's still time,' Olivia says. 'And if anyone can persuade him to marry, it will be you!'

The *Golden Grove* arrives on 15 October 1788 and, in one fell swoop, more than triples the population of the island to sixty-four. There's huge excitement as the crew and passengers bring news of Sydney Cove and everyone there. The residents show them around the island and point out all the work they've done. The newcomers are wide-eyed and can't seem to believe how orderly everything is, and how much food there is for everyone, and compare it to the deprivations they've left behind at Port Jackson.

Gidley King is heartened to hear their excitement and notes it in his daily journal.

'And one of the convicts said there's a lot of thieving going on in Port Jackson because everyone's so hungry,' Ann tells Gidley King. 'They're amazed there's nothing like that here.'

'Good, good,' Gidley King replies, writing feverishly. 'And what else did people say?' He knows Ann has a foot in both camps—as his lover she's accepted by the other officials and the mariners on the island, while, as a convict, she also has the confidence of her peers. Consequently, she's the perfect person to inform on them all.

'Another said that the governor is punishing those he catches more and more harshly. I suppose, poor man, he's at his wits' end,'

The Governor, His Wife and His Mistress

Ann replies. 'But it's hard when people are hungry. They'll risk everything.'

'Mm-hmm,' Gidley King replies absent-mindedly.

'On the same day as the *Golden Grove* set off for here,' Ann continues, 'he sent the *Sirius* over to the Cape of Good Hope to buy flour and more breeding livestock. I guess things are getting pretty desperate. He's even given convicts the day off on Saturdays to forage for more food.' She pauses for a reaction, but none comes. There's only the sound of Gidley King's pen scraping on the page. So she continues. 'Work has also started on building the new Government House to replace the canvas tent he has now. Apparently, the tent lets in the wind and rain so he's very uncomfortable.' She laughs. 'We're probably much more cosy here than he is there, don't you think?'

'Probably.'

'It's going to be quite a grand affair with two storeys. Some people over there think *too* grand. He's also drawing up a town plan for Sydney, but no one knows if he's making any headway. The town is growing more quickly than plans can keep up with. And, oh yes, they've had a lot of rain there which damaged the brick kiln and many of its bricks, and made the roads impassable.'

Gidley King looks up at that. 'They've probably been having similar weather to those incredible storms we've had here,' he says. 'But I suppose the difference here is that they fell some of those giant trees and, when they fall, they cause untold damage.'

'Not so much to damage there. But another interesting thing, one of the convicts said he'd discovered gold!'

'Gold?' There's real excitement in his voice for the first time. 'Where? How?'

'Outside Sydney Cove, in the forests somewhere,' Ann says vaguely. 'He said he'd show the officials where it was if they'd give him, and the woman he was living with, a free pardon.'

'And?' Gidley King is rapt. If there is gold in the colony, how much easier would this whole experiment be! England would be sure to send over more supplies of everything if they felt there was something of real value at stake.

'Sorry!' Ann says. 'They discovered he'd been lying. He'd melted down some brass buckles and said it was gold.'

'But surely Governor Phillip would have seen that for what it was?'

'He was away. He'd left someone else in charge.'

'So what happened to the fellow?'

'He was given three hundred lashes and had to wear a coat with the letter R on it. R for Rogue.'

Gidley King snorts with laughter. 'Serves him right,' he says.

Ann stands up then and moves behind Gidley King's chair to peer over his shoulder at his scrawl of notes. 'Can I ask you something?' she begins shyly.

'Yes, what is it?'

'Do you ever mention me in your journal?'

He can feel the start of a flush on his face. 'Ann, sorry, no, but this isn't the place for anything like that. This is an official government report.'

She nods. 'Well, how about in your letters to the governor?'

He shakes his head. 'That's all business, too.'

The Governor, His Wife and His Mistress

'But couldn't you perhaps mention me just once?' she perseveres. 'It could make a huge difference to me.'

'What do you mean, my dear? What difference could it possibly make?'

She takes a deep breath. 'He might someday offer me a pardon and then . . . And then I would be free to return to England for my children.'

Gidley King frowns. 'All in good time,' he says, finally. He's trying to speak gently, but even he can hear the faint note of irritation in his voice. 'But what about our baby? Shouldn't you be thinking of our child now?'

20

WHAT WE DO IN THE SHADOWS

Ann Inett

6 JANUARY 1789, NORFOLK ISLAND

The whispers are growing louder by the day. The thirty-two convicts who'd arrived on the *Golden Grove* are continually having meetings with each other under cover of darkness, passing notes during the day and talking in low, urgent voices.

Ann Inett, unable to sleep because of the discomfort of her baby sitting lower in her abdomen, is now in the habit of taking in the night air while pacing the clearing in front of Government House. When she's there, she frequently spies figures creeping around the settlement in the shadows, and catches regular glimpses of the flicker of candlelight through the canvas tents and in the gaps in the mud walls of huts.

She wonders if there's anything going on, but if there is, no one's talking to her about it. It seems to involve only the new arrivals, who don't appear to have taken anyone else into their confidence.

The Governor, His Wife and His Mistress

'Do you think there's something afoot?' Ann asks Olivia the next time she sees her. 'Have you heard anything?'

Olivia shakes her head. 'I haven't, but I'll ask Nathaniel. He knows everyone and seems to have made quite a few friends among the newcomers.'

In the meantime, Ann casually mentions her suspicions to Gidley King. 'I don't have much to base it on, but I do have an idea that the new group of convicts are up to something,' she tells him.

'Why on earth would you think that?'

'It's just a feeling I have. And at night, there seems to be far more people walking around than usual.'

'Well, we do have more people here now,' Gidley King replies flatly. 'You might expect that.'

'But not like this,' she persists. 'They're sneaking around, as if they're hiding something. And during the day, there are a lot of whispered conversations that stop whenever you are near.'

Gidley King passes a hand over his brow, and Ann can see how tired he's looking. She tends to judge how anxious he is by the amount of port he drinks each night. Lately, that has gone up to two, to three and sometimes even to four glasses.

'It is difficult,' he says eventually. 'These thirty-two new convicts take the total number to forty-six. There's only four of us free men from the original *Supply*, plus twelve more from the *Golden Grove* after the captain and one other returned to Port Jackson. A total of sixteen. They outnumber us nearly three to one.'

Ann doesn't like to think of the population of Norfolk Island in terms of free men and convicts. Some days, living here in Government House with Gidley King, she almost manages to

145

forget her status—or lack of it. Other times, like now, she's sharply reminded.

'Maybe they're just getting together as they're so far from home?' Ann realises it sounds weak even as she says it.

'Even so, we have to take measures to make sure we're safe,' Gidley King replies. She wonders if she's included in that thought. But he continues, regardless. 'It's proving very hard to supervise the work of so many convicts effectively all the time, and I fear many of them are slackening off as a result. I'm going to have to rethink how I organise everything.'

'That won't mean drastic change, though, will it?' Ann asks fearfully. Her memories of being kept in chains in gaol in England, and being loaded onto the transport in manacles, are still very fresh. She'd hate to see anything like that on Norfolk Island.

Gidley King doesn't seem to notice the tinge of alarm in her voice. 'I'll work out what to do,' he says. 'We might have to curtail people's freedom a lot more.'

Immediately, Ann starts to regret ever mentioning anything to him.

It's proving a long, hard birth and, by the end of six hours of pushing on 8 January, Ann Inett is absolutely exhausted. She'd been expecting an easy time of it since this would be her third child, but it isn't to be.

'You've got to remember, Ann, you're older now than you were when you had Thomas and Constance,' Olivia tells her as she weeps

The Governor, His Wife and His Mistress

with the pain and the despair that it will never end. 'You were in your twenties before, and now you're in your thirties. And this time, you were worn out before you even started, remember? It's little wonder you're having such a rough trot.'

'But how much longer?' Ann cries, squeezing Olivia's hand so tight, her friend flinches. 'Do you think the baby's all right?'

Olivia has no idea; this is all so new to her and, being seven months pregnant herself, she is, frankly, terrified. Gidley King has told her to send a messenger to fetch *Sirius* surgeon Thomas Jamison if anything goes awry, but she has no way to tell if this is perfectly normal—or not. She'd tried to ask, but he'd vanished almost as soon as he'd finished issuing her with her orders.

So, instead, she sits patiently, trying to reassure her friend and giving her the odd nip of rum for the pain, and then taking one herself for her nerves. 'I'm sure it won't be long now,' she says, trying to sound confident. 'Keep going.'

Olivia is just dozing off when a terrible shriek rents the air. She sits up as if shot and, to her relief, sees a baby emerging onto the bedsheet in a pool of blood. She picks it up immediately to check it's alive. There's a terrible moment of silence, and then, thankfully, it howls. She turns to Ann to see her sitting up and looking anxiously towards her arms.

'It's all right, it's all right,' she tells Ann. 'You have a beautiful baby—' she looks more closely at the squealing mass in her arms '—boy. He looks perfect. Congratulations!'

Olivia takes the knife she's patiently sterilised in the fire and, with her eyes half-closed, cuts the umbilical cord and ties a knot with string over the end. Then she carefully washes him in the water she's been warming for the past three hours. 'Here he is,' she says, eventually, handing the baby over to his mother. 'I'll go and find his father.'

Gidley King is lurking in his study and comes immediately, when summoned, to Ann's side. She passes him the child, and he stares down into his face. He's quiet for so long, Ann worries there's something wrong.

'Gidley,' she says, 'is everything all right?'

He wrenches his eyes away from his son back to her. She can see tears in them. 'Everything is perfectly all right,' he answers. 'Perfectly.'

'Now we have to decide on a name,' she says. 'I was thinking Samuel after my father or Philip after yours.' Her voice grows softer. 'Or maybe Joseph . . .'

She can see his eyes darken, just fleetingly, at the last suggestion.

'But you might have ideas, too,' she says quickly.

'How about Norfolk?' he replies. 'He's the first child born on Norfolk Island, so maybe we should honour him in that way.'

Ann is silent for a few moments, gazing at her perfect newborn in his father's arms. She has an odd taste at the back of her throat and realises it's disappointment. This new colony at the far side of the world has taken everything away from her, and now it has claimed her new child, too.

As soon as Ann has recovered her strength, she writes yet another letter to her parents for Thomas and Constance, and then visits Olivia and Nathaniel at their hut, taking the swaddled Norfolk with her.

The Governor, His Wife and His Mistress

They both coo over the new arrival, with Olivia confessing how scared she'd been and how much she is now also dreading her impending childbirth.

'Honestly, you forget the pain very quickly,' Ann reassures her. 'And you are a few years younger than me.'

'Only seven years younger,' Olivia protests. Nathaniel puts his arm around his wife. 'You'll be fine, sweetheart,' he says, giving her shoulders a squeeze. 'And I'll be right here beside you—with Ann, too, of course.' Then he kisses her tenderly on the forehead.

Ann watches the pair silently. How she envies their open shows of easy affection for each other! Gidley King is caring when he's alone with her, particularly if he wants to bed her with his new set of lovemaking skills, but when he's occupied with his government affairs, he barely speaks to her. And when they're in the company of others, he tends to talk to her as if she's only his housekeeper; nothing more.

Olivia catches Ann's eye and playfully pushes Nathaniel away. 'So how is everything with Gidley now he has a son?' Olivia asks her friend. 'Is he any different? Will we hear wedding bells—or whatever the equivalent would be on this damned island?'

Ann shrugs. 'He's the doting father,' she says. 'I can't fault him there. He obviously adores Norfolk. I sometimes catch him talking to the baby as if he's a grown-up. He loves playing with him, too. I've seen a completely different side of him with our son.'

'But any talk of marriage?' Olivia persists.

Ann shakes her head. 'I've tried to raise the subject a few times, but he either doesn't understand what I'm trying to say or is choosing to ignore it.'

'Men aren't terribly good at picking up hints,' Olivia says, looking meaningfully at Nathaniel.

Her husband smiles at her. 'I have no idea what she means,' he replies.

Ann hesitates. Olivia notices. 'Come on, Ann,' she says. 'Is there something else you're not telling us?'

'Oh, it's probably nothing,' Ann replies. 'But . . .'

'Yes?'

'Well, I read his official daily journal the other night when he was out. He wrote in there about Norfolk.'

'It's good that he's mentioned in there, isn't it?' Olivia asks.

'Yes, of course,' Ann says, her voice suddenly trembling. 'But it was *what* he wrote. He simply wrote, *Light winds with a swell, people all employed as before. 1 male child born. Norfolk*, and that was it. Nothing more about him; not who the father is, or the mother. Nothing.'

Olivia and Nathaniel are silent.

Ann can see neither knows what to say and she's feeling very much on the verge of tears. So she abruptly changes the subject. 'Now I was also wondering whether you've heard anything more about the rest of the convicts on the island? Are they actually plotting anything?'

She sees Olivia and Nathaniel exchange glances and immediately realises something is indeed up.

Ann frowns. 'What is happening?' she asks. 'Do you know?'

Ten days later, on the Sunday, Gidley King presides over his weekly service, which this week includes the baptism of his own child.

Ann has sewn a new dress for the occasion, from the lengths of cotton brought over on the *Golden Grove*, as Gidley King appears again in his best naval uniform. Ann has dressed baby Norfolk in an embroidered white cotton gown.

It's a simple, but beautiful, little ceremony with the baby's head being dabbed with water from the nearby spring. Gidley King formally proclaims his name as Norfolk, and everyone on the island crowds around for a sight of the infant and to offer their congratulations.

'He certainly looks the proud father!' Olivia whispers in Ann's ear. 'A son is the greatest gift a woman can ever give a man. I'm sure he'll soon reward you for it.'

Ann isn't convinced. 'Maybe,' she says. 'Only time will tell.'

That evening, when Gidley King goes to bed, she sneaks another look in his journal. He's written that he *performed divine service and baptised the newborn infant by the name of Norfolk, he being the first born on the island.*

Ann's heart sinks.

Over the following week, Gidley King makes a number of changes in the colony. He gathers a small band of the free men on the island together and equips them with firearms. Together with the marine corps, he then gives them lessons on how to use them.

'It's just if the worst happens,' he confides to Ann. 'If anyone tries to overrun us, we'll be ready to fight back.'

Ann bites her lip. It could well be too little, too late. But she's in a quandary. Nathaniel told Olivia, and Olivia confided in Ann that a mutiny is being plotted by the convicts. Apparently, they'd originally hatched a plan during the voyage to Norfolk Island to take over the *Golden Grove* and sail off to who knows where. But they'd ditched that and were now scheming to stage a revolt on the island itself.

Convict William Francis, who'd been transported for fourteen years for highway robbery in England, is scheduling the mutiny for shortly after the arrival of the next ship to the island, either the *Supply* or the *Sirius*. He plans to steal into Government House when the commandant isn't home, take all the firearms and hand them out to the convicts. Then they'll tie up Gidley King on his return, together with the other officers, and load all the convicts in the ship and make good their escape.

Ann listens to the plot in horror. How on earth can they hope to get away with it? But maybe they will. And perhaps, after their planned first stop in Tahiti, they'd even manage to sail all the way back to England.

She's absolutely torn. Should she tell Gidley King what's going on? Does she owe him that? They've been together for nearly a year and she's become genuinely fond of him, and she believes he feels very much the same about her. As the father of her child, and also as her likely husband-to-be, shouldn't she be loyal? In addition, she has to consider her own interests, and Norfolk's. Revealing the plot could well also win her even more favour with the commandant. Is he likely to be so grateful for her faithfulness that he'll start thinking more seriously about making her his wife and giving Norfolk a much more respectable start in life?

Might he even arrange a pardon for her with the governor and then take them with him when he's finally summoned back to

England? And, perhaps even more importantly, might taking his side be the *right* thing to do?

On the other hand, can she truly betray her fellow convicts and the confidence she's received from her only true friend, Olivia? Wouldn't that be the ultimate treachery? And if the ringleaders are discovered and caught, would they be hanged for treason? She knows Gidley King doesn't favour capital punishment but, at the end of the day, the decision might not rest with him. Could she possibly live with that on her conscience?

It's a horrible position to be in. She tries to shake off the sense of foreboding that's gathering over her head like a dark cloud, but she can't help wondering about the consequences of saying nothing; she might even do better to throw in her lot with the other convicts. After all, what has England ever done for them but tear them away from their families for minor misdemeanours, threaten to hang them and then banish them to the other side of the world? She hadn't received anything like justice in the hands of the British legal system, and it's likely everyone else is in the same position, too.

Yet could the convicts really pull off such a daring escape plan? And, if so, could this be her best chance ever to return to England to reunite with her other two children?

That night, Ann doesn't sleep a wink. She tosses and turns in a feverish panic and is in a constant state of wonder that the man in bed beside her sleeps so soundly. His life could well be in her hands. But he has absolutely no idea.

21

A TRAITOR IN THEIR MIDST

Philip Gidley King

12 FEBRUARY 1789, NORFOLK ISLAND

Philip Gidley King is astounded; he can't believe what he's being told. But this seaman seems absolutely sincere, and he's been here, working with them on Norfolk Island as a gardener, since their first day.

'Are you sure this is true?' Gidley King asks him. 'Where did you hear about this?'

Seaman Robert Webb looks grave. 'I heard it from my mistress, Elizabeth Anderson,' he says. 'As a convict, she has the ear of the others, and decided to tell me about it.'

Gidley King sits back in his chair. Elizabeth Anderson! He'd seen her just the day before, talking to Ann in one of the laneways leading off Government House. They'd both looked furtive as he approached, and Elizabeth had scurried off as soon as he drew level.

The Governor, His Wife and His Mistress

Ann had a strange expression on her face and he'd meant to ask about it later when they were both home, but he'd forgotten.

'Thank you, Robert, for bringing this to me,' Gidley King says to Webb. 'This is a very serious situation. I don't doubt that the convicts, in such numbers, would have been able to take possession of the island if they'd have stolen our firearms, but I don't think they'd have been able to take one of our ships as well. But it's perfect that we've been able to nip this in the bud. I am beholden to you.'

'I believe a number of the convicts were against the plot,' Webb replies. 'They appreciate the kindly way you govern. So they shouldn't all be punished. Elizabeth, for instance. And some of them took fright when you had that other convict, Tom Watts, flogged yesterday for refusing to work. Suddenly the consequences, were the mutiny to fail, came home to many of them.'

'That's a very good point, thank you again,' Gidley King says, rising to his feet. 'But I shall have the ringleader William Francis and his cohorts arrested and clapped into irons. That should see off the threat.'

Webb gives a neat bow and heads out. Gidley King calls together his new little army of free men, along with a few of the seamen, and they head to where they know Francis, and his co-conspirators, should be working. There, they confront them, arrest them and march them away to be put in irons. Everyone else watches on in amazement, presumably some in horror and others in relief.

There's something still worrying Gidley King, however. A nagging thought at the back of his mind. Had Ann been an accomplice to the plot? Was she a traitor in their midst? What on earth had she been talking to Elizabeth Anderson about?

As soon as he arrives back in Government House, he calls her. She arrives at his side promptly, Norfolk in her arms, looking flushed. When he sees his son, his expression softens. Is it possible to ever love an infant so much?

He wrests his attention back. 'Ann, could you sit down?' he asks her. 'I have something I want to talk to you about.'

She sits but starts speaking immediately. 'Did you catch Francis and the others? Oh, I do hope so!' she says. 'What a terrible thing they were all plotting. How on earth did they think they'd get away with it?'

Gidley King is speechless. So she did know about the plot! And could she have played a part in it? He can't bear to believe it might be true, but he knows there is honour among thieves and all that. He hates himself for thinking it, but if this mutiny had succeeded, what would have become of him, his son and the new colony?

'Now, Ann,' he starts slowly, trying to recover lost ground, 'I need to know—were you aware of this plot? Be truthful, *please*.'

Ann looks him straight in the eyes. 'Yes, I had just found out,' she says. 'You saw me talking to Elizabeth yesterday. She was telling me and I urged her to tell Webb so he could tell you.'

Gidley King is confused. 'But if you found out yesterday, why didn't you think to tell me?' he asks.

'Of course I did,' she replies. 'How could you possibly doubt it? But I thought it would be better coming from someone else. I think you value the information I bring from the convicts. If I'd told you about this, they would never trust me again.'

'So you weren't ever going to tell me?'

'If Elizabeth had refused to tell Webb, then I would have told you,' she says. 'But Elizabeth agreed, so that kept my cover intact.'

Gidley King nods. Ann is always so much cleverer than he often gives her credit for. She's right: it works well for him that she is able to converse so freely with the convicts and report back, without anyone suspecting she is betraying their confidences. Why had he leapt to the worst possible conclusion so quickly? She's had his son, for God's sake. He feels sure that she'd never consider jeopardising either Norfolk's future or that of his father. He was wrong to doubt her and feels thoroughly ashamed.

He stands up, reaches out his hand, and pulls Ann, still holding Norfolk, to her feet. 'I'm so sorry, Ann,' he says, a tremor in his voice. 'I am so sorry for ever mistrusting you.'

And then he gathers them both in his arms.

The next few days are a frenzy of activity. All the trees around Government House are cut down, as Gidley King is now worried that, if another uprising is ever planned, it would be hard to see a rabble approach. He orders that some of the fresh logs be chopped into posts so a fence can be built around the house with a small guardhouse to vet visitors. He also appoints a bodyguard to try to ensure his safety.

Then he assembles the entire population and talks publicly about the intended mutiny, and how foolish it was. He points out what a comfortable life most of them have, far from the privations being suffered at Port Jackson. He promises that those convicts who work hard will be rewarded, while those who don't will be punished. A new daily rollcall system will now be implemented and, for the meantime, an evening curfew—just in case.

But the good news is that it won't be long before they should have more ships visiting them too. The *Golden Grove* was due to return to England after going back to Port Jackson, but they still have their two ships that connect them to the outside world, the *Supply* and the *Sirius*, hopefully soon to be back from the Cape. They will bring with them more updates on the progress in Sydney, news from home in England and even more supplies.

Everything has just settled down again when, ten days later, on 25 February, a massive cyclone slams into the island. It hits around noon with a heavy gale that steadily builds in strength. Twelve hours later, it shifts direction and then blows with even greater fury, as the heavens open to a great deluge of rain. That continues until noon the next day, with the heaviest rain anyone ever imagined possible.

The force of the cyclone tears many of the lofty pine trees and huge oaks up by their very roots. Some, as tall as one hundred and eighty feet and as wide as four feet in diameter, are sent flying through the air by the tempest, while heavy rocks are also picked up by the winds and flung this way and that. Other trees, too heavy, and with roots too deep, come crashing to the ground instead. One smashes the newly built granary to smithereens.

As Gidley King, Ann and Norfolk shelter in Government House, he records the disaster in his journal.

> *In addition to the horror of this scene . . . the gale now raged with most*
> *violent fury, which defies all description: whole forests seemed, as it*

*were, swept away by the roots, and many of the trees were carried to
a considerable distance. By one o'clock in the afternoon, there were as
many trees blown down round the settlement as would have employed
fifty men for a fortnight to cut down ... everything in the gardens
was nearly destroyed, and an acre of Indian corn, which was in a
promising state, and nearly fit for reaping, was laid flat and covered
with water four feet deep.*

Conditions didn't ease until three o'clock, when the wind veered around to the south and, by sunset, things had quietened down so much, it felt like the cyclone had been simply a bad dream. Until, that is, the little family ventured out of the house, went past their fortifications, and could see the widespread devastation.

'If I wasn't here myself, I would never have believed such a thing were possible,' Gidley King remarks in astonishment.

'It felt like the end of the world,' Ann agrees.

As the great clean-up operation gets underway, the weather continues to be unsettled and Gidley King worries about the future of his little colony. 'We've faced everything so far, and we haven't even been here a whole year yet,' he muses to Ann one evening over yet another glass of his favourite port. 'I can't imagine what else here could possibly go wrong. But maybe I shouldn't tempt fate.'

22

A DEVASTATING BLOW

Ann Inett
6 MARCH 1790, NORFOLK ISLAND

Time passes quickly and, by the end of the second year, around one hundred acres of land have been cleared for growing vegetables and grain. About one-fifth of that, however, is taken up with tree roots, and pests also claim far more than their fair share of any crops. But, still, the produce includes wheat, rice, barley, pumpkins, potatoes, turnips, artichokes, lettuce, onions, leeks, celery, parsley, bananas, orange trees and sugar cane. The seas are also teeming with red snapper, although it's exceedingly hard to catch them in the sloppy surf from the island's sole two boats—a small leaky one and a cutter—and so many tempted to try are fearful of being swept onto the rocks. Even though it happened nearly two years ago, John Batchelor's death has affected everyone.

The Governor, His Wife and His Mistress

The huge harvests of flax that were envisaged during the early days haven't come to fruition, either. The plants are quite different from those known in Europe and are proving extremely difficult to harvest. The pine trees, too, are a bitter disappointment. Although they're tall and straight and reach up to two hundred and twenty feet high, the upper part of the trunks are too knotty and hard to be useful. They're also too brittle to make good masts, with different branches intersecting at the same level leaving the trunk weak at the joins, while they're very heavy which would upset a ship's centre of gravity. In addition, attempts to process the milky-white sap from the bark, since there's none in the timber, have found nothing of any practical use, as it will neither melt nor burn. As a last resort, Gidley King oversees an experiment to burn the spongey timber of the trees to make pitch or tar, but because there was no turpentine in the wood that didn't work either. The only practical value of the wood seemed to be in sawing it up for planks for house-building.

Yet there has been remarkable progress in the development of the island. There's now a road from Sydney Bay to Anson Bay, via Mount Pitt, and wood has been sawn to construct a number of buildings. With limestone located at the western end of Turtle Bay, mortar and plaster can now also be produced, as well as the bricks from the hastily repaired kiln.

But the one major problem remains: the lack of a good, safe harbour. Ann Inett knows that is Gidley King's greatest frustration and she listens for hours to his plans to try to create one. He talks about having the convicts pick up the many rocks littering the shallows, build piers, create a breakwater and force a wider opening in the reef—anything.

'We're His Majesty's smallest, most remote colony, yet we could be among his most valuable,' Gidley King says. 'If only we had a way of easily exporting our many goods, and bringing fresh supplies onto land. But the lack of a harbour frustrates us at every turn.'

Ann listens patiently but her thoughts are elsewhere. Their boisterous son Norfolk is now fourteen months old, and taking up most of her time and energy. She's also five months gone with their second child and frequently feeling deathly tired.

Gidley King was delighted when she told him she was expecting again, and she was thrilled that he was so overjoyed. Again, she started hinting at marriage; again, it seemed to totally pass him by.

'Maybe he'll propose when this baby is born,' she confides to Olivia, who's already nursing her second baby.

'He should do it now,' Olivia replies. 'This is ridiculous. Are you sure his intentions are pure?'

'What do you mean?' asks Ann, confused.

'Well, he won't walk out on you one day, will he?'

Ann laughs. 'Oh no, not Gidley,' she says. 'We're very close. I have every confidence in him. He's just not quite ready to commit. Give it time.'

Olivia looks uncertain. 'How much time does he need?' she asks. 'It's been two years and it'll soon be two children, too.'

'I just need to be patient,' Ann says firmly. 'And speaking of patient, surely the *Supply* and *Sirius* should be visiting us soon to bring news of home and of Port Jackson, and fresh provisions? Just think, it's been nearly three years since we left Portsmouth. It feels like a lifetime ago.'

The two ships finally sail in on 6 March but, to everyone's disappointment, they bring little of what's been hoped for. It turns out that no ships have made it to Port Jackson from England so there's no news from home, nor extra food and supplies. Sydney Cove is in such dire straits, with the failure of its harvest and poor weather, they can't afford to send much of anything, either—except for more hungry convicts.

Both ships anchor near Cascade Bay and start unloading their passengers and their luggage. It's not long, however, before the wind whips up and they're forced to stop the operation and sail back out to sea to avoid being dashed against the rocks.

As the island's residents help the fresh batch of newcomers wade through the surf from the rowboats to shore, they can only watch on helplessly as the ships and all the provisions move away. There are some cattle, pigs and chickens on board, they're told, but they will have to wait for the wind to drop and for it to be safer to approach. In the meantime, Gidley King counts the new arrivals—sixty-five officers and free men, six free women and children, one hundred and sixteen male convicts, sixty-seven female convicts and twenty-seven children. It's another huge leap in the island's population, by more than five times, to around three hundred and fifty, with all the island's babies. The convicts and their children again outnumber the free men and women by nearly three to one.

Among the new arrivals are Governor Phillip's deputy, Captain John Hunter; the commander of the marines on Port Jackson, Major Robert Ross; Captain Lieutenant George Johnston and—joy of joys!—one of Ann's friends from the First Fleet, Esther Abrahams.

When the two women see each other, they rush into each other's arms. 'It's so wonderful to see you again,' Ann laughs through her tears. 'And Rosanna, you are so grown up now! And who do we have here?'

'This is baby George,' Esther answers.

'From George Johnston?' Ann asks, wide-eyed. 'I'd heard you were going to be his housekeeper.'

Esther smiles. 'And a great deal more than that now,' she replies. 'He's a good man, and we're very happy together.'

'That's wonderful! We seem to be leading almost parallel lives. I'm Commandant Gidley King's housekeeper, and as you can see from young Norfolk here and from the little one here,' she pats her belly, 'we're a growing family.'

'Congratulations!' Esther says.

Ann seizes her hand. 'Now come up to Government House. It's not very grand, I'm afraid, but we can get you dry and I'm dying to catch up on all the news.'

There is a huge amount of news from Port Jackson, but not much of it is good. Although Captain Hunter and the *Sirius* arrived back safely from the Cape eleven months before with four months' worth of flour and seeds, still nothing has come from England. Governor Phillip had been pleading with them for more supplies but to no avail. Once the *Sirius* has delivered its goods to Norfolk Island, Hunter intends to sail on to Batavia for fresh supplies. But back in

The Governor, His Wife and His Mistress

the colony, everyone is apparently waiting on tenterhooks for a ship from home and any time there's a thunderclap or an animal loudly belches or breaks wind, people rush to the shoreline to see if a ship has fired a cannon in greeting on its way in. One of the lieutenants had been staring at the horizon for so long, he mistook a cloud for a square sail, and set up almost a stampede. For famine looks to be on its way without more supplies, and all rations have been cut to four pounds of flour a week, one and a half pounds of rice and two and a half pounds of salt pork.

'But how do the men manage to work on such empty stomachs?' Ann asks.

'They often can't. The governor has cut their hours of work to six a day and is encouraging everyone to grow their own vegetables to relieve pressure on the provisions put aside.'

'Is that why he's sent so many of you on the ships?'

'He told George that you're much better off for food here, so he's divided the colony almost in half and sent us here in the hope that we won't all starve to death. We've been hungry for the past three months.'

Ann looks thoughtful. 'We've been doing all right so far,' she says. 'But I'm not sure we'll have enough food for so many people.' She's silent for a moment, and then brightens. 'I forgot to say, Olivia's also doing well here. She married another convict, a really good man, and they've just had their second child. She will be so pleased to see you.'

With Gidley King constantly in meetings with Hunter and Ross, Ann learns all the news and gossip from Port Jackson over the next few days. Relations have improved generally with the natives but there have also been some severe setbacks. Johnston had been ordered to capture an Aboriginal man as a warning to the others who'd been attacking settlers to protect their traditional hunting grounds. He'd brought back a young warrior called Arabanoo who'd ended up dining at Government House with Phillip. Sadly, however, he'd succumbed to the smallpox which had arrived in the colony and spread quickly through the native population, killing at least half of them very quickly. The governor was still determined to obey his orders from the king to open communication with the natives, so then sent someone else out to capture another native. This one was called Bennelong.

Ann asks how their other friends from the First Fleet, Ann Green and Nancy Yeates are faring.

'Ann Green was heartbroken when Captain Sever left,' Esther tells Ann. 'Sever was adamant that he had to return; after all, he had a wife waiting for him in England. But she had her baby, Letitia Green, who's a toddler now. But now Ann is with a man called Dennis Considen, who was the surgeon on the *Scarborough* with the First Fleet, and they had a daughter just before we left,' Esther tells Ann. 'She called her Constance.'

'Constance?' echoes Ann, thinking of her own daughter back in England. 'That's lovely. And is she happy?'

'She seems to be, as much as any of us are happy there,' Esther says. 'The surgeon is a nice man. She's done well.'

'And Nancy? How is she doing?'

Esther smiles broadly. 'She's done extremely well. She's now with the judge advocate David Collins; in fact, she's having a baby with him.'

166

Ann is amazed. 'But doesn't he have a wife?'

'Back in England, but that doesn't seem to dampen his enthusiasm any over here.'

'No, and these men don't seem to be too keen to take wives over here,' Ann says gloomily.

'That's true,' Esther replies. 'But you never know. I've mentioned the possibility a few times to George, and he hasn't dismissed it out of hand.'

'I've also spoken of it with Gidley, but it doesn't seem to make much of an impression. Maybe one day. But in the meantime, well done, Nancy! She'll end up doing better than any of us.'

'Oh, don't be too sure about that,' Esther says. 'My George seems to be in Governor Phillip's favour, but your Gidley seems to be a man destined for greater things.'

It takes two weeks before the weather settles down enough for the ships to drop anchor and start unloading their cargo into the rowboats to bring them to shore. Ann curses that damned lack of a safe harbour again! It's still windy and pouring with rain, but everyone is impatient for the valuable food, and livestock, to be delivered. Many of the islanders watch the perilous operation anxiously, knowing there is so much at stake for them all.

Suddenly, a cry goes up. They can see the wind has shifted and is blowing both ships towards the treacherous reef. The lighter *Supply* is nimble enough to tack away, but the *Sirius* is too bulky and heavy and careens backwards towards the jagged teeth and smashes into them.

From the shore, Ann can hear Hunter shouting on board for the masts to be cut down in the hope the raging surf will lift his ship higher in the sea up off the reef, but sadly she looks stuck. Then Ann can see him gesticulating for all hands to abandon the ship; it's obvious to everyone that it's now sinking. The marines run into the pounding surf to see what they can do to help and a cable is set up from ship to shore, with a pulley system to land the stores and so those on board can cling to it as they make their way to safety on land. As the ship then starts to break up, casks of supplies are tossed into the sea in the hope that some of them can be picked up, and livestock either swim—or drown.

The flagship of the First Fleet is lost.

It's a devastating blow. Quite apart from the disaster of losing so many supplies, the *Sirius* was their main link to the outside world, and now both colonies are left only with the small *Supply*, which can carry just fifty people at best. Hunter and the entire crew of the *Sirius* are also now stranded on the island. It feels as if the whole island has gone into mourning.

The next day dawns bright and blue, mocking the misery of the past two weeks. The crew of the *Sirius* are given jobs to do helping build houses and other public works, and are also tasked with removing some of the rocks that obstruct the passage through the reef at Sydney Bay. Yet the biggest problem is now how to feed everyone, especially with all the extra people on the island.

But that very day, something extraordinary happens. A flock of large birds darkens the skies above, hovers over Mount Pitt and then lands with a thud almost in front of the startled settlers.

The birds turn out to be a species of petrel which, as they're seabirds, are only at home taking flight from the water. On land, they're awkward, ungainly and often have huge problems taking off, because they find their long wings so difficult to spread. As a result, they're easy to catch and everyone soon discovers they make good eating for the nearly four hundred hungry people now on the island. They're quickly nicknamed 'mutton birds' and 'flying sheep' because of their fatty taste that's akin to mutton. That first flock turns out to be only one of many, and they continue to arrive in their thousands on their annual migration in March. Their arrival is so timely, one officer dubs them the 'Birds of Providence', believing they were sent by God to save them.

That evening, with Hunter resting at Government House, Ann is taken aside by Gidley King.

'I have been given some important news,' he says. 'I am being sent back to Sydney and then on to Britain to report on the new settlements and negotiate more government support.'

Ann feels as though she's had all her breath knocked out of her. She is so dizzy, she has to quickly sit down. She keeps a hand on her belly, where she can feel the little one kicking in fright. Is this the end? Is he now going to abandon her and their two children here?

She glances up at him and sees he's looking puzzled.

'But what . . .' she starts. 'What is going to happen?'

He's now smiling as if he understands. 'Ann,' he says gently, 'will you come with me?'

23

A BROKEN PROMISE

Philip Gidley King
24 MARCH 1790, NORFOLK ISLAND TO PORT JACKSON

It's with excitement, and not a little anxiety, that Philip Gidley King sails away from Norfolk Island on the *Supply*, with Ann and Norfolk standing by his side. He's pleased that he's been chosen to go to London to take Governor Phillip's dispatches and to deliver a verbal report on the progress of the two colonies of Port Jackson and Norfolk Island, and that he's been recommended for a promotion. He's also energised by the thought that he'll soon be back in England. He allows himself the luxury of daydreaming about the gentle green countryside, the cosy taverns, seeing his family again and the company of both men and women with similar interests and standing.

At the same time, however, he acknowledges a tinge of worry about what will happen to Norfolk Island in his absence. He's very proud of everything he's achieved there, against all the odds, and, as the birthplace of his son and where his second child had been conceived, it had begun to feel like home. He glances at the woman next to him. Thanks to her, he's experienced love for the first time, and is profoundly grateful. He reaches down and takes her hand as they watch Mount Pitt disappear in the distance.

The island is now in the hands of Major Robert Ross, the officer in charge of the First Fleet garrison of marines, and the newly appointed lieutenant governor of the settlement. Gidley King is not so sure how he feels about him. His conversations with Captain John Hunter about Ross haven't exactly filled him with confidence about how the island will fare under his command. Captain Hunter had confided that Governor Phillip found him a huge irritant, mostly because of his refusal to provide men to help supervise the convicts in their work, insisting that the marines' narrow role was simply to keep the peace, maintain order among the convicts and protect everyone from any attacks by hostile natives. Ross would also apparently find fault with Phillip wherever he could, resisting following his instructions and proving obtuse and difficult whenever he was able. In addition, he declared to anyone who would listen, that this new part of the world was barren, forbidding and had no possible future. He even wrote back to the Admiralty in England as much, directly contradicting Phillip's much more positive outlook. Against such a barrage of negativity and obstinacy, Phillip took the easiest way out and sent him far away to Norfolk Island.

Even there, from what he'd observed so far, Gidley King felt the signs were ominous. Ross had said he intended to govern so many people on such a small island with martial law, since the convicts so comfortably outnumbered everyone else, which meant that anyone committing a serious offence could be dealt with on the spot, rather than being sent back to Sydney for a criminal trial. He also introduced capital punishment. Gidley King had spoken out against both measures, but they'd been introduced, regardless. In addition, Ross planned to cut rations and outlaw the hunting of mutton birds.

Gidley King tries to pull his attention away from island affairs, and to what the future may hold. 'It'll be strange being back in Port Jackson,' he says to Ann. 'I wonder how much it will have changed in the past two years?'

'Hopefully, a great deal,' she replies. 'I'm looking forward to showing it to Norfolk.'

'Me too. But I am hoping that England will have sent a ship by now to deliver more provisions. It seems so cruel that they haven't. It feels a little as if they've turned their backs on us.'

It's an uneventful voyage and, when they finally sail through the heads, they can immediately see that the first settlement is indeed very different from when they left it. Back then, the land was just being cleared and it was filled with tents and the most basic of huts. Now, there are a number of sturdy buildings, including a white-washed Government House looking down on the harbour, a few other individual houses, storerooms, fortresses, gaols and a handsome block of officers' quarters.

As their ship arrives, the governor is rowed out to meet them. He climbs aboard and greets his old friend Gidley King warmly, shakes hands with Hunter, and nods to Ann and Norfolk. Then he listens to the news of the wrecking of the *Sirius* under Hunter's command with a strained expression. Finally, the men take their

The Governor, His Wife and His Mistress

leave to be rowed back to Sydney, leaving Ann and Norfolk in the care of another officer who's come on board.

Once on shore, Hunter departs for a meeting with David Collins, while Gidley King accompanies Governor Phillip to Government House. Once there, he sits down at his desk and puts his head in his hands. Gidley King feels for him. How much bad news can one man cope with?

'Norfolk Island could prove a great asset to this settlement,' Gidley King says, trying to cheer him, 'but if only we could provide a safe harbour. Without it, we are hamstrung. Although Captain Hunter believes Cascade Bay could be made into a decent landing place.'

'Yes, I understand,' says Phillip, tiredly. 'That's good. And how are your supplies of food? I hear growing conditions are good.'

'They're not bad,' Gidley King replies. 'We have to stay on top of the pests there, but the soil is good. We've also had flocks of what we call mutton birds migrating which have given us meat. As for the flax, I'm still hopeful that, if we could get a flax dresser to come out from England, we might find a way of turning that into cloth. At the moment, everything we've done has failed.'

'I will ask for a flax weaver along with all our other demands,' Phillip says. 'It's been so long since we heard from England that I have to assume a ship was sent out but has met with some accident. When you arrive in London, I would like you to stress how desperate the situation is out here, and how badly we need more provisions and support.'

'Yes, sir, I will.'

'And I'd like you to leave for England as soon as you are able. We don't have a day to spare. Take the *Supply* to Batavia and then find another ship there to take you on to England. I'll have the *Supply* come back with as much food, grain, livestock and medical supplies as it can carry to keep us going. In the meantime, I'll have to cut the rations again. And King?'

'Sir?'

'Come and see me again before you sail.'

That evening, staying in a room in the officers' quarters, Gidley King watches Ann as she starts to unpack their trunks. She's plainly excited to be back on dry land in Sydney again and is chattering about taking Norfolk to see the friends she came over with on the First Fleet while she has the chance.

'There's no rush,' says Gidley King. 'Take your time.'

'But, Gidley, I'm so excited to see them,' she says. 'It's been over two years. So much can happen over here in such a short period of time. I'm going to miss Olivia and Nathaniel and their babies so much, but hopefully it might not be too long before they come back to Sydney too. But now I want to see Ann and Nancy and hear all their news. And I want them to meet Norfolk.'

'Of course,' Gidley King says, only half-listening, pouring another glass of port. He feels tired and irritable but is trying not to show it. 'Of course.'

'The baby will be coming soon, too,' she adds. 'I wonder if it will be a girl or a boy? We should think of names. Maybe Utricia after your mother, or Ann; Philip after you or your father or—'

The Governor, His Wife and His Mistress

'How about Sydney?' he says suddenly. 'We have Norfolk, and Sydney would do well for his brother or sister.'

Ann stares at him, and he can see she is shocked by the suggestion.

'I don't see anything wrong with that name,' he says defensively. 'It's a fine name.'

'But . . .' Ann starts.

'But what?' he asks, more sharply than he intended.

'It's just a surprise,' she says softly.

'Norfolk got his name from Cook who called the island after the highest-ranking peer in England,' Gidley King says stiffly. 'It's a very noble name. Likewise, Sydney was named by Governor Phillip after the Baron of Sydney, the Home Secretary, who planned the First Fleet and made him governor. You couldn't get two more distinguished names.'

Ann hangs her head. 'I suppose so,' she says.

'Well, that's settled then,' he says. 'Now I'm going to bed. I'm very tired.'

'Of course, Gidley.'

He can see she's hurt and he hates himself for it. But he has so many important things to do between now and the departure for London, he doesn't have the time—nor the inclination—for idle chatter.

The pair barely see each other over the next week. Gidley King is busy with constant meetings and endless arrangements for the voyage over to Batavia, and then to London, with the date for departure from Sydney set for two days' time, on 17 April. Ann spends her time seeing her friends and showing Norfolk the colony, marvelling at the new buildings, such as the observatory at the foot of the

175

hill at Dawes Point; Government House, the only building with stairs in the colony; the food storehouses under heavy guard; the soldiers' quarters by the Tank Stream; and the lines of convict huts. Norfolk is wide-eyed. He's never seen anything like this before. Ann is similarly taken aback by the number of people walking around barefoot and in rags, due to the acute shortage of clothing and shoes.

Finally, on 15 April, Ann and Gidley King sit down for dinner together.

'How are all the preparations coming along?' Ann asks. 'Are they going smoothly?'

'As much as these things ever do,' he replies glumly.

'Oh, cheer up,' she urges him. 'It's going to be a great trip!'

'I don't know about that at all.'

'I do!' she persists. 'I can't wait to be gone! I know it's going to be difficult, with the baby coming, but I am so thrilled to be going back to England. I'm already half-packed. It's going to be wonderful. I can't wait to introduce Norfolk, and hopefully Sydney, to Thomas and Constance. It'll be such a marvellous reunion!'

Gidley King looks at her sharply, as if he's never really seen her before. Her eyes are shining and she's hugging herself in excitement. He feels the colour drain from his face, but he hopes she doesn't notice. He's in a state of absolute shock.

The next morning, Gidley King goes to visit Phillip at Government House. As he's shown into the drawing room to wait, he sits, then stands, then paces up and down. By the time the governor enters the room, he's worked himself up into a state.

The Governor, His Wife and His Mistress

'Whatever's the matter?' Phillip asks him. 'You look so red in the face. Don't tell me there's a problem with the *Supply*?'

'Oh no, nothing like that,' Gidley King reassures him. 'Everything is fine with the *Supply*. We've fully equipped her ready for the voyage and we plan to leave tomorrow.'

'Excellent!' says Phillip. 'And do you have Lieutenant Ball in command of the ship?'

'I do, and I'm very happy with that. He's a fine fellow.'

'So, my dear boy, what's wrong?' the governor asks him, as he takes a seat next to him on the couch.

'Well, the problem is . . .' Gidley King starts. 'The problem is . . .'

'Spit it out, man!'

'It's Ann.'

'Your convict mistress?'

'That's right,' Gidley King replies, colouring slightly.

'So, what of her?'

Gidley King hesitates. 'She seems to have got it into her head that she's coming to England with me.'

'And that's a problem because . . . you don't want her to?' Phillip asks.

'In some ways, I would quite like her to come, but then again . . . not,' Gidley King says. 'I have grown very fond of her these past two years, I'm not afraid to admit, and, of course, we have Norfolk and another baby on the way. But my mother would be very shocked by the idea of me with a convict woman, and probably my friends and my farm workers, too.'

Phillip sighs. 'I see,' he says.

'And then there's the Admiralty. I don't think it would go down very well with them at all.'

'No, you're quite right. They would frown at the very notion.'

'I imagine they realise such things go on,' Gidley King continues, 'but they'd probably prefer not to have it in their faces.'

Phillip nods. 'So why don't you just tell her she can't go?'

'She's set her heart on this voyage so much, it's going to be hard. She's suffered a lot in her life and I don't want to be the one to bring her more pain.'

Phillip is silent for a moment, gazing out of one of the windows towards the harbour. 'Then don't,' he says finally. 'Tell her it's me who has forbidden her to go to England. She is a convict after all, and serving a seven-year sentence I believe?'

Gidley King nods.

'So say I have forbidden her to leave. Besides, the high seas is no place for a pregnant woman. I wouldn't like anything to befall your next child. And this is a vital mission I'm sending you on. I don't want you to have any distractions. Tell her that, too.'

Gidley King feels overcome with gratitude. 'You won't mind if I tell her that?' he asks.

'Not at all. Tell her we'll give her a little house to use while you're gone, and we'll take good care of her, your son and your baby in your absence.'

Gidley King stands up and salutes Phillip. Then he places a hand on his shoulder. 'Thank you, sir,' he says. 'Thank you.'

The Governor, His Wife and His Mistress

When Gidley King returns to the officers' quarters and tells Ann that she's not allowed to leave with him, she's inconsolable. She weeps, she wails and she curses Phillip and his inhumanity.

'But I was so looking forward to going home,' she cries, as Gidley King puts a comforting arm around her shoulders and strokes her hair.

'I know, my love, I know,' he whispers. 'I am so sorry. I was looking forward to having this time together, too. I absolutely love being at sea, and it would have been wonderful to be sailing with you and Norfolk by my side.'

'But you promised I could go. You *promised*!'

'I did promise you could come to Sydney with me, but I didn't realise the governor would stop you leaving the country.'

'Can't you try to persuade Phillip to let me go?' Ann pleads. 'Did you really try?'

'I tried, I really did,' Gidley King says. 'But there was no swaying him. His mind was made up. I'm as devastated as you.'

24

THE DEPARTURE

Ann Inett

17 APRIL 1790, SYDNEY COVE, NEW SOUTH WALES

Early the next day, Ann Inett and Norfolk go down to the shoreline to wave his father goodbye. Ann's eyes are already red from crying the whole night, and Norfolk is whining as he knows something must be terribly wrong.

When Philip Gidley King kisses him goodbye, his son wraps his arms around his father's leg and refuses to let go until Ann gently prises him off. As Gidley King embraces Ann for the last time before boarding, he holds her chin up and kisses her lightly on the lips.

'Take care, my dear,' he says. 'If you need anything, ask the governor. He says he'll look after you.'

Ann feels a bolt of alarm. 'Gidley, you will come back to me?' she asks him. 'You will come back to me and your children?'

The Governor, His Wife and His Mistress

'Of course,' he says. 'I will be back as quickly as I can, hopefully within not too much longer than a year. I just have to deliver my reports to London and plead with them for as many supplies as they can possibly muster to send over. Then I will be back as soon as is possible.'

'Promise me you'll be back,' she says, feeling a familiar ache in her heart she recognises from when she'd learned of the death of Joseph, and then when she'd lost her first two children. '*Promise* me.'

'I promise,' Gidley King says, and she's pleased to see tears glinting in his eyes. 'You and my son mean everything to me. You can't possibly doubt that.'

She hangs her head. 'I don't,' she says. 'But it's going to be so hard without you. Having this child alone, waiting for you. And if anything were to happen to you . . .'

'It won't,' he says with as much certainty as he can summon. 'The time will go quickly, you'll see. I will be back before you know it.'

'And then will you consider making an honest woman of me?' she asks, with a shy smile.

'Oh, Ann,' he says, wrapping his arms around her. 'Yes, let's think of that too.'

'*Really?*'

'Yes, really.'

And with one last kiss for his mistress and his son, he turns away and boards his ship.

She stands with tears streaming down her face of either sadness or happiness, she can't be sure which, and waving long after the ship has disappeared through the heads.

THE ARRIVAL

Ann Inett

21 SEPTEMBER 1791, SYDNEY COVE, NEW SOUTH WALES

It has been a gruelling one year and five months since Philip Gidley King left Port Jackson when word finally reaches Ann and her two sons, Norfolk, now nearly three years old, and Sydney, fourteen months, that he is about to arrive. The whole colony has been waiting impatiently for the arrival of HMS *Gorgon* and the much-needed supplies she is bringing after so many long months of hunger and drought.

Governor Phillip had ordered all rations at both settlements to be reduced by a third, and everyone was close to starvation. But more convicts kept on coming.

The six ships of the non-naval, privately owned and managed Second Fleet had arrived in dribs and drabs from 3 June 1790, carrying settlers, convicts and some supplies. There were far fewer supplies, however, than everyone had imagined, and far more convicts.

The Governor, His Wife and His Mistress

In total, one thousand and thirty-eight convicts, around three hundred of them women, had been loaded aboard the ships in England, but about a quarter of them had died in the appalling conditions on the profit-driven ships, and around forty per cent of the survivors had arrived in Sydney in such a terrible state, they were dead within the first six months. The sudden presence of so many dying, sick and frail, unskilled convicts had put enormous pressure on food supplies at the settlement and outright famine looked a distinct possibility many times.

Like everyone else, Ann had to scrabble for food to feed herself and her two young children. There were moments of absolute despair. She hated the way she had to send Norfolk to bed on an empty belly so many nights, and she'd never forget the screams of her hungry baby when her milk started to dry up.

There'd been plenty of other crises, too, in the colony. Bennelong, the kidnapped Aboriginal man, had escaped in May the previous year, and then had been spotted in Manly Cove in September with a group of natives. Governor Phillip and his men had approached but a spear had been thrown that pierced the governor's right shoulder near the collarbone and came out close to his backbone. Everyone retreated, then, not long afterwards, Bennelong re-appeared to enquire after the governor's health and became a go-between between him and the other natives. A small brick house was built for him and his second wife Barangaroo on the eastern headland of Sydney Cove. At the same time, however, another Aboriginal warrior—this one known as Pemulwuy—had speared Phillip's gamekeeper, who'd later died of his wounds. A search to find him had returned empty-handed and the governor, in a rage, ordered the capture of two

Aboriginal men and the killing of ten more, whose heads would be put on public display as a lesson for the locals. Expeditions to follow his orders also failed, and they were later quietly dropped. Ann simply can't wait to share all the news with Gidley King, and hopes that her little family's days of hunger will soon be behind them when he returns.

The *Gorgon* was expected long before now but with the Admiralty's continual changes of plans there's been delay after delay. The ship is now going to be coming in as part of the Third Fleet; one that will, hopefully, contain a lot more provisions than new convicts and settlers.

When the ship finally travels between the heads and down through the harbour, her sails billowing in the cool winds, it feels as if the whole colony is rejoicing.

Ann puts on her best frock, dresses the children, and walks straight down to the Sydney Cove harbour, to the place where she's spent so many long days since her lover departed, watching for his ship to come in. It feels strangely familiar, until she realises that this was how she felt nearly eight years ago, when she'd gone into town to wait for Joseph to arrive home. She shakes her head to rid herself of the thought. That was then, and this is now.

When the ship nears the shore, she feels her heart lift. The nightmare of living in Sydney alone, battling to provide enough food for her two young children, will soon be over. She cranes her neck for a sighting of Gidley King on the deck but there are so many people there, and so many now crowding around her on the shore, she can't even catch a glimpse of him.

The Governor, His Wife and His Mistress

When the ship drops anchor, a stone's throw from the jetty, she pushes her way to the front of the horde, hand in hand with Norfolk and with Sydney tucked under her other arm. She can't wait to see Gidley's face when he catches sight of Norfolk and sees how tall and strong his son has grown, and when he looks into her arms to meet Sydney. A shiver of delicious expectation works its way down her body.

And then, finally, miracle of miracles, she sees him sitting up at the bow of the first longboat, looking so handsome in his uniform and yet so heart-warmingly familiar.

'Gidley!' she calls out. *'Gidley!'*

Ann steps forward, just as the longboat draws alongside and Gidley King stands to disembark. She's only about six feet away as he pauses to offer his arm to the young woman beside him. The woman looks up at him and smiles, and he bends down to kiss her on the lips, placing a proprietorial hand on her swollen belly.

Ann stops dead in her tracks, her own smile frozen on her face, and her heart icing over.

Part three

AMBITION

AN ILL-STARRED PASSAGE

Philip Gidley King

17 APRIL 1790, EN ROUTE TO ENGLAND

When Philip Gidley King waved Ann Inett goodbye, as he set off on his long voyage back to Britain, he had no intention of doing anything other than arriving safely, delivering his report, loading as many supplies as he could, visiting his mother in Cornwall and then coming straight back to Sydney. But life has a strange way of tricking you—and often when you least expect it.

The long voyage back, for a start, is a nightmare. With the old, and by now leaking, *Supply* under the command of Gidley King's old friend Lieutenant Henry Ball, who'd helped him land on Norfolk Island that first time, the initial part of the voyage, to Batavia, is all smooth sailing. They arrive at the port headquarters of the powerful Dutch East India Company within three months and congratulate themselves on their feat. Then they begin the hard negotiations with the traders for supplies of food, livestock, seed and medical supplies.

That done, they're both eager to be off on their separate journeys, but it takes four weeks to hire a second ship, also laden with goods, to accompany the *Supply* back to Sydney, and it's even harder for Gidley King to find another ship to take him to England. Eventually, the pair are assured a 300-ton Dutch mercantile brig, the *Waaksamheyd*, will be available to transport food to Sydney, while Gidley King could pay to board the medium-sized Dutch six-gun *Snelheid*.

But before they leave, officers from the *Supply* start going down with a mysterious fever, experiencing headaches, chills, weakness, nausea and a rash all over the body. Gidley King recognises the signs immediately. This is the same 'gaol fever', or typhus, he'd seen affect some of the women on the *Lady Penrhyn* on the First Fleet. But there is little he can do and gradually more and more men succumb to the fever. Even Lieutenant Henry Ball catches it at one stage but while he, thankfully, recovers, a number of others die.

Gidley King is eager to get away from such a dangerously unhealthy port and is relieved when the *Snelheid* finally sets sail on 4 August 1790. His relief, however, is short-lived. On the fifth day at sea, six crew are taken ill with the fever and not long afterwards, the captain is also struck down, then his two mates, and finally all the sailors—bar four—become so sick, they don't have the energy to leave their bunks. Even worse, the ship's surgeon falls to the fever and, Gidley King notes in despair in his journal, *was so ill that he could not even help himself.*

The Governor, His Wife and His Mistress

Desperate times require desperate measures and Gidley King takes it upon himself to assume command. He summons the remaining four healthy sailors onto the upper deck.

'I will never go below to see the sick men, except where it might be absolutely necessary, and then I'll take every possible precaution to protect myself from the fever,' he tells them. 'And I want you to promise me you'll do the same.'

'Yes, sir!' the four chant in unison.

'Now, it is my aim to keep the remainder of us healthy, to avoid making the sick any sicker and to make sure we all safely reach the next port. Are you with me, men?'

'Yes, sir!'

At that, Gidley King orders the four to dose themselves up on port wine, with two teaspoonfuls of ground bark in each glass as a preventative, and to stuff their nostrils with tobacco. He also arranges for them to rest each night below a tent rigged up on the quarterdeck. And then he sets their course across the Indian Ocean for the island of Mauritius, a French colony, three thousand nautical miles away.

'Ann, I'm so glad you didn't come,' he mutters to himself one evening into the wind as he looks back in the direction of Port Jackson. 'I miss you, my dear, I can't pretend I don't. I could make good use of your wise counsel now. But I would have hated to have put you through this. Not to mention Norfolk and our new child. You may not think it now, but Governor Phillip did us both a great favour. And I will tell you that when I return to you.'

The fatalities keep coming, however. Very soon, three of the sick men below are discovered dead, covered in the telltale purple rash. Gidley King instructs his healthy men to plug their noses with fresh tobacco and go down below to lash the bodies into their hammocks and throw them overboard, and then wash themselves thoroughly in vinegar to get rid of any lingering scourge. More deaths quickly follow, and when three or four of the sick sailors below go out of their minds, threatening the others, they're also lashed into their hammocks until they die.

The ship and its motley crew finally limp into Mauritius, east of Madagascar off the coast of Africa, by 29 August and come alongside the wharf at the harbour. The captain and three more sailors die as they're being carried to shore.

Gidley King and his little band of survivors stay in Mauritius for three weeks to recover from their ordeal. He has the ship scrubbed clean and recruits a fresh crew. Finally, they sail again on 21 September, with only four sailors from the twenty-six who originally left Batavia. The remainder are all dead or deposited at the hospital with little hope of recovery.

Gidley King eventually reaches England just before Christmas on 20 December and reports straight to the government. He goes to see the Secretary of State for the Colonies, Lord Grenville, who tells him about the bloody French Revolution across the English Channel that took place the year before, and hands over the dispatches from Phillip and stresses how much extra help they need, particularly with the loss of the *Sirius*. He is told that a ship, the HMS *Guardian*, was sent over to Port Jackson in September 1789, laden with crops, livestock and other supplies, as well as twenty-five convicts, passengers and a number of superintendents who were to work in Sydney. Gidley King informs him that it hadn't arrived by the time he'd left the colony eight months later. Lord Grenville looks grave.

'We learned in April that the *Guardian* never made it,' he says. 'After leaving the Cape of Good Hope in December last year, the ship struck an iceberg in the fog at night on the way to New South Wales.'

'Oh my God!' Gidley King exclaims, his hand flying to his mouth.

Grenville continues. 'Captain Edward Riou and some of his crew heroically tried to save their ship by pumping seawater out of the hull, trying to repair the damage and tossing guns and livestock overboard to make it lighter, but many people were lost. He eventually managed to get it to drift within sight of the Cape and rescue boats came and picked up the survivors. That's why the ship never arrived.'

'How terrible. We had no idea.'

'Well, how could you?' Lord Grenville asks. 'I'm sure you might have thought we'd abandoned you.'

'Oh no, sir,' Gidley King replies, but even he can hear the lack of conviction in his voice.

The Second Fleet had then been sent to the colony, comprising six ships full of convicts, as well as supplies and a military force in the form of the New South Wales Corps, all supplied by private contractors so the cash-strapped Admiralty could build up funds against French revolutionaries. Most of the ships had left at the start of 1790 and the government hoped they might have already arrived by June that year, so they would provide some relief.

Gidley King is also due to see the Admiralty Under-Secretary Evan Nepean, but the official's secretary tells him he is simply too busy with the French threat. Gidley King is outraged and immediately writes Nepean a furious letter outlining everything he has been through to reach England. Nepean soon makes the time.

'Governor Phillip has made numerous recommendations about you,' Nepean tells Gidley King. 'He is full of praise. Apparently, your leadership on Norfolk Island has been exemplary, and has made a huge contribution to the survival of the main colony at Port Jackson. As a result, we wrote to tell you about your promotion to Commander and Lieutenant Governor of the colony of Norfolk Island, but perhaps the letter hadn't reached you before you left.'

'No, sir,' Gidley King replies. 'Thank you, sir.'

He is careful to keep his demeanour composed, but he's absolutely thrilled. This appointment means he will be able to take command from Major Ross and leapfrog many of his superiors. There is obviously still Governor Phillip and Captain Hunter over him, but as for everyone else . . .

'Many congratulations,' Nepean chimes into his thoughts. 'You have an important future in front of you. We would like you to return to the colony as soon as is possible to continue to play a role. It sounds as if Governor Phillip relies on you and we will be sending more food and supplies as soon as we can.'

Flushed with success, Gidley King takes the time to visit Sir Joseph Banks, with an introductory letter from Phillip. Banks is a genial host and invites his visitor to his house in Soho where he shows him a number of his botanical specimens, including an example of the flax plant Gidley King is trying to process on Norfolk Island. It's the start of a lifelong friendship which he knows will stand him in very good stead.

While he is in London, he also calls on the well-known artist and poet William Blake. Gidley King shows the painter some of his own watercolours and receives a tour through Blake's collection of works at his home in North Lambeth. Blake is fascinated by some of Gidley King's sketches and paintings from Port Jackson, and even copies one of a native family, and publishes it as a postcard. It is the first illustration from the new colony. Finally, Gidley King calls on one of the other most important men in his life—his agent, whom he instructs to send him an annual shipment of port, no fewer than thirty-six dozen bottles each time, more than a bottle a day.

With his business successfully completed in London, Gidley King returns home to Launceston. His mother is delighted to see him and demands to hear all his news.

She listens silently, wide-eyed, as he tells her about the voyage of the First Fleet, the new colony at Port Jackson, his time at Norfolk Island and then his horrendous journey back to England.

'But, Mother, don't you already know most of this from my letters?' he asks, as he drains his third cup of tea at the kitchen table. 'I've already written of many of these things.'

'It's not the same as hearing it from your own lips,' she says. 'It's been nearly four years since you left us, four years since I've heard your voice. Can't you indulge your old mother?'

He laughs. 'Of course. What else do you want to know?'

'What did the Admiralty tell you when you came back to London before you came here?' she asks. 'Can you stay, or do you have to go back?'

'Sorry, Mother, I know you hoped I'd stay, but they're keen for me to return as soon as is possible.'

Her face falls and he realises she is close to tears.

'But don't be upset,' he says, putting his hand over hers. 'It probably won't be till the middle of March. I have a couple of months yet at home to see you and look over the farm. Do you know, by the way, how that's going?'

'I think very well. Jethro drops in every few weeks and gives me an update. He's an excellent manager and a very thoughtful man.'

'I'm glad to hear it. And, Mother, I nearly forgot, I have some good news, too.'

'What's that?' she asks, as she looks back up.

'I've been promoted to Commander and Lieutenant Governor of Norfolk Island.'

'What does that mean?'

'It means that I'm set to be a very important person within the new colony and, when I return to England, I shall probably be richly rewarded.'

'And when will that be?' she persists.

'I really don't know,' Gidley King says.

There are a few moments of silence, while he watches his mother digesting the news.

Then she smiles. 'You're not getting any younger, Philip,' she suddenly says. 'You're thirty-two now and still have no other family to your name. It's time you started socialising more.'

ARE THERE KANGAROOS?

Philip Gidley King

6 JANUARY 1791, LAUNCESTON, CORNWALL, ENGLAND

By the time Anna Josepha Coombe celebrated her twenty-fifth birthday, her parents had started despairing. Her twin sister, Theodosia, had already married, but there was still no serious suitor in sight for Anna Josepha. Their elder brother, John, had introduced a number of his friends to his sister, but none seemed particularly keen on wooing her, either.

'I know she's no raving beauty,' her mother, also Theodosia, confides one day to her sister Utricia. 'But she has a lovely temperament. She would make someone such a loving, caring wife. Her sister Theo's been so outgoing and lively since the day they were born, she tended to steal all the limelight. And as life for her became brighter, Anna Josepha seemed to fade.'

'I've always had a soft spot for her,' Utricia says. 'She's terribly thoughtful and sweet. She could be a valuable asset to the right man.'

'I know, but first we have to find that man.'

That conversation had started Utricia thinking and when her son, Philip Gidley King, returns from New South Wales, she wonders whether the pair might make a good match. He doesn't seem to be pursuing anyone in the new colony—there probably wouldn't be too many good women to choose from over there anyway—so maybe the cousins could be perfect for each other. He seems to be doing so well and no one would ever doubt that a good wife would enhance his prospects of advancement even more.

She invites Theodosia and her daughter Anna Josepha over to tea one morning, and then casually mentions it to her son.

'Philip, I know I shouldn't interfere in matters of the heart,' she begins.

'Yes?' he replies, puzzled.

'But, as your mother, perhaps I should.'

He raises one eyebrow. He has no idea what is coming.

'Your cousin Anna Josepha is dropping in tomorrow for tea. Do you remember her? She's seven years younger than you, but her family has always lived close by, and we used to all have picnics together.'

'She was one of twins, wasn't she?' Gidley King asks. 'I remember one was enormous fun, and the other was a bit quiet and mousy.'

Utricia is surprised he remembers but she moves on quickly before he can enquire which one it is who's calling by. 'That's right,' she says. 'She's coming to tea tomorrow and is so excited to see you again. Is that all right?'

'Why are you asking my permission?'

The Governor, His Wife and His Mistress

'I thought it would be nice for you to meet her again.'

'Oh,' he says, realising what she means. 'It sounds as if it's already arranged so I guess it will have to be all right.'

That afternoon, Gidley King goes out to his farm to meet with Jethro, who tells him how well everything is going. He looks over the accounts, inspects the dairy herd, and then decides to go for a long walk around the whole farm, telling Jethro he doesn't need to be accompanied. He trudges off, his hands thrust deep into his pockets to try to keep them warm. He is no longer used to the bitter chill of an English winter, he realises. So often in the last three years, he'd daydreamed about walking over the soft green lands of England. But he'd forgotten how cold it could be. That had never been part of his reverie.

A terrible storm hit the whole of England before Christmas, and there's plenty of evidence of its wrath here in Cornwall. There are still huge branches lying where they've been ripped off trees by the gale force winds, the odd blackened tree trunk that's been struck by lightning and deep pools of water in the muddy fields. It reminds him of Norfolk Island after the cyclone two years before. He wonders how the island is faring now, with Ross in charge. He dreads to think. The man behaves like a bull at a gate, yet with far less reason. Surely, however, there will have been nothing done that he won't be able to undo and put right on his return? Being its new lieutenant governor would give him much greater powers to act, especially now he has personally met the minister and the Admiralty under-secretary and knows he has their ear, and approval. He silently thanks Phillip once again for the introduction.

199

He wonders how long it will be before he receives notification that a ship will be ready to take him back to Port Jackson, and then on to his island. It could be any time, he supposes, from February to April. It might be nice to see spring arrive here at home before he sets off. There'd be plenty he could do at the farm, meetings to attend in London, friends to catch up with and it would be nice to spend more time with his mother. She's aged shockingly in his absence, and she obviously misses him terribly. But he hasn't been able to bring himself to tell her she is a grandmother with hopefully, by now, two healthy grandchildren.

He absent-mindedly tries to brush some mud off his breeches, and instead realises he's rubbed it in further. Damnation! Perhaps his mother's maid would be able to wash it out. He hopes she'll be as good as Ann at getting his clothes clean. At that, his mind swivels back to Ann, waiting for him in Port Jackson. Why has he been so reticent to tell his mother about her? He isn't sure. He's terribly fond of Ann, and enormously proud of Norfolk, of course. But coming back to England has made him acutely aware that a lower class convict woman like Ann won't fit in with his family and friends, and, perhaps even more importantly, with his career ambitions. What would the Admiralty think? Surely, they wouldn't approve. It was one thing to take convicts over to the new colonies, it was quite another to bed them and have children with them.

While Ann is often quite unlike the other convict women, she obviously does have a criminal record, that convict stain. She also now has four children, unwed, with two different men. He quickens his pace. In some ways that feels an unfair black mark against her, especially as she was, at first, unwilling to submit to his advances. And he knows she is keen on marrying him, but he's always somehow managed to avoid the subject. Could he really judge a woman badly on that? Despite his misgivings, he is acutely aware that he does.

The following morning, Anna Josepha and her mother arrive at 11 am promptly. Utricia notes that the young woman is wearing one of her prettiest frocks and has rouge daubed on her cheeks. She has to admit Anna Josepha has improved with age. She is still rather plain, but well turned out in the latest fashion; a pale peach gown with a tight grey bodice to the waistline, pleated lengths of uncut silk in the skirt and elbow-length sleeves. As she is presented to her cousin, she gives a little curtsey and Gidley King feels himself colouring.

'No need for formality,' he tells her. 'I remember you well from our childhood. But it must be ten years since we last saw each other?'

'I think it's more like twelve,' Anna Josepha replies with a shy smile. 'You were home, briefly, from the American War. You'd distinguished yourself after the sinking of the *Liverpool* and then you'd captured an enemy ship from the *Renown*. We all used to follow your adventures.'

Gidley King is taken aback by how much she so evidently knows about him. He had no idea that young ladies would be fascinated by affairs at sea. Ann has never shown the slightest interest in his naval career before the First Fleet. He feels oddly touched. He's noticed the gown too—uncharacteristically for him, he has to admit—and how elegant and distinguished it looks. It would be wrong to compare it to Ann's clothing, of course, as, despite her skill with the needle, she has little access to such fine materials and knowledge of London fashions, but he simply can't help it.

His mother and hers exchange smiles. Utricia has confided to her sister that the way to her son's heart is through his naval career, and Theodosia has coached her daughter well. Anna Josepha is a good student and now knows every twist and turn of Gidley King's career, right up to his most recent promotion.

The little foursome sit down in the drawing room for tea to be served. 'Now, tell me, cousin, what have you been up to in the intervening ten . . . twelve years?' Gidley King asks kindly.

'I fear nothing as exciting as you,' she replies. 'I had a most excellent tutor who gave me a huge love of reading and writing and music, so I have tended to pursue those interests.'

'Ah, what do you like writing?'

'I love to keep a daily journal,' she replies. 'I find it's a great way to keep track of the changes in life and of your own thoughts.'

Gidley King sits up straighter. 'That's wonderful,' he says. 'I, too, keep a daily journal of everything that happens. I find it's an important discipline. Hard to do some days, but generally it's excellent to have a record of events.'

'I often find it difficult to do every day.' Anna Josepha laughs. 'It can be tiresome some days and I have been known to fall asleep at night over my writing.'

'I've done that, too,' Gidley King smiles, 'and probably far more often than you.'

The Governor, His Wife and His Mistress

'Oh, but you would have far more interesting things to say in yours. I'm sure that keeps you awake!'

'Not always. My journal is often more of an official record of everything that happens wherever I happen to be. For instance, in my most recent posting, on Norfolk Island, which is about one thousand miles from our new settlement at Port Jackson, I've been meticulous about keeping it up every day. One day it will tell the complete story of a place that is much more important than anyone ever thought it would be.'

Anna Josepha leans forward in her chair. 'Tell me what Norfolk Island is like,' she urges him. 'Are there kangaroos there?'

He can't help laughing at her enthusiasm. 'Sadly, no,' he replies. 'The only animals we have are rats, and lots of them.' He sees her face fall and moves quickly on. 'But it's a very beautiful place. Lots of tall pine trees, lovely wildflowers and craggy cliffs surrounded by an ocean so blue it's simply unbelievable.'

'It sounds gorgeous,' Anna Josepha enthuses. 'A real island paradise. I understand you're going back as the lieutenant governor. Will you stay there long?'

'As long as they need me,' he answers. 'But it certainly won't be forever. I started building a good settlement there, despite the difficulties, and I'm keen to continue.'

'I'm sure you must be. What an amazing challenge for you. You must be so proud of all you've achieved and are set to achieve in the future.'

'Well, yes, I am,' he says. 'Thank you.'

'And maybe one day you'd permit me to read your journal?' Anna Josepha continues. 'I would find it absolutely fascinating.'

Gidley King smiles at her. What a delightful young lady this cousin has turned out to be!

28

THE CHARMING COMPANY OF WOMEN

Anna Josepha Coombe
20 FEBRUARY 1791, HATHERLEIGH, WEST DEVON, ENGLAND

She hadn't known quite what to expect when her mother suggested she go to tea at her aunt's to meet a cousin she only faintly remembered who was now enjoying a spectacularly successful naval career and seemed destined for even greater things. Anna Josepha Coombe hadn't been keen at first. If he was in the navy, and particularly high up, he was bound to be boring and pompous and have no time for young women with little experience of the outside world.

As children, she could recall Philip Gidley King playing with her elder brother, John, just five years younger than him, but not having much time for herself or her twin. That was understandable. Everyone doted on John who was a lively, confident young boy. While her twin sister, Theodosia, took after him in many ways, also brimming with self-assurance and a sense of fun, Anna Josepha felt very much the wallflower. She'd always preferred her own company and loved to sit quietly and read and write, and daydream of what life could be like far away from the suffocating confines of the family home in the small market town of Hatherleigh in West Devon.

She'd often go out walking on her own, something her mother duly scolded her for, but she liked the solitude. She'd wend her way across the moors, around the farms, and into the woods, and then sit on a blanket and read, surrounded by trees and birdsong. That was her idea of heaven.

Unlike her sister, she loathed parties and social gatherings, and often found herself tongue-tied and stuttering when anyone spoke to her.

'Come on, sis,' Theo would say to her. 'You look like you've found a farthing and lost a crown. If you sit there looking like you'd rather be somewhere else, no one's going to take the time to get to know you.'

'I don't care,' Anna Josepha would stubbornly reply. 'I don't like having conversations that mean nothing. And anyone worthwhile will see through all this forced gaiety and seek out those who aren't constantly pandering to it.'

Theo would sniff and turn her back on her sister. She liked being seen out with her—being a twin always sparked interest and lots of questions—but sometimes Anna Josepha wasn't worth the effort.

So Theo continued to be courted by all sorts of highly suitable, and most desirable, beaus, while Anna Josepha sat on the sidelines, disinterested in being similarly wooed. When her sister became engaged, her only faint irritation was that, for a while, she was besieged with her twin's cast-offs.

'Why don't you agree to meet with a couple of them?' her long-suffering mother would chide her. 'Please? You're going to end up an old spinster, if you're not careful.'

'But I can keep you and Father company for longer,' she said, unperturbed. 'I'm quite happy on my own, with my reading and writing. I don't need company.'

When, however, her mother said her cousin had travelled around the world and had been living on a tiny island in the middle of the South Pacific Ocean, Anna Josepha couldn't help, despite herself, being just a little intrigued. She still wasn't eager to meet him, but he didn't sound like her usual kind of suitor, and she doubted he'd be a suitor at all, if he was living such an adventurous, exotic life.

Her mother, however, seemed to have different ideas. She'd been talking to her sister, his mother, who had regaled her with tales of Gidley King's achievements, and how unusual his life was now. As much as she didn't want to admit it, Anna Josepha found it fascinating. She listened carefully to everything her mother said and couldn't help a little flutter of excitement when the day of their tea dawned. Of course, it would lead to nothing, but it should be a most entertaining morning.

Gidley King turns out to be nothing like she expected. A quiet, serious man, who tilts his head to listen carefully whenever she says something—she finds him quite charming. Considering everything he has achieved, he isn't at all boastful either. In fact, he seems almost ready to play everything down.

The morning tea flashes by in a flurry of conversation. She asks him about his daily journal, Norfolk Island, Port Jackson, Governor Arthur Phillip and the sinking of the *Liverpool.* He asks her about her journals and which books she likes most and why, and what she does in Hatherleigh to amuse herself. She talks about walking alone through the countryside, noticing her mother scowling beside her, but then quickly rearranging her face when Gidley King also confesses to a love of wandering through the wilds.

'Did you ever think life would turn out for you like this?' Anna Josepha asks him at one point, when she offers him a scone laden with jam and cream.

'You mean attending a cream tea?' he asks.

'No, I meant . . .' she begins solemnly, until she catches a mischievous glint in his eye and a smile on his lips. 'Ah, you're playing with me.'

'Apologies, yes,' he replies. 'I remember, as children, you loved to joke.'

Anna Josepha is about to correct him, and say that was her twin, when she catches a warning look from her mother. 'That's right,' she says, instead. 'We all used to joke and play around.'

'I so clearly remember the time when your brother put a frog in the pocket of your governess's apron,' Gidley King continues, seemingly not noticing her hesitation. 'How she screamed! But then, happily, she saw the funny side.'

The Governor, His Wife and His Mistress

'She was wonderful about it. I'm not sure I would have liked it back then, but these days I wouldn't mind.'

Gidley King grins. 'All that walking alone through the countryside?' he asks.

'Absolutely,' she says. 'I'm made of far sterner stuff now.'

She notices how approving he looks at that. In fact, he looks pretty much like that at everything she says, and at everything about her. When she first walked into the room, for instance, she caught the admiring glance he gave her gown, and she couldn't help ruffling the silk a touch more than necessary when she sat down. She also observes how closely he watches her table manners and she's careful to behave exactly as she's been taught by her tutor. He compliments her on her style, as well.

'You know, life is so different for us in the colonies,' he says at one point. 'I used to dream of having tea like this, with such exquisite little scones and jam and cream and cake. You'll have to forgive me if my table manners are a little rusty.'

'Not at all,' his three companions murmur.

'Oh, I think they are!' he insists. 'We've endured periods of famine in both Port Jackson and Norfolk Island and sometimes good food is hard to find. Any guest invited for a meal at Government House in Port Jackson is asked to bring their own bread to the table, rations are so short. And if I never had to eat salt pork again, I'd be most happy.'

Gidley King's mother and aunt join in his laughter, and Anna Josepha does, too, even though she doesn't really know what they're laughing at. Surely, every meat tastes better with the addition of salt? Why would that be such a strange thing?

'I'm also not used to the company of women, and such charming company at that,' he says, looking straight at Anna Josepha.

She can feel a blush on her cheek, and silently admonishes herself for being so easily flattered. But he just continues smiling at her as her mother rises to her feet.

'Well, it's been a delightful morning,' says Theodosia, 'but I'm afraid we should not outstay our welcome, and we must be off.' She kisses her sister lightly on the cheek, and then holds up her cheek for her nephew to kiss.

He duly obliges, then steps aside so he's directly in front of Anna Josepha. He catches her hand and lifts it to his lips. 'I've had a wonderful time,' he says. 'I do hope we shall meet again while I'm in England.'

'How much longer will you be staying?' asks Anna Josepha, suddenly feeling downcast at the prospect of this man disappearing from her life as quickly as he's appeared.

He shrugs his shoulders. 'I am not sure,' he says. 'I'm waiting for the Admiralty to inform me when they have a suitable ship for my passage back. It could be any time.'

Anna Josepha knows she looks crestfallen, but she makes no effort to disguise it. 'Well, I hope it's not too soon, cousin,' she says. 'I have enjoyed meeting you again, and there's so much more I would love to talk to you about.'

'And me you,' he says, with an intensity that makes her heart leap.

29

THE PROPOSAL

Philip Gidley King
6 MARCH 1791, LAUNCESTON, CORNWALL, ENGLAND

Over the next two weeks, Philip Gidley King meets Anna Josepha three more times: once for dinner at her parents' house; another time for tea at his mother's; and on the third occasion, they arrange to go on a walk together through the woodlands near her home.

He's pleased that she enjoys walking so much and takes great delight in talking about the type of flora and fauna in Port Jackson and Norfolk Island, and comparing it with what they're seeing. She's a good audience and asks many thoughtful questions, not all of which he can answer. He realises, halfway through their stroll, that he's never had a conversation with anyone about the animals and plants of New South Wales, beyond fretting about the uselessness of the pine trunks and the lack of flax. Ann never seemed particularly interested in their surroundings, he muses to himself. But then, he has to admit, she did have her hands full looking after him, as well as Norfolk, her next pregnancy and reporting to him on what the convicts were up to. And her mind always seemed to be half back among the green hills of middle England, with her lost children.

But Anna Josepha seems cut from completely different cloth. She has a strong Christian faith, just like him, and writes him letters after each of their meetings, thanking him for his company and saying how much she enjoyed their talks. He's absolutely charmed by such manners. He's never received a letter from a woman before, and is entranced by everything about hers, from the delicate perfume that wafts out as he opens the envelopes, to her elegant handwriting, her poetic use of language and the warmth with which she addresses him. 'King', she calls him each time on the page, and he finds he likes it.

His mother, Utricia, watches on with obvious pleasure. 'You seem quite taken with Anna Josepha,' she remarks one morning after breakfast. 'Are you seeing her today?'

'Not today,' he says. 'I didn't feel too well yesterday afternoon, so I thought I should stay in.'

'What's the matter?'

'I'm not sure. I have a fever and I feel quite fatigued and stiff. My knees and one of my feet are swollen, too.'

'Maybe you've been overdoing everything?' his mother suggests. 'You had a long and difficult journey and you could have picked up anything. You look pale. Why don't you go back to bed and see if you feel better later?'

'I think I will,' he says, not putting up any fight, which he can see she finds odd. 'I will get up later, I need to speak to you.'

Late in the afternoon, he finally wakes, dresses and goes back downstairs. His mother is waiting with chicken soup and hot tea. 'Are you feeling any better?' she enquires anxiously.

'A little,' he replies. 'Some of the stiffness is still there, but maybe I'll go to bed early again tonight.'

'And you said you had something to talk to me about?'

'Ah yes, I've had news from London.'

She raises an eyebrow. 'Good news, I hope.'

'It is the news I had been waiting for, but suddenly I am no longer sure whether it's good or not,' he replies. 'I don't quite know . . .'

'What is it, Philip?' she asks, more sharply than she intended.

He looks up at that bite in her voice. 'I received a letter from the Admiralty. It says I am to depart for Port Jackson on board the HMS *Gorgon*, as part of the Third Fleet to go over to the colony. I'll be sailing under Commander John Parker and—'

'When?' his mother breaks in abruptly. 'When will you be leaving?'

He's surprised again by her tone, but puts it down to her reluctance to see him go. 'In nine days' time,' he replies. 'On the fifteenth of March.'

Utricia looks crestfallen. 'That's not long at all,' she complains. 'I would have thought they could give you a little more notice than that.'

'Mother, this is the Royal Navy we're talking about.' He smiles. 'It's a huge beast with many moving parts. They will not be waiting on my convenience!'

'So what are you going to do?' she asks.

'What do you mean? I'll be sailing on the fifteenth of March, as I've been ordered to.'

'Yes, yes,' Utricia says impatiently. 'I realise that. But what are you going to do about Anna Josepha?'

'What do you mean?' he asks, genuinely baffled.

She sighs and looks at him like he's very stupid. 'I mean, what are your intentions towards her?'

'I don't have any intentions . . .'

'But why not?'

'Why should I?'

Utricia snorts in frustration. 'Oh Philip,' she says. 'It's obvious to me that you think a great deal of Anna Josepha, and she, in turn, looks absolutely entranced by you.'

'Entranced?' Gidley King repeats, still not understanding.

'Haven't you seen the way she looks at you? The poor girl is in love with you.'

Gidley King is dumbstruck. 'Really?' he asks. If he had to admit it, he's a tiny bit in love with Anna Josepha, too. But this wasn't meant to happen. He has someone back in Port Jackson, a woman who's borne, hopefully by now, two children by him.

'What is it?' asks his mother sharply. 'What is it you're not telling me? Anna Josepha looks perfect for you and for your career. What is stopping you?'

'Nothing,' he mutters. Even now, with two children and the undertaking he's made to Ann that he'll be back for them, even after his promises that he'll consider making an honest woman of her, he still can't bring himself to admit to his mother that he has been sleeping with his housekeeper, a lowly convict woman. He just can't do it.

As her son and only child, he's always been the apple of his mother's eye. He couldn't stand to see her face crease with disappointment if she found out what he's done. She's always been so proud of him, boasted about his exploits at sea, and now his latest promotion. She'll be heartbroken and would no longer be able to hold her head high in the village.

No, he can't do it.

'I don't know,' he eventually says.

Utricia places her hand on his. 'Look, I know you're used to being on your own,' she says. 'And it'll be hard for you to share your life with anyone after all these years. It'll be a big period of adjustment. But it will be worth it, I promise you.'

He looks at her hand. It used to be so smooth and warm, and now it's wrinkled with blue veins. She has aged so much since his father's death, and his own absence in New South Wales. She might not have long left. Could he really deny her the pleasure of seeing her son make a good marriage?

She isn't giving up. 'Think, Philip, of what a good asset she could be for your career. She's clever, you've seen that for yourself, she'd make a great hostess for someone in your position, and she'll be so devoted to you, she'll make a wonderful wife. And children. She's so much younger than you, so she has years ahead of her . . .'

Gidley King blanches at that thought. How many more children could one man really want? But his mother is right in so many ways. Anna Josepha he could imagine charming the Admiralty, bewitching his mentor Phillip, and being most acceptable to people in the government like Nepean. Ann Inett, on the other hand . . . No. As good a woman as she undoubtedly is, she could end up dragging him down. Besides, he could imagine Anna Josepha being utterly devoted to him, while Ann still often mentions her children to another man back in England; her other life, one he had no part in.

'So,' he asks his mother eventually, 'what do you think my next move should be?'

The following day, feeling in marginally better health, Gidley King arrives at Anna Josepha's parents' house and asks Theodosia if he can have an audience with Anna Josepha's father, John Coombe. Theodosia looks thrilled to see him and he briefly wonders whether she knows why he's here. But that's silly. How could she?

He's shown into the drawing room, where Coombe is already sitting. He rises at the sight of his visitor and the two men shake hands.

'Good morning, sir,' Gidley King starts hesitantly, realising suddenly how nervous he is. 'I'm here to ask you something.'

'And good morning to you, too,' Coombe replies, evenly. 'How can I help you?'

There's a pause while Gidley King composes in his mind what to say. He's been practising all the way over, but now his words seem to have deserted him.

Coombe takes the initiative. 'Would you like some tea?' he asks. 'I'll have the maid bring us some.'

'No,' Gidley King finally says, still standing awkwardly before his host. 'No, thank you. I've actually come to ask if you might

The Governor, His Wife and His Mistress

permit . . . you might agree . . . to giving me your daughter's hand in marriage.'

Coombe smiles and doesn't look in the least surprised. Again, Gidley King has the odd feeling that he's been set up.

'Why, yes!' Coombe says. 'Good man! A splendid notion!'

'I haven't spoken to Anna Josepha of this yet,' Gidley King says. 'I obviously need to speak to her. She mightn't agree.' Even as he's saying it, he can hear the doubt in his voice. Does he not want her to agree? In some ways, it would make everything so much easier if she doesn't. He could then get on his ship and sail alone back to Port Jackson, to Ann and his children waiting for him. It would be so simple. But, of course, he does like the idea of Anna Josepha as his wife, too. She would be an undeniable asset.

He's so lost in his thoughts, he jumps when Coombe advances and slaps him on the back. 'Nonsense!' Coombe says. 'She'll be delighted. What young woman wouldn't?'

Gidley King smiles at him ruefully. 'But there is one problem,' he ventures.

'You're already married?' Coombe asks.

Gidley King feels like he's been winded. How does this man know? How could he have possibly found out about Ann? He is utterly speechless. But then he sees Coombe's face, and watches as his prospective father-in-law doubles up in laughter. It's evidently a joke and John Coombe had no idea how close he was to the truth. Gidley King forces a weak smile.

'Very funny,' he says, as his host wipes the tears of laughter from his eyes with an oversized handkerchief. 'No, it isn't that. Of course it isn't that. It's . . . I have to go back to sea in eight days, back to

217

New South Wales. So if Anna Josepha, and you, agree, the wedding would have to happen quickly.'

Again, Coombe doesn't look in the least surprised. 'I'm sure that can all be arranged,' he says.

'May I see your daughter now?' Gidley King asks. There's still a chance that she might refuse him; his pride would be wounded, but his life would be much easier.

Alone at last with Anna Josepha in the drawing room, with her father having thoughtfully withdrawn, Gidley King faces his moment of truth. As he watches her sit down, the pale yellow silk of her gown scrooping with her movement, her face turned expectantly to him, he feels a rush of affection towards her. She is so young, so innocent, so fresh. Life with her could be a whole new beginning for him.

But then he still feels fondly towards Ann. Is it possible to be in love with two women at once? He wishes his father were still alive, so he could ask him. It might one day be a conversation with Captain Phillip, too, although the captain isn't known for his success with women. Ann is eleven years older than the woman now before him, and so much more worldly. He likes that about her in some ways but, in others, Anna Josepha's youth has a certain appeal; he knows he could mould her so much more completely.

'King, I didn't expect to see you today,' Anna Josepha is saying, and he snaps his attention back to her and the task at hand.

'Neither did I,' he replies. 'But I just heard from the Admiralty, and my ship is due to sail on the fifteenth of March.'

The Governor, His Wife and His Mistress

Her face falls, and he's heartened, somehow, that she is so obviously upset. Gidley King moves towards her, kneels at her feet and takes her hands in his. 'I am so sorry, but I have to do my duty,' he says.

'I understand,' she whispers. 'But it is so soon. I thought we'd at least have another month together . . . getting to know each other . . .'

'So did I. But sadly, it isn't to be.'

She hangs her head and he can see a tear glisten on her cheek.

This isn't going the way he imagined. He takes a deep breath. 'Anna Josepha, I wondered if you'd consider coming with me to New South Wales?'

She looks up sharply.

'As my wife, I mean. Would you do me the honour of marrying me?'

A beatific smile slowly spreads over her face. 'King!' she exclaims. '*Really?*'

He's taken aback and utterly charmed by the innocence of her response. But at the same time, he can't help a splinter of misgiving. How on earth will this all end?

30

BETTER THE DEVIL YOU KNOW

Anna Josepha King
15 MARCH 1791, PORTSMOUTH, ENGLAND

As the forty-four-gun man-of-war *Gorgon* sets sail from Portsmouth, bound for New South Wales, Anna Josepha King feels both excited and fearful. A week ago, her life was quiet and humdrum, moving to a steady rhythm of books, afternoon teas and walks in the country. Today, it's been turned completely upside down.

Just four days ago, she married a man she barely knows in an intimate ceremony at London's grand neoclassical church St Martin-in-the-Fields by the King's Mews, and now she's setting off with him on the adventure of a lifetime. Neither event was in her plans. If she was ever to marry, she imagined she'd be doing it in a church in her local parish, surrounded by family and friends. Instead, she ended up in the church that serves the Royal Navy, with a service so

The Governor, His Wife and His Mistress

hastily arranged, she was able to let very few of her circle, beyond her immediate family, know in enough time that they could attend.

At least, however, she didn't have to worry about the bridal dress. Her new husband's mother, Utricia, had bequeathed the stunning gown she wore for her own wedding, in a gorgeous pearl-studded sheath of ivory satin supplied by her late husband's drapery business. The first time Anna Josepha tried it on, she gasped to see herself in the mirror. And when her father walked her down the church aisle as she clasped her bouquet of pink and white roses, peonies and sweet peas, and Philip Gidley King turned to greet her, she could see the admiration in his eyes, too.

It was, in the end, a beautiful day, despite the rushed preparations and her last-minute nerves. At one stage, she'd told her mother that maybe they should call it off; she wasn't ready. Her mother wouldn't have a bar of it.

'Don't be silly, dear,' she'd admonished her. 'Philip will be the best match you could ever hope to make.'

'But we hardly know each other,' Anna Josepha protested. 'We've probably spent ten hours in each other's company, at most. How can I make a lifetime commitment with so little knowledge of him?'

'Nonsense!' her mother snorted. 'We've known Philip all his life. We know everything about him, and better the devil you know than the devil you don't. What sounder way to get to know him, anyway, than during a long voyage to the other side of the world?'

'That's what I'm worried about. We might discover we hate each other. Maybe we could meet again when he returns to England, and then we could get to know each other more.'

'And do you really think he'd wait for you?' Theodosia replied scornfully. 'When he's such a fine young man nearing his prime, and has the choice of so many eligible women?' She stopped and put an arm around her daughter. 'Look, it's natural to be nervous, of course it is. But this is such a great opportunity for you, you must seize it with both hands.'

The couple spent their wedding night in a London hotel, where Anna Josepha was ragged with nerves. Perhaps she shouldn't have worried so much though, she thought later. Her new husband turned out to be a thoughtful and gentle lover. She assumed, as a sailor, he must have lain with many women before to be so expert.

But now the day of their voyage has finally arrived and she and Gidley King stand on the open deck of the *Gorgon* watching as the fortifications of Portsmouth and the four turrets of Southsea Castle disappear into the chill March mist as they approach the open sea. She shivers.

'Are you cold?' Gidley King instantly asks her. 'Shall we go down below?'

'No, I'm fine,' she replies. 'Just a little anxious about the voyage.'

'That's perfectly natural,' he reassures her. 'You'll soon get used to the movement of the sea. It can be very soothing.'

That afternoon, they meet their fellow travellers. Captain John Parker is in command of the ship, and has brought along his wife, Mary Ann, while there's also a botanist, a surveyor and a chaplain on board, as well as the seventeen-year-old son of a friend of Governor Phillip's, William Chapman. He'd begged to be allowed to accompany Phillip on the First Fleet, but his mother had insisted he was too young. Finally, he's managed to join the Third Fleet.

Also on board are members of the British Army regiment of the New South Wales Corps, set to join the first contingent sent over with the Second Fleet to relieve the First Fleet's Marine Corps, together with its Scottish captain William Paterson and his wife, Elizabeth. Together with thirty convicts that makes it a total of two hundred and eighty passengers and crew. The ship is also carrying six months' worth of provisions for nine hundred people in New South Wales, and livestock, and has been ordered to collect the salvaged stores from the wreck of the *Guardian* at the Cape.

Anna Josepha takes an immediate liking to Mary Ann, who also loves to make notes in her journal, and she can see Gidley King is smiling broadly to see the tightly packed containers of provisions below deck. She imagines the locals at Port Jackson will welcome him warmly when they see everything he's managed to bring them. She only hopes her welcome will be half as warm.

The ship follows the usual route, and arrives in Tenerife on 15 April. The little group, together with some of the officers and their ladies, are invited to dine at the home of the governor. They force their way through the unfamiliar oil-laden Easter week dishes and assume dinner has finished, when a huge roast turkey is served. Everyone groans. If only they'd known at the start!

Anna Josepha feverishly writes notes in her journal every day, describing the sounds, sights and smells of the ports they visit, and the people, their clothes and their customs. Sometimes Gidley King escorts her around the city of Santa Cruz, pointing out some of the buildings he'd looked at on his first visit, like the homes for the poor, orphans and unmarried women. Then, at the end of each visit, over a port or two for Gidley King—it helps with the recurring stiffness in his joints, he tells her—the pair discuss the events of the day and write together in their separate journals, comparing notes. As this is all so new to his wife, Gidley King praises her on how much she notices saying it's often far more than he does.

They're regularly accompanied on these excursions by young Chapman, who seems to have attached himself to the lieutenant governor and his wife. He's good company, funny and enthusiastic about everything, and the Kings enjoy being with him. Gidley King also spends a lot of time with Captain Paterson, who's keen to collect botanical and insect specimens for Banks, and Anna Josepha with Elizabeth.

'The new corps are going to be vitally important to the future of New South Wales,' Gidley King tells his new bride one evening. 'Captain Paterson tells me that he is to order the marine corps back to England on the *Gorgon*'s return trip, which will mean the departure of a man I personally have no time for, a Major Ross. He took over Norfolk Island when I left, but Governor Phillip is known to dislike him, and he's an excellent judge of character.'

'I like the captain's wife, too,' Anna Josepha says. 'Hopefully, we shall see plenty of them in the new colony. It's nice to be arriving knowing I've made at least one friend.'

The couple also often join the others to walk around the city, eat and explore further afield by donkey, although Mary Ann's mount bolts at one point and leaves her rolling down a hill. Happily, she is unhurt and finds it hilarious.

The Governor, His Wife and His Mistress

After ten days, it's time to be back at sea, and the ship departs for the next stage of the voyage towards the Cape of Good Hope. Some of the seamen catch sharks to eat their tails, while everyone watches porpoises rolling in the waves and dolphins leaping over them—enjoying discussing the differences between the two species. Great flocks of seabirds and flying fish are spotted, until the fleet is hit by squalls of wind and rain that have them battening down the shutters to prevent the ingress of water and eking out their days in the half-light.

By 19 June, the ship docks at the Cape of Good Hope and there's more dining and excursions and official engagements, while Captain Parker oversees the unloading of provisions from the wrecked *Guardian* onto the *Gorgon*. Some of the salvaged stores have been sold by the ship's captain to set up a fund to help support other captains, which Gidley King decides on his own initiative to utilise. He takes a slice of the special fund to buy some cattle and sheep at the Cape, always available for a good price, to take back with him to the colony. He also crosses paths with an officer who'd earlier sailed with Captain Cook, Captain George Vancouver, who has a storeship on its way to Port Jackson to deliver more livestock. He may be stopping at New Zealand and Gidley King reminds him of a request from King George III that he might procure 'two natives of New Zealand' during his visit to bring them to Norfolk Island to instruct the settlers on how to prepare flax.

When he boards that evening, happy to have conducted good business, Anna Josepha seems restless and he asks her if she's all right. 'I think so,' she says. 'But I have news.'

'Yes?' he asks, having no idea to what she's alluding.

She takes a deep breath. 'How would you like to be a father?'

For a moment, he's confused. He *is* a father. But then he remembers who he's with. 'What do you mean, my darling?'

'King, we're going to be parents!' she announces, laughing.

He blinks. 'When?' he asks.

'I think around November or December.'

'But that means . . .'

'Yes, probably that first time,' she replies, shyly. 'Or maybe the second or third.'

He comes to his senses quickly and pulls her close, kissing the top of her head. 'That's wonderful! I am thrilled.'

He's been searching for the right time to tell her about Ann, Norfolk and Sydney all the way through the voyage, but realises that now he may have missed his chance. He curses himself for his stupidity. He knows he'll have to tell her soon, but not now. They should both be free to treasure this new development in their relationship for a while yet.

They set sail again but run into trouble almost immediately. In a bad storm, a man falls overboard, and the cutter sent out to rescue him can't find him. Then one of the rescuers falls into the heaving sea and vanishes. The mood on board verges on melancholy.

Close to the end of the voyage, as the coastline of New South Wales is coming into view, there's another tragic fatality, a midshipman who'd fallen ill shortly after leaving the Cape, followed quickly by the death of another seaman.

The Governor, His Wife and His Mistress

'King, I can't wait for this voyage to be over,' Anna Josepha tells her husband that night. 'So much death, so much suffering. It has been fine for us, but for so many others . . .'

'Hush,' Gidley King says soothingly, rubbing her back. 'We'll be arriving in Sydney Cove soon. There's not much further to go. And then you'll be much more comfortable in your condition.'

His wife cries herself to sleep that night, with Gidley King tossing and turning through the hours of darkness, wondering how on earth he's going to break his terrible news to her now.

They expect to drop anchor at Port Jackson the next morning, but a storm blows up and lasts for three interminable days with off-shore westerlies blowing hard and preventing them from sailing into the harbour. Everyone's so eager to get to shore and deliver all this much-needed food, but there's nothing that can be done except to wait until the tempest blows itself out and the wind changes direction. It appears to be growing stronger with every minute that passes, however, with rain sheeting down and lightning striking the main mast, shattering the top into a thousand pieces. Then bolts of lightning strike all around, giving everyone on the quarterdeck a sharp electric shock and knocking down nearly every man standing. The sea foams up and leaves the ship shuddering in its wake.

Eventually, the wind swings around to the east and the sea settles down once more, and on 21 September, the *Gorgon* is finally able to pass through the heads of Port Jackson. Sydney Cove is at the far end of the harbour, and Anna Josepha stands with Gidley King on the deck, watching the welcome sight before her. It's spring and the hills are a rich verdant green, the sea a brilliant glittering blue, and suddenly, there's not a cloud in the sky.

'There it is!' says Gidley King, pointing out the little settlement coming towards them, with a crowd of people quickly gathering along the shoreline. 'They will give us a hero's welcome!'

As the ship drops anchor and the couple climb down into the ship's longboat and are rowed to the makeshift jetty, they can hear the clamour from the crowd. Gidley King smiles to hear the excitement in people's voices. 'Welcome to New South Wales, my dear,' he says to his wife, offering her his arm, and bending down to kiss her. 'And to our child,' he adds as he places a hand on her belly.

The very next moment, a woman forces her way through the crowd to stand directly in front of them, blocking their way. Anna Josepha smiles at her, but Gidley King just stares.

'Welcome to Sydney,' the woman says, thrusting a wriggling infant into his arms. 'Meet your new son.'

31

LOST FOR WORDS

Philip Gidley King
21 SEPTEMBER 1791, SYDNEY COVE, NEW SOUTH WALES

Horror-struck, Gidley King looks from one woman to the other, and then back again, completely lost for words. This is his absolute worst nightmare. It's been haunting him ever since he proposed to Anna Josepha six months before, and now it's become his shocking, ghastly and utterly unthinkable reality.

Time slows to a crawl. He can see the confusion on his wife's face and the fury on Ann's. He remembers again what pretty blue eyes his mistress has when she's happy, but the light seems to have gone out of them now to be replaced by a sharp, flinty grey. Anna Josepha's features, however, look as if they're softening, as understanding slowly seeps in and her face crumples.

'Oh, God help me,' he silently prays. 'I know I've done wrong, But please, *please*, help me.' He wants to be struck down by a thunderbolt, swallowed up by a tidal wave, or swept away by the crowd pressing in on all sides. But nothing happens, and instead he stands there stupidly, rooted to the spot and opening and closing his mouth, as if gasping for both air and inspiration. He feels the weight in his arms and looks down at the squirming child he's been passed. His new son looks up at him, curiously. Gidley King gasps. This should have been such a happy occasion, the first meeting between father and son. But now it's one of the most shameful, humiliating episodes of his life.

Anna Josepha is the first to come to her senses. 'Let's get out of this crush so we can talk,' she says suddenly. Ann nods, snatches the infant back out of Gidley King's arms, and starts to push her way through the crowd. Anna Josepha takes her husband's arm and propels him in the same direction. It's only then that he notices the little boy trailing after Ann, his hand in hers, with a mop of dark hair and big blue eyes staring at him.

The little group finally emerge from the crush and stand in the bright sunlight, looking at each other. Gidley King knows this is his mess, and realises he has to be the one to clear it up. He takes a deep breath. Where to start? At that moment, Sydney starts to scream, giving Ann the opportunity to jiggle him in her arms and coo soothingly to him.

'How old is he now?' Anna Josepha asks Ann softly.

Ann looks up. 'Fourteen months,' she replies.

'He looks quite a handful.'

'Sydney is that all right. He's got to the age he doesn't like to be carried anymore.' Ann puts him down on the gravel path and props him up on his feet.

The Governor, His Wife and His Mistress

'Sydney?' Anna Josepha repeats. 'That's a nice name. And pray, who have we here?' She touches the shoulder of the little boy shyly clutching at his mother's skirt.

'This is Norfolk, he's two and a half.'

The boy scowls. 'No, Mama, two and *three-quarters*!' he insists firmly. 'Nearly three!'

Both women laugh. Anna Josepha reaches out to shake his hand. 'Well, hello, two-and-three-quarters-year-old Master Norfolk. My, what a handsome, grown-up boy you are!'

Norfolk grins and reaches for her hand, which he shakes gravely.

Gidley King is mesmerised by the scene. Do the two women actually understand who each other is? How can they be so friendly with each other? He should say something, take control, but he can't think of anything he could do or say to make this terrible situation any more bearable.

Anna Josepha glances at her husband, and then looks back at Ann. 'I'm so sorry, how rude of me.' She smiles. 'I should introduce myself. My name is Anna Josepha.'

To Gidley King's surprise, Ann smiles back. It seems she can't resist his wife's beautiful manners. 'And I am Ann,' she says. 'Ann Inett. I would say I'm pleased to meet you, but my manners, I'm afraid, don't stretch that far.'

'Of course,' Anna Josepha replies. 'I could hardly be less surprised about that—or more surprised to be meeting you and your children.' She looks pointedly at Gidley King. 'King told me nothing of this. I assume both are his?'

Ann nods. 'So,' she then says, in a voice that sounds as if she's trying to keep it as even as she can, but can't help a small quiver in the middle, 'in turn, I must ask, are you and Gidley . . . are you two . . . married?' She too trains her eyes on Gidley King.

He looks away from them both, towards Government House luminous in the bright sunlight fifty or so yards away. If only he and Anna Josepha had been able to make it there safely, he could have broken the news to her inside and, together, they could have devised a plan. Governor Phillip might even have been able to help. But now it's too late. The unimaginable has happened and it feels as if the situation's only getting worse by the minute.

Again, his wife takes up the slack. 'I am so sorry, Ann, but we are,' she says. 'I can only assume by your demeanour that this is going to be bad news to you. We were married shortly before we started this voyage. We had only known each other for two months.'

'*Two months?*' Ann sounds incredulous. 'Well, he has known me for three and a half years now, and you can see the evidence of our relationship in our two sons. When he left here, he implored me to wait for his return and promised me we'd then discuss marriage. I didn't imagine that would mean I'd end up discussing his marriage to someone else.'

She looks very close to tears, and Gidley King's heart goes out to her. What a rat he was. At the same time, he can't help admiring how well Anna Josepha is handling this. He steals a sideways glance at her. Unfortunately, she also seems to be struggling to keep her composure.

'I'm very sorry, Ann,' she says. 'If I'd have known—'

'And when is your little one due?' Ann breaks in.

Anna Josepha looks down. 'I have about two months to go,' she whispers, and Gidley King sees a tear drip onto the dusty ground by her feet.

The Governor, His Wife and His Mistress

Later that day, in the safe haven of Government House, Gidley King introduces his new bride to the governor.

Phillip gives her a little bow and regards her approvingly. 'So it wasn't all business and no play over in England,' he says, slapping his old friend on the back. 'You must have been pretty busy.'

Gidley King can see Anna Josepha forcing a weak smile at the joke.

'I met Anna Josepha through family connections,' he says. 'She is my cousin, the daughter of my mother's sister. We knew each other as children, but it had been many years since we'd seen each other.'

'And you look as if you make a fine pair,' Phillip says. He turns to the young woman. 'How was the voyage over?' he enquires kindly.

'It was very comfortable, thank you, Your Excellency,' she replies. 'We had pleasant stops at a number of ports along the way, which broke up the voyage. We also made friends with some other passengers on the ship who I understand will also be going to Norfolk Island with us. The Patersons and William Chapman.'

'Ah yes, the young fellow,' Phillip says. 'He's eager for experience, and that will certainly be an experience! And Elizabeth Paterson will be good company for you, my dear, while her husband serves as the Commander of the New South Wales Corps on Norfolk Island. Now, we have put aside a small house for your use in Port Jackson while you're here, before you sail again. Can I have someone show you to it, while I steal your husband to bring him up to date with developments in the colony?'

'Of course.'

'And I will see you tomorrow for our dinner party?'
'Thank you, I would love that.'

As soon as the two men are alone together, Phillip pours him a port, and congratulates him on his promotion to lieutenant governor. The men click tumblers. He then asks him about everyone he saw in London and what they said about New South Wales. 'Obviously, you acquitted yourself well, judging by the amount of provisions you brought with you on the ship,' Phillip tells him. 'The government has finally been a little more generous with us.'

Gidley King informs him about the *Guardian*'s fateful voyage and how they salvaged more supplies from its wreckage on the way past the Cape. Over a second glass of port, he brings up the subject of the extra livestock he'd bought there with the special fund. Unfortunately, all the bulls and three-quarters of the rams had died on the final leg of the voyage to New South Wales.

Phillip frowns. 'We're very glad to have extra livestock, but did you have permission from the navy to do that? You know how difficult they can be, like the official rebuke you received over the *Renown* affair.'

Gidley King swallows. 'I thought we needed supplies so badly.'

'And so we do,' Phillip says. 'But the navy works on rules, and you don't want to get a reputation as someone who's ready to flout them.'

Gidley King quickly changes the subject. He says he saw Banks while in England, who wanted to pass on his good wishes to Phillip, and the artist Blake who seemed terribly interested in his sketches. The governor is pleased to hear of both; the more attention New

The Governor, His Wife and His Mistress

South Wales can garner back home, the better it will be for them all. Gidley King also informs him that the rest of the Third Fleet, when they arrive, will hopefully bring more skilled settlers and even more supplies.

'Yours is the sixth ship that's arrived out of the eleven coming,' Phillip says. 'That also means so many more mouths to feed, so we'll need Norfolk Island to continue supplying us with as much food as you can manage. The news from the first ship to arrive, the *Mary Ann*, was that one thousand, eight hundred and eighty-nine male convicts had boarded in Portsmouth, and one hundred and seventy-eight females. Who knows what the final number of the living will be? But, so far, it doesn't seem that the death rate is anywhere near as high as it was with the Second Fleet.'

'That's good news,' Gidley King says. 'And how are things on Norfolk Island?'

Phillip's face clouds. 'From what I've heard, Major Ross isn't making himself very popular. But you'll be the better judge when you get over there. And with the New South Wales Corps relieving the marines, Ross will be back on his way to England soon, so he won't be a problem for either of us.'

Gidley King smiles. Obviously, Ross hasn't done anything to endear himself any more to the governor.

'And King, you dark horse, tell me about your new wife.'

'Not much to say,' Gidley King says quietly. 'She's a very nice young woman, and I think she'll adapt well to life over here.'

'I don't doubt that,' Phillip says. 'But what of your other woman, the convict? Don't you have a couple of children with her?'

'Yes,' says the younger man. 'We're trying to sort that out.'

'Good luck with that! I found I had enough trouble with one wife, but with two . . .'

By the time Gidley King arrives back at the officer's house they've been given, Anna Josepha is already asleep. He's relieved. He pours himself another port and realises he's so tired he can't face whatever she might have to say to him just yet. At least in the morning things might look better, and he might not feel like a condemned man preparing for his execution. Somehow, he doubts it, but he can live in hope.

He doesn't sleep well, however. All night he sees the faces of the two women he loves, both scored with the anger, misery and disappointment he has caused them. He curses himself for not summoning the courage to tell Anna Josepha during the voyage about his predicament in New South Wales. He feels sure he could have made her understand, and then roped her into helping smooth over the situation with Ann.

He thinks too of his two boys, the little lad looking at him, no doubt wondering who he was, having been so small when he left, and then the toddler regarding him curiously. He feels a lump in his throat contemplating them. Such good-looking, well-mannered little boys. They were a credit to Ann. And how had he repaid her? He could hardly bear to consider it.

32

THE RECKONING

Anna Josepha King
22 SEPTEMBER 1791, SYDNEY COVE, NEW SOUTH WALES

Anna Josepha barely slept a wink. She spent the evening writing in her journal, trying to sort out her feelings about everything that had happened. Writing things down always made her feel calmer and more in control. But this time, the more she wrote about this bizarre situation, the more she felt everything was spiralling further and further beyond her grasp. After half an hour, she threw down her pen in despair, curled into a ball on the bed and gave in to the racking sobs that had been threatening to come to the surface from the moment they set foot in this damned place. Her world could never be the same again.

When her husband came in, she pretended to be asleep. From the smell of him, he'd been drinking heavily, too. She was dumbfounded. Why would King think that might be a good thing to do now?

By the time the sun rises and the morning starts to heat up, she slips quietly out of bed so as not to disturb him. She feels no better. Yesterday, she'd been the happy new wife of a man who seemed kind and smart and loving, with both of them on the verge of a thrilling new adventure together. Today, she feels empty, deceived and betrayed. She doesn't even know who he is anymore.

She can hear her husband getting washed and dressed, so she sits at the table and steels herself to face him. When he walks into the kitchen she can see he's bleary-eyed from the previous night's port. Normally, she'd make allowances for that. He's a man with a lot of responsibility and under a lot of pressure. But not today.

'Good morning, my love,' he opens, and she can see the uncertainty in his eyes. 'How did you sleep? Well, I hope.'

'No, I didn't,' Anna Josepha replies, curtly.

'No, me neither.' King slumps into a chair opposite her.

For a moment, at the look of complete despair on his face, her heart begins to melt a little. But then she reminds herself of what he has done, and her heart hardens once more.

'Anna Josepha,' he begins, 'I am so, so, so sorry. I meant to tell you, and have been trying to work out how to tell you from that very first time we met again at my mother's house.'

'So why didn't you?' she asks, icily.

His shoulders slump. 'I just couldn't find the words. I didn't know what to say. And I liked you so much, then I fell in love with you and I guess I was scared.'

'Of what?'

The Governor, His Wife and His Mistress

'Of losing you.' He reaches over the table and puts his hand over hers. She pulls her hand away as if his very touch revolts her. He brings his hand back to his side and looks forlornly down at his palm. 'So have I?' he asks.

'Have you what?' she asks.

'Have I lost you?'

She sighs deeply. 'I don't know yet. But you have to be honest with me, King. I think I deserve that. Tell me about Ann. Tell me about your children. Tell me why you've brought me here.'

Gidley King breathes heavily and she can see a tiny vein throbbing in his temple. 'I never intended any of this to happen,' he starts. 'When I came here with the First Fleet, Ann was one of the female convicts on one of the transports. I was told I should choose a few of the women to accompany me to Norfolk Island and the assistant surgeon selected some of the best behaved. Ann was one of them. I asked her to be my housekeeper and . . . one thing led to another.'

'So you were sleeping with her?' Anna Josepha asks. She bites her lip. Obviously, he was. That was a stupid question.

He doesn't seem to notice. 'I was lonely, it was a hard job, I had no idea how long I'd be there for. She was lonely, too.'

'And were you thinking of marrying her?'

'No, I wasn't.'

'Why not? She had your children, didn't she?'

'It's complicated.' He sighs. 'Over here, so far from home, everything is very different. Men and women get together, they have children, and few of them ever marry. They're thrown together by circumstance, and they try to make the best of it. If Ann and I were back in England, I'd wager neither of us would ever have even considered the possibility of being together.'

'So is that your excuse?'

'I think it's my reason,' he says. 'I'm being absolutely honest with you.'

'And do you love Ann?'

He looks straight into her eyes. 'No, I don't,' he says. 'I love you.'

'But you must care for her?'

'Of course, I do. She's the mother of my children. But it's a completely different kind of love that I feel for you. I fell in love with you, and it was you I asked to marry me, and you I married. Anna Josepha, you are everything I've ever wanted in a woman.'

'But were you ever going to tell me about Ann?'

'I thought every day about confiding in you. But every time I tried, I got scared, and then I put it off.'

It's Anna Josepha's turn to sigh. 'So what are you going to do now?' she asks.

He looks down at his hands again. 'To be truthful, my love, that depends very much on you.'

She cocks her head to one side. 'What do you mean?'

'Well, I realise I've broken your trust in me. You might not want to continue with me on this side of the world. I could not blame you if you did not.' He puts his head in his hands and his voice is muffled. 'I want to tell you how sorry I am to have put you through this. You do not deserve it. And I do not deserve you.'

Anna Josepha sits at the table in silence for a long time. At one point, Gidley King even looks up, presumably to check she is still

The Governor, His Wife and His Mistress

there. When he sees she has not moved, he looks back down again at the table. It seems he is waiting for an answer from her, for some kind of sign.

She doesn't know what to do. Yes, she was stunned to realise that he had hidden this other life from her, and had not had the courage to tell her earlier. But he seems to be genuinely repentant. She could see how these relationships might develop so far from home. Men were not meant to live alone. They were not good at it. Still, she feels hurt that she hadn't been told the truth right from the very beginning. But if she had, would she be here today? Would her mother and father have permitted it?

When she examines her situation closely, she knows she loves King, and feels sure he loves her, too. They have a child on the way as well. Could she really throw all of that away just because of a dalliance of convenience before she came onto the scene?

She coughs, and her husband looks up again. 'I can't pretend this hasn't shocked me and pained me terribly,' she says.

He nods, anguish plain on his face.

'But if you solemnly promise never to lie to me again—'

'But I never actually lied to you about this, my darling,' he protests.

She silences him with a withering look. 'You lied by omission,' she says sharply.

'You're right,' he admits.

'So if you promise never to lie again to me, then we shall find a way through this mess. I don't know how, but we will.'

He looks so pathetically grateful that she holds out her hands and he grasps them so firmly it feels as though he'll never let them go.

That afternoon, Gidley King and Anna Josepha return to Government House for the dinner party Phillip is holding to welcome them, the Patersons and the Parkers to the colony, and to celebrate the end of the famine with all the extra supplies that have arrived on the *Gorgon*.

The governor also invites Elizabeth Macarthur, the wife of a lieutenant of the New South Wales Corps, John Macarthur, who came over in the Second Fleet. Phillip has argued with him over his purloining of a cask of spirits and, as a result, he is no longer welcome at Government House, but the governor confides he has a lot of time for the cultured Elizabeth.

The group have a relaxed evening, dining on kangaroo—Anna Josepha finds she doesn't mind the taste—and swapping stories of their voyages. She's charmed by the warmth and friendliness of Mrs Macarthur and vows to seek out her company later.

Towards the end of the meal, the governor makes a toast of welcome.

As he takes his seat, Anna Josepha speaks up. 'Your Excellency, I would like to ask you something.'

'Yes, my dear, anything!'

'King and I would be honoured if you would agree to be the godfather of our new child when he or she arrives,' she says. 'And if you agree, and it is a boy, we would love to ask your permission to name him Phillip.'

When the couple return to their house, they sit down again at the table to discuss what they should do. They'll be sailing off to Norfolk Island in four or so weeks, so they don't have long to come up with a plan.

Gidley King is ready to suggest one first. 'Darling, I don't know how you might feel about this,' he starts, cautiously. 'But I think Norfolk and Sydney would have a much better start in life if they were brought up by us. We can give them the kind of opportunities Ann could never hope to.'

Anna Josepha ponders his words. She can see the sense of them, but how would she feel bringing up another woman's children? The birth of her own first child isn't far off, and she hopes to have plenty more. She was one of only three—after the death of her parents' first-born—and she'd always wanted a house full of children, listening to music, reading books, going out walking together, supporting each other. Would two more children make that much of a difference?

She clasps her hands together as if in prayer and rests her chin on them. 'You're right, King,' she says finally. 'We're in a far better position to provide for them. I will be happy to bring them up as my own. But what do you think Ann would say to that?'

Her husband grimaces. It's clear he knows exactly what she'll say.

33

DO YOU LOVE HER?

Ann Inett

23 SEPTEMBER 1791, SYDNEY COVE, NEW SOUTH WALES

The minute Ann hears someone knocking on her door, she knows instantly who it is. She's been waiting for two days now. And she recognises Gidley King's footfall, the way he raps impatiently on every door he's ever wanted to pass through, and how he calls out if admission isn't instant.

'Ann!' comes the voice. 'It's Gidley! Please let me in. I need to see you.'

She trudges to the door and opens it. She sees from his reaction that he's shocked by her appearance. Ann knows her eyes are puffy from lack of sleep, and red-rimmed from all her tears. But he doesn't look much better. In the two days he's been back in Sydney Cove, he looks as if he's aged ten years.

'Come in,' she says dully. 'The children have been waiting for you.'

The Governor, His Wife and His Mistress

He looks past her to Norfolk who's now rushing to the door to meet him, and Sydney, who's gurgling as he wobbles over, imitating his brother.

'Papa!' Norfolk shouts as he reaches his father and grabs on to his leg—just like he did at the harbour when Gidley King was leaving for England seventeen months before. Sydney makes a noise that sounds vaguely similar—after all, it's not a word he's ever attempted before—and clamps on to his other leg. Ann can see, not without some satisfaction, that Gidley King's eyes have filled with tears. She's coached the boys well.

He drops the package he's been holding, kneels down with his sons and gently removes their little fingers from his legs. 'Why hello, Norfolk!' he says first, gathering the boy in his arms. 'Do you remember me?' He looks into his son's face. 'You were only very small when I left.'

Norfolk's face is blank and Ann can see it's upsetting his father that he doesn't recognise him. 'He was only fifteen months old when you left,' she says. 'I talked about you every day but, for a child, it's never the same as seeing someone.'

'Of course,' Gidley King murmurs. 'Of course.' He then turns to Sydney and sweeps him into his arms. 'And hello to you, too!' he says. 'You're a fine fellow as well. How old are you now?'

'He's a year and two months,' Ann says.

'And how have you all been?' Gidley King asks, turning to face Ann, still with both boys squirming in his arms. 'Have you been managing all right?'

She tosses up whether to preserve the last vestiges of her pride, or to be brutally honest. She decides the latter. 'No, not really,' she answers. 'It's been pretty tough out here. There hasn't been enough food, and I hated seeing the children go without. They're too young to understand.'

He nods. 'Hopefully that should be much better with all the provisions the government has now sent over,' he says. 'And look,' he reaches for the package he's put on the floor, 'I've brought the children a gift. Boys! Do you want to see what it is?'

He pulls off the paper to reveal a small, brightly painted wheeled-horse pull toy. The boys yelp with excitement. Norfolk grabs the string and pulls it around the room, with Sydney excitedly toddling in his footsteps.

Ann regards him coldly. 'That's our compensation, is it?' she asks. 'You're not coming home to be a father to your children, nor to finally marry the woman who bore them, but you are giving them a toy? And we're meant to be happy with that?'

She can see her words have hit their target from the way he looks immediately deflated. 'Gidley, honestly, what did you expect? You've treated us appallingly. I just can't believe you would do such a thing.'

'Ann, my dear—'

'Don't "my dear" me,' she snaps. 'I'm not your dear, or anyone else's.'

'I'm sorry,' Gidley King says. 'I'm only trying to make everything right.'

'And how on earth do you propose to do that? Are you thinking of abandoning your new wife, as you did me, and coming back to us?' She looks at the shock registering on his face. 'No, I didn't think so.'

The Governor, His Wife and His Mistress

'Ann, I'm so sorry,' he starts again. 'I didn't mean for this to happen.'

She can feel her temper rising. All that time she spent as his housekeeper and lover, she was always careful to be deferential to him, no matter his behaviour. But that time has passed. She may well have nothing more to lose. 'So it happened by accident, did it?' she snarls. 'You accidentally met a younger woman in England, accidentally married her, accidentally bedded her and are now, again accidentally, having a child with her?'

Gidley King colours. 'I'm so sorry, Ann,' he repeats.

'And, from the looks of it when you arrived, you hadn't even told her that we exist!' Ann continues. 'How could you sink so low, Gidley! How *dare* you!'

He hangs his head.

'Tell me what happened. I deserve to know that at least.'

He looks up at her. 'Do you really want . . . ?'

'I do.'

'My mother introduced us. Anna Josepha's my cousin and I knew her from my youth. My mother is getting older, and she was keen to see me wed.'

'But she didn't want you to marry me, the mother of her grand-children?' Ann interrupts him.

Gidley King again looks beaten.

'Oh, don't tell me,' Ann continues, realisation dawning, 'she didn't know about us!'

'That's right.' Gidley King speaks so quietly, she can barely hear him.

She shakes her head in wonder. 'Go on,' she urges him.

'Mother felt she was a fine woman, and marriage to her would be good for my position.'

'And what did you think?'

Gidley King raises his eyes to her. 'I agreed.'

'So marriage to Anna Josepha would look much better for your prospects than marriage to the poor convict woman who'd been keeping your bed warm, and looking after you, and making sure all your needs were satisfied, all those years before?'

He says nothing.

'I understand,' she says. 'And do you love her?'

'Very much,' he says.

'More than you ever loved me?'

Gidley King looks trapped. 'I loved you, honestly I did,' he says. 'And I still care for you, of course. But she is my wife, and I have made a pledge to her.'

Ann feels all the fight drain out of her. So he loves this new woman, and only 'cares' for her. A wave of sadness sweeps over her, leaving her struggling to breathe. She'd hoped that when he saw her again, reunited with Norfolk, and met Sydney, that he'd have second thoughts about this marriage of his. That he'd come back to her. But it seems that he is lost to her.

She puts her head in her arms and can't help sobbing as if her heart is broken which, she realises, it is. Norfolk, hearing his mama so upset, runs over to her and puts his head in her lap to try to comfort her.

Gidley King sits motionless and she remembers how hard he finds it—like many men—when women are emotional in front of him.

The Governor, His Wife and His Mistress

After a minute of listening to Ann weeping, however, he stands up and comes over to her, putting his arm around her shoulders. She flinches, but he only holds her more firmly. Ann's shocked and turns her face up and, without even thinking about it, lifts her lips to his. Gidley King responds and the pair kiss; a long, loving kiss that seems to dissolve time and all the hurt and the waiting.

Then he suddenly jumps back as if he'd touched hot coals. 'No, Ann, no,' he says. 'That wasn't meant to happen. I'm sorry.'

Ann is encouraged, however, by the warmth of his lips and wonders if all is not lost. She dries her eyes with a handkerchief tucked into the pocket of her apron. 'But if you still care for me . . . maybe . . .'

Gidley King looks sad. 'No, that can't be,' he says firmly. 'That was a mistake. Forgive me. For that and everything else.'

Ann makes an effort to regain her composure. Norfolk's head is still in her lap, and Sydney is playing on his own with the toy horse in the corner.

'So what do we do now?' she asks him. 'You're presumably going back to Norfolk Island soon?'

'There's a ship leaving Port Jackson in a little over four weeks on the twenty-fourth of October,' he says, obviously relieved that the conversation has taken a more businesslike bent. 'I'm now the lieutenant governor of the island. I received a promotion.'

'I heard,' she says. 'I suppose congratulations are in order. But it's a shame you're not staying longer so you can get to know your children a little.'

'That's another reason I wanted to talk to you today,' Gidley King says. 'We—that's Anna Josepha and I—believe that we can offer the children so many more opportunities than you could, in your position. How would you feel at the prospect of them coming to live with us? And, of course, that would leave you much freer to have your own life. Men could be wary of taking on a woman with two children by another man.'

Ann stares at him in absolute shock. Her whole body is trembling. What on earth is he proposing? Does he honestly expect her to give up their two children when he knows full well how much it shattered her to be forced to give up Thomas and Constance when she was brought here? And he thinks a new man would make up for the loss of her sons?

'Get out!' she says. 'Get out now! And don't ever darken our door again.'

34

THE HARDEST DECISION

Anna Josepha King

24 SEPTEMBER 1791, SYDNEY COVE, NEW SOUTH WALES

From Gidley King's demeanour when he returned from Ann's house the previous evening, Anna Josepha knows the conversation couldn't have gone as well as he'd hoped. She can't say she's surprised. What woman would willingly give up her children to another, especially after the shock she's just had?

When she met Ann on their arrival, she'd judged her to be a reasonable woman. Of course, being jilted for another would test the temperament of even the most saintly, but add into the torrid mix two children and another pregnancy . . . Yes, Anna Josepha can envisage the torment that Ann must be going through.

If only King had confided in her before, they could have devised a strategy together to have minimalised Ann's heartache and brought about the best outcome for everyone. But that bird had flown, and now they had to do the best they could to salvage something from the mess left behind.

'I don't think there's any way she'll agree to us bringing up the children,' Gidley King tells her the next morning. 'She had two children before, in England, but she had to leave them behind when she was transported here. That was absolutely terrible for her, and she's never recovered from it.'

'So it's natural she'll cling on to the children she's had here, with you,' Anna Josepha says thoughtfully. 'She wouldn't want to lose Norfolk and Sydney on top of the first two.'

The pair sit in silence, both thinking over the dilemma. Anna Josepha cracks first. 'King, would you mind if I tried to talk to her myself, woman to woman? It might not do much good, but I should try.'

'I'd love you to!' he says, his relief obvious. 'Are you sure you wouldn't mind? This is asking a lot of you, I know, and especially after—'

'It's fine,' she cuts in before he can bring up again the pain of the past few days. 'I will talk to her. I can't promise it will help, but I shall do my best.'

From the expression on his face, she knows she has said the best thing she possibly could. She wonders where she's getting all this strength from, then she looks down at her belly—probably from her unborn child. She has to do everything for him or her that she can to make King happy, to keep their family together and to preserve the peace with everyone on this side of the world.

The Governor, His Wife and His Mistress

Ann looks surprised to see Anna Josepha at her door, and invites her in. The two women are polite but formal. Ann offers her tea and Anna Josepha accepts as if she's been offered the keys to the kingdom of heaven.

'To what do I owe this pleasure?' asks Ann warily when the two women are sitting down, and the children are drawing in the corner.

'I know we didn't get off to the best of starts,' Anna Josepha says, 'but I would like us to get on.'

'Why?' asks Ann bluntly.

'Well, like it or not, we are both important parts of King's life. And our children will always be important to him, too.'

'But probably your children more than mine,' Ann retorts.

Anna Josepha can hear a trace of bitterness in her voice. 'I disagree,' she says. 'Norfolk and Sydney are very important to him, and he would love to get to know them better.'

'Really?' asks Ann. 'So important that he never even told you about them?'

'We both know how much he regrets that now.'

'Does he?' Ann asks.

'I truly believe so,' Anna Josepha replies evenly. 'Since he's seen Norfolk again, and has now met Sydney, he talks of little else.'

The two women gaze at the two figures bent over their artworks, chattering away to each other. 'They are beautiful children,' Anna Josepha says. 'You must be very proud of them.'

'Oh, I am,' Ann replies, her eyes looking misty. 'We've survived some hard times in the colony but they're bright little boys, and so brave.'

'I don't doubt it. I hope my own child takes after them.'

They smile at each other. Then Ann takes the initiative. 'Did Gidley tell you what happened when he came round here yesterday?'

Anna Josepha nods. 'He told me he'd apologised to you and suggested that we bring up the children.'

'And anything else?'

'He said that was a notion that didn't appeal to you at all.'

Ann looks as if she's about to say something but then thinks better of it.

'He also told me you had two children back in England who you'd been forced to leave. That must have been terrible.'

Ann's face falls and she appears to be struggling to decide what to say. 'Thomas and Constance,' she says eventually. 'Thomas will be thirteen now, and Constance ten. They are being brought up by my parents, but they have refused to write to me to tell me how they are. I write to them as often as we can send letters, but I've heard nothing back.'

'Oh my dear!' Anna Josepha gasps. 'That would be awful. Why will they not write?'

'It's a long story. My parents and I disagreed about my choice of suitor. They wanted me to marry one man, but my heart was with another. I left home as a result.'

'What did you do then?'

'I lived with him. We had no money, so we put off the wedding for later. He went off to the American War to earn money but then ... then ...'

Anna Josepha clamps her hand over her mouth in fear of what Ann will say next. 'He was killed in action,' Ann finishes. 'He never came home to us. To me and to his children.'

The Governor, His Wife and His Mistress

'What a terrible tragedy! I don't think I could ever cope with something like that. How on earth did you manage?'

'It was very hard. But I had dressmaking skills and earned a modest living until one of my customers refused to pay for a dress I made for her. Without that money, one thing led to another and I was sent over here with the First Fleet.'

Anna Josepha feels tremendously moved by Ann's story, and shakes her head in despair. 'It is amazing to me that you have managed to keep going, despite so many setbacks. You are a very special person.'

'Thank you,' says Ann, visibly touched by the concern, and sympathy.

'I can completely understand why you told King he could not have these two children. But I wonder if I could possibly talk to you about that?'

Ann nods. It appears as if Anna Josepha has won her confidence.

'As you know, King is now the Lieutenant Governor of Norfolk Island and he has the confidence and support of Governor Phillip, the Admiralty back in Britain and the government there,' she says. 'So it would seem he has a very bright future. Our children, yours and mine, I am very confident, will have the best education money can buy, and will have a choice of profession and every advantage in pursuing that.'

She looks at Ann's face and can see she's taking it all in. 'I will be prepared, when the time comes, to be separated from our children, for the sake of their futures,' she continues. 'It will be very hard, I am sure of it, but when they are old enough, they will be sent to school in England, with the support of family over there to ensure that all goes well. If the boys opt to join the Royal Navy, like their father, he will do everything he can to advance their progress.'

'But what does that have to do with Norfolk and Sydney?'

Anna Josepha takes Ann's hands in her own and is pleased when Ann makes no move to take them away. 'We would love to give exactly the same opportunities to your sons,' she says. 'We would like to see them succeed in life, and would do everything in our power to warrant that. We want to educate them and, if they want to join the navy, to help them.'

'But that means taking them away from me!' Ann exclaims.

'Not forever,' Anna Josepha replies. 'We would take Norfolk with us to the island when we sail there soon, and start on his home education. Then, when he is ready, we would send him to England to school. It will be a wrench to see him go, but there's no other alternative. But in the meantime, he will live with us in Government House, he will have an extremely comfortable childhood, and I will treat him as my own.'

'*Your* own?'

'What I mean is that I would treat him no differently from my own children. He will grow up with his half-brothers and half-sisters as one big happy family. But Norfolk will always know you as his true mother, and I will write regularly to let you know how he is getting on, I will read to him any letters you write, and you will be free to visit him on the island whenever you'd like. King will see to that.'

'Has he agreed to this?' Ann asks, wide-eyed.

'He will,' Anna Josepha says firmly.

'But what of Sydney? He's too young to leave me just yet.'

'I agree, absolutely. He should stay with you here, and then come and join us later. We will do exactly the same for him as we will do for Norfolk, and any children of our own.'

Ann is thoughtful, and Anna Josepha squeezes her hands. 'I know this is a difficult decision,' she says, 'so take your time thinking about it.'

'I find it hard to even think of life without my boys,' Ann says. 'But I understand what you're saying and I thank you for it. I am aware that Gidley has the power to just take them from me.'

'That will not happen,' Anna Josepha breaks in. 'You have my word on that. This will be your decision and yours only. We will respect the choice you make.'

'Thank you,' Ann says looking into her eyes. 'I will give this much thought. I don't want to let them go, and they need their mother's love. But I do realise that you and Gidley could give them a much better future than I could ever offer them in such a far-flung colony. It makes sense, but I am not sure I have the courage to let them go.'

Exactly one month later, on 24 October, Gidley King and his wife, Anna Josepha, depart Port Jackson on board the *Atlantic* for their new life on Norfolk Island. They are accompanied by Captain William Paterson and his wife Elizabeth; William Chapman; senior assistant surgeon William Balmain, who'd been working in

Port Jackson since arriving with the First Fleet; chaplain Reverend Richard Johnson; and a small boy by the name of Norfolk. He waves goodbye to his weeping mother on shore, and his younger brother, until he can no longer see them.

DISCORD AND STRIFE

Philip Gidley King
2 NOVEMBER 1791, NORFOLK ISLAND

As Norfolk Island looms up in the distance, Gidley King feels his heart lift. He is excited to be back. Swinging round to the south side of the island, Sydney Bay looks much the same, with its cliffs and beach ringed by rocks leading up to dark green hills with pine trees climbing steeply behind. But he can spy a number of new buildings on the clearing to the front and it looks as though the plantations of wheat, corn and vegetables nearby are thriving.

'This is going to be your new home,' he says to Anna Josepha, who's standing next to him on the deck, staring out at the vista before them. 'I do hope you'll be happy here, my dear. It's a beautiful land with so much potential. It could be our own personal paradise.'

She smiles and looks down at Norfolk, holding her hand and watching intently as the ship pulls closer to the shore. Gidley King bends down so his eyes are level with his son's. 'Do you remember this, Norfolk? You were only young when we left here, but this is where you were born. You'll love it here, you'll see.'

For the first time, the ship has no trouble landing as the weather is uncharacteristically calm, and Gidley King has a huge grin on his face as he helps his wife and son out of the small longboat that rowed them from ship to shore. The party are greeted by Major Ross and are welcomed back to Government House. It's little how he remembers it, however. As he pulls a bottle of his prized port from a case to toast their safe arrival, he reflects that when he'd first come onto the island it had felt almost a palace after his long voyage on the First Fleet, his short stay at Port Jackson and then his nights of sleeping through storms in a makeshift tent. Now he can see how ramshackle it has become, particularly, he imagines, without Ann caring for it so diligently. It seems to have shrunk, too, but Norfolk was so much smaller when he'd been there before, and young William Chapman had been invited to live with them now as well. He drinks deeply from his glass.

Walking around the next morning, he's startled to find the atmosphere on the island much changed in the twenty months he's been away. Before, there'd been a tiny population, all pulling together—apart from that one incident of foiled plans for a mutiny—but now there's around one thousand people, comprising so many more convicts, new settlers and officials. Each group of people appear to be at each other's throats, with the soldiers and settlers vying for ascendancy and the convicts resenting the authority of both.

'It feels to me that the mood before of hard work, a willingness to muck in and the desire to do well has gone,' Gidley King confides to Anna Josepha. 'In its place is an air of fear, argumentativeness and aggression. I wonder if that's the result of Major Ross? It can't have helped that he introduced martial law and much harsher penalties for transgressions, as well as capital punishment! That wretched man has done much more damage than good.'

'Hush, King,' she tries to soothe him. 'The place is back under your control now and, hopefully, you'll be able to change it. You and Captain Paterson should be more than a match for the task.'

Gidley King is still so annoyed, however, he decides to inform Nepean at the Admiralty back in London. *I found discord and strife on every person's countenance and in every corner of the island,* he writes in his letter. *I am pestered with complaints, bitter revilings, back-biting, and almost everything to begin over again.*

In a bid to start afresh, on his first Sunday he has everyone turn out to hear the reading of his commission as the new lieutenant governor, followed by three cheers for King George III. Then there's a joyful mass wedding ceremony and christening conducted by Reverend Johnson. Looking out at everyone, particularly the eight hundred convicts, Gidley King vows to re-establish good relations between the citizens and confers a general pardon on convicts who've committed minor offences while there, gives twenty-seven of them permission to become free settlers, and grants everyone a day's holiday.

He also draws up a plan of reforms, including establishing a school and an orphanage—like the one he'd seen in Tenerife—as there are ninety-eight children on the island now. In addition, he orders that no husband or father can leave the island without first making sure his wife and children have enough to live on. Then he wants to see lots of roads and bridges built, and some of the dilapidated wooden houses replaced with stone. A new Government House also needs to be constructed—and nearly three times bigger than the original.

He'd like the island to have its own court system, too, rather than having to send lawbreakers, and then witnesses to their crimes, to Port Jackson, especially when there could be as long as nine months between ships. So a courthouse and a gaol are planned and, with law and order still a problem, he imposes an 8 pm curfew on the island, and supplies the settlers with firearms. As well as the main area of the island, Kingston, near Sydney Bay, Gidley King sets up two more settlements—Queenborough in the centre and Phillipsburg to the north, where he finds the young Chapman a job as a storekeeper.

Anna Josepha is eager to see as much as she can and meet as many of the islanders as possible before she has her baby and will find it harder to get out and about. She walks along the paths that have been laid between the settlements, hand in hand with Norfolk, and often with Chapman joining them, and sometimes Elizabeth Paterson. They stop to talk to people they pass, whether convicts, settlers or soldiers, making no distinction between their standing. Gidley King takes great delight in how well they're received.

One day, she returns home to tell him that a woman carrying two infants in her arms, with one little girl straggling behind her, stopped them. 'Norfolk! Is that you?' the woman asked the boy. 'My goodness how tall you've grown! I don't suppose you'd remember me; I'm a good friend of your mother's.' She suddenly seemed to remember herself and stopped dead. 'Oh, I'm sorry, ma'am,' Anna Josepha recounted to her husband. 'No disrespect intended.'

The Governor, His Wife and His Mistress

'And none taken.' Anna Josepha laughed. 'You're a friend of Ann's? How lovely. It's nice to meet you. And you are . . . ?'

'My name's Olivia,' said the other woman, bobbing a shallow curtsey. 'And this is Ann,' she indicated the little girl behind her, 'and these two here are my twins, Sarah and Mary.'

'How delightful!' Anna Josepha exclaimed. 'But tell me, how do you know Ann?'

'I came over on the First Fleet with her,' Olivia replied. 'And I was with her for this one's birth.' She chucked Norfolk affectionately under the chin, and he giggled. 'Quite a lot of trouble he gave his dear mama, too!'

Anna Josepha smiled. 'I don't doubt it,' she replied. 'He's a big boy.'

'And you must be due soon?' Olivia asked.

'Any day now, and I can't say I'm looking forward to it. But I'm struggling in this heat.'

'It'll be over and done before you know it. Look at me, I've got three now, and another on the way. I wish you lots of luck with it. And . . . you have Norfolk here. Is Ann all right? Is there any news of her?'

'Ann and Sydney are well. Norfolk is with us for a little while before he goes to school in England.'

Olivia nodded as if she understood the situation only too well. 'Good day to you,' she said. 'I wish you and your husband well.'

Gidley King listens to his wife's story of their meeting silently. 'Olivia . . . she's a good woman,' he says, finally. 'And her husband, Nathaniel, is one of the best, too. They have always been close to Ann.'

Even as he says it, he's overjoyed that Anna Josepha is making such headway—even among those who'd be most loyal to Ann.

The baby arrives on 2 December, a healthy boy they name Phillip Parker, after both the governor and the sea captain who brought them from England. Norfolk is entranced with his new half-sibling and Gidley King realises he must be missing Sydney.

'But he's a smart little boy and he seems to be settling down well with us,' Anna Josepha reassures her husband one evening as she sits nursing their newborn, and he nurses a glass of his beloved port, with Norfolk safely tucked up in bed. 'He's managing well. But I'll write to Ann to tell her how he is, and give her our news, and ask how she is faring, and young Sydney.'

Gidley King is amazed, yet again, at his wife's generosity of spirit. He could never have dared to imagine that things could work out so well between the two women in his life. A few days before, he'd overheard Chapman, who's become devoted to Anna Josepha, describing her as almost an angel. He smiled when he heard that, but he thinks he is right.

'That sounds an excellent idea,' he tells his wife.

Gidley King beams at her yet can't help the slightest feeling of unease about how well the two women seem to be getting on. He still burns with shame when he remembers the kiss he gave Ann in her house. He'd be mortified if his wife ever found out.

The Governor, His Wife and His Mistress

Despite the arrival of more food on the island, life is still hard. No one knows much about agriculture and there continues to be an acute shortage of tools, just like when the First Fleet arrived. Gidley King gives some convicts permission to clear small plots of land to grow food for themselves, and gives others pigs to breed to help increase the amount of pork meat available.

Hunger still drives some to stealing food, however, and there are fights over rations between the different groups. Gidley King has to resort to draconian punishments to keep the peace between the warring factions and provide a deterrent to future crime. The lash is used to teach offenders a painful, and very public, lesson; people are clamped in leg irons; and one woman is executed for robbery; while others have their heads shaved and are whipped for blasphemous language. At the same time, he restricts the freedom of settlers and soldiers to unfairly persecute convicts, saying they're entitled to the same rights of humanity as everyone else, and continues in his rehabilitation efforts. When their terms expire, he announces, they'll be permitted to leave the island as free people with a ticket of pardon.

Life gradually becomes a great deal more peaceful on the island and Gidley King allows himself to relax a little. But one day in August 1792, while sitting in his study at Government House, he hears a commotion, and sees someone racing up. He goes to the door to see what the problem is. It seems there's been a terrible accident involving Ann's dear friends Olivia and Nathaniel.

He pulls on his coat and makes his way to their house. Nathaniel had been felling a big tree, the breathless messenger tells him, when it fell the wrong way onto their house. By the time Gidley King arrives, the assistant surgeon Balmain is already there, tending to Olivia, with Nathaniel kneeling by their side, watching on in tears.

'Is she all right?' Gidley King asks Balmain. 'Are there any other injuries?'

Balmain lowers his eyes, and Gidley King notices, for the first time, two small bodies lying half-covered by a sheet on the clearing by the house. Just as he realises they must be two of her children, Anna Josepha comes running up. He stands in her way in the hope of preventing her seeing the bodies, but it's too late.

'Oh no!' she cries, seeing the lifeless twins, Sarah and Mary. 'But how about Ann? And Olivia's baby, William? Are they . . . ?'

Nathaniel looks up at the sound of the names and sees the lieutenant governor and his wife. He hauls himself to his feet. 'Ann was out playing so she is fine and Olivia managed to save William,' he says in a broken voice. 'She shielded him with her body as she heard the tree falling. But the two little ones . . .'

'And how is Olivia?' Anna Josepha asks.

'She's pretty badly hurt,' Nathaniel says, hanging his head.

Balmain butts in. 'But I think we can save her.'

'Please God,' Anna Josepha says.

'Yes,' Gidley King whispers, almost to himself. 'We need all the good men and women we can lay our hands on in a place like this.'

36

MONOPOLISING TRADE

Anna Josepha King
1 SEPTEMBER 1792, NORFOLK ISLAND

The tragic loss of the children comes as a big shock to the little colony, but Olivia gradually regains her strength. Anna Josepha visits her as often as she can, usually bringing Norfolk and Phillip along with her. Norfolk plays with young Ann, while the two babies gurgle at each other.

On one of her visits, Olivia mentions she has received a letter from Ann Inett.

Anna Josepha is instantly interested. 'I received a letter from her, too, but it didn't contain much news,' she says. 'She said how much she misses Norfolk, and that young Sydney is doing well. But not much else. She would love to visit us here, but there are so few ships calling at the island, it's very difficult to arrange.'

Olivia nods. 'Did you know that I named my eldest after her?' she asks. 'I don't know if I ever told you that.'

'No, you didn't. But how lovely. I'm sure Ann was delighted.'

'She was.'

'And did she say anything more to you than she said in her letter to me?'

Olivia smiles and shifts her position in bed. 'She said she's very grateful to you for keeping her in touch with everything Norfolk is doing. She wasn't sure if you would keep your promise. But she's worried that you might be sending him away to England to school soon. She's dreading that.'

'Of course,' Anna Josepha says. 'I can understand that. It'll be the same for me when Phillip's time comes.'

'But for her, it'll be the third child she's lost. That's hard.'

'Absolutely. She must be such a strong woman to have withstood all she has.'

'She certainly is. She constantly surprises me, too, and none more than with her latest news!'

'There's more?' asks Anna Josepha.

'Yes! She has met someone and has fallen in love.'

Anna Josepha feels her heart lift. That is wonderful news indeed. She realises there must have always been a little fear tucked away, somewhere deep within, that Gidley King might one day return to his first lover, the mother of his two sons. But, happily, no more.

'That's marvellous!' she says to Olivia. 'And who's the lucky man?'

'Apparently, his name is Richard John Robinson. He came over with the Second Fleet. He's from London.'

'A convict?'

'He was tried at the Old Bailey for stealing a horse and given a death sentence that was commuted to life transportation. Ann met him when he first arrived, and says he's a fine man, kind and thoughtful and ambitious to get ahead in the colony. He also treats her son Sydney as his own.'

'He sounds perfect.'

'They're hoping to marry in November.'

Anna Josepha has a sudden thought. 'I know Ann is a dressmaker, did she say she has any plans to make her own gown for the wedding?'

Olivia frowns. 'She didn't say, but they can't get much material over there, so she probably won't be able to.'

'I have my wedding dress with me. The material came from King's father. She has as much right to it as me. Do you think she would like to wear it?'

Olivia grins. 'I'm sure she would love that,' she replies. 'That's very kind of you. Are you sure?'

'Of course! It's not much use to me on Norfolk Island, is it? And I would like to do something nice for her. I will package it up and hope the next ship arrives in time for her to receive it ahead of the wedding.'

It gives Anna Josepha a great deal of pleasure to think of Ann's face when she receives that gorgeous sheath of satin. She tells Gidley King about Ann's upcoming wedding and he seems pleased too, but somehow she doesn't find the right moment to mention the dress.

In any case, she's expecting another little one, which will be a good distraction as she's increasingly worried about her husband's health. He keeps having recurrences of the joint stiffness Balmain has now officially diagnosed as gout—and the port he's drinking to deal with the pain doesn't seem to be helping.

'You know, King, maybe the port is making it worse?' she ventures one day. 'It seems the more you drink of it, the more pain you're in.'

'I drink more when the pain becomes intolerable,' Gidley King replies. 'I don't think I could get through it otherwise.'

His general mood has become darker as a result of the news from Sydney Cove that the governor is sailing for England in December to seek medical attention. Phillip has been ill for some time, with an acute pain in his side that sometimes makes it impossible for him to walk. The surgeon at Port Jackson has diagnosed kidney stones, but has said Phillip needs to go back home for treatment. The loss of Gidley King's long-time mentor and keenest supporter will cut him deeply. He's also just received papers from pen-pushing bureaucrats in the Admiralty admonishing him about the unauthorised purchase of livestock at the Cape. He is clearly feeling insecure in his position.

'I'm sure everything will be all right,' she tells him one evening. 'They say Paterson will be leaving Norfolk Island to return to Port Jackson to take the governor's place until he returns, and he's our friend.'

'It's not him I'm worried about,' Gidley King says morosely. 'It's the man above him, the overall commander of the New South Wales Corps in Port Jackson, Major Francis Grose. We don't see eye to eye on a lot of things. He's a soldier and resents me as a navy man.

I'm worried he will favour his soldiers above anyone else and will give them a lot more power.'

To Anna Josepha's alarm, it seems her husband is right. Grose gradually moves the colony from one run by a civil administration to one controlled by the military, even replacing the magistrates with military officers. He issues them with land grants and gives others farms, with an allocation of ten convicts each to help work them. He also allows his soldiers to engage in trade, especially in liquor, with rum a major commodity.

Moreover, Phillip had left Gidley King alone to manage Norfolk Island as he thought best, but Grose is interfering more and more, and demanding Gidley King run any plans and projects past him before they're implemented. He then takes the opportunity to deny him permission for many, like his schemes to give the convicts more land to allow them to grow more crops. Grose also doesn't seem to approve of the lieutenant governor being so entrepreneurial on the island, organising teams of people to catch more mutton birds, to fish and to grow a new crop, sugar cane. Grose sees Norfolk Island as an adjunct to his Sydney settlement, both under his control and running in parallel fashion, rather than as an independent little colony thriving as best it can.

Gidley King and Anna Josepha become even more worried when Paterson leaves the island in March for Port Jackson. Now they won't even have his protection.

The couple try to take a few days off from their worries to mark the birth of their first daughter on 22 April 1793. It's a joyous occasion, and much less traumatic than her brother Phillip's arrival. They name her Anna Maria. Gidley King looks over the moon to have a daughter to finally add to his brood of three boys.

But it's still a busy time for him. He's back on his mission to produce the longed-for flax with the arrival the next month of two Māoris captured on a New Zealand beach by Captain Vancouver's storeship. They were lured on board because they were curious to see inside, and the ship abruptly upped anchor and sailed away with the kidnapped men. In Port Jackson, they were transferred to another ship bound for Norfolk Island. Gidley King meets them off the vessel and tries to explain that he wants them to show him how to prepare flax. The whole affair, however, quickly turns into an unmitigated disaster. Flax-making, they finally manage to convey, is women's work. They have no idea.

The two men, Tookee and Woodee, who turn out to be a warrior and a priest, beg Gidley King to take them home, but with no ship going that way for some time, he ends up inviting them to stay at the new Government House, and eat meals with the family. Anna Josepha is thrilled with the diversion. Her husband learns some words of their language, and they of his, and they all start communicating, after a fashion. There are moments when the Māoris threaten suicide if they're separated from their families for much longer, but everyone tries to console them.

Finally, the *Britannia* storeship, which has been chartered by military officers for a trip to India to buy food and rum that they're then bringing back to Sydney to sell for a profit, arrives at the island.

It's an arrangement Anna Josepha knows her husband abhors. 'The worst thing Grose seems to be doing is giving officers land

The Governor, His Wife and His Mistress

grants, and allowing them to run trade, almost as a monopoly,' Gidley King confides in her one day. 'He allows them to buy food, provisions and alcohol from the trading ships that arrive, depriving everyone else of the right to buy the goods. Then they sell them to people at vastly inflated prices. They're lining their own pockets at our expense. This won't end well, mark my words.'

As a result, Gidley King boldly decides to commandeer the *Britannia* to take the Māoris back to the beach at the Bay of Islands, where they'd been captured. He takes leave and, with Chapman by his side, returns the men to their homes.

When he gets back, he regales Anna Josepha with tales of how incredible the experience has been. 'They sang a song at each sunset about going back to their wives and families, which I found very affecting,' he tells her. 'When we anchored, they sang a long song to everyone there, telling them where they'd been, what they'd seen and what had happened to them.'

'That must have been amazing!' she responds, wishing she'd been able to accompany the little expedition.

'We exchanged gifts before we left again. Look!' He shows her two greenstone clubs, shaped like teardrops. 'I shall always treasure these and remember that experience.'

It wasn't long, however, before he was given even more reason to never forget it: a furious censure from Grose. The military commander was outraged that Gidley King had had the temerity to leave his post and take his officers' ship to return two lowly 'savages' to their homeland. As part of the payback, the angry officers start stopping ships en route for Norfolk Island and buying up everything on board, so no more provisions arrive.

Anna Josepha peeks into his diary one evening after he's spent a furious hour writing. *I cannot help remarking that if this secure exclusion is meant to disgust those who are on this island with their place of residence*, he's written, *it certainly has in a great measure answered this intent.*

Money is also a constant worry and, with so few ships calling by, the lieutenant governor's salary often arrives several months late. Phillip had always given him leave to manipulate the accounts so he could loan himself money when it was overdue and his family was in need, but Grose is distrustful. After having so much freedom to run the island, and his own affairs as he sees fit, Gidley King finds the new layer of supervision beyond the pale.

He takes comfort in spending time with his family, however, and Anna Josepha always tries to make it as relaxed as possible. Yet she realises it can't be this way for much longer and, with the news that another ship is on its way to Norfolk Island ready to return to Port Jackson, Gidley King acts.

'I'm sorry, my dear, I know how attached you've become to young Norfolk, and how much he dotes on you,' he tells her one day. 'But he's nearly five years old, and it's time for him to go to England, to start school. He can go to his mother's for a few days before the next ship leaves Port Jackson for Portsmouth.'

'I suppose we always knew this day was coming,' Anna Josepha says. 'I'll be very sad to see him go, but Ann will be thrilled to see him again.' She'd actually received a letter from Ann two weeks before, wondering if Norfolk might be coming back soon since he was now getting to school age, and warmly thanking her for the dress.

The Governor, His Wife and His Mistress

'But I do have a favour to ask you, my dear,' Gidley King says hesitantly. 'I wonder if maybe he could go and stay with your parents in Devon, and they could sort out schooling for him?'

She's startled. 'Why's that?' she asks. 'I would have thought your mother would be delighted to have the company.'

She notices now how sheepish he looks. 'To be honest, my mother is not aware he exists.'

Anna Josepha is stunned into silence. 'What do you mean?'

'I never actually told her about Ann—or the children.'

'I can't believe it!' she says. 'You didn't tell her when you were in England before, and you still don't plan to let her know?'

She notices her husband has the grace to hang his head in shame. 'I couldn't do it to her,' he mumbles.

'But would you deprive her of the joy of knowing she has two other grandsons?'

'She'll be happy when the time comes to meet Phillip and Anna Maria,' he says quietly. 'Until then, I'd prefer her not to know.'

Anna Josepha looks at him in silence. It is simply astonishing, she thinks, that such a fearless, clever man in some ways could be so unutterably awful in others.

37

A SON RETURNS

Ann Robinson
15 DECEMBER 1793, SYDNEY COVE, NEW SOUTH WALES

It's been two years, one month and twenty-two days since Ann waved goodbye to her son Norfolk as he sailed away from Port Jackson. She's never managed to stop counting.

Now, waiting at the dock and casting her eyes over the passengers disembarking their ship, she begins to panic that he's not there. And then, finally, she spies him. A tall boy—much taller than when he'd left—holding a small sea trunk and looking lost in the surge of people. Ann gives herself a minute to enjoy the sight of him, then plunges into the crowd.

'Norfolk!' she calls. *'Norfolk!'*

The boy looks over uncertainly, then sees his mother and his face breaks into a broad grin. He waves and starts running towards her.

She crouches down, opens her arms wide and he tumbles right in. 'Oh my darling,' she murmurs in his ear. 'Oh my darling, how I've missed you!' She hugs him as if she'll never let him go. 'It's so wonderful to see you again! I can't believe this day has finally come.'

Suddenly, her whole body is heaving with sobs that she's unable to stop. She clings to her son and the two remain frozen to the spot while everyone else pushes past them. 'I'm so sorry, Norfolk,' she says. 'I promised myself I wouldn't cry.' She releases her grip on him and pulls back. 'Now let me have a proper look at you.'

She looks into her son's face, and is surprised to see it streaked with tears, too. She ruffles his hair affectionately. 'Aren't we a pair!' she exclaims. 'Look at us!'

Norfolk makes a sound halfway between a giggle and a sob, and then they both laugh. 'It is so good to see you, son,' she says. 'You are a sight for sore eyes.'

'It's great to see you too, Mama,' he replies. 'And where's Sydney?'

'He's waiting for you at home. We live in Parramatta now, a little carriage trip to the west. He wanted to come and meet you, too, but I told him he couldn't as there'd be too many people. He was very annoyed. He can't wait to see you either!'

Hand in hand, the pair move away from the foreshore and then climb into the open wagon waiting to take people the fifteen miles to the settlement west of Port Jackson. Ann has made sure they have booked seats; nothing is too good for her son. Besides, this is a monumental day, and they won't have long together before he'll be back on another ship, sailing far, far away.

'My, you have grown so tall,' she says when they're seated. 'And you look so grown up, like a proper little gentleman.'

Norfolk laughs, obviously pleased at her words. 'Well, I am four now, nearly five,' he says importantly. 'I am grown up.'

Ann laughs. She's pleased to see that, in some ways, he hasn't changed a bit: still making sure everyone knows exactly how old he is, and keenly anticipating his next birthday.

It takes them two hours to reach Parramatta, travelling along the side of the river, and on dusty carriage tracks fringed with luxuriant greenery either side that slaps the horses' flanks as they pass by. In the distance, they can see acres of rolling grasslands, dotted with small farms helping grow the food Port Jackson needs to survive. Ann entrances her small son with stories of some of the things he's missed while he was away, like the twenty-one convicts escaping, with a plan to walk to China.

'You can't walk to China from here, can you?' Norfolk asks, wide-eyed.

'You most certainly can't! But apparently they believed that China was just the other side of the Blue Mountains, west of Sydney.'

'What happened to them?'

'Sadly,' says Ann, 'some became completely lost in the wilderness and some others perished.'

'That is sad,' he says, looking thoughtful. 'We've had people trying to escape at Norfolk Island, too, but there's nowhere for them to go there either.'

'But it is possible to get lost wherever you go in the world,' Ann says. 'We've had visitors from France here looking for a French captain called La Pérouse. Your papa met him a few years ago when

The Governor, His Wife and His Mistress

they were both in Botany Bay, but he disappeared after that, and hasn't been seen since. No one knows where he might be.'

Norfolk nods, taking this in.

Ann considers what else has been happening, like the raids on the settlers by the natives of the so-called 'Woods Tribe', led by Pemulwuy, but decides that could be too much bad news. Instead, she asks brightly, 'And do you remember Bennelong, the native who became a friend of Governor Phillip and then speared him in the shoulder?'

'I do.'

'Well, he went back to England with the governor, taking a young friend of his with them. Can you imagine them in the fine houses of London, meeting important people?'

Norfolk laughs. 'Do you think he'll wear proper clothes?'

'I hope so,' says Ann. 'He'll find it pretty cold otherwise.'

When they finally stop at the centre of the new farming settlement, they clamber out, and Sydney, now three and a half, scampers up at full tilt, almost crashing into his brother in his haste.

'*Norfolk!*' he yells at the top of his voice.

'And *Sydney*!' Norfolk yells back, mocking his younger brother. He picks him up and swings him around as Sydney screams in delight. 'My, you've got heavy! What are they feeding you?'

Ann puts a hand on Norfolk's arm. 'There's someone else I'd like you to meet,' she says. 'Norfolk, meet Richard Robinson. He lives with us now.'

Norfolk holds out his hand in a very grown-up way. 'It's good to meet you, sir,' he says. 'I've heard all about you.'

Ann and Richard exchange smiles over his head, and Richard takes his hand and shakes it. 'And I have heard all about you too, Master Norfolk,' he says. 'Please just call me Uncle Richard.'

'And you can just call me Norfolk,' says the boy with a cheeky grin.

The next three days pass like the happiest of dreams for Ann. She adores having Norfolk back home, and he gets on so well with Sydney and Richard. She watches the three together of an evening, wreathed in smiles. Ann thinks she's the happiest she has ever been in all her life. If only it could always be like this!

She's haunted by the thought that the next ship to England will be calling soon, and she'll have to take Norfolk back to Port Jackson to say another painful goodbye.

'Maybe we should keep him here with us,' she says on the second night, in bed with Richard. 'Maybe he doesn't have to go to England for school.'

Richard frowns. 'Didn't you make a deal with his father to allow him to go?'

Ann immediately knows she's strayed onto boggy ground with Richard. He's well known for being one of the most principled men in the colony. In England he'd received a death sentence for the theft of a bay gelding. He'd bought it on behalf of another man, he said, who'd then failed to come up with the ten guineas. Afterwards, he'd been among more than a hundred convicts offered transportation rather than the death sentence, but caused a sensation when he was one of eight who'd refused, on principle.

'No, I will go to my sentence,' he'd famously declared. 'I find I am in the hands of men.' It was only the chaplain at Newgate Prison who eventually made him change his mind, and he'd ended up travelling to New South Wales aboard the deadly Second Fleet.

Richard still takes great pride in holding firm to his values. 'Gidley King sounds as if he has been fair to you, so maybe you should respect that.'

'He was fair up to a point,' Ann replies. 'But don't forget he did betray me very badly.'

'But that's all in the past now. You have to get over it. And if it hadn't have happened, you might never have met me!'

'Well, that's true enough.' Ann smiles, lifting her head from the pillow so he can put an arm around her shoulders. 'That would have been a shame.'

'Tell me how much,' he says, pulling her closer. 'I want to know *exactly* how much.'

The notion of keeping Norfolk home is a thought, however, that Ann can't seem to shake. She loves having him around so much, she's loath to give him up again. Also, she feels sure that very soon Gidley King will be sending for Sydney to come and join him and Anna Josepha on Norfolk Island, and then also dispatching him to England for school. Losing her two sons like she'd lost Thomas and Constance feels unthinkable. She hadn't had any choice the first time, but this time she does. Wouldn't it be far more responsible to keep the two boys with her? They need their mother, she is sure they do. They mightn't thank her later for letting them go.

Richard is supportive and sympathetic, but firm. 'Annie, you know it makes sense to let Norfolk go,' he says the next morning, going back to their interrupted conversation. 'We have to think of him. He's the most important person in this. Boys these days need a good education to get on. What would he do here without one?'

'He could make do. You're doing all right.'

'But I'm not a young man starting out with no schooling at all. When I worked at the farm back in the Midlands, I did the accounts, and the buying and selling, as well as the hard toil on the land. I couldn't have done that without having been to school.'

'I suppose so,' she says begrudgingly.

'And now, working as a clerk at the public barn and granary here in Parramatta, my qualifications have come in extremely handy.'

'Maybe they'll start building more schools out here? The Reverend Johnson opened one in February in Sydney, after returning from Norfolk Island, in that makeshift wattle and daub shelter he built to be a church near the harbour in Port Jackson.'

'But how long will that take? And where will all the teachers come from?'

Ann tries a different tack. 'How will Norfolk get on in England? He doesn't know anyone there.'

'Hasn't Gidley King organised for him to live with Anna Josepha's family?'

'Yes, that's true,' she's forced to concede. 'And from how saintly she is, you'd have to imagine they're good people. It was so lovely of her to lend me her wedding dress for our wedding.'

'And I'm sure you looked much more beautiful in it than her.'
'Oh, get away with you!'
'But didn't you yourself tell me that she's rather plain?'
'I suppose I did. But she glows with kindness and good intentions. Gidley's done well for himself there, even if I hate to admit it.'
'Don't you find it odd that he's not suggested Norfolk lodge with his own family?'
'I imagine they still don't know me or our children exist.'
Both fall silent. Richard speaks first. 'At the end of the day, it wouldn't do any good to make an enemy of such a powerful man on this side of the world,' he says eventually. 'He has the ear of everyone in charge, like Grose and Paterson. It wouldn't do to cross him.'

They finally agree simply to make the most of Norfolk's time while he's with them. They show him around Parramatta's farms, market gardens and fields of grain, point out the massive one-hundred-acre land grant given to the controversial Captain John Macarthur earlier that year, and the Elizabeth Farm homestead he's building for his wife and children, as sheep graze peacefully all around. Then they picnic by the river with Sydney showing his older brother how to swim.

'But you were living on an island!' Ann exclaims. 'Didn't you ever swim off the beach?' she teases him.

'No, Mama, I was never allowed,' he answers. 'It's too dangerous.'

She smiles. 'Yes, good boy! You're quite right. Tell Sydney what it's like.'

'The surf breaks on the rocks. It can get really scary. Many people have lost their lives there,' he explains solemnly.

The little family also visit St John's Church in Parramatta, where the couple married. 'It was such a lovely day,' Ann reminisces to her elder son. 'I wish you could have been here.'

'You should have seen your mother,' Richard says. 'She looked absolutely beautiful.'

Ann is a study in casualness. 'So tell us, Norfolk, what was your life like on Norfolk Island?' she asks him. 'How is your father and how is Anna Josepha?'

'They're fine,' he says, with complete disinterest.

Ann persists. 'And how is it having a new little brother and sister?'

'It's all right, I guess,' he answers obediently. 'But Anna Maria cries a lot.'

'Babies do.' Ann smiles. 'And does Papa play with you much?'

Norfolk shrugs. 'He's busy in his office a lot of the time and he's often cross and shouts at people, and we have to be quiet,' he reports. 'Anna Josepha says it's very difficult being in charge of the island at the moment. And sometimes he has to go to bed as he's not well.'

'What's wrong with him?'

'I don't know. She doesn't say, and we're not allowed to ask him.'

She knows she's being uncharitable, but Ann is immensely cheered by the news. She's powerless to prevent Norfolk leaving the next day, but maybe, just maybe, Gidley King will be too preoccupied to call for Sydney to join him on Norfolk Island. She lives in hope.

38

PUT EVERY MAN TO DEATH!

Philip Gidley King
20 DECEMBER 1793, NORFOLK ISLAND

It's the spark that lights the powder keg. A fresh batch of soldiers on the island are brazenly bullying the male convicts—eating, drinking and gambling with them, and then trying to lure their wives away for sex. There are a number of fights and the combatants are either punished under harsh military law by Lieutenant Edward Abbott if they're a soldier or, if they're a convict, by Gidley King, according to the much more lenient criminal law. Both the crimes and their punishments then create a huge amount of ill feeling.

The antagonism comes to a head one night when the island's convict coxswain objects to a soldier's advances on his wife and beats him up. The New South Wales Corps come to the defence of their comrade and demand that his aggressor is flogged, rather than merely fined the regulation twenty shillings.

285

Soon after, at Christmas, four soldiers are spotted holding aloft a burning torch, heading for the convict's farm. Someone tries to stop them, and the torch is thrust into his face. Gidley King is outraged, and has the offending soldier arrested. That evening, in revenge, two more soldiers attack the convict and bludgeon him almost to death. Despite the brutality of the assault, the badly injured man begs the governor to let the soldiers off. If he doesn't, he pleads, he's sure there'll be even more vicious reprisals. Gidley King is appalled at what's happening to his beloved island home.

'How did everything here go so wrong?' he asks Anna Josepha later that night. 'This was a model colony when we started here. It's always been a tough place where we had to battle the elements, but not each other. The soldiers are ruining it. And Grose is doing nothing to help.'

'You'll find a solution, King, you always do,' she replies evenly. 'I know you. You do like a challenge.'

'But often *after* it's been solved.' He pours a ruby red glass of port, and sniffs it with appreciation before sipping. 'It doesn't help that I've always got Grose breathing down my neck, looking for any sign I'm favouring anyone over his damned soldiers. I do miss Governor Phillip! Where is this ever going to end?'

To try to patch over this latest crisis, he comes up with an ingenious plan: he demands both sides sit down and drink a gallon of rum together.

'But I still don't think it's done any good,' King confides in Anna Josepha the next day. 'They had a good time together, but that animosity is still simmering away under the surface.'

A few nights later, a play takes place, staged by some of the free settlers and convicts. Gidley King and Anna Josepha attend, with a number of officers, but notice an unkempt soldier sitting nearby in the audience, refusing to take off his hat. Afterwards, when they are nearly back at Government House, Gidley King hears a commotion back in the direction of where the play was performed, with shouting, the sound of people being hit, and one blood-curdling yell, 'Put every man to death!'

There are men running back towards the playhouse brandishing weapons and so Gidley King races there, too. He looks around and quickly sizes up the situation. The man bellowing the terrible threats is the dishevelled soldier, so he seizes him by the shoulder and hauls him over to the Sergeant of the Guard. The man challenges him to a duel, but Gidley King ignores him and orders that he be confined to the guard house. It turns out that the disturbance is the culmination of a fresh bout of enmity after a dispute over seats between Anna Josepha's convict servants and the soldiers. Another attack on that poor convict coxswain had been planned, and then a wholesale armed mutiny, with a conspiracy to 'butcher' a number of the ex-convict settlers.

Gidley King is forced to act quickly. He insists that twenty mutineers are arrested, and a temporary armed militia is formed of free settlers and marines to keep the peace. The insurgents are then sent to Sydney Cove for a court martial.

The acting governor Grose, however, is outraged by his actions. He refuses to back him and goes on the attack instead.

'No provocation that a soldier can give is ever to be admitted as an excuse for a convict's striking a soldier,' he declares. But then he goes even further. 'No soldier can ever be arrested,' he rules, 'or tried by a civilian judge or magistrate, even if he breaks the law.'

'This is absolutely ridiculous!' Gidley King fumes to his wife. 'It means that soldiers are now free to act with absolute impunity towards anyone they please. They are above the law.'

'Surely the British Government won't agree to this,' Anna Josepha replies. 'You can't sit back and let this happen.'

'I'll write to the Secretary of State for the Colonies and inform him of what happened and what Grose is now dictating as a result.'

Although the letter takes many months to reach London, and then for the reply to arrive, it finally turns out, happily, to be a victory for the beleaguered lieutenant governor. Grose is forced to withdraw and apologise.

Life doesn't get much easier, however. Food thefts continue, soldiers steal money from convicts and one group of runaway convicts terrorises the community, until they are finally caught and lashed. In a bold effort to frighten everyone into obeying the law, Gidley King finally threatens to banish anyone pilfering food to lonely Nepean Island, eight hundred yards south of Norfolk Island, with its high cliffs and stark landscapes. That proves a very effective deterrent. In the meantime, Gidley King also continues to push for a separate legal court to operate on the island so he can bring offenders to justice quickly and efficiently.

The Governor, His Wife and His Mistress

Eventually, tensions on the island begin to ease, and life quietens down once again. Then comes good news: Grose finally departs for England in December 1794, troubled by old wounds he'd received in the American War. Then, there's even better news: the new governor is to be a naval officer rather than a military one, Gidley King's old friend and colleague from the First Fleet, Captain John Hunter. He arrives back in Port Jackson in September 1795 to assume control.

Gidley King feels he's finally on a winning streak. The next month, the British Government agrees that he can set up a court on Norfolk Island, and gives him permission to make that happen. That means a triple celebration as the decision comes a few days before the birth of his second daughter, Utricia, named in honour of his mother.

But the strain of the past three years is beginning to tell on him, and Anna Josepha is worried. The painful intermittent bouts of gout he's suffering from are worsening. 'He complains of a searing pain in both his lungs and his stomach,' she confides in Olivia, who is recovering well from her injuries. 'He constantly feels unwell. I am very concerned about his health.'

'Perhaps he needs a break from the island,' Olivia suggests. 'There are many of us here who can't leave, but he has that option.'

'That's true. It could be good for him to get away for a while. He's had a very difficult time.'

'We don't want to see him go. The convicts are grateful that he's tried to protect us against the soldiers. But maybe now is the time for him to think of himself—and his family.'

Anna Josepha considers that carefully and, as her husband grows sicker, she suggests he apply for leave to go to England to see his doctor. He's reluctant but with his condition deteriorating fast, and she and Chapman putting his affairs in order—just in case—he finally agrees. Governor Hunter, a major supporter who's now had a book published in London using part of Gidley King's journal and his dictionary of Aboriginal words from around Sydney, encourages him to write to London for permission.

After nearly five years at the helm of one of the most remote islands in the world, he's ready to go home.

The storeship *Britannia*, with Gidley King, Anna Josepha, Phillip, Anna Maria and little Utricia on board, sets sail on 22 October 1796 for Port Jackson, where they've arranged to pick up Sydney, despite Ann's entreaties, and then on to England. As some small compensation, Gidley King has agreed to take some more letters from Ann for Thomas and Constance, as well as for Norfolk. He's also carrying letters from many of the convicts and settlers on the island for their families back home, including from Olivia's husband, Nathaniel. Then he's packed on board more specimens for his mentor Banks, while their friends William and Elizabeth Paterson are also sailing with them.

Sydney, now six years old, is tearful at leaving his mother and Richard—the closest to a father he's so far known—but Anna Josepha befriends him quickly, and makes sure the small boy feels an integral part of the family. He's excited at the thought of meeting up with Norfolk again in England and gets on well with his new half-brother Phillip, just a year younger, and is thrilled to meet his two half-sisters. He quickly settles down.

The Governor, His Wife and His Mistress

Arriving at the Cape of Good Hope, Gidley King goes ashore with Paterson, and learns that an old acquaintance is selling their flock of Spanish sheep. He inspects them and is given a gift of three, and then manages to persuade two officers who'd arrived from Port Jackson to pick up supplies to buy the remaining twenty-six.

They catch another ship, the *Contractor*, for the rest of the voyage. Anna Josepha is anxious—she is by now heavily pregnant. But the ship is comfortable, and the crew welcoming. The captain and his mate even deliver her baby, another daughter the couple call Elizabeth, on board in February 1797. Fortunately, it is a much easier birth than Utricia's, who's still a delicate infant. Elizabeth, by contrast, seems much more hale and hearty.

The ship finally docks in Portsmouth in May, and Gidley King immediately attends his doctor. His ailments are indeed all related to gout, and he's told to cut down his drinking, which will only make it worse. If he drinks less or, even better, stops drinking altogether, he'll see an instant improvement in his health.

Anna Josepha is relieved. 'I know drinking port was an excellent way for you to relax,' she says. 'But now that we know it's not doing you any good, it will be wise to stop. You *need* to, King. I don't want to lose you, and neither do your six children.'

'I understand,' he says gloomily. 'If I could get rid of this wretched pain, I suppose it will be worth it.'

'It will be more than merely worth it,' she insists. 'It could save your life.'

But even as he starts to make a slow recovery, there doesn't seem to be much to be cheerful about in England. He's by now almost broke—his salary would only go so far, as well as the revenue from a thirty-acre plot of land he leased on the island. To his credit, he'd been meticulous about never engaging in trade, like the military officers, or doing anything untoward to increase his income. But such honesty, in the midst of so much rampaging profiteering, has cost him dearly.

He needs to find work again but, everywhere he turns, he hits a brick wall. The navy seems only to be interested in young, vigorous officers to command convoys in the face of French aggression under Napoleon Bonaparte, so his requests for a rise in rank in acknowledgement of his achievements are turned down. At the same time, the Admiralty doesn't appear particularly interested in his comprehensive report on the affairs of tiny, remote Norfolk Island.

Needing help, he visits his old friend Phillip, who has successfully recovered his health in England and is now advancing his way up the naval hierarchy, commanding ships in anticipation of an all-out war against Napoleon. His love life has made a turn for the better, too. His wife Margaret died in 1792, the year he returned to England, so he took a second wife, Isabella Whitehead in 1794. Margaret had been seventeen years his senior; his second wife is thirteen years his junior.

He's delighted to see his protégé. 'King, you are a most welcome visitor!' Phillip exclaims. 'How the devil are you? But you look pale, my man.' He takes two glasses from his drinks cabinet and pours two generous serves of port. 'I remember how much you love this stuff. Here, let's drink a toast to us both.'

Gidley King hesitates only a moment before taking the glass. 'Thank you, sir,' he says, taking a good mouthful after Phillip proposes his toast. 'It is good to see you, too.'

The Governor, His Wife and His Mistress

He explains why he's there, that he's having trouble finding a new naval position and wonders if Phillip can put in a good word for him.

'I don't know if you know,' Phillip replies, 'but I recommended you for the post of New South Wales Governor when I returned here, but they ignored my advice and appointed Hunter instead.'

Gidley King is taken aback. 'That was very kind of you,' he says.

'Nonsense! You were the best possible candidate. You'd done magnificently on Norfolk Island and, in my opinion, would have made an excellent governor.'

'That's all very well, but if I don't get a position now, I'm going to have to pick up my spade and go back to working on my farm in Cornwall.'

Phillip grimaces at that; the farming life never really suited either of them. 'I'll put in another commendation for you but, in the meantime, why don't you write to Sir Joseph Banks? He still holds great sway in matters of the colony.'

The next day, Gidley King does just that. He sends Banks the new specimens of plants he has collected for him, and writes of his nine years of devoted service since leaving with the First Fleet and how he feels that he might now have to resign his commission of lieutenant governor, and return to his farm.

While he awaits a response, he visits his mother in Cornwall and introduces her to his family . . . or most of them. He's already dispatched Sydney to join Norfolk at school in Yorkshire so he still doesn't have to tell his mother his shameful secret, or face any awkward questions. But while baby Elizabeth is thriving, little eighteen-month-old Utricia falls sick. She's never been strong, and now she gradually fades away. The day she falls asleep and wakes no more, both Gidley King and Anna Josepha are devastated. Her mother-in-law comforts her as she weeps for a full day, before wiping her eyes and resolving to be strong for their other children.

In the meantime, Gidley King applies for a casual role inspecting some new ships that are being offered for use in the New South Wales colony. He approves only one, the *Buffalo*, so the navy commissions a second to be built, the *Porpoise*. On the day he goes to inspect that, he is aghast, and says work on it should not proceed as it's so badly designed. His employer says he was the one who approved the design, and Gidley King wonders if he's going to be forever out of favour.

But then, on 1 May 1798, a few days short of a year since the family reached England, and nearly eleven years to the day Gidley King had first set out with the First Fleet to Botany Bay, he receives news.

John Hunter is to be removed as Governor of New South Wales, and Philip Gidley King is to take his place.

Part four

POWER

39

HAVE YOU HEARD THE NEWS?

Ann Robinson

21 DECEMBER 1798, PARRAMATTA, NEW SOUTH WALES

It's a busy Friday night in the lead-up to Christmas, and Ann is fair rushed off her feet.

'Another one over here, landlady!' shouts one man in the corner, at the same time as a group of farm labourers charge in through the doors. 'A nip for every man,' yells one of the new arrivals.

Ann looks towards her husband, Richard Robinson, who's similarly racing around, balancing a tray full of glasses. He glances back towards her and, for a brief moment, their eyes meet and they share a smile. They each know exactly what the other is thinking.

When Governor Hunter announced two years ago that he was going to issue ten liquor licences in a bid to control the military officers' rum monopoly, it was Ann's idea that they apply. Her seven-year transportation sentence had just expired and, with Norfolk and Sydney both in England, she knew she had to do something with her time. If she could earn good money, then she might one day have enough to be able to achieve her dearest dream: to return to her homeland.

Her two sons with Gidley King, now nine and eight years old, could possibly never visit this part of the world again, she reasons, so she will need to go to them. And, of course, there's still Thomas and Constance. There's not a day goes by when she doesn't imagine reuniting with her first-borns. Her son would now be twenty, and her daughter, eighteen. Would they still be living somewhere close to their grandparents? Might they be married? Could they even be starting families of their own? Have they ever received all the letters she's sent them, and still writes? Do they think of her, too? One day, she'll find out, she vows. One day.

Richard also wants to go back to Britain at some point in the future but, with his sentence being for life, he knows he'll have to make a significant contribution to the new colony in order to earn a pardon, so the couple can return together.

Running a public house to help keep the making and selling of illicit liquor in check could qualify as something of a public service and be quite a profitable pursuit to boot. It's something, they agreed, they'd be happy to try. With Richard now having been promoted from a clerk to the Superintendent of Government Mills, his wages and some extra she'd been earning from dressmaking since Sydney left meant they had some savings. Also, having lived in Parramatta a few years now, they knew the area well. Many of the locals worked hard, and liked to drink just as hard, and there were more arrivals—free settlers, officials and convicts—every year choosing to settle out west as Sydney was now so crowded. They could see a good future for the town.

'How about calling it The Yorkshire Grey?' Richard asked Ann after they'd painstakingly filled out their application.

'What does that mean?'

'It's a type of horse, a big horse, the ones who pull brewery drays. A lot of pubs in England are called that. I used to go to one in the Tottenham Manor in the centre of London. It was a great little place, very classy; all dark wood and etched windows.'

'I'm not sure we can afford that.' Ann laughs. 'But it's a good name. It might well be that a lot of people coming over associate that name with hotels, and will want to go somewhere with a name they recognise.'

'Apparently a fair few people have applied for licences, but they say they'll only give out five for Parramatta,' Richard replies. 'But I reckon Hunter would know your name from Gidley King, so we might be lucky!'

And now, much to their surprise, the pair are running one of the busiest establishments in the settlement, despite strong competition from The Freemasons Arms Inn, Salutation, Crown and Ship. They find they love the frenetic pace, the way they work for themselves without supervision and, mostly, the great atmosphere of people enjoying a break, a drink and the opportunity to let off steam. They can hardly believe they're so successful.

Their closest rival establishment is The Freemasons Arms Inn, run by another convict, colourful Jewish merchant James Larra, sentenced to death for stealing a tankard worth five pounds. He was transported instead on the Second Fleet, on the same ship as Richard, the *Scarborough*. He'd been granted a conditional pardon after serving on the night watch and, after a spell as a farmer, had turned to the much more lucrative liquor trade instead. With nearly everyone drinking spirits—all known by the shorthand 'rum'—there's a lot of money to be earned, particularly through the sale of 'grog', or spirits watered down with molasses.

At The Yorkshire Grey, Ann has a great way of charming customers. They respond well to her easy, down-to-earth manner and suspect she must have had a tough life, although she rarely talks of it. A few know she came over with the First Fleet and occasionally ask her about that, but she's always pretty non-committal.

'I don't want to go back there,' she tells Richard when he asks her why. 'It was such a miserable, hopeless time. I'd been torn away from my children, and I had no idea what was happening or what was to become of me. It was a pretty desperate period in my life. I remember spending a lot of it just wanting to die.'

'I know what you mean,' Richard says. 'Whenever anyone brings up the subject of the Second Fleet . . .' He shudders. 'Those times are best forgotten.'

'Let's look forward to a good future,' Ann says, 'either here or in England.'

This evening, The Yorkshire Grey is packed with revellers preparing for a good Christmas in the colony. It's been a warm day and is an even warmer evening, and the smell of sweat and spirits mingles with the aroma of roast beef from the kitchen.

Ann's in an excellent mood: she received a letter from Norfolk this morning. He says he's missing his dear mama but is working hard at his lessons and he likes the family he's been billeted with in Yorkshire. He's thinking he might join the navy, especially as his father has promised to help—and wouldn't that mean he'd be able to visit her one day? She smiles happily at the thought. Quite possibly.

She's serving as fast as she can, and enjoying the friendly banter from customers, when a man bursts through the doors and shouts loudly to his mates, 'Hey! Have you heard the news?'

The hubbub quietens down. There's something about the urgency in the man's voice that makes everyone want to hear what he has to say.

'What is it?' someone calls over.

'Governor Hunter is to be recalled to London!' the man yells. 'They don't reckon he's doing a good enough job!'

The noise from the bar rises once more as everyone excitedly discusses the revelation and tries to work out what it will mean for them, and the colony.

'But you'll never guess who's going to take his place!' he shouts over the din.

Again, the conversations stop and there's an expectant hush. Ann and Richard both halt what they're doing and wait to hear what he's got to say.

'It's Philip Gidley King!' the man announces. 'He's coming back!'

Ann gasps for breath and can feel the colour drain from her face. Gidley! She can't believe it. She'd successfully put that part of her life behind her—apart from Norfolk and Sydney, of course—and had honestly believed she would never see the man again. But now he's going to return, and will again be back in charge, not only of Norfolk Island but of the whole of New South Wales.

She can feel Richard sidle up to her. 'Are you all right?' he asks, putting a hand on her arm. 'You've gone white.'

'It's just such a shock,' she says. 'It's like the past coming back to haunt me.'

Richard nods. 'I can understand that. But this might be good for you, for us. He's always been a reasonable man from what I understand, and he still seems fond of you. He might be inclined to reward our entrepreneurship.'

Ann tilts her head. 'You mean a pardon for you?'

'That mightn't be a bad thing to start with,' Richard answers. 'But I meant that when he gives out the land grants, he might put you, the mother of two of his children, into the mix.'

'I suppose so,' she says, hesitantly.

'Think what a good thing that would be! If Norfolk and Sydney do one day come back, you'll be able to offer them a comfortable home.'

She smiles. She hadn't thought of it like that.

'And maybe he'll have the power to bring them back, and give them jobs in the colony.'

'That'd be a way away. They're still so young.'

'True. He could build some decent schools here and bring over some schoolteachers. He probably won't like being separated from his sons either.'

Ann's mulling that over when one of her regular customers, a man she knows from her days on Norfolk Island, approaches.

The Governor, His Wife and His Mistress

She can tell from his gait that he's already had far too much to drink, and he looks at her with an ugly leer.

'Hey, Ann,' he says, slurring his words. 'Gidley King! Fancy that! Do you think he might like to pick up where he left off?'

40

A PRIVILEGE AND A CURSE

Anna Josepha King
22 DECEMBER 1798, PORTSMOUTH, ENGLAND

Anna Josepha is beginning to despair. It's been more than six months since Gidley King was told he was to be the new Governor of New South Wales, but he still seems no closer to taking up the post.

They've completed all the heart-breaking tasks, like deciding that their seven-year-old son, Phillip Parker, and their five-year-old daughter Anna Maria should stay in England for the sake of their education, and saying a very tearful goodbye to them. They've also written letters of warm farewell to Norfolk and Sydney. But they still have nothing to show for such sacrifice. Now they, together with little Elizabeth, not yet two years old, are living on a broken-down ship in a dry dock in Portsmouth, having no idea when they might finally set off for New Holland.

The Governor, His Wife and His Mistress

'This is ridiculous,' she fumes to her husband. 'It'll soon be Christmas but how can we possibly celebrate it under these circumstances?'

He shrugs his shoulders sadly. He's been complaining to everyone in the British Government and the Admiralty he can think of, but he doesn't seem to be making any progress. They all seem to be fixated on the potential war with France instead. 'I suppose we just have to be patient,' he replies mildly. 'It surely can't be too much longer before something's done and we can head off.'

It had been a comedy of errors ever since Gidley King was informed about his new position. He, of course, was delighted to be given such an important post and the chance to play a significant role in the new colony. He'd written both to Phillip and Banks to thank them warmly for their commendations which, presumably, brought him such a fine result. Anna Josepha was considerably less thrilled. She'd been looking forward to settling back in Devon, near her parents, and spending her time bringing up her family. Now she was heading off again to the other side of the world to . . . who knows what?

That was the plan, anyway. So far, it has been nothing but an unmitigated disaster. It started with the French Revolution and that damned Napoleon, which made the British fearful of a full-scale invasion and nervous about sending ships anywhere they might encounter hostile French forces. But even after the French naval fleet was nearly decimated by the new British hero Lord Nelson in August 1798 at the Battle of the Nile, and the coast was declared clear, things didn't improve. And that's because the family was, astonishingly, given the very same ship for the voyage whose design Gidley King had criticised so volubly: the *Porpoise*.

The next delays were caused by a huge six-foot by twelve-foot plant-cabin being built on the *Porpoise*'s deck, to hold a huge number of plants chosen by Banks to take to New South Wales, including fruits, grapevines, hops, cactus, camphor and ginger. When that was finally finished, the *Porpoise* set sail with much fanfare down the Thames in September 1798 and out into the Channel—only to hit a huge gale, which rendered the ship almost completely inoperable. Eventually, it managed to stagger into Portsmouth where it was put into dry dock for work on the keel and rudder. It's here, on board, that Anna Josepha, her husband and daughter are forced to live in cramped quarters for a whole year to save money, while they're waiting for their voyage to begin.

When that day eventually comes, in September 1799, they're thrilled to get away. But their elation doesn't last long. A few hours into her journey, the ship's steering gear starts to break down and she has to be escorted back to port. She can't even get clear of British waters, let alone travel around the world.

This time, the family transfer to the 330-ton whaler *Speedy*, carrying fifty female convicts, and in November 1799, they're finally on their way.

'They should have listened to you in the first place,' Anna Josepha says to Gidley King. 'We could have been there by now. If they're so keen to get rid of Hunter, I hate to think what's happening over in Port Jackson and, in the year wasted, it will only have grown worse.'

The Governor, His Wife and His Mistress

Within two days of the start of their voyage, Gidley King falls ill with a terrible cold, rheumatism and another ferocious attack of gout. His condition deteriorates steadily until Anna Josepha records tremulously in her journal that he is now 'dangerously ill'.

She tends him affectionately, heaving a big tin bath onto the deck, filling it with warm water, helping him in to make sure most of his body is covered and then laying a sail cloth over him for modesty. It helps to ease his symptoms and the bath becomes such a well-known sight, everyone knows who's on board as soon as the *Speedy* approaches a port.

It's not only Gidley King who suffers on the trip, though. Little Elizabeth contracts prickly heat from the warmth of the tropics as they pass through the equatorial waters south of Tenerife, and another child, two women and the master-weaver who was due to take charge of turning the flax into linen in Port Jackson all die, while the ship's doctor 'becomes insane'. Terrible weather also assails them, with high winds, monstrous waves and lashing rain drenching the convicts below and leaving everyone else falling around their cabins and on the deck. Elizabeth takes a tumble and is quite seriously hurt; Anna Josepha's maid falls down the stairs and is so badly bruised she can barely move; and a female convict splinters her leg plummeting down a hatchway. The animals being carried to the colony also fare badly. Sheep, chickens, hens, ducks and geese perish; a hog falls down a hatch and breaks ribs; a goose tumbles through an open skylight onto the dinner table; and a pair of ducks are mysteriously discovered in the Kings' quarters. And all the time, Anna Josepha is terrified they might come across one of the many hostile French ships patrolling the North Atlantic and be taken captive.

It doesn't get any easier, either, when they near New South Wales. As they approach Van Diemen's Land, an incredible storm breaks, with the raging wind sluicing waves up and over the ship, tearing away the railings on the deck, the boat cranes, water casks and, sadly, that far-famed tin bath.

When they finally make it ashore at Sydney Cove in April 1800, the little party is met by Governor Hunter who seems oddly pleased to see them. It's only a few sentences into his welcome speech that Anna Josepha realises the reason: he doesn't know that his old friend Gidley King has come to replace him. She nudges her husband in the ribs to try to warn him, but he's totally absorbed in what Hunter has to say and doesn't pick up on any of her frantic signals.

It's only when Gidley King hands him the notice effectively dismissing him from his post that Hunter finally realises what's going on. He looks devastated, then angry. Anna Josepha attempts to take his arm and steer him away, with chatter about how much Sydney has changed during their absence, but he refuses to be sidetracked. Instead, he blusters to his successor about how his enemies have obviously got into the government's ear in London to undermine him and what an outrageous way it is to treat a loyal servant of the king, someone who's faithfully served the British Government for over forty-six years. Privately, Anna Josepha agrees, but better it's her husband who replaces him, she reasons to herself, than someone far less respectful and courteous.

She only hopes that when the time comes for Gidley King to leave the post, he's treated much more civilly.

Ex-Governor Hunter is now under orders to return to England by the first suitable ship. The difficulty lies, however, in the definition of the word 'suitable'. He decides an acceptable vessel will be the *Buffalo*—but only after it is completely refitted, a process that will likely take months. Anna Josepha is crushed. It means that the family can't move into the spacious Government House but end up staying with the Patersons for a few days, until conceding there simply isn't enough room to breathe for four people and a small child in their home, and then finding another modest house in the colony to move into.

While Gidley King starts getting to grips with the state of the colony, and trying to manage his predecessor, realising he can't take the title, or powers, of governor until Hunter has gone, Anna Josepha determines to get on with another kind of business. As soon as she is able, she takes a carriage, with Elizabeth, to Parramatta.

It's been eight and a half years since they'd spent that month in Port Jackson when she first arrived from Britain, and three and a half years from the time they'd last left Norfolk Island to go back home. She's anxious to see Ann Inett, or Robinson as Ann's now known, she reminds herself. The pair had exchanged numerous letters during their time on the island, particularly when Norfolk was with them, and Anna Josepha also wrote during their voyage to Britain with Ann's son Sydney and then during their two and a half years in England. She'd heard back regularly from Ann, too, and the letters had been growing increasingly warm in tone between the two women. But she knew Ann would welcome news of her sons in person.

The carriage races along the dirt tracks and finally stops outside a handsome, honeyed sandstone building. Anna Josepha steps out, helping Elizabeth down the step, and looks up at the front in wonder. 'The Yorkshire Grey' says the sign. When Ann had described her and her husband Richard's new venture, she hadn't mentioned that it was on quite such a grand scale. But how wonderful! Ann really does appear a quite exceptional person; the very embodiment of Gidley King's hopes of what a fresh start could achieve for Britain's unwanted.

A window opens up above, and there's a shout of recognition. 'Just a moment!' calls a voice that strikes a distant chord in Anna Josepha's memory. 'I'm coming down.'

A minute later and Ann strides out the door. Anna Josepha uncertainly half holds a hand out to be shaken, but Ann brushes past it and hugs her. The two women stay in the embrace for far longer than either had intended.

'My, it is so good to see you,' Ann eventually says, when the pair break off. 'You haven't changed a bit!'

'But I think your eyes have grown older.' Anna Josepha laughs. 'You obviously haven't noticed all the extra wrinkles in the years since we last met. But, goodness, you look so well. Clearly, the life of a wife—and a successful businesswoman—suits you.'

'It's not so bad,' Ann says. 'I have been lucky to fall on my feet.'

'You are too modest. Luck has nothing to do with it. I'm sure it's all about hard work, and vision.'

The Governor, His Wife and His Mistress

'Well, bad luck brought me to New South Wales, but I like to think that good luck brought me my husband and the means to do something like this. And look,' she squats down on her haunches, 'you must be Elizabeth! How do you do, my dear?'

Anna Josepha smiles and puts her hand on the little girl's head. 'I think having my children since we met, and losing one, made me really understand how you must have felt with your children,' she says.

'I was so sorry to hear about little Utricia,' Ann says, 'that would have been hard.'

'Thank you, it was. We still miss her every day. And for you, I'm so sorry we took Norfolk and Sydney away. But I wanted to come here as soon as we arrived to let you know how well they are doing with their studies and that they are both growing up healthy and strong. Of course, they are missing you terribly and looking forward to one day being with you again.'

Ann's eyes, she notices, are filling with tears, but she sees how hard she's trying not to let the dam waters break. It's a moment before she replies. 'Yes, and I thank you from the bottom of my heart for this,' Ann says. 'I'm so grateful, too, for the way you've always sent me news of them. Your mother also kindly wrote when Norfolk was staying with her and would send me little pictures he had drawn of me and Sydney and Norfolk Island, and now their schoolmaster in Yorkshire writes regularly. Of course, the two of them are old enough now to write letters themselves, which is wonderful.'

Anna Josepha nods. This is the life she's now going to have with Phillip and Anna Maria left in England for their schooling. She doesn't know how she's going to bear it.

311

Ann is obviously thinking the same thing. 'It will be easier for you,' she reassures the younger woman. 'They will always leave a hole in your heart but you have Elizabeth here to console you. And you are safe in the knowledge that you will be reunited one day, either over here or back at home.'

'I suppose so,' Anna Josepha murmurs, now also struggling to control her emotions as she can feel her lower lip trembling. 'But I already miss them both so much.'

'I know,' Ann says, taking Anna Josepha's hands in hers. 'Being a mother is both a great privilege, and a terrible curse.'

41

FULL OF FIERY POISON

Philip Gidley King
28 SEPTEMBER 1800, SYDNEY COVE, NEW SOUTH WALES

It's an ineffably long six months before Hunter departs on his refurbished *Buffalo*, and Gidley King can finally assume command of the colony as governor. He's found the wait exasperating.

The two men ended up arguing about everything, from the way the colony was being run to the way it *should* be run, from how to curb the growing power of the military's out-of-control rum trade to what to put in its place, from Hunter's own record in the job to Gidley King's qualifications to take over. Hunter, now sixty-three, felt that Gidley King, forty-two, had a surfeit of ambition for the paucity of his years and experience. Gidley King saw Hunter as having worked hard, but ultimately as having failed in his duty. Miserably, from being good friends on the First Fleet voyage, they became sworn enemies, and during the final two months of Hunter's presence, the two men never even spoke.

As Gidley King takes over the role of governor on 28 September 1800, however, he feels incredibly relieved, and determined to do his duty, to the best of his abilities, to the colony and to the British Government. The colony's very first newly anointed First Lady Anna Josepha and their daughter Elizabeth are also delighted to be able to move into Government House and to finally unpack all their trunks and boxes.

During their absence, the Sydney settlement has been completely transformed. Gidley King can see some changes are enormously gratifying, and others, less so. The two-storey white-washed Government House is still commanding the harbour from the ridge but it's been joined by dozens of new buildings stretching up from the water, with nearly all the trees along the foreshore now cut down. The Tank Stream is crossed by a new bridge, while there are houses, a stone windmill, a gaol, hospital buildings, the military barracks, officers' quarters and a brick granary. The old wattle and plaster shelter that had served as a church and schoolhouse was burned down by convicts, incensed that Hunter had ordered them to attend every Sunday two years earlier. In its place is an old weatherboard storehouse that serves for worship instead. And in the midst of it all, a clock tower stands tall, overlooking all the activity.

For it is certainly busy. There are convicts still working in gangs; convicts who've finished their sentences now working for the government or setting up their own businesses; settlers conducting trade or coming into town for supplies; and soldiers, soldiers, nearly everywhere. The population, Gidley King finds out, is now standing at over five thousand, with over three thousand men—seven hundred of those being the military—nearly one thousand women and the rest made up of children. The colony is still far from being able to provide enough food for so many people, and most continue to be dependent on provisions of salt pork, wheat and sugar brought by ships.

The harbour, too, is now dotted with vessels of all shapes and sizes. While his ship, the *Speedy*, is in dock, awaiting its next cargo, it's been joined by another visiting whaler and schooners that have been constructed locally, which go up the river to Parramatta, sail to the new Hawkesbury settlement, and off to Coal River to the north.

During the final months of Hunter's occupation, Gidley King had carried out a major muster of people, stock, work done and work being done in New South Wales for both the British Government, and for himself, to get to grips with everything going on. It means he's been able to travel throughout the colony on horseback and by boat, talk to people, and gain a comprehensive picture of the state of the place.

What worries him most, as a devout Christian and humanist, is the escalation in the trade, and drinking, of rum. *The cellars from the better sort of people in the Colony to the blackest characters among the convicts are full of that fiery poison* he writes in one letter back to England. *The children are abandoned to misery, prostitution, and every vice of their parents, and in short, nothing less than a total change in the system of administration must take place immediately.* Ironically, however, he omits to make any mention of his own affection for port.

Instead, Gidley King vows to get to work straight away. There's also the increasing number of native raids on farms, often for food, or as payback for atrocities committed by settlers, like the kidnapping of Aboriginal children. The leader of one raid at Toongabbie, Pemulwuy again, had been tracked and injured but had managed to escape. Something has to be done. But first, Anna Josepha asks that he address one more concern.

'As you know, I went to see Ann Inett, now Robinson, and met her husband, Richard, and saw the public house they're running in Parramatta,' she says.

'Yes,' he replies, having no idea as to what might be coming next.

'Well, I think we—or you—owe them,' she says. 'She gave you Norfolk and Sydney and many years of her life. She's not able to have any children with Richard but she's now served out her sentence and is doing very well. But I believe there is something you could do for them.'

Gidley King says nothing.

'You could give them a land grant,' she continues, undaunted by his silence. 'And maybe even consider pardoning her husband. He seems a very fine man, completely reformed.'

'Let me consider it,' he finally says.

As governor, he feels as if he has a huge amount to do, and as quickly as possible. The most important task in front of him is to try to dry up the quantity of spirits washing around the colony with all their ill-effects. As a result, he slaps an immediate ban on military and civil officers trading in rum, forbidding them from

The Governor, His Wife and His Mistress

either buying or selling it, and certainly from continuing chartering ships to bring in more. In his first year of rule, twenty-two thousand gallons of rum landing in Sydney Cove are turned away—enough to supply every man, woman and child with an astonishing volume of nearly four and a half gallons each—and by his second year, only one-eighth of what had arrived the previous year turns up.

To consolidate this success, he also introduces the colony's first currency to replace the informal one, involving the exchange of bottles of rum.

Another priority is to rein in the soldiers who were granted land and farms by their former commander, Major Grose, and often give themselves far more than their permitted number of convict labourers. They usually don't pay for the extra help and too quickly resort to the lash to punish their workers. Gidley King persuades the British Government to back him in prohibiting the military to also work as farmers.

He is also driven to make the colony self-sufficient in food, and to require less money from Britain, something that would make him immensely popular with his colonial masters. He also explores options for developing a local whaling and sealing industry. Unfortunately, seeing the threat he might now pose to their profits, the British East India Company complains to the British Government, and this enterprise is halted. There are other countries to trade with, however, and Gidley King explores the possibilities, bringing fresh pork in from Tahiti, and also looking at the potential for trade with New Zealand, particularly for fish, as well as with Fiji and even with China.

In the meantime, he sends fleeces from New South Wales to England in the hope of establishing a wool industry, examines timber as another possible export, and begins some mineral exploration projects.

At home, Gidley King wants to instigate a big crackdown on crime and is keen to work harder on rehabilitating convicts, and at least double the number of pardons issued every year from the current measly thirty-six.

He's in no doubt that he'll face plenty of opposition in the coming days, months and years, as well as plots to undermine him and destabilise his rule, and possibly even attempts to get rid of him, so he'll need as many allies as he can possibly get onside.

That evening over dinner—with just one port to follow, having cut down on doctor's orders—he brings up a subject he knows Anna Josepha has been waiting to discuss.

'I've been thinking about what you said about Ann,' he says. 'You're right: I do owe her.'

His wife looks pleased and clasps her hands together.

'It sounds as if she and her husband are excellent cases in point of convicts who've been successfully rehabilitated by this place. I'd like to encourage others by highlighting their example.'

'Good idea!'

'I thought I should grant Ann thirty acres of land near Sydney Cove, and also another site at Pitts Row—by the pits made for the Tank Stream.'

'That would be wonderful. She'll be thrilled!'

'It means she'll be free to farm the land, or lease it out, or set up a new business or another orderly public house here in town.

The Governor, His Wife and His Mistress

'But there's something more,' Gidley King says. 'I also want to give her husband a pardon.'

Anna Josepha gets up from the table and puts her hands affectionately on his shoulders. 'That is so generous of you,' she says. 'They will be forever beholden to you.'

He turns his head and kisses one of her hands, thoughtfully. That is exactly what he had been hoping. Issuing that pardon would have the additional benefit of boosting the number of civilians in the colony, compared to the number of soldiers, too.

And that could never be a bad thing, he reasons. As it turns out, it will soon be very prescient indeed.

WAIFS AND STRIFE

Anna Josepha King

1 APRIL 1801, SYDNEY COVE, NEW SOUTH WALES

There are two new projects of Gidley King's that excite Anna Josepha more than any others. The first is his plan to repair and extend Government House. It's looking distinctly shabby and, while it feels big enough to her—much, much more spacious than the Government House where they spent so many years on Norfolk Island, with their children Phillip and Anna Maria, and Norfolk for a while—Gidley King is adamant they need more room. He starts drawing up plans for a new roof and extensions.

The second scheme is even more thrilling. The pair had set up an orphanage on Norfolk Island when they were there, along the lines of the one they'd visited in Tenerife on Anna Josepha's first voyage to New South Wales.

'But there's an even more urgent need for one here,' he says to Anna Josepha one morning. 'Just think, there are nine hundred and fifty-eight children here in Port Jackson and many of them are illegitimate, and a huge number have been abandoned.'

'I feel for them,' she replies, 'especially with winter coming. How do they manage?'

'We are obliged to care for them, nurture them and educate them if they're to have any hope of a decent future,' says Gidley King.

'So what do you propose?' Anna Josepha feels her heart quicken at the prospect of doing such good work, and making an important contribution to the colony's future, as well as to the children's.

'Captain Kent is going back to England and his house will soon be vacant. I've a good mind to buy it for the government. What do you think?'

'That would be wonderful There's also a lovely garden there that the children could play in,' Anna Josepha exclaims, her eyes sparkling. 'And who could we get to run it?'

Gidley King looks at her intently.

She suddenly understands what he's not saying. 'Me?' she asks, putting a hand to her chest.

'You are the most qualified person I can think of, my dear. You have children of your own, you have looked after children from another mother as if they're your own, and you are the most giving and loving woman I have ever met.'

'Oh, King!' she says, blushing. 'That's so sweet of you. But do you think I'd be capable?'

'Why ever not? But why don't you ask your friend Elizabeth Paterson to help you, too, and we can always appoint a few more members to a board. I'd suggest we start with maybe one hundred little girls who are orphans, or whose parents are not fit to bring them up.'

'I'd absolutely adore that,' she says. 'And I'm sure Mrs Paterson would love to be involved, too.'

While Anna Josepha already counts Elizabeth Paterson as one of her dearest friends from their time together on the two voyages from England to New South Wales, and then their stay on Norfolk Island, she welcomes any opportunity for them to become closer still. Quite apart from enjoying her company, and wanting to turn the planned orphanage into a success with her, she is all too aware that her husband is facing possibly his greatest test: wanting to reform the New South Wales Corps. With Lieutenant Colonel Paterson now the officer in overall charge of the so-called Rum Corps, any chance to persuade the Patersons to be more loyal to her husband shouldn't be passed up.

She knows it's a tricky task. Gidley King relies on the military to do his bidding in the colony and, if they turn on him, all would be lost. He's starting to form a little private army of free men and reformed convicts, as he did on Norfolk Island, but they'll be no match for the superior numbers of the heavily armed corps. He's under pressure, too, from the settlers who want him to do more about the native raids on sheep and their threats to murder 'all the

The Governor, His Wife and His Mistress

white men they meet'. So, on 1 May 1801, he issues a government and general order declaring that anyone can shoot at 'bodies of natives' around Parramatta, George's River and Prospect Hill. Later, he also offers a reward for the death or capture of Pemulwuy. The settlers are delighted.

Yet his new restrictions on the soldiers trading, farming and trafficking spirits are already inviting resentment from the corps and it's lost on no one that a naval officer is dictating to the military, two forces who've traditionally been rivals. Some officers are even ignoring his directives, including the Commandant of Parramatta and the effective second-in-command of the entire corps, Captain John Macarthur. He'd fallen out with Governor Phillip over allegations that he purloined a cask of spirits, then been given a one-hundred-acre land grant by his military mate Grose in the gap before Hunter arrived, and then had complained about Hunter to London. As the biggest landowner in the colony, now with nearly four thousand acres to his name, and the most successful farmer, with nearly three thousand sheep, he has a huge amount of influence—and is never averse to using it to create trouble.

Anna Josepha had met his wife, Elizabeth Macarthur, at her first Government House dinner at Sydney Cove before she'd departed for Norfolk Island, and is careful to renew her acquaintance. The two women get together whenever Mrs Macarthur is in town, or Anna Josepha visits Parramatta, and they find great common ground in talking about their respective children. It seems to ease relations with her short-tempered husband, too, and, at first, all seems to be going well. Macarthur is conciliatory towards Gidley King and indicates that he'd like to sell his interests, including his land and sheep, to the government and return to England. Gidley King can think of nothing he'd like better. He also has a special interest in those sheep as they've been bred from the Spanish rams he'd sent over from the Cape when leaving New South Wales in 1796. But the British Government refuses his request. Moreover, the pair clash over a court case and, as a result, Gidley King declares his intention to take the courts out of the hands of military officers and replace some of the military with civil officers.

Anna Josepha is distraught by the row, especially when Macarthur says none of the military should speak to her husband or to her, as a way to force him to back down. She immediately goes to see Elizabeth Paterson.

'What do you think of this?' Anna Josepha asks. 'Is it true that none of them will ever speak to us again?'

'Hush,' Elizabeth replies. 'We will continue to socialise with you, and very publicly, just to show them how foolish and spiteful this is. I'm sure it'll all be over very soon.'

Gidley King is delighted when his wife informs him that the most important man in the military, and his wife, will be ignoring the boycott. But Macarthur is quick to seek revenge. He filches a letter from his wife's desk written to her by Elizabeth Paterson and reads it aloud to his fellow officers, mocking the poetic prose. She's mortified, especially as it says she hopes to influence Anna Josepha, and hence Gidley King, to favour herself and her husband, and to persuade him to act against Macarthur who's always flouted Lieutenant Colonel Paterson's command.

The Governor, His Wife and His Mistress

As soon as Anna Josepha hears what has happened, she makes straight for Elizabeth's home, close by Government House. She ignores the parts of the letter where Elizabeth hopes to influence her; after all, that's what she's doing to her friend, too. 'Oh my dear!' she exclaims. 'I'm so sorry to have embroiled you in this sordid mess. How could Macarthur stoop so low?'

Elizabeth is close to tears. 'He could do a lot worse,' she says. 'And he might well do so. I know William is outraged. I'm afraid of what might be coming.'

Anna Josepha agrees. Tensions are by now running so high in the colony, she has no idea how it will end.

But neither woman has to wait for long. Paterson, determined to defend his wife's honour, challenges Macarthur to a duel on 14 September 1801. Unfortunately, however, he comes off a very poor second best with a terrible wound to his shoulder, from which it takes him many months to recover.

When Gidley King learns what has happened, he's furious and puts Macarthur under house arrest, then sends the man he now calls 'The Rich Botany Bay Perturbator' to England for a court martial for wounding a superior officer. He pens a warning to London at the same time: *If Captain Macarthur returns here in any official character it should be that of Governor, as one half of the colony already belongs to him and it will not be long before he gets the other half.*

Macarthur eventually leaves a month later for London but never receives the punishment Anna Josepha and her husband feel he so truly deserves. The papers for the case against him are lost in a shipwreck, the duplicate papers being carried by another ship are suspiciously mislaid, and the third set are entrusted to the ship on which Macarthur is sailing and don't, unsurprisingly, arrive either.

'How lucky can one man be?' Anna Josepha later asks Elizabeth Paterson. 'He has caused so much trouble for us both, yet they say he'll be on his way back here soon. Then Lord help us all!'

43

NOTORIOUS, SEDITIOUS
AND REBELLIOUS

Ann Robinson
16 DECEMBER 1801, PARRAMATTA, NEW SOUTH WALES

There's a frisson of excitement going all through Parramatta, and it's so intense that Ann can almost touch it. A new ship has just docked at Sydney Cove and the rumour mill is in full throttle that it's bringing even more Irish convicts to the colony.

Listening to people's conversations at the bar that night, Ann knows something is up. There are so many whispers, so many furtive glances, so much huddling in the corners, all her senses are on high alert. And all talk is of one thing: plans for another revolt.

'I'm going into Sydney today to see Anna Josepha,' Ann says to Richard the next morning.

He nods. 'I think that would be wise.'

'I want to warn her that something's up. If trouble starts out here, they'd have no idea and by the time they find out, it could be too late to stop it.'

'Be careful, though,' Richard warns her. 'It wouldn't do you any good for people to know you might be reporting their conversations to the governor's lady. Or our business!'

'I'll be discreet,' she says. 'But I think we owe them that, don't you?'

It has been a year since Ann had received the proclamation that she was being given two big land grants, and her husband a pardon. Anna Josepha had called by soon after Gidley King made the decision to let her know, and Ann had been overcome by the news. She could hardly believe it. She had no doubt in her mind, either, that this was all Anna Josepha's doing. Even though she knows Gidley King to be a very fair man, she also realises he'd be far too busy running the colony in the face of so much enmity to think of such a thing.

Not for the first time, she congratulates herself for never letting on to the woman she once saw as her rival for his affections about that one shared kiss when he first arrived back to take over Norfolk Island. She had been sorely tempted at the time, but Anna Josepha had been so unexpectedly thoughtful and kind, she hadn't been able to tell her. Ever since, Anna Josepha has proved herself a wonderful ally.

The land grant had given the pair rich new sources of income. They'd set up Pleasant Farm on thirty acres north of Parramatta at Toongabbie Creek, and had employed a number of farm workers, including convicts, to look after it for them, later buying the

The Governor, His Wife and His Mistress

twenty-five-acre Wherret Farm next door, too. On the Pitts Row grant, they were planning another public house with a restaurant attached. They'd never dreamt they could one day be in such a position of influence and wealth. And if Ann can repay Anna Josepha with more than her silence on a stolen intimacy with her husband, she'd very much like to.

She knows how much pressure Gidley King is under, but one of his biggest challenges is the threat from some of the disaffected Irish convicts.

It had started back in their homeland with the Irish Rebellion of 1798, an insurrection organised by the Society of United Irishmen against the British crown. A series of uprisings around Ireland were quelled, a sympathetic French invasion was headed off by the British Navy and then the Act of Union in 1800 brought Ireland firmly under British control.

But, since then, huge numbers of Irish activists and leaders of the rebellion have been transported to New South Wales as political prisoners. In September the previous year, plans were foiled at the last minute 'to overturn the Government by putting Governor King to death'. After the plot was discovered, Gidley King began to expand his private army of free men and reformed convicts, which became known as the Loyal Associations, to help protect him and his government. But over the next few months, several more schemes are uncovered while even more Irish convicts arrive.

As Ann rides in her carriage towards Sydney, she thinks about the trouble afoot. From the snippets of hushed conversations she's overheard, it sounds like a fresh plot is being hatched and this time, it isn't concentrated on the settlement of Sydney, it would also involve

Parramatta and some of the outlying areas. She asks her coachman to hurry. It may well be there's no time to waste.

Anna Josepha isn't at home when Ann reaches Government House, but she knows where she'll probably be. She asks the coachman to head to the building that's now become known as 'Mrs King's Orphanage'. She arrives before lunch and finds Anna Josepha sitting in a corner with five little girls, going through their alphabet.

'Good morning!' she exclaims as she sees the pleasure on Anna Josepha's face at seeing her.

'And good morning to you, too. This is a most unexpected surprise!' She rises to her feet and tells the children to go and wash their hands ready to eat, then loops her arm into Ann's and walks her outside into the garden. 'What brings you here today?'

'I'm so sorry to disturb you,' says Ann. 'It's just that there are some terrible rumours going around Parramatta about another possible disturbance.'

A cloud immediately passes over Anna Josepha's face. 'What kind of disturbance?'

'A new ship called the *Minorca* arrived two days ago, with one hundred and one convicts aboard, many of them from Ireland, apparently.'

'Oh no!' Anna Josepha whispers. 'And it is they who are plotting yet another revolt?'

'From what I'm hearing in Parramatta, I think it involves them. I don't know any details, but it seems it is going to be more widespread, not just in Sydney.'

The Governor, His Wife and His Mistress

'This is terrible news. Did you hear that the other plots involved assassinating King?'

'I did, and that's why I wanted to come and tell you straight away. I have no idea when they might be plotting to overthrow the governor, but it sounds as if it's a real threat. And there are so many Irish here now, which makes it very dangerous.'

Anna Josepha sighs. 'King was saying only last night that the numbers of United Irishmen were becoming very worrying.'

'I know you're friends with Mrs Macarthur,' Ann continues. 'I've never met the lady; she wouldn't associate with someone like me. But people say she's very nice and fair and so . . .'

Anna Josepha sits up straight. 'Does the plot involve her, too?'

'I think so,' Ann replies. 'I heard someone saying there was a plan to set light to her house so that the soldiers would immediately come to rescue her and the rebels could then take over the barracks with ease.'

Ann notices for the first time how weary her friend looks. In some ways, it might be easier for Gidley King to face these pressures as he, at least, can take measures to subvert them. But his wife can only sit and worry. Ann realises why Anna Josepha spends so much time at the orphanage and decides to change the subject.

'I had letters from Norfolk and Sydney a month ago,' she offers. 'They both seem to be going well.'

'I'm so glad,' Anna Josepha says. 'I still feel terrible about taking them away from you, but at least they are getting a good education. From what King says, Norfolk might have a position waiting for him in the navy, too.'

331

'He mentioned that in the letter,' Ann replies. 'Something else I need to thank you for!'

'It is the least we could do under the circumstances.' She purses her lips and Ann wonders what's coming next.

'I also feel very bad that, when we were in England, we didn't make any attempt to find Thomas and Constance for you,' Anna Josepha says softly. 'We should have done.'

Her words take Ann by surprise and she's shocked to feel tears stinging her eyes. Will she ever get over the loss of her children? She hadn't even thought of the possibility of Anna Josepha searching for her lost son and daughter. She now wishes she had.

Discord continues to keep bubbling among many of the Irish convicts, particularly around Parramatta, and then Castle Hill to the north-west of the Sydney settlement, where many have been sent to work on the public farm. Ann does her best to ignore it but she can't help feeling terribly unsettled by the restlessness.

'Why can't we all just get on?' she asks Richard one evening. 'We've all suffered, we've all had our troubles, but now is the time to come together and build new lives for ourselves.'

Not everyone agrees, however, and in April 1802, another rebellion in Castle Hill is successfully headed off, and the leaders are separated from the men they were planning to command.

Ann suspects that's unlikely to be the last of the troubles. Gidley King is building up his loyalist army and trying to set up networks of informants. Ann hopes, by keeping an ear open in Parramatta, she'll

The Governor, His Wife and His Mistress

also continue to be of assistance. And, finally, it's from Parramatta that the most important snippet of information comes. On 3 March 1804, an Irish convict tells the local commander that a full-scale revolt is being organised for the next day.

Ann hears about it almost immediately and is terrified. That night, she and Richard close up their hotel early and stay indoors with the lights out. Nothing happens, and she allows herself to breathe again until, the next evening, a house in Castle Hill is set ablaze and three hundred and thirty-three men, armed with guns, cutlasses, pitchforks, pikes and sticks, march on the local military garrison and capture their headquarters. Then they set out for Hawkesbury, planning to capture that settlement as well, before moving on to Parramatta.

'What do they plan to do here?' she asks Richard, as they shelter in their cellar.

'I have no idea,' he admits. 'But I think we just happen to be on the route to Sydney.'

He turns out to be right; from Parramatta they march on to Sydney, by then planning to be a thousand-men strong, where they intend murdering Gidley King and taking over the government.

Ann immediately fears for her ex-lover, but knows that a messenger is on his way to Government House late that night. When he arrives, she later finds out, Gidley King immediately leapt onto his horse, sounded the alarm, declared martial law, assembled the loyalist army, ordered Lieutenant Colonel Paterson to defend Sydney with his troops and sent Major George Johnston to lead a detachment of the New South Wales Corps to intercept the rebels marching towards Sydney. Gidley King then set off for Parramatta, riding through the dark night, and then on towards Hawkesbury where he took command of the military and his army of free men.

In the bloody battle that followed, Ann hears that fifteen of the rebels were killed outright, many more were injured and twenty-six were captured.

It seemed, indeed, that the plan was to set Elizabeth Macarthur's house ablaze to act as a decoy for the military. Mrs Macarthur takes refuge in Government House during the troubles and is full of gratitude to Anna Josepha for the advance warning she gave her.

'But it wasn't me,' Anna Josepha tells her. 'It was a good friend of mine.'

Elizabeth looks at her, mystified, then her face clears. From that moment on, whenever Ann's path crosses Elizabeth's in town, the older woman smiles warmly at her. The two women might well inhabit different realms of society, but they know they'll always look out for each other.

As a result of the foiled rebellion, seven of the leaders are hanged, nine are flogged, thirty-four are sent to Coal River to work in the mines, and three others are exiled to Norfolk Island.

'I think it's time for us to go back to Sydney,' Ann tells Richard the day of the hanging. 'Let's open our second hotel there. It feels much safer now than it has for some time. Until, of course, something else happens.'

44

EXPLORING THE UNKNOWN

Philip Gidley King
13 JUNE 1804, SYDNEY COVE, NEW SOUTH WALES

It's a wondrous thing for Gidley King to have two women in his life who have miraculously become his most valuable allies.

Anna Josepha, his young bride, knew little of life before he swept her away to the other side of the world. Here, she could so easily have floundered in the rigours of surviving one of the most ambitious experiments humankind has ever seen but, instead, she has thrived. Her sweet nature seems to endear her to everyone. No one would have any idea how beautifully she uses it in Sydney to win confidences, influence people and make steadfast connections.

And whoever could have suspected that Ann, his former mistress, would also have blossomed into such a force in the colony? Or that, via his wife's friendship rather than enmity, she would become another precious confidante? He wonders what she looks like these days. Would her eyes still be as cornflower blue? Her figure as neat? He shakes his head to try to rid himself of her image.

He hasn't seen Ann now since that terrible time in Sydney when he'd visited her to explain how he'd returned with a wife in tow, and suggested that she give up their children. His face still burns with shame to think of that day, that kiss. He wonders if she even remembers it, now she's happily married, by all accounts. From her loyalty to his governorship, with the vital information she feeds Anna Josepha from Parramatta, maybe she has forgiven even if she hasn't forgotten. He's studiously avoided ever meeting with her, despite his wife's entreaties. But he would like to see her again. One day.

For the meantime, he has plenty to occupy his time. It's not simply about reacting to difficulties and trying to solve problems as the new colony begins to take shape, either. He's determined to tap into the potential of this new land and try to make it a vibrant, dynamic off-shoot of Britain that can make, and pay, its own way in the world. It's not only idealism that drives him. The French are staking a claim on great tracts of the globe, and it's part of Gidley King's role to stop them claiming any of New Holland. In addition, there's always a need for more food and, with the soil in Sydney not as good as hoped, the search for richer and more fertile terrain is a constant endeavour.

Under his stewardship, the population pushes north into Newcastle on the Coal River, south with new settlements in Van Diemen's Land, and he plans to set up another settlement on the upper eastern part of the coast to grow cotton to export to China. Some of the exploration is intensely personable and pleasurable,

The Governor, His Wife and His Mistress

like riding through the bush with Anna Josepha to the Nepean River, which flows from south-west of Sydney Cove up west of Parramatta until it joins with the Hawkesbury River. The couple cross the river several times to view the wild cattle, descendants of the two bulls and five cows brought out on the First Fleet which wandered off and were lost. By 1804, it's thought the wild cattle in the area number up to five thousand. Despite the fierce reputation of the Mountains Tribe in the region, Anna Josepha is fearless, and is heralded as the first and only European lady to cross the Nepean.

Most times, it's left to others to mount expeditions to see what's out there. Gidley King commissioned Acting Lieutenant John Murray to continue the exploration of the south coast, and in 1802, he chanced upon a major bay and hoisted a Union Jack there to take possession. He wanted to name it King's Bay in honour of the governor, but Gidley King insisted it be named after his mentor, instead, as Port Phillip Bay. He then sent the judge advocate David Collins—the ex-lover of Ann's old First Fleet friend Nancy Yeates— to lead a settlement there. Collins chose to site it at Sorrento, with poor sandy soil, instead of at the mouth of the Yarra River. By the time Gidley King sent a message asking Collins to check alternative sites, he'd already left for Van Diemen's Land. Collins became the founder of Hobart, where he invited his son and daughter by Nancy to visit him.

Van Diemen's Land also attracts the interest of the Home Office in London, who start pressing Gidley King to transfer some of the settlers and convicts there from Norfolk Island—which, without a good harbour and its remoteness, they feel might never be the successful second colony they'd hoped. The governor resists. He believes in the island's future and is determined to see it saved. But Van Diemen's Land continues to fascinate everyone. Explorer Matthew Flinders, for instance, is the first to be able to confirm, along with surgeon and explorer George Bass, that it's actually an island, separated from the mainland by what comes to be known as the Bass Strait. Flinders then leads the first in-shore circum-navigation of New Holland, which he suggests should be called Australia. On stops in Port Jackson, he develops a friendship with both Gidley King and Anna Josepha, and becomes fond of their small daughter.

'It feels like he's found the family he's always wanted,' Gidley King remarks to his wife one day. 'He has a good marriage, and wanted a family of his own, but the Admiralty never allowed him to bring her with him, and Banks agreed.'

'Why ever not?' asks Anna Josepha.

'They believe that having a wife on board means men can't concentrate on their scientific work and will be distracted.'

'I am sure the wives would often be of great help,' she replies with indignation.

'As I am certain I couldn't have survived so long on Norfolk Island, and now here, without your company.'

'So poor Flinders left his wife behind?'

'Yes,' says Gidley King, sighing. 'And I get the feeling he's a very lonely man as a result.'

'He's so solicitous with little Elizabeth, he looks as though he'd make an excellent father.'

'If only he'd stay home long enough to try.' Gidley King smiles.

The Governor, His Wife and His Mistress

'How about we ask him to be Elizabeth's godfather instead?'

Banks is another man always making headlines. He's so powerful that everyone is keen to court him and Gidley King writes him regular letters about the colony and continues to send him all manner of plants and animals for his personal collection, or his Royal exhibition at Kew. Ships en route to Britain are stocked with waratah seeds, caged birds, kangaroos, emus and black swans and, at times, the heads of Aboriginal people. When the fearsome warrior Pemulwuy is finally tracked down and shot dead, his head is cut off and promptly dispatched to Banks, too. Another time, King sends over a duck-billed platypus, preserved in a keg of spirits, to convince the doubters that such an animal does, in fact, exist.

Meanwhile, Flinders remains on the move and, in 1802, met the French explorer Nicolas Baudin on a similar coastal mapping expedition for his government. Despite both of them believing their countries are at war, they swap details of their discoveries in a south coast bay Flinders names 'Encounter Bay'. By the time Baudin's ship reaches Port Jackson, however, the two nations are at war, but with all Baudin's crew being almost dead from scurvy and dysentery, Gidley King takes pity on them and supplies them with food, including some from his own personal rations, and treats the worst affected in hospital. Baudin praises the governor's 'benevolence' and gives Anna Josepha a gift of fifty pounds for the female orphanage, and later sends the couple a French fine china dessert service. But when Flinders is later forced to put in at the French island of Mauritius because of the poor state of his ship, he receives nothing like the same consideration, and is instead detained for over six years—despite Gidley King's pleas that he be treated the same as he'd treated Baudin—giving the Frenchman time to publish his finds first.

From Port Jackson, Baudin heads south and Gidley King worries that he might be planning to plant a French flag in Van Diemen's Land. As a result, he sends a vessel after him for His Majesty's colours to be planted at the Frenchman's campsite on King Island, which is successfully done, albeit upside down.

Much of the exploration is also done as part of Gidley King's desire to find mineral deposits. He dispatches an expedition to the north to examine the newly discovered coal deposits. It's reported that the coal is equal to any found in Britain and although his team want to call the new settlement Kingstown, again he demurs and it's named Newcastle after the British coal city. Exports of the black gold begin almost immediately, to India and the Cape, and start to provide a very promising source of revenue.

The hunt for good grazing and growing land never ceases, and Gidley King finances an expedition to cross the Blue Mountains in the hope of being able to open up a path across them to whatever lies beyond. Sadly, his explorer fails twice, finding his way barred by yet more mountains as provisions come close to running out.

But much as he would love to see how his fervent desire for the colony to become far more than a depository for Britain's criminals pans out, he realises his health may not last much longer. He's still plagued with regular bouts of gout and, despite drinking much less, it disables him every time. He's forty-five years old and he always imagined he'd be home within five years when he left in November

The Governor, His Wife and His Mistress

1799. An enormous amount has been achieved during his three years as governor, but he's growing tired and sick and he wants to go home. In May 1803, he pulls out a sheaf of paper and begins writing a letter to the Secretary of State for War and the Colonies, Lord Hobart, seeking leave to retire.

THE BEST-LAID PLANS . . .

Anna Josepha King
2 JULY 1803, SYDNEY COVE, NEW SOUTH WALES

The first time Anna Josepha overhears someone talking about her, referring to her by a new nickname, she is crushed. The next time, she worries. And the third time, she is appalled.

'King, do you know what they're calling me now?' she asks her husband over breakfast.

'No?' he replies absent-mindedly. 'What's that, dear?'

'Wait for it . . .'

He looks up expectantly.

She pauses, uncertain of what his reaction will be.

'Come on, Anna. Tell me!'

'It's . . . Queen Josepha,' she says.

Gidley King's face creases, then he bursts into laughter. 'That's very funny!' Then he sees his wife's face. She looks absolutely distraught. 'No, no, don't be upset,' he says. 'You should be flattered.'

The Governor, His Wife and His Mistress

'Why?' she asks. 'Maybe they think I carry on like I'm royalty.'

He shakes his head. 'Nobody would ever think that. I'm sure it comes from a place of fondness for you. It also makes sense to call the wife of a King, a Queen. And, besides, people like you and admire you. They see you doing all that work for the girls in the orphanage and they know you have a good heart.'

Anna Josepha blows her nose. 'Do you really think so, King?' she asks.

'Absolutely!' He laughs. 'I have no doubt whatsoever. I may have many critics and people who don't like me, but you, my dear, are seen as absolutely blameless for my sins. Besides, no one can call me King King.'

She's mollified, but still doesn't like to think her husband has so many enemies. To her, he seems to be doing everything the British Government and the population of New South Wales could ever expect, and usually a great deal more. The supply of food in the colony has increased dramatically, there's a lot more land being used for crops, there's a vast number of cattle, pigs and sheep being kept, and prices of fresh pork and grain are fixed at a much lower level than before. As a result, far fewer people are now reliant for food on the Government Store and, by 1803, the governor has even told Britain he no longer needs them to send over salt meat. In addition, goods are bought officially by the government from visiting ships and sold off at little profit, and the economy is fast diversifying, with a variety of new industries, such as milling, salt-making, tanning, coalmining, timber-cutting, shipbuilding and a small amount of whaling.

The population seems to be thriving, too. For convicts, pardons have become much more frequent, with one hundred issued in 1803 compared to thirty-three the year before. As for settlers, London is now considering Gidley King's plea to send over 'a better class' of them to engage in business and trade. There are also schoolhouses to educate the young, although very few teachers, while everyone knows more about what's going on with the colony's first newspaper, the *Sydney Gazette and New South Wales Advertiser*, beginning weekly publication in March 1803. Copies quickly become sought-after, both at home and in Britain, with both the Secretary of State for War and the Colonies—and Banks—putting in a regular order.

Anna Josepha's also doing her bit to help the population, with her continued devotion to the young girls at the orphanage. One is doing particularly well, a ten-year-old who's now being adopted by Elizabeth Paterson. The girl's father, a close friend of the Patersons, had disappeared at sea, and her mother had abandoned her when she met another man to marry.

The next year, Anna Josepha actually boosts the population of free citizens. At Christmas 1804, she says she has a special gift for both Gidley King and Elizabeth, now aged seven. Both try to guess. Neither of them are right.

Finally, she holds up her hand, laughing, to stop the flow of increasingly wild ideas. 'Elizabeth,' she says solemnly, 'you're going to have a new baby brother or sister.'

Elizabeth looks confused, but Gidley King beams at her. 'That's excellent!' he says, taking both of them into his arms. 'So unexpected after all this time, but wonderful. A new baby will keep us both young!'

'Let's hope so,' she answers, delighted by his reaction. 'I'll write to Phillip and Anna Maria tonight to let them know. It'd be wonderful if the government lets you retire soon and we could have the baby in England, all together as a family.'

He looks suddenly tired. 'That would indeed be wonderful,' he says, 'but I doubt it will happen. It's now over a year since they agreed I could retire but they're still saying I have to wait until they have a replacement. And they don't seem to be in any hurry to find one.'

'We can live in hope,' Anna Josepha says, smiling. 'And maybe it's a compliment that they're finding it so hard to replace you.'

He smiles at her, but she can see the smile doesn't quite reach his eyes. She knows he's under enormous pressure. There have been more native raids on settler farms and crops, and a mounting toll of deaths on both sides. Eventually, he tells her he has to take decisive action again, and this time issues another government and general order in April 1805 to send detachments from the New South Wales Corps to protect outer settlements. He confesses his fear, however, that this will simply lead to more bloodshed.

Just under a month later, on 1 May 1805, they welcome a beautiful little baby girl into their lives. They name her Mary. Anna Josepha and Elizabeth are thrilled. Gidley King looks even more haunted. Predictably enough, they are still in Government House in Sydney.

A month on, the event they've all been dreading finally comes to pass: the return of John Macarthur to the colony. Anna Josepha has visited his wife, Elizabeth, a few times at their farm in Parramatta, usually calling in to see Ann as well, and so she's kept up with his progress in London. She reports each twist and turn in his fortunes to her husband.

Neither of them could ever have imagined he'd fare so well. Because of the missing paperwork, it was decided there was too little evidence against him for a court martial and, with the help of influential patrons and friends, he appears to have got off scot-free for injuring his superior officer, Paterson, in the duel.

To add insult to injury, he'd taken some fleeces from his own flocks to London precisely at a time when Britain was desperate for new sources of wool because of sharply rising prices from the Napoleonic Wars. Cloth merchants examined his wool and declared it to be 'of a very superior quality, equal to the best which comes from Spain'. Within days, Macarthur had drawn up a statement about the capacity of New South Wales to produce wool and campaigned to become the head of the new colonial industry. As a result, he was granted permission to resign from the army to return to New South Wales to take up farming, along with a grant of another five thousand acres—the largest land grant ever given—of some of the best pasture land discovered in the colony, in Cowpastures in the south-west of Sydney, an allocation which would be doubled, the government promised, if the results were good enough.

Anna Josepha knows Gidley King is in two minds about the whole affair. On the one hand, Macarthur is well known as a troublemaker, who upset both Phillip and Hunter, and has caused so much trouble for him. 'The Perturbator' did, after all, once say, 'If King were a man's enemy, there could not be a stronger inducement to make Macarthur that man's friend.' But on the other hand, both men share the same enthusiasm for the idea of a future for New Holland as a major wool producer. Gidley King is delighted that his purchase of those Spanish rams from the Cape improved the quality of the fleeces so significantly and he's increased the government flocks and encouraged farmers to build up their numbers, now sitting at a record twenty thousand sheep. He also appreciates that Macarthur is a very competent and driven man and, despite his undoubted ego and feistiness, is just the kind of person who might be needed to drive the industry.

'But I'm still hesitant about agreeing to such a massive land grant,' he confides to Anna Josepha. 'I think I'll tell him he can occupy it provisionally while I discuss it with London. It's the best land we have, and it seems wrong to give it all to one man, and especially a man like him.'

Anna Josepha is pleased that her husband isn't backing down, but is being so conciliatory, at the same time, to the man he once so bluntly derided.

She has an idea. 'I saw Elizabeth Macarthur last week, and she and her two daughters are waiting for him at Elizabeth Farm on their own,' she says. 'We have so much room here, how about we ask them if they would like to stay with us in Government House for a while, so they'll be right at the harbour to welcome him when he does arrive?'

Gidley King looks surprised, but then thoughtful. 'You know, that's not a bad idea,' he replies. 'It means we'll get off on the right foot with him straight away. That wouldn't do any harm.' He grins at his wife. 'There's a reason I have my own nickname for you as well.'

She laughs. He often refers to her these days as the 'undersecretary' and, she has to admit, she quite likes it.

Anna Josepha sends a messenger to Parramatta with the invitation, and he rides back that afternoon with a politely written note from Elizabeth saying that she'd love to stay with them. As a result, by the time Macarthur's ship comes into the harbour on 8 June 1805, they're almost extended family. Indeed, they feel so warmly towards each other, that the Gidley Kings even invite Macarthur himself to stay for a few days, before he rides back to Parramatta.

Much to everyone's surprise, he agrees, and one of the most unlikely friendships in the colony is finally sealed.

The news Anna Josepha and her husband have been waiting for so keenly finally comes: London has appointed a successor so Gidley King will soon be free to leave the colony. It's been an interminable two years since he first asked for permission to retire but, at last, the end is in sight and he's going to be able to go home. Anna Josepha is relieved; she's just lost her dear friend Elizabeth Paterson who, with her new daughter, has moved to Port Dalrymple in northern Van Diemen's Land to join her husband who's been appointed the lieutenant governor of the penal outpost there.

But then, out of the blue, comes disaster.

In June 1805, it starts to rain and rain until it looks as though it will never stop. The rain continues through spring, summer and into the autumn. Planting has to be delayed, then put off completely; the maize crop is rotted through and grain in the storerooms is found to be damp. And the Hawkesbury River simply doesn't stop rising.

There'd been floods in the Hawkesbury many times before. When Hunter first explored the area in 1789, as it was decimated, ironically, by drought, he noted the presence of debris lodged in trees up to forty feet above the river. Ten years later, in March

The Governor, His Wife and His Mistress

1799, the river rose fifty feet above its regular level and overflowed its banks, with the torrent of water carrying away houses, livestock and provisions, and drowning one man. In March the next year, the area again flooded and swept away the last of the wheat harvest, pigs and poultry, while in March 1801, half the stacks of wheat and nearly all of the corn harvest were destroyed and most of the swine were drowned. But the 1805 rains were a different matter entirely. By October 1805, they'd flooded around one thousand acres of land planted with wheat and maize, and in November the river rose twenty-seven feet in nine hours, and again inundated the farms.

Finally, in late March 1806, the rains come in such torrents that the river level rises rapidly, everything is submerged in water and it's only the actions of the chief constable, ex-convict Andrew Thompson, rescuing people from their rooftops and straw rafts, that save around a hundred lives. The night of horror, the newspaper, says is *almost inexpressible*. They're the worst floods ever seen, and they change everything.

Anna Josepha watches on in misery as her husband has to declare a state of emergency, reintroduce rationing and bring in more food supplies. After all his work, after all the misery, after the incredible toll it's had on his health, this is a truly miserable end to his period of rule. For the first time, he's beginning to look like a broken man, and her heart feels bruised for him.

46

MEMORIES OF THE PAST

Ann Robinson
2 APRIL 1806, SYDNEY COVE, NEW SOUTH WALES

The latest copy of the *Sydney Gazette and New South Wales Advertiser* is lying on the table when Ann walks into the drawing room. A story on the front page immediately catches her eye. A new governor has been appointed for the colony. His name is Captain William Bligh.

The British Cabinet, it says, had its hands full with grave matters close to home, the war with Napoleonic France to wit, so the responsibility for choosing the best man for the position was handed over to Banks, the man largely responsible for the scheme of transporting convicts that had brought the colony into existence in the first place.

'Richard! Have you seen the newspaper?' Ann calls to her husband.

'No,' he says, walking into the room. 'Anything interesting?'

350

The Governor, His Wife and His Mistress

'A new governor has been appointed,' she tells him. 'William Bligh.'

'Bligh . . .' he repeats. 'Where do I know that name from?'

'The mutiny on the *Bounty*? It was the year after I got here, 1789, when his crew rose up against him and set him adrift in a little boat with his loyalists.'

'Oh yes! Of course,' Richard says. 'I was still in Portsmouth when that happened. They called him the *Bounty* Bastard. From what I heard, he was a vicious man, cold-hearted and hot-tempered. Good job he wasn't put in charge of either of the fleets we came on, but Lord help those in the one he's on now! Do they say when he's going to be here?'

'It says they're expecting him to arrive in July or August,' Ann replies. 'So not long now. I imagine Gidley will be leaving as soon as Bligh gets here. From what Anna Josepha says, his health isn't so great, and they're all longing to go home.'

'You can't blame them for that,' Richard replies. 'They've had a tough few years.'

'I must make sure to see them before they go,' Ann says. 'I shall miss Anna Josepha. I've become very fond of her.'

'And the governor has been very good to us, too,' says her husband, 'with those land grants and the pardon. We'd still be struggling if not for him.'

Ann looks out of the window of their home above their new inn and eating house in Sydney, at Pitts Row. She can see the merchants gathering ready for their day's work, a gang of convicts being marched off with pickaxes over their shoulders obviously set for hard labour, and a woman dragging along a screaming toddler by his hand. It's a moment before she responds.

'We have been very fortunate.' She turns back to look at her husband and smiles. 'Everything is going well. Parramatta is still busy and the maize crop is looking good on the farm, and the pigs are fat and healthy. So perhaps I should go to see them to say thank you while I can.'

'Both of them?'

'It's such a long time since I've seen Gidley. I don't know. I think the last time I saw him was just before he went over to Norfolk Island and took our first-born. I haven't even seen him since he's been governor here.'

'Well, maybe this would be a good time to say goodbye,' Richard says, coming over and putting his arm around her waist. 'I know you're still probably angry with him and, God knows, you have every right to be. But maybe seeing him again would be good for you. It could bring you peace.'

'I suppose so,' she says, her voice heavy with doubt. 'I imagine it can't do any harm.'

A few days later, Ann bumps into Anna Josepha in the street. The governor's wife is wearing a dark navy, shapeless frock, and a bonnet is tightly tied over her ringlets. Ann can't help noticing how tired she looks and—although she hates herself for thinking it—old. Why has she never thought before to offer to make her a more flattering, stylish gown that would suit her far more than the old-fashioned, matronly ones she seems to favour these days? Anna Josepha is eleven years younger than Ann but today looks older. Could that be the result of having another baby so late in life, Ann wonders, or the worries of being queen of the colony? Ann smiles to think of her friend's nickname. She knows how much she hates it, but she thinks it's apt. There's something quite stately about Anna Josepha, although nothing a better gown wouldn't fix.

The two women embrace warmly. Anna Josepha is holding Mary in her arms, and Ann kisses her on the cheek. 'Hello, my darling,' she coos. 'Gosh, you're looking pretty today.' The infant giggles at her. 'And where's Elizabeth?'

'At school, thank goodness.' Anna Josepha smiles. 'It's too hard when I have the both of them together.'

'I remember,' Ann says. 'You don't get any time to yourself. Mind you, you do have the advantage of maids these days.'

'As do you!' her friend remonstrates. 'My dear, you seem to be doing so well. I hear you now employ so many workers on your farm, and so many servants. Your eating house is said to be marvellous, too. Congratulations. What an excellent businesswoman you are. I must confess, I would be hopeless at anything like that. I think my role on earth was always to be a wife and mother.'

'And you're making an excellent job of that!' Ann says. 'Being wife to the governor wouldn't be so easy. He's had a lot on his plate. But I hear you're going to be leaving us soon?'

Anna Josepha's face lightens, and Ann catches a glimpse of the bright young woman she met the day she arrived. 'The new governor is on his way here now, and it should only be a couple more months.'

'We read in the newspaper the other day . . . Captain William Bligh. How do you think he will go?'

'Oh, I have never heard of him,' Anna Josepha says. 'I'm sure he'll be fine. King knows of him, and says he's not so sure but, as I tell him, that's no business of ours now.'

'What does he say to that?' Ann asks, raising an eyebrow. From what she knows of Gidley, he'd be terribly concerned that his legacy could be overshadowed by an incompetent successor.

'He doesn't listen to me,' she replies. 'He's busy writing out pages and pages of information and instructions for Bligh. I tell him not to bother, but he doesn't listen.'

Ann nods sympathetically. 'Of course, I'll come to see you before you go,' she says.

'You must!' her friend replies. 'We should come to your eating house one day!'

'You would be most welcome. But I was also thinking of coming to see your husband one afternoon, to bid him farewell.'

'Please do,' Anna Josepha says. 'How about tomorrow afternoon? He'll be home then. Any time after lunch.'

The next day, Ann dresses carefully. It's now been over fourteen years since she and Gidley last set eyes on each other and she wants him to know how well she's done since; and that his desertion, however heartless, had never held her back. She puts on a new outfit that she only finished two days before, a slim-fitting, pale blue muslin gown with puffed sleeves in the latest fashion, with a darker royal blue velvet cape draped around her shoulders. Her maid comes into the bedroom as she finishes.

'Madam, you look stunning!' the young woman gasps.

Ann regards herself in the mirror. Yes, she does. Of course, she old now—nearly fifty-two—while Gidley will be forty-eight in a few days, but she knows she could pass for ten years younger. Maybe it was having her children so early, she thinks. Or maybe it was not having the strain of bringing any of them up for long. She'd been deprived of that pleasure every time.

But now is not the moment for bitterness. Now is the time for a final farewell to Gidley and all the hurt of the past he caused her. Then will come the time for a new beginning.

As Ann is shown into Gidley King's study at Government House, she is shocked at his appearance. She'd always thought of him as a tall man, and good-looking with classic dark features. Today, she mightn't have recognised him. He stands to greet her and she tries not to react to how round-shouldered, overweight and hunched he's become, at how slack his jowls now are and at how his shock of dark hair has receded into thin lines of grey on his almost bald head. His nose is also streaked with vivid red spider veins. She wonders if he's still drinking as much port as he used to.

As she approaches, she can see her reflection in his eyes, and his admiration.

'Ann!' he exclaims. 'How wonderful to see you again after all these years!' He clasps her hands in his and looks, at first, as if he's going to kiss her but thinks better of it. Instead, he raises her right hand and brushes it with his lips. 'You look . . . so beautiful. You've hardly changed.'

'And you—' she starts.

polite,' he interrupts her, laughing. 'We've known

ough to be honest. This place, I have to admit,

me. I've had long bouts of illness and want to get home

while I still have the strength.'

'I'm sorry to hear that,' she says, folding her gown underneath her as she takes a seat on the other side of his desk. 'How have you been, Gidley?'

'Oh, you know,' he starts. 'This land would try the patience of a saint. But I'm managing. I've made it this far, and not too long now to go. But how are you? From what Anna Josepha tells me, it sounds as if you are doing magnificently!'

'Life has turned out much better than I would one day have thought,' she says guardedly. 'And I want to thank you for the land grants and for my husband's pardon. That was very kind of you.'

'It was no more than you deserved,' he replies, waving his hand as if it were nothing. 'I was very glad to be able to do something for you. After all, you did so much for me.'

There's a short silence as both allow the memories of the past to float up between them before Ann pushes hers firmly down.

'And now you're about to go home again,' she says steadily.

'Yes, but it will be hard to leave some people here.' He looks at her full in the face and Ann realises, with a start, that he's including her. 'You know I am still so sorry about what happened between us,' he says.

She looks down at her hands. She can see they're twisting, almost unbidden, in her lap.

He takes a breath and continues. 'I often wonder about the choice I made,' he says. 'Was it the right one? Should I have remained faithful to you? Could we have had a future together if I'd have had the courage?'

Ann says nothing. There seems to be no point.

He, however, appears untroubled by her silence. 'I did love you, you know. I love our sons. I enjoyed our time together. But I was a coward. I felt it would be frowned upon to have a convict wife. Now I realise I should have ignored those people in my ear. I should have gone with my heart. You are still so lovely, Ann, I—'

Ann rises abruptly to her feet. 'Enough!' she says, in a voice that brooks no dissent. 'You chose Anna Josepha over me all those years ago. We can't go back to that time, and neither should we.'

'But—' Gidley King seems to be taken aback.

Ann sweeps straight on. 'I think you made the perfect choice. Anna Josepha is everything you could wish for in a governor's wife—kind, courteous and thoughtful. You are very lucky to have her. That woman is a saint and you should be careful to treat her as such. She is absolutely devoted to you, as you should be to her.'

It's his turn now to fall silent.

She barely hesitates. 'I came to say thank you and farewell, and I consider I have done both those things,' she says. 'Now I will go home to my husband, the man who has never doubted me, the man I would never betray. Good day, Governor King.'

47

WAITING TO LEAVE

Philip Gidley King
8 AUGUST 1806, SYDNEY COVE, NEW SOUTH WALES

The *Lady Sinclair* drops anchor and, once they are ashore, Bligh and his daughter Mary are greeted with all due pomp and circumstance, passing through a New South Wales Corps guard of honour before being met by Gidley King and Anna Josepha waiting near Government Wharf.

Gidley King has prepared a little speech of welcome, but Bligh doesn't seem particularly interested. He's regaling the governor with tales of how bad the voyage over was, and what a nightmare the convoy's Captain Joseph Short made it. Gidley King isn't terribly surprised. The captain had arrived earlier, come straight to Government House and had similarly accosted him with stories, this time, of Bligh's ill-temper and despotic ways. Out of the corner

The Governor, His Wife and His Mistress

of his eye, he can see Anna Josepha leading Mary into the house and envies her the far easier role.

Eventually, despite the torrent of angry words, he manages to steer Bligh into the drawing room where the servants have laid out tea. He gives the man who is about to take his place a run-down of the past years in the colony, since his arrival in 1788. Bligh seems to be impatient for him to end, however, and eventually Gidley King pauses his flow to find out what his successor might want to say.

'And what of this John Macarthur?' Bligh asks. 'You've had trouble with him?'

Gidley King nods. It seems Bligh has been well briefed by Banks, who's never liked 'The Perturbator', and the new governor-to-be is obviously spoiling for a fight. As Gidley King listens to Bligh's bluster, he sighs. Where will it all end?

He tells Bligh that he granted Macarthur the land at Cowpastures only provisionally and is still awaiting confirmation from London. In the meantime, Macarthur has taken on thirty-four convict labourers to work his lands and is also proposing to manage the herds of wild government cattle in the district. Gidley King will, very gladly, leave a decision on that to his successor.

He and Anna Josepha, Elizabeth and Mary will stay for Bligh's investiture as governor five days from now, and then will board their ship, the *Buffalo*, where they'll sleep a few days before setting sail back to England.

The absolute last thing he wants to do is hang around to prevent the next governor taking over, as Hunter had done to him with, ironically, the very same ship.

Bligh is installed and the family is preparing to board the *Buffalo* ready to leave the colony. Gidley King has farewelled his friends, said a formal goodbye to his officials and staff and cleared up all his paperwork. Anna Josepha has undergone a tearful parting from all her little orphans and has had Mary promise to take over as patron of the orphanage in her place. Both she and Ann had apparently wept when they left each other.

'It was so sad,' she tells Gidley King later. 'I said that maybe we'll meet again someday in England, and she said she'd love that when she can take time out from her business interests and has saved the fare. But we agreed to keep writing to each other and hopefully one day we'll have a reunion there. I promised to give both her boys a kiss from her when we arrive.'

Her husband nods. Ann's farewell to him hadn't ended anywhere near as fondly, but he can't begrudge her that. And today, the way he's feeling, he wonders if he'll even make it to Britain.

As he finally boards the ship, he can feel his legs stiffen and he has to lean heavily on his wife for every step. He's been dreading getting another attack of gout, but this feels exactly what might be happening.

Two days later, he collapses on the ship and the surgeon is called. The verdict is grim: he's far too sick to travel. He's carried off into lodgings but, still wanting to keep as far out of Bligh's way as he can, he tells Anna Josepha they should stay at Government House in Parramatta, and leave the new governor to it, until he's well enough to leave. It's his worst nightmare realised. Hunter had hung around

The Governor, His Wife and His Mistress

for six months, and now Gidley King has no idea how long it will be before he's well enough to depart.

He resolves, however, to still be of some use, and dictates letter after letter to Bligh to help guide him. His diligent note-taking holds him in excellent stead as his journals have a record of nearly everything that's happened. Luckily, he also has his 'under-secretary' in Anna Josepha who, in the absence of his secretarial staff now he's no longer governor, takes every word down for him. She writes of the rules and regulations of the colony, how far they are permitted to be varied from those of Britain, and about all the building projects that are now underway.

In addition, he advises his successor on how to treat the native population.

Much has been said on the propriety of their being compelled to work as Slaves, but as I have ever considered them the real Proprietors of the Soil, I have never suffered any restraint whatever on these lines, or suffered any injury to be done to their persons or property—And I should apprehend the best mode of punishment that could be inflicted on them would be expatriating them to some of the other settlements where they might be made to labour.

He also tells Bligh how he'd never tolerated any injustice or wanton cruelty to them, and believes that the further they are driven away from their native hunting grounds, the more angry and violent they might well become. He makes no mention, however, of the times he did actually encourage reprisals against them, and doesn't notice his wife's sharp glance as she loyally writes down his words.

One of Gidley King's main worries during the time he's recuperating from his illness is money. While in New South Wales, he was being paid one thousand pounds a year for his role, albeit still only half the salary of Bligh, but he was also drawing full pay as principal commander of one of the colonial ships. Both ceased the moment his successor stepped ashore. And while Phillip and Hunter are each receiving a pension, there's no guarantee he'll collect one.

Fearing that he could well be destitute by the time he reaches Britain, with his wife and six children to support, he tries to shore up his position in any way he can. Three years before, he'd written to the British Government to make a claim on three hundred of the wild cattle from the government herd, which had strayed from Sydney. He's never heard back, so takes them anyway.

Then he makes an arrangement with Bligh for the exchange of land grants. As the outgoing governor, he awards land to Bligh and, in turn, Bligh gives him a grant. Gidley King's land is out past Parramatta, with Anna Josepha calling one of the blocks, 'Thanks'.

Gidley King dearly hopes that, when he does eventually make it to England, owning this land will help stave off financial ruin, which is looking more likely by the day.

48

THE WORST VOYAGE

Anna Josepha King
10 FEBRUARY 1807, SYDNEY COVE, NEW SOUTH WALES

The day the Gidley Kings are due to sail—almost exactly six months on from their original departure date—a wrapped parcel is delivered by messenger to Anna Josepha on the *Buffalo*. She examines it curiously, and sees it's from Ann. There's a note with it too: *Do not open until you are on your way!* it says.

Anna Josepha smiles and puts it to one side. She'll look at it later, as instructed, when things have settled down. At the moment, her husband is nursing a sore head from his favourite port he insisted on drinking at the farewell dinner party they held on the ship the night before, and she's still organising the cabin for the children. They're due to hoist the anchor at midday and set off, with a flotilla of small boats from the colony sailing with them out past the heads to bid farewell. Among the people she sees on the harbour in their boats, cheering and waving, is the unmistakeable figure of John

363

Macarthur. She can still hardly believe the way he's been turned from enemy to friend. All testament to her husband's skill at diplomacy.

The other passengers on their ship include Captain Short, the man who'd been in charge of the convoy that brought Bligh and his daughter over. It seems he's become the first casualty of Bligh's rule. Incensed that Short was put in charge of the convoy, rather than he, Bligh had argued with him at every opportunity. Now Bligh is in control of New South Wales as governor, he'd ordered Short back to England to face a court martial. So instead of starting a new life as a farmer in the colony with his wife and their six children, as they'd been promised as payment for taking charge of the voyage, they're all facing a bleak and uncertain future. Anna Josepha feels desperately sorry for them, and wonders if this is a sign of things to come from Bligh's rule. Diplomacy is obviously far from his forte.

She writes in her journal that she hopes their ship will visit Norfolk Island on the way home, so she can have one last glimpse of the couple's first home together, and say goodbye to her friends there, too. Gidley King writes in his that he hopes they'll be able to sail through the Bass Strait that Flinders discovered during his time as governor. That, too, will be a fitting finale.

The couple stand on the deck waving goodbye to their friends in Sydney, as the ship passes through the heads. But a storm approaches, and their little flotilla is forced to turn back. And then the prevailing winds mean they have to turn south-east. As they pass New Zealand and then head out across the Pacific Ocean towards Cape Horn at the bottom of South America, they're forced to miss both Norfolk Island and the Bass Strait.

The Governor, His Wife and His Mistress

The voyage continues as wretchedly as it began. There are howling gales, massive storms and a fireball that lands on the quarterdeck, knocking over the crew like skittles, and then drops down the main hatchway. It sparks panic as everyone fears it will burn a hole in the ship's hull and they'll all be lost. After an extremely tense wait, during which no one draws breath, it happily vanishes as mysteriously as it appeared.

There are also heaving seas that form great walls of water that smash over the ship and soak everyone, and everything, on it. Anna Josepha worries constantly about her husband's health. Despite his six months' convalescence, he's still far from well and she's fearful of any setbacks. He spends most of the time aboard resting in their cabin, and she brings back news of everything else—usually bad news—happening on the ship.

'Most of the plants we're taking back for Sir Joseph have been drowned in seawater,' she reports one day. 'They aren't looking good. I think they're all going to die.'

Another day, another tragedy. 'The birds Governor Bligh asked us to take to England for him are no more. A wave came right over the quarterdeck and swept them away and drowned my poor little favourite bird in its own cage.'

And then the worst piece of news: the death of Captain Short's ailing wife. 'And the horrible thing is,' Anna Josepha relates to Gidley King, 'she told her husband that if she were to die at sea, she wanted her body preserved and taken to England for burial. So the only way of doing that was to take out her entrails, put them in a small case and toss them overboard, and then place her body in a cask of pickles. It was dreadful. Had she reflected before her death what was necessary to be done for the safety of all our health, I am sure, poor soul, she would much rather have consented to a watery grave.'

'Poor woman!' Gidley King says, looking shocked.

'And poor Captain Short!' Anna Josepha sighs. 'He's left alone with their six children, and the youngest is only about a year old, younger than our Mary.'

'God help him.'

'Please, King, if God should take my life on the sea, I shall not care what becomes of my body provided it all goes together.'

Despite himself, Gidley King laughs. 'That's not going to happen,' he says, reassuringly. 'We will all of us, hopefully, reach England in one piece. And if the unthinkable does happen, you have my word, I will not stand by to see you end up in a jar of pickles.'

That's by no means the end of the disasters, however. A few days later, Gidley King falls off the stairway between decks and sprains both his wrists. Despite that, they celebrate his forty-ninth birthday on 23 April with a dinner party on board, followed by singing and the dancing of reels.

Two weeks later, Anna Josepha has the fright of her life. A sail is spotted late at night coming towards the *Buffalo* and, with England and France still at war, the alarm is sounded in case it's an enemy ship ready to attack. All the women are ordered down into the ship's bread-room, a dark airless cabin below the gun-deck, where Anna Josepha is confronted by the biggest rat she has ever seen. *It frighted* [sic] *me more than the fear of coming to action*, she writes in her

The Governor, His Wife and His Mistress

journal. *Never did I experience such a heat and had we not been released by the Commanding Officer, I think I must have fainted with fright and fear.* In the event, it turns out a false alarm. It's a British warship on its way to Buenos Aires. But while the warship's captain presents Anna Josepha with some gingerbread and a leg of mutton—which sadly goes off before anyone has a chance to eat it—it doesn't turn out such a happy encounter. Gidley King climbs down the hull of the *Buffalo* and jumps into a longboat to visit the warship but sprains his ankle as he does so. It brings on another horrendous attack of gout.

With no tin bath on this ship, the surgeon John Macmillan gives him two pills. They're supposed to abate his agony but have an even worse effect. His head swells, he can't swallow food for nine days and he can't speak for a week. There's nowhere to go ashore, either. There's no wind in the South Atlantic and the ship is becalmed, fast running out of food, with little to eat besides tripe and salt fish, and much of the other stores ruined by a rat plague on board. And, to add even more misery to the mix, one of the children of the already grief-stricken Short dies.

All the time, the ship is also leaking badly, and the fore top-mast and its yards have snapped off and vanished overboard. Everyone is rapidly running out of hope.

Miraculously, the ship manages to limp into Rio's harbour, and everyone is able to go ashore to rest and recuperate, while the ship is repaired. Then, in August, it sets off again and, even though the same leaks seem to spring up very quickly into the voyage, it crosses the North Atlantic and arrives safely in Spithead, Portsmouth, on 8 November 1807.

Anna Josepha, who's exhausted from nursing her husband during the voyage, can't actually believe they have made it. Yet it's only when she's clearing their cabin, ready to go ashore, that she notices, in the corner, the forgotten package from Ann. She takes a moment to sit down, and then tears off the paper.

When she sees what's inside, she gasps. She reaches in, lifts it out and holds it up to its full length. It's a stunning gown, with a fashionable waistline just under the bust, curving back seams, a short train and puffed sleeves. And it has been carefully cut and sewn from the most gorgeous pearl-studded ivory satin.

49

SOUND AND FURY

Ann Robinson
8 NOVEMBER 1807, SYDNEY COVE, NEW SOUTH WALES

There's barely a day goes by that Ann doesn't wonder how her dear friend Anna Josepha is faring on her voyage back to England.

She'd slipped onto the foreshore to see their ship depart from Sydney, but considered she'd already said her farewells, and didn't want to prolong the agony. She'd watched as Anna Josepha stood, smiling, on the foredeck and waved to the crowd, sadly in another dark and dowdy outfit that did nothing for her. Gidley King stood at her side, looking so pale and haggard, Ann's heart went out to the pair.

The former governor, whatever his faults, had done a huge amount for the colony, and deserved a peaceful and happy retirement, but he still had this ordeal to overcome before he could even start to relax. And Anna Josepha . . . how would she fare on what would probably be her last voyage? Still, at least when she arrived, she'd look good. Ann hugged herself to think of the gown she'd made. It had taken long nights of unpicking, re-cutting and sewing, but the end result, even if she said so herself, was nothing short of fabulous.

Today, she still smiles to think of it, especially as fashion has recently become very much more a talking point in the colony, thanks to Mary Bligh, the governor's daughter. Unlike the last consort, she is a huge fan of fashion and had nearly caused a riot back in February when she wore the latest style from London to church one Sunday.

It was a gauzy blue gown, almost transparent, from what everyone says. Of course, that might be all very well in the dark drawing rooms of London society but over here in the strong sunshine, it was a different story entirely. When Mary had stood up in church for the hymns, everyone behind her could see right through her dress to her pantaloons underneath. It had caused an uproar, with the soldiers behind Mary and her father snickering, an incensed Bligh ordering them out of the church to soundly berate them, and Mary fainting on the spot, to be carried away by her husband, John Putland.

Ann's First Fleet friend Olivia and her husband, Nathaniel Lucas, have come to live in Port Jackson after seventeen years and thirteen children on Norfolk Island, minus the twins who were killed in the accident. Nathaniel seems to be busier than ever, now working as a private builder and superintendent of carpenters in New South Wales, in charge of a number of big construction projects. Whenever Olivia can leave her children with friends, she loves to get out, and Ann adores seeing her.

The Governor, His Wife and His Mistress

'Oh, poor Mary Putland and that dress!' Ann says to Olivia when she visits for the day. 'I so wish I'd been in church that day. I would have loved to have seen both the dress and the scene it caused.'

'I'm not so sure,' Olivia replies. 'It must have been awful for her.'

'Of course, you're right. It's unkind of me. But it does sound very funny.'

She smiles. 'I suppose it would have been,' she admits. 'But the consequences haven't been so comical for many of us.'

Ann nods. She's right. Governor Bligh's temper tantrum with the soldiers has only caused a further deterioration in his relations with the military. He now seems to have lost much of the goodwill that Gidley King managed to build up with the New South Wales Corps and John Macarthur, and both Bligh, and the colony, are now suffering for it. He seems to be charging full bore ahead with reforms, many of which he'd be better off negotiating carefully and introducing slowly. As a result, Sydney is tense, waiting for the next round of arguments, the next explosion of Bligh's famous temper. For example, he's made an order which prohibits the exchange of spirits or other liquor for any payment, with punishments from a fifty pound fine for a settler to one hundred lashes and hard labour for a year for a convict. It's hasn't endeared him to anyone. In addition, he's threatened to take Macarthur's land at Cowpastures away from him.

In both Ann's public houses, in Sydney and in Parramatta, over many serves of rum, she has heard his words to the soldier-turned-wool-farmer being repeated ad nauseum with glee by customers, in impersonations of vastly variable quality.

What have I to do with your sheep, sir? What have I to do with your cattle? No, I have heard of your concerns, sir, you have five thousand acres of land in the finest situation in the country but, by God, you shan't keep it.

'He'll be lucky to keep his post,' Ann sighs one day, when she hears that Bligh has dismissed Macarthur's appeal about a promissory note he'd been given for wheat without even giving him a chance to state his case, and is challenging another lease of his on land near Government House. 'He's making so many enemies. You'd think he'd have learned from the *Bounty* mutiny but he's asking for more trouble. Mary's the one I feel sorry for. She has to put up with a father like that, and continue being his official consort, and I hear her husband is very sick at the moment.'

'It can't be easy for her,' Richard agrees.

'I wonder what she really thinks about it all,' Ann muses. 'I'd love to know!'

It's a strange Christmas that year, with the colony enormously unsettled under Bligh. It feels like a tinderbox and no one wants to plan anything as trouble could break out at any moment. The governor spends time in the Hawkesbury with the farmers who are the most loyal to him—after all, he is giving them a lot of aid to get over the terrible floods—while Mary stays behind at Government House, looking after her ailing husband. On 4 January, the news filters through the colony, later confirmed by the newspaper, that he has died of consumption.

The Governor, His Wife and His Mistress

Yet Bligh doesn't seem to let anything get in the way of his politicking, and his rows with Macarthur grow more heated until the news spreads like wildfire through Sydney that Macarthur has actually been arrested. Then, on the evening of 26 January 1808, the twentieth anniversary of the arrival of the First Fleet, a procession of three hundred armed soldiers march to Government House, led by the hero of the Castle Hill uprising Major George Johnston, the lover of another of Ann's First Fleet friends, Esther Abrahams, intent on revolt. The only person who tries to stop them at the gates is little Mary Bligh, dressed in mourning black, who, despite all the loaded muskets, tries to beat back the forces with her parasol.

Of course, she's overwhelmed, and the soldiers swarm through the house and place Bligh and his daughter under house arrest, in an episode that soon becomes widely dubbed 'the Rum Rebellion'. As a result, Johnston becomes the Acting Governor of New South Wales, and Esther his de facto First Lady.

As soon as the smoke clears and the situation grows clearer, Ann writes to Anna Josepha to tell her the incredible news. Bligh and his daughter are being held in Government House, and there's a stalemate between the overthrown governor and the military rebels. Bligh eventually says he's prepared to leave and return to England, but only if he's given his flagship *Porpoise*. The problem is that Norfolk Island is finally being evacuated, with the settlers, convicts and military being moved to Van Diemen's Land, and the *Porpoise* is in use for that.

It looks an insoluble problem. 'It certainly does,' confirms Esther, the next time she visits Ann in Sydney from the couple's farm in

Annandale. 'No one knows what to do. As you'll be aware, Bligh is such an unreasonable man and he's really digging his heels in.'

'Mary's with him there, too, isn't she?' Ann asks. 'She seems terribly brave.'

'I imagine growing up with a father like that, you couldn't be any other way,' Esther answers and the two women can't help laughing.

Ann pictures Anna Josepha receiving her letter and reading it to Gidley King. She imagines he'll be both horrified and heartened. He'll be appalled that the colony has come to this, after all his hard work building it up. On the other hand, this could only increase his standing with the British Government and the king. From talking to Anna Josepha and reading the newspaper, Ann's always had the distinct impression that neither appreciated what a clever leader Gidley King had always been, trying to weave his way through the conflicting interests of the colony, and constantly coming up with ways to accommodate everyone.

So if Bligh's overthrow isn't going to go down in history as Gidley King's most resounding validation, she doesn't know what will.

50

THE HOMECOMING

Philip Gidley King

9 NOVEMBER 1807, LONDON, ENGLAND

By the time Philip Gidley King stumbles ashore in Portsmouth, he's an absolutely broken man. He no longer has the strength to work, yet he has a big family still to support and only his continuing half-pay as a naval captain and the interest on some minor savings to keep them all afloat.

The knowledge of his land grant and ownership of wild cattle in New South Wales is some comfort. He could perhaps lease out some land, have it farmed or use it for the cattle to graze and increase in numbers? But soon the news reaches him that controversy is swirling around both the land and the cattle. All large land grants made by governors are meant to be approved by England first but neither he nor Bligh had mentioned theirs to the British Government, or even officially recorded them. And there's now doubt that he has a fair claim on any of the cattle, either.

He and his family take up lodgings in Norton Street, Marylebone, and there's a heartwarming Christmas reunion with his eldest children by Anna Josepha: Phillip Parker, now sixteen, and about to enter the navy, and Anna Maria, fourteen. He'd seen neither for nine years since leaving them in England and is shocked at how grown-up they now are. He can see in their eyes, however, that they're just as taken aback at his appearance.

They're delighted to see Elizabeth again, though. They last saw her as a small baby, and she's now ten, and they are eager to meet their new sister, two-year-old Mary.

'I imagine I have aged enormously in the last ten years,' he says sadly to Anna Josepha on Christmas night after their first dinner together. 'I just hope I have more time to get to know them all over again.'

'I'm sure you will, King,' his wife replies. 'Now we're home, we can concentrate on building your health back up.'

After the Christmas holiday, Gidley King also contacts his children by Ann Inett—Norfolk, just turning nineteen, and Sydney, seventeen—who are now both officers in the British Navy, and they make arrangements to catch up with their father when they're next on shore leave. He tells them their mother is well, she misses them dearly and hopes to either visit them one day in England, or to see them if ever they make it back to New South Wales.

'It would be wonderful to get all the children together again,' Gidley King says wistfully. 'Norfolk, Sydney and Phillip got on so well as children and, while they are still in contact, writing to each other regularly as I requested, I don't think they have physically met for some years.'

'Let's try to do that then,' Anna Josepha says. 'Maybe when the weather grows warmer?'

With his family commitments now fulfilled, Gidley King doubles down to business. His first task is to pen a letter to the Secretary of State for War and the Colonies, Robert Stewart, the Viscount Castlereagh, asking to be granted a pension. He knows Phillip receives five hundred pounds annually, and Hunter three hundred pounds, even though he served for only a short time and left under a cloud. Gidley King dearly hopes he'll be awarded more.

To his mounting despair, he hears absolutely nothing back.

Gidley King's homecoming has happened at the worst possible time. Britain is in turmoil. It is still fighting in the Iberian peninsula against the invading forces of Napoleon's France, and working with its Spanish and Portuguese allies to hold the superior French numbers back. All the country's politicians are focused on the war effort, and few have much time to spare for the retiring governors of remote colonies.

In addition, many of the politicians who supported and championed Gidley King during his time in New South Wales have by now disappeared. Prime Minister William Pitt the Younger had died in January 1806, a new Whig administration came to power the next month, and then the Tories snatched back government in March 1807, with a very different Cabinet. In addition, his old mentor Banks is no longer as influential as he once was. Also sick from gout, he's almost lost the use of his legs entirely, and is wheeled in a chair to meetings. Phillip is not a well man, either. He's had a stroke and is partially paralysed but Gidley King goes to visit him in Bath anyway, to wish him well.

The former governor's shipmate on the voyage over, Captain Short, is in court and is very successfully blackening Bligh's name but, as yet, no one has any idea of the Rum Rebellion. Neither the news of the overthrow of the governor, nor Ann's letter, have yet arrived.

Gidley King is now in absolute agony from his gout, and spends days confined to his bed. His joints are red and swollen and he wakes in the middle of the night, feeling like his body is on fire. For every waking hour, he's racked with excruciating pain.

His mental torment is growing, too. He's overwhelmed with anxiety about his family's welfare if he has no pension to draw on, and he frets about how Anna Josepha will cope. Sometimes, his bitter resolve to get a pension feels like the only thing that's keeping him going.

He decides to give it one last go. He writes again to Viscount Castlereagh, outlining all his achievements and every single reason he can think of for why he deserves to be given a pension after his more than six years as Governor of New South Wales. He says he has *served His Majesty on sea and land nigh on forty years*, and that he's worked in the best interests of the colony from its foundation, over twenty years before. His service had been long, devoted and fruitful, with many great successes in keeping the peace in New

The Governor, His Wife and His Mistress

South Wales and expanding its range of industries, improving the quality of wool produced, developing cattle farming, whaling and mining, and introducing new exports while moving it towards becoming self-sufficient in food. He'd also built new schools and the orphanage, increased the colony's population of free men and women as well as convicts, and launched the colony's first newspaper. Then he'd explored the land beyond Sydney and set up new settlements in Newcastle and Van Diemen's Land, as well as highlighting Port Phillip Bay as a potential site. Moreover, he had created many artworks that had charted the lives of the native inhabitants as well as all the newcomers, and illustrated the making of the colony, as well as keeping a comprehensive daily journal that supplied the British Government with everything they ever needed to know.

He brings up the time King George III asked the Viscount to express *His Majesty's entire approbation of the conduct of Governor King as manifested in the important charge committed to him and His Majesty's satisfaction at the great improvements which the colony has received under his superintendent.* He has been proud to serve his country, Gidley King writes, but he now needs some certainty about *future provision and support.*

It's a long and comprehensive letter, forceful, persuasive and well argued. Unfortunately, Viscount Castlereagh doesn't receive it. Gidley King dies on 3 September 1808, at the age of just fifty, before it can be posted.

TOO LITTLE, TOO LATE

Anna Josepha King
1 OCTOBER 1808, LONDON, ENGLAND

Anna Josepha is left devastated by the death of her husband. She's now forty-three and has six children to support, as well as her ailing mother-in-law. Without any kind of pension for her husband, she despairs. In the space of a year, she's gone from being the most important woman in one of Britain's fastest-growing colonies, with a good husband, a fine house, servants and maids, to a widow eking out an existence in cramped lodgings, with no power, no influence and certainly no hope. She feels close to giving up.

It's at that point that she receives Ann's letter telling her about the Rum Rebellion against Bligh. She can barely believe it. But Ann's words stir something in her soul. *Bligh's downfall,* she writes, *will surely show the British Government what an excellent governor his predecessor had been to avoid such a terrible fate in his similar battles against the New South Wales Corps. It can only serve to illustrate, in the most compelling way imaginable, Gidley King's immense value in terms of his wisdom, strength, resolve and tact.* Ann signs off wishing them a happy and healthy retirement, and saying she hopes to catch up with them both in the years to come.

Anna Josepha puts the letter to one side. Her tears on the paper are making the ink run, and she has a feeling that she'll be reading it over and over in the days and weeks to come. For now she feels herself filled with a fresh resolve. Ann is right. Bligh's defeat holds the promise of being her own late husband's triumph, and only she has the power—and now the determination, too—to make that happen.

She starts tidying the papers on Gidley King's desk to make room for her to sit and write a letter to the government. As she shuffles all the documents, her eye falls on one with her husband's distinctive signature. It's his magnum opus—his long letter to the Secretary of State for War and the Colonies, detailing every single one of his great achievements that was, somehow, never actually posted. Anna Josepha stares at it in horror. She feels sick to her stomach. This could have made all the difference. How could it possibly have been missed?

After reading and rereading the letter, with all its memories of life in the colony, both the soaring highs and the desperate lows, she folds it, finds an envelope and seals it inside. Then she sends it with a messenger to the Viscount Castlereagh. This time, there'll be no chance that he doesn't receive it.

A small life annuity of two hundred pounds a year is finally granted to Anna Josepha. Viscount Castlereagh has read her letter and, together with the news of the rebellion against Bligh brought to England by John Macarthur's youngest son, Edward, in dispatches from the colony, decides that Philip Gidley King is indeed something of a hero, and that his widow is immensely deserving of the pension.

The government issues a declaration saying that he served as Governor of New South Wales under *peculiarly trying circumstances* and that he'd *assumed control of the colony at a time when the gravest abuses were at their height.* It was also recognised that *these difficulties that were faced by King were identical to those which overwhelmed Bligh,* and *it was doubtful if any Governor of New South Wales had greater difficulties to contend with. Gidley King,* it announced, had *proved himself an able, fearless and upright administrator.*

Anna Josepha writes to Ann to give her the good news. She's heartened by the British Government's praise for her husband but is saddened that it's come too late for him to have heard it.

He would have loved to know that his work was being so appreciated, she writes. *It would have given him great comfort in his last days. Instead, he died in an agony of uncertainty, not knowing whether his widow and his family would survive without him. How can anyone think that was a fair way to treat someone who's given so much for his country?*

The annuity has now given her enough money to live on—but only just. Looking after the children, as well as Gidley King's mother, means she doesn't have anything left over each week.

The Governor, His Wife and His Mistress

But she's eager to thank Ann for the news of Bligh that came at exactly the right time and, always, for her stalwart encouragement. She tells her about the annuity she's now received and Ann's part in that. She also describes seeing both Norfolk and Sydney recently, and how they're a credit to their mother. They're tall and strong and look so handsome in their navy uniforms!

Anna Josepha pauses midway through her letter, pen in hand. She pictures Ann bustling around her public house, and then walking in one of her splendid gowns through the dusty streets of Sydney, and is suddenly overwhelmed with a longing to return. It's in New South Wales, after all, where she had her happiest times, where she got to know her husband after such a brief courtship, where she brought up her children and where some of her fondest memories reside.

Sitting at her late husband's desk, she gazes out of the window at the busy London streets, the horses and carriages and all the people walking under the dark wintry skies. It's cold and there's the threat of icy rain. But this time of year will be gorgeous in Sydney, she thinks; sunny and bright and warm.

A thought abruptly seizes her. The pension could still be paid to her even if she's in New South Wales, and she'd have the land from Bligh's grant to live on and their wild cattle, too. It's likely that she'd be much better off than here in England. Besides, her children are all growing up and soon will no longer need her.

Of course, she has no idea how New South Wales will fare into the future. Doubtless a new governor will be appointed soon but it's unlikely to be someone cut from similar cloth to Bligh; it's far more probable that it'll be a man much more like her husband. She smiles at the thought. That would be good to see.

Anna Josepha continues to stare out of the window but no longer sees what's out there. England feels so much a stranger to her these days. It's New South Wales, she now realises, where she believes she truly belongs. It's an unsettling thought, but it's one certainly worth considering: going back home.

REUNION

Ann Robinson
26 JUNE 1809, SYDNEY COVE, NEW SOUTH WALES

Anna Josepha's letter arrives at Ann's on a bright Monday morning just after the start of winter. Ann breaks open the wax seal and reads it eagerly. She's already heard about Gidley King's death from the *Sydney Gazette* and has been warmed by the outpouring of grief in the colony for the man everyone now remembers with ever more fondness after Bligh's brutally brief reign. But she wants to hear how his widow is faring, and hopes she may have news of Norfolk and Sydney.

Ann is heartened by her friend's news, and gratified that maybe she has played some small part in helping her secure the pension that is so rightfully hers. And the idea of Norfolk and Sydney in their naval uniforms . . . she simply can't imagine it. When she'd sent them off, they were only small boys; it's so hard to think of them as men.

One day, she thinks, she will return to the place of her birth. She's determined to see both boys again, as well as to try to trace Thomas and Constance.

She continues reading and smiles to hear how Anna Josepha is longing to return to New South Wales. How strange life can be! While she wants to come back to this side of the world, Ann has always dreamt of her own return to England. Hopefully, somewhere, somehow, they will see each other again—either in this part of the world, or in the other—as both strive to realise their dearest wish.

That evening, she tells Richard about the letter. 'I still want to go back to England,' she says. 'I need to see my children. Do you think we might do that?'

'Absolutely,' he replies. 'Very soon we shall have enough money for two passages back. We should start thinking of selling our businesses and either leasing, or selling, our land.'

Ann beams at him. 'Really?' she asks. 'Can we do that?'

He laughs to see her delight. 'Of course,' he says. 'We have done well here; we have made our fortune. There is no reason to think that we won't continue to thrive in England. I would like to see my family, too, and meet your other children. Lord knows, I feel as though I already know them well from everything I have heard of them.'

'Thank you!' Ann says, drawing her husband close. 'Thank you!'

Everything is still very unsettled in Sydney, with Bligh at last gone, although it's reported he's in a ship somewhere off Van Diemen's Land rather than arriving in Portsmouth. The military is in firm

The Governor, His Wife and His Mistress

control of the colony now, with Gidley King's old friend Lieutenant Governor William Paterson installed as the Acting New South Wales Governor, and his wife, Elizabeth, Anna Josepha's helper with the orphanage, as First Lady. No one quite knows what will happen next, but with rumours circulating that he's being extremely generous with land grants, Ann and Richard apply. They're then awarded a further one hundred acres of land, as reward *for working hard and leading a clean life.*

As a result, they're left with huge parcels of land, as well as their farm and inn and eating house businesses in both Parramatta and Sydney. Gradually, they start to advertise it all for sale.

They divest themselves first of their interests in Parramatta, selling their fields of maize, their pigs and now cattle and sheep, and letting many of their farm workers and servants go.

They have to work through the whole process slowly, to avoid attracting too much attention from the military. But when a new governor is appointed in London, Lieutenant Colonel Lachlan Macquarie, a soldier this time instead of a naval man, things begin to quieten down and everyone feels more confident of the future. Macquarie lands in Sydney on 31 December 1809 and takes over officially as governor the next day, with Bligh returning from Van Diemen's Land with his tail between his legs, to leave soon after.

Macquarie appears a fair man, and he and his wife, Elizabeth, tend to favour the convicts who have served their terms, the so-called emancipists, so Ann and Richard feel they can finally relax. They continue with their land and hostelry in Sydney Town until at last Ann says the time is right, and she can wait no longer. She writes to both Norfolk and Sydney to let them know she is soon to be back in England, and to Anna Josepha as well.

Eventually, in 1819, Ann, almost sixty-five, and Richard, sixty, place a notice in the *Sydney Gazette*, announcing that he has bought a passage on the ship *Surry* and is due to depart the colony on 31 July. Ann is remaining for another eight months to oversee the sale of their Pitt Row property—the inn, eating house and their home—on a site which has by now been renamed Pitt Street. She leaves on the *Admiral Cockburn* at the beginning of March 1820, along with a cargo of fine wool bound for the London markets.

Ann's long anticipated arrival back is everything, and more, that she has ever hoped for.

Richard is there waiting at the docks in Portsmouth to meet her off her ship and she's so relieved to see him, and to finish the voyage, she falls straight into his arms. He holds her for a few minutes, kissing her hair, until he pulls himself away.

'Ann, wait!' he says. 'I've got some people here who want to meet you.'

'No,' she groans, trying to bury herself back in his arms. 'I don't want to meet anyone. I just want to be with you.'

He laughs and eases himself out of her grip. 'You will want to meet these people, Ann.'

She turns her face up reluctantly, and he gestures over his shoulder. Two handsome young men are standing there, one in a naval uniform. She stares. They seem familiar but . . . 'Oh my God!' she cries. 'It's my boys!'

They step forward in unison, their faces split into two wide grins. 'Mother!' says Norfolk. 'I can't believe you didn't recognise us!'

She's still frozen to the spot, her hand over her mouth in disbelief, as Sydney laughs. 'Come on, Mama,' he says. 'Can't we have a hug?'

The next four days in Portsmouth, with both men on leave, pass in a whirl of news, chatter and reminiscing. She knows most of what's been happening with them from their letters, but she demands to hear it all again from their lips. Both had reached the rank of lieutenant in the navy, with Norfolk, now thirty-one, serving as the first New South Wales–born British naval officer, and receiving awards of distinction for his conduct in the Dardanelles in 1807. He'd been captured, however, during the Anglo-American War in 1814, and after a period as a prisoner of war, he resigned from the navy and now runs trading ships in the West Indies and Africa.

Sydney, thirty, remained in the navy after the Napoleonic Wars and also served as part of the naval guard on St Helena, when Napoleon was imprisoned there. Still in active service, he has now changed his name to Sydney Inett King, just as his father had also taken his own mother's name.

On the fifth day, the little family travel up to London, and Ann, Richard and Sydney attend Norfolk's wedding to Philadelphia Montague. In the church, there's yet another surprise waiting—Anna Josepha. The two women are thrilled to see each other again, especially at such a special time for a man both have treated as their son. The two women hold hands as Norfolk and Philadelphia say their vows, and Ann believes her heart might burst with happiness.

Two days later, Richard tells Ann they are now to go on another outing, to visit her old home in Grimley, Worcestershire. They climb into a coach and she turns to him excitedly.

'Maybe I can start to look for Thomas and Constance while we're there,' she says. 'Maybe someone will remember them. Mrs Thompson might still be alive, or a neighbour of my parents . . .'

Richard's face is grave, and he puts an arm around her shoulders. 'Ann, I have some bad news,' he tells her. 'I'm sorry.'

'What is it?' she asks, suddenly afraid.

'I managed to track down Thomas, but I'm so sorry, he passed away two years ago.'

Ann looks at him, dumbfounded. 'He's dead?' she asks, stupidly.

'Yes.'

'But he would have only been in his early forties.' She looks out of the carriage window at the once-familiar countryside rushing past. This was always her worst fear. Poor Thomas. She didn't come back soon enough for him, and now he is gone.

She can feel Richard looking at her, and she nods her head slowly. 'Thank you for finding him,' she whispers.

The pair travel the rest of the way in silence until they finally arrive at another well-known sight for Ann, the twelfth-century Worcester church of St Clement.

She can feel the cold hand of fear grip her. 'Is this where . . .' she starts, but is unable to complete her sentence.

Richard nods, but then climbs out of the carriage and helps her down. 'But there's something else first,' he says. 'Let's go for a quick stroll to stretch our legs, and then I will show you.'

The Governor, His Wife and His Mistress

The pair amble down the eastern side of the River Severn. The path has been improved, she thinks to herself, remembering how muddy it used to be. There are also a lot more houses. But it has been thirty-five years since she was last here, she reminds herself. She's shocked to realise it was so long ago.

'Now, Ann,' Richard's voice breaks into her thoughts, 'are you ready to go back?'

She sighs and tucks her arm in his. 'Let's get this over with.'

They walk back to the church but now there are carriages outside and horses stamping impatiently. There's a soft glow of light and a buzz of conversation from inside. Ann makes for the graveyard, but Richard steers her towards the entrance.

She turns away. 'We can't go in there now, there's something on,' she says. 'We mustn't intrude.'

'We won't be intruding, I promise you,' he says.

'No, no, we shouldn't,' Ann insists.

He frowns. 'Yes, we should,' he says even more firmly, propelling her through the doorway.

He marches her in and she can see a christening is about to take place. A baby in a long white gown is being held by its mother, while the father stands proudly beside her. When the parents see Ann walk in, they both break into smiles, and the woman walks towards her.

'Hello, Mother,' she says. 'Meet your granddaughter, Mary Ann Robinson Guy. We've named her after you.'

AFTERWORD

Ann Inett-Robinson died in England in 1827, aged seventy-three, and was buried close to her son **Norfolk King**'s home in Stepney, East London. He died there in 1839, aged fifty, and it's believed he and his wife were childless. **Sydney Inett King** married Worcester girl Mary Butler in 1825 and they had seven children. Their first was called Ann, and their seventh, Philip Gidley. Sydney died in 1841, aged fifty-one, but his wife, Mary, long survived him, dying in London in 1880. Constance Inett went on to have six children with her husband, William Guy, but no further record of her exists.

Anna Josepha King endured a long wait to return to New South Wales, but finally made it back in 1832, when her son, **Phillip Parker King**, after a period of distinguished naval service, returned for good to the colony. By then, her eldest daughter, **Anna Maria**, had also gone to live in Sydney as the wife of John Macarthur's nephew Hannibal Hawkins Macarthur, and her youngest daughter, **Mary**, had gone over with her husband Robert Lethbridge. Only **Elizabeth** stayed on in London. Anna Josepha died in Parramatta in 1844, aged seventy-nine.

Philip Gidley King, after his death in 1808, aged fifty, was buried in Tooting Bec, London. In 1988, the year of Australia's bicentenary, his great-great-great-grandson, historian and author Dr Jonathan King, who'd just produced a re-enactment of the voyage of the First Fleet from London to Sydney, also shipped out the former governor's gravestone to St Mary's Churchyard in St Marys, near Penrith, in deference to his request, 'I wish to end my days in New South Wales.' The gravestone has been placed next to his wife Anna Josepha's grave. Gidley King's mother, **Utricia**, survived him by five years, moving in with Anna Josepha and dying in 1813 at the age of eighty-eight.

Anna Josepha's friend **Elizabeth Paterson** sailed with her husband, William, to England in 1810, but he died mid-voyage and she was denied a pension as he'd refused to reinstate William Bligh after the Rum Rebellion. In 1814, she married her husband's former commanding officer, Lieutenant Francis Grose, who died two months after their wedding. She died in 1839 at the age of sixty-nine.

Olivia Gascoigne-Lucas had thirteen children by her husband, Nathaniel Lucas, of whom eleven survived. Nathaniel was appointed superintendent of the government lumber yard in 1813, with sixty-one men under him, and was involved in the building of the Rum Hospital in Sydney, built the parsonages in Liverpool and

Parramatta, and St Luke's Church in Liverpool. He argued with government architect Francis Greenway, who accused him of being 'addicted to the bottle', about both the hospital and the church, and he died shortly afterwards in 1818, his death thought to be suicide. His widow, Olivia, immediately moved to Van Diemen's Land with six of her children and died in 1830, aged sixty-nine.

Ann Green had eventually been abandoned by her surgeon lover Dennis Considen, with their baby, just as she'd been deserted by Captain Sever, with his. But she'd married fellow convict William Blady, who arrived on the Third Fleet, and they had a son, Thomas, and a daughter, Jane. After her sentence expired, she received a fifty-acre land grant and the couple lived on their farm, while she also worked as a midwife, and finally as a housekeeper at Government House, Windsor. She died in 1820, aged sixty-seven.

Nancy Yeates was similarly dumped by her man, the judge advocate David Collins, to whom she'd borne two children, when he returned to England and to his wife in 1797. On the plus side, he did leave her his hundred-acre farm as compensation. Then, in 1800, she married Scottish convict and former lawyer James Grant in St John's in Parramatta, the same church where Ann and Richard married. He died in Sydney in 1812. No further records have been found of her.

Esther Abrahams-Johnston became the unofficial 'first lady' of New South Wales when her lover Major George Johnston became acting lieutenant governor after the overthrow of Governor Bligh in the 1808 Rum Rebellion. She finally married him in 1814, with her daughter Rosanna bearing witness. The couple had seven children. Johnston died in 1823 and bequeathed his estate of Annandale to

The Governor, His Wife and His Mistress

Esther, which was contested in court by one of their sons. Esther died in 1846, aged either seventy-five or seventy-nine; no one knew for sure.

Arthur Phillip spent his last years in retirement in Bath, Somerset, and was promoted to Admiral of the Blue in 1814. He was cared for following his stroke by his second wife, Isabella Whitehead, thirteen years his junior, whom he married shortly after the death of his first, estranged wife, Margaret Denison, who'd been seventeen years his senior. He died in August 1814, and an annual service of remembrance is held at the Bath church where he's buried by the Britain–Australia Society.

William Bligh, the governor who took over from Gidley King, was never given another important command after being unseated by the Rum Rebellion, but was promoted in 1814 to Rear Admiral of the Blue. He later charted Dublin Bay in Ireland. He died of cancer in 1817 at the age of sixty-three, and has a tomb crowned by an eternal flame at St Mary's Church, Lambeth, near his London home.

John Macarthur, after working to destabilise Gidley King and then instigating the military coup against William Bligh, successfully managed to undermine the next governor, Lachlan Macquarie, too. His huge land grants and wool exports soon made him the richest man in New South Wales but his behaviour became increasingly erratic and in 1832 he was officially declared 'a lunatic' by later governor Richard Bourke. He died a prisoner at his Camden Park Estate home in Sydney in 1834, at the age of sixty-seven, and was buried in the grounds.

Jean-François de Galaup, Comte de La Pérouse disappeared from Botany Bay after meeting with Philip Gidley King in 1788.

It wasn't until 1828 that it was discovered that his ship had been wrecked off the remote Solomon Island of Vanikoro. Some believe he was captured and eaten by the local natives; others say he escaped to be wrecked on the Great Barrier Reef. It is said that King Louis XVI, on his way to the guillotine in 1793, enquired of his captors, 'Is there news of La Perouse?'

AUTHOR'S NOTE

We know the details of Ann Inett's crime and punishment, but we can't be certain why she did what she did. The premise in this novel, however, fits all the known facts.

FURTHER READING

Bassett, M., *The Governor's Lady*, Melbourne University Press, 1940

Brooke, A. & Brandon, D., *Bound For Botany Bay: British Convict Voyages to Australia*, The National Archives, 2003

Clune, D. & Turner, K., *The Governors of New South Wales*, The Federation Press, Sydney, 2009

Coleman, D., *Maiden Voyages and Infant Colonies*, Leicester University Press, 1999

Courtenay, A., *Three Sheets to the Wind*, ABC Books, Sydney, 2022

Cox, P. & Stacey, W., *Building Norfolk Island*, Thomas Nelson Australia, Melbourne, 1971

Gill, J.C.H., *Norfolk Island: The First Phase, Journal of the Royal Historical Society of Queensland*, 1976

Heney, H., *Australia's Founding Mothers*, Thomas Nelson Australia, Melbourne, 1978

Hill, D., *1788: The brutal truth of the First Fleet*, William Heinemann Australia, North Sydney, 2008

Hughes, J., Liston, C. & Wright, C., *Playing Their Part: Vice-regal consorts of New South Wales 1788–2019*, Royal Australian Historical Society, 2020

Hughes, R., *The Fatal Shore*, The Harvill Press, London, 1987

King, A.J., *Journal of a Voyage from England to Australia in the Ship* Speedy, *19 November 1799–15 April 1800*, King Family Papers, Mitchell Library, State Library of New South Wales. ML MSS 8565

King, A.J., *Journal on HMS* Buffalo *1807*, King Papers, Mitchell Library, State Library of New South Wales. MLMSS 1973X

King, J. & King, J., *Philip Gidley King: A Biography of the Third Governor of New South Wales*, Methuen Australia, North Ryde, 1981

Nobbs, R. (ed.), *Norfolk Island and its First Settlement, 1788–1814*, Library of Australian History, Sydney, 1988

North, J., *Esther*, Allen & Unwin, Sydney, 2019

Parker, M.A., *A Voyage Round the World in the* Gorgon *Man of War: Captain John Parker*, Illune Press, London, 1795

Pembroke, M., *Arthur Phillip: Sailor, Mercenary, Governor, Spy*, Hardie Grant, Melbourne, 2013

Williams, S., *Elizabeth & Elizabeth*, Allen & Unwin, Sydney, 2021

Williams, S., *That Bligh Girl*, Allen & Unwin, Sydney, 2023

ACKNOWLEDGEMENTS

I loved meeting, and getting to know, Ann Inett, Anna Josepha and Philip Gidley King during the writing of this book, and it was my immense good fortune to later make contact with Dr Jonathan King OAM, the great-great-great-grandson of Anna Josepha and Philip Gidley King.

An acclaimed historian and prolific author, who penned a biography of his ancestor, the governor, with his father, John, in 1981, he was incredibly generous with both his knowledge and his time, and kind enough to go through the pages and make many invaluable editorial contributions to the text. I could never have found a more expert historical reader and a more patient and helpful consultant! Thank you, Jonathan. This novel is all the richer for your excellent advice.

I'm also very grateful to my dear friend Robin Walsh for going through the pages, too, and making some splendid suggestions. He's been by my side through the writing of all three of my historical novels now, and each would have been impossible without his enormous knowledge and reassuring presence giving me the confidence to continue. I could never thank him enough.

Thanks are due as well to Aboriginal historian Dr Stephen Gapps for his advice and comments on the parts of the novel that touched on the First Nations' experience of the early colony, and their resistance to the incursions of many of the settlers. I pay my respects to many of the brave men and women in these pages, including Pemulwuy, Arabanoo, Bennelong and Barangaroo.

I'd also like to mention my good friend Virginia Addison who is another excellent reader, and always ready to generously give up her time to help.

The team at Allen & Unwin have been a huge support in allowing me to indulge this fascination with history, and trying to bring it to life by channelling fiction to fill in the gaps between facts. I've so enjoyed the various challenges, and they've always been there for me.

Great thanks, of course, to my publisher Annette Barlow, whose enthusiasm for a good story and great characters has taught me so much. And editor Christa Munns, whose sharp eye, flair for both story and words, and incredible encouragement have been absolutely priceless. Thanks also to Deonie Fiford for her beautiful copyedit, which has made the text all the richer, deeper and more fluid, and to Christa Moffitt for another incredibly irresistible cover.

I'd also love to thank my agent Fiona Inglis for her unstinting support and patience, and wonderful ability to make deals to allow me to keep writing.

And last, but certainly not least, I couldn't have done any of it without the love of my life, Jimmy Thomson—or his crime novelist alter ego James Dunbar—by my side. I'm so lucky to have the both of you with me!

ALSO FROM ALLEN & UNWIN

Elizabeth & Elizabeth

SUE WILLIAMS

'Well-written, rich in historical detail and engaging . . . a lovely novel and recommended reading especially for those interested in Australia's past.'
Book'd Out

There was a short time in Australia's European history when two women wielded extraordinary power and influence behind the scenes of the fledgling colony.

One was Elizabeth Macquarie, the wife of the new governor Lachlan Macquarie, nudging him towards social reform and magnificent buildings and town planning. The other was Elizabeth Macarthur, credited with creating Australia's wool industry and married to John Macarthur, a dangerous enemy of the establishment.

These women came from strikingly different backgrounds with husbands who held sharply conflicting views. They should have been bitter foes. *Elizabeth & Elizabeth* is about two courageous women thrown together in impossible times.

Borne out of an overriding admiration for the women of early colonial Australian history, Sue Williams has written a novel of enduring fascination.

ISBN 978 1 76106 753 2

That Bligh Girl

SUE WILLIAMS

'**Superb narration and engrossing drama.**'
Tom Keneally

Mary Bligh is no shrinking violet. After an horrific six-month sea voyage from Britain, she proves as strong-willed as her bloody-minded father, the newly appointed Governor William Bligh. The pair immediately scandalise Sydney with their personalities, his politics and her pantaloons.

When three hundred armed soldiers of the Rum Rebellion march on Government House to depose him, the governor is nowhere to be see. Instead, Mary stands defiantly at the gates, fighting them back with just her parasol.

Despite being bullied, belittled and betrayed, Mary remains steadfast, even when her desperate father double-crosses her yet again in his last-ditch attempt to cling onto power. But will Mary turn out to be her father's daughter and deceive him in pursuit of her own dreams and ambitions?

Sue Williams returns to the untold stories of the women of colonial Sydney with another fascinating, meticulously researched historical novel.

ISBN 978 1 76106 588 0